PENGUIN BOOKS
The *Time Out* Book of London Short Stories

Maria Lexton was formerly books editor of *Time Out*.

The *Time Out* Book of

London Short Stories

Edited by Maria Lexton

PENGUIN BOOKS

PENGUIN BOOKS

Published by the Penguin Group
Penguin Books Ltd, 27 Wrights Lane, London w8 5tz, England
Penguin Books USA Inc., 375 Hudson Street, New York, New York 10014, USA
Penguin Books Australia Ltd, Ringwood, Victoria, Australia
Penguin Books Canada Ltd, 10 Alcorn Avenue, Toronto, Ontario, Canada m4v 3b2
Penguin Books (NZ) Ltd, 182–190 Wairau Road, Auckland 10, New Zealand

Penguin Books Ltd, Registered Offices: Harmondsworth, Middlesex, England

First published in Great Britain by Penguin Books 1993
10 9 8

Filmset in Monophoto Bembo
Typeset by Datix International Limited, Bungay, Suffolk
Printed in England by Clays Ltd, St Ives plc

CONTENTS

Notes on Contributors vii

Preface xi

PIDGIN AND THERESA *Clive Barker* 1

THE DOG THAT ROARED *Nicola Barker* 13

THE CRIME AND SUICIDE OF HARRY D'SOUZA *Ronan Bennett* 18

SUNSHINE *Anne Billson* 29

THE GIFT THAT UNWRAPS ITSELF *Glyn Brown* 39

A MAP OF THE HEART *Julie Burchill* 51

MEMORIALS *Gordon Burn* 60

WAITING TO WAVE *Jonathan Carroll* 71

MOTHER OF THE CITY *Christopher Fowler* 76

COLD COLOURS *Neil Gaiman* 89

WRITTEN ON MY HEART *Steve Grant* 96

S/HE *Robert Grossmith* 103

THE RED LINE *Charles Higson* 116

FAITH *Nick Hornby* 126

FUCK OFF *John McVicar* 134

HARLEY STREET *Hilary Mantel* 145

LOVE'S SWEET DAUGHTER *John Milne* 156

THE BLITZ SPIRIT *Kim Newman* 170

DRUG SQUAD SMEECHED MY HOOVER *Lawrence Norfolk* 181

NEWMAN PASSAGE *or* J. MACLAREN-ROSS AND THE CASE OF THE
   VANISHING WRITERS *Christopher Petit* 185

A SHORT HISTORY OF THE ENGLISH NOVEL *Will Self* 196

NOTHING BUT BONFIRES *Adam Thorpe* 209

NIGHT MOVES *Mark Timlin* 219

TURNING THIRTY *Lisa Tuttle* 229

THE GIFT *Nigel Watts* 237

NOTES ON CONTRIBUTORS

CLIVE BARKER is a playwright turned short-story writer turned film-maker whose work is at once fantastical, erotic and horrific. He shot to fame with the publication of *The Books of Blood* in the seventies and moved into film directing in 1987 with *Hellraiser*, followed by *Hellraiser II*, and *Nightbreed*; the release of *Hellraiser III* is imminent. He now lives in Los Angeles where he is working on a sequel to his novel *The Great and Secret Show*.

NICOLA BARKER was born in 1966 in Ely, Cambridgeshire, and is currently working as a diet cook at The Queen Elizabeth Children's Hospital, Hackney. Her first collection of short stories, *Love Your Enemies*, was published by Faber in February.

RONAN BENNETT was born in 1956 and was brought up in Belfast. With Paul Hill (one of the Guildford Four) he co-authored *Stolen Years: Before and After Guildford*. His first novel, *The Second Prison*, was shortlisted for the 1991 *Irish Times*/Aer Lingus First Fiction Award and for the 1991 David Higham Award, and is being adapted for a BBC Screen One drama by Lynda La Plante. His 1992 novel, *Overthrown by Strangers*, is now a Penguin paperback.

ANNE BILLSON is film critic of the *Sunday Telegraph* and author of two film books and a novelization. Her first novel, *Suckers*, was published earlier this year and was chosen as part of W. H. Smith's Fresh Talent promotion. She is currently working on a second novel and a screenplay.

GLYN BROWN was born in London in 1956 and is now a freelance journalist. She won the 1991 *Time Out* Short Story competition. Her stories have appeared in various publications and she is currently working on her first novel, provisionally titled *The Fabulous Wild*.

JULIE BURCHILL was born in Bristol and has lived in London since

1976. She is a newspaper columnist, novelist, screenwriter and critic. Her books include *Love It Or Shove It, Damaged Goods, Girls On Film, Ambition, Sex And Sensibility* and *No Exit*. She is co-founder of *The Modern Review*.

GORDON BURN is a London-based journalist whose books include *Somebody's Husband, Somebody's Son: the story of Peter Sutcliffe* and *Alma Cogan: A Novel* which won a Whitbread award. He is currently at work on a new novel which will be published next year.

JONATHAN CARROLL is the author of seven novels, *The Land of Laughs, Voice of Our Shadow, Bones of The Moon, Sleeping In Flame, A Child Across The Sky, Outside The Dog Museum* and *After Silence* and a short story collection called *Die Panische Hand*. He lives in Vienna.

CHRISTOPHER FOWLER was born in London in 1953 and to date has published four horror novels: *Roofworld, Rune, Red Bride* and *Darkest Day*, and three short story collections: *City Jitters, The Bureau of Lost Souls* and *Sharper Knives*.

NEIL GAIMAN is best known for his work in comics as author of the bestselling adult fantasy series *The Sandman* and, with artist Dave McKean, *Signal to Noise* and the forthcoming *Mister Punch*. A collection of his short fiction, poetry and essays, *Angels and Visitations* will be published later this year.

STEVE GRANT was born in 1947 and was educated at Hull and Manchester Universities. He joined *Time Out* in 1976 where he has stayed, with one short break, ever since, give or take the occasional bout of freelancing. He has written five plays, and published poetry in Britain and America. He is *Time Out*'s executive editor. He is currently working on his first novel.

ROBERT GROSSMITH was born in Dagenham, Essex, in 1954, and took a BA in Philosophy and Psychology at the University of Keele and in 1987 completed a doctorate on Vladimir Nabokov. His stories have appeared in publications in England and America; his first novel, *The Empire of Lights*, was published in 1991.

CHARLES HIGSON was born in Somerset in 1958, was the singer in the seventies' pop group The Higsons, then took up writing for Harry Enfield and Craig Ferguson's Harry Enfield's television programmes. His published work so far includes *Wad and Peeps – The Xmas Loadsamoney and Stavros Rip-off Book*, and two novels: *King of The Ants* (1992) and *Happy Now* (1993). He is currently working on a couple of film scripts.

NICK HORNBY was born in Surrey in 1957 and now lives in London where he works as a freelance journalist and author. He has had two books published: *Contemporary American Fiction* (1992) and *Fever Pitch* (1992).

JOHN MCVICAR was born in London where he lives and works as a freelance journalist.

HILARY MANTEL was born in Derbyshire and has lived and worked in Africa and the Middle East. In 1987 she was awarded the Shiva Naipaul Memorial Prize for travel writing. She is the author of five novels, *Every Day is Mother's Day, Vacant Possession, Eight Months on Ghazzah Street, Fludd*, and *A Place of Greater Safety* which won the 1992 *Sunday Express* Book of the Year Award.

JOHN MILNE was born in Dockhead, went to school in Blackheath and attended art school in Blackheath. He has written for television (*Bergerac, Sam Saturday, The Bill, Lovejoy, Eastenders* and others) and is now working on *Alive and Kicking*, his eighth crime novel featuring London PI Jimmy Jenner.

KIM NEWMAN was born and lives in London where he works as a critic, editor and writer. His many novels include *The Night Mayor, Bad Dreams* and *Anno Dracula*. Forthcoming is *The Original Dr Shade and Other Stories*.

LAWRENCE NORFOLK was born in Richmond, London, and now

lives in Chicago. His first novel, *Lemprière's Dictionary*, was published in 1991.

CHRISTOPHER PETIT is a writer and film-maker; director of *Radio On*, *An Unsuitable Job for a Woman*, *Flight to Berlin*, *Chinese Boxes*, *Miss Marple: A Caribbean Mystery*, plus several documentaries for television. His first novel, *Robinson*, was published earlier this year.

WILL SELF was born in the old Charing Cross Hospital in 1961, brought up in East Finchley, London, and now lives in Shepherds Bush. His collected cartoons were published in 1985; his story cycle *The Quantity Theory of Insanity* in 1991 and his twin novellas *Cock and Bull* in 1992. His first novel, *My Idea of Fun*, was published in September.

ADAM THORPE was born in Paris and brought up in India, Cameroon and England. He has published two collections of poetry: *Mornings in the Baltic*, which was shortlisted for the Whitbread Prize for Poetry, and *Meeting Montaigne*; his first novel, *Ulverton*, was published last year.

MARK TIMLIN was born in London where he now lives and works as a full-time writer. Eight of his crime novels featuring south London private eye Nick Sharman have been published by Headline. His ninth, *Ashes by Now*, is published in October by Gollancz.

LISA TUTTLE was born in Houston, Texas, moved to England in 1980, spent ten years in London before moving to Scotland. She has edited anthologies, written non-fiction as well as short stories and novels, the most recent being *Lost Futures* in 1992.

NIGEL WATTS is the author of three novels, *The Life Game*, which won the Betty Trask Award in 1989, *Billy Bayswater* and *We All Live in a House Called Innocence*. His next novel, *Twenty Twenty*, is being written as part of a Ph.D. at the University of East Anglia.

PREFACE

Time Out has had an enviable reputation for publishing bold, innovative, barrier-breaking fiction penned by bold, innovative, barrier-breaking writers, ever since it made its first foray into fiction with the publication of a short story by the then unknown Ian McEwan, in the early seventies. So a collection of original short stories seemed the ideal vehicle with which to celebrate the magazine's twenty-fifth birthday. And just as *Time Out* has faithfully – and fearlessly – recorded London life in all its varied aspects and pursuits, so we were determined that this, our first ever venture into fiction in book form, would reflect wildly differing views of our capital city. With that in mind, we approached writers who have, over the years, been associated with *Time Out* either as journalists or interview subjects, and others – both new and established – whose work is much admired by readers and staff alike and whose voices echo the diversity of London life. The resulting collection of stories by twenty-five of the most exciting contemporary British writers is an intriguing mix of names and styles, each story offering its distinctive and individual image of London in the late twentieth century, or what the great Irish short-story writer William Trevor defined as 'the art of the glimpse'.

We are proud to present first stories by Gordon Burn and Nick Hornby. We are equally proud to include contributions from Hollywood-based prince of darkness Clive Barker; fellow horror-mongers Christopher Fowler, Kim Newman and Anne Billson; cult fantasist Jonathan Carroll; the inimitable Julie Burchill; Brit crime supremos John Milne and Mark Timlin; graphic novelist wunder-kind Neil Gaiman; nineties literary laureates Will Self, Adam Thorpe, Hilary Mantel and Lawrence Norfolk; rising stars Nicola Barker, Glyn Brown, Robert Grossmith and Nigel Watts; former *TO* film editor turned director Christopher Petit; *Time Out*'s Executive Editor, Steve Grant; Belfast-born superior thriller writer Ronan Bennett; reformed Public Enemy Number One John McVicar; category-defying Charles Higson, ex-musician, comedy scriptwriter and thriller-writer; and the darling of the SF set, Lisa Tuttle.

A thrilling line-up guaranteed to fire the imagination and alert the reader to a series of vividly drawn visions of London they wouldn't otherwise have discovered; signposts of the past and present, penned by a host of writers rich in talent raring to kick-start English fiction into the twenty-first century.

Maria Lexton
Time Out
May 1993

PIDGIN AND THERESA

Clive Barker

The apotheosis of Saint Raymond of Crouch End took place, as do the greater proportion of English exaltations, in January. Being a murky month, January is considered in celestial circles a wiser time to visit England than any other. A month earlier, and the eyes of children are turned heavenward in the hope of glimpsing reindeer and sleigh. A month later, and the possibility of spring – albeit frail – is enough to sharpen the senses of souls dulled by drear. Given that angels have a piquancy which may be nosed at a quarter-mile (likened by some to the smell of wet dog-fur and curdled cream) the less alert the populus the greater the chance that an act of divine intervention (such as the removal of a saint to glory) can be achieved without attracting undue attention.

So January it was. January 17, in fact; a Friday. A damp, cold, misty Friday; ideal circumstances for a discreet apotheosis. Raymond Pocock, the saint-to-be, lived in a pleasant but ill-lit street fully a quarter-mile from Crouch End's main thoroughfare, and given that by four in the afternoon the rain-clouds had conspired with dusk to drive all but the dregs of light from the sky, nobody even saw the angel Sophus Demdarita come calling.

Sophus was no naif when it came to the business at hand. The child-healer Pocock would be the third soul she had removed from the hylic to the etheric conditions in a little over a year. But this afternoon there was error in the air. No sooner had she stepped into Raymond's squalid flat – intending to claim him silently – than his gaudy parrot, perched upon the window-sill, rose up shrieking in alarm. Pocock sluggishly attempted to hush it, but the bird's din had already set the occupants of the flat below and beside his yelling for some hush. When they didn't get it they came to the Saint's front door, threatening both bird and owner alike, and one – finding the door unlocked – threw it open.

Sophus was a pacifist. Though there were many amongst the Sublime Throng who enjoyed causing a little mayhem if they could get away with it, Sophus's father had been a legionnaire during the

Purge of Dis, and had told hi daughter such gruesome tales of those massacres that she could not now picture blood-letting of any sort without nausea. So instead of dispatching the witnesses at the door – which would have solved so many problems – Sophus attempted to snatch Pocock from his sordid state with sufficient speed and light that those at the threshold would not believe what they had seen.

First she bathed the joyless room in such a blaze of beatific light that the witnesses were obliged to cover their eyes and retreat into the grimy hall. Then she embraced the good man Raymond and laid upon his forehead the kiss of canonization. At her touch his marrow evaporated and his flesh lost all but its spiritual weight. Finally, she lifted him up, dissolving with a glance the ceiling, beams and roof above them, and took him away into paradise.

The witnesses, speechless with confusion and fear, hurried away to their rooms and locked their doors to keep this wonder from coming in pursuit of them. The house grew still. The rain fell, and the night came with it.

In the Many Mansions Saint Raymond of Crouch End was received with much glory and rhetoric. He was bathed, dressed in raiments so fine they made him weep, and invited before the Throne to speak of his good deeds. When he protested mildly that it would be immodest for him to list his achievements, he was told that modesty had been invented by the Fallen One to encourage men to think less of themselves, and that he should have no fear of censure for his boasts.

Though it was less than an hour since he'd been sitting in his room composing a poem on the tragedy of flesh, that squalid state was already a decaying memory. Asked to recall the living creatures with whom he had shared that room, it is unlikely he would have been able to name them, and unlikelier still that he'd have recognized them now.

'Will you *look* at me?' the parrot said, peering at himself in the tiny mirror which had been the Saint's one concession to vanity. 'What the hell's happened?'

His feathers lay in a bright pile beneath his perch. The flesh their shedding had revealed was scabby and tight, and it itched like the Devil, but he wasn't displeased. He had arms and legs. He had

pudenda hanging in his belly's shadow that were impressively large.
He had eyes in the front of his head, and a mouth (beneath a
beakish nose) which made words that were not some babble recited
by rote, but his own invention.

'I'm human,' he said. 'By Jesu, I'm *human*!'

He was not addressing an empty room. Sitting in the far corner,
having first shed her shell and then swelled to four feet eleven,
was the sometime tortoise Theresa, a gift to Raymond from a
little girl who had been cured of a stammer by the Saint's tender
ministrations.

'How did this happen?' the parrot, who'd been dubbed Pidgin
by Raymond in recognition of its poor English, wanted to
know.

Theresa raised her grey head. She was both bald and uncom-
monly ugly, her flesh as wrinkled and scaly in this new incarnation
as ever it had been in her old.

'He was taken by an angel,' she said. 'And we were somehow
altered by its presence.' She stared down at her crabbed hands. 'I
feel so *naked*,' she said.

'You *are* naked,' Pidgin replied. 'You've lost your shell and I've
lost my feathers. But we've gained so much.'

'I wonder . . .' Theresa said.

'What do you wonder?'

'Whether we've gained much at all.'

Pidgin went to the window, and put his fingers on the cold glass.
'Oh, there's so much to *see* out there,' he murmured.

'It looks pretty miserable from here.'

'God in Heaven –'

'Hold your tongue,' Theresa snapped. 'Somebody could be
listening.'

'So?'

'Parrot, *think*! It wasn't the Lord's intention that we be trans-
figured this way. Are we agreed on that?'

'We are.'

'So if you raise your voice to Heaven, even in a casual curse, and
someone up there hears your cry –'

'They may turn us back into animals?'

'Precisely.'

'Then we should get out of here as quickly as possible. Find ourselves some of Saint Raymond's clothes and go out into the world.'

Twenty minutes later they were standing on Crouch End, perusing a copy of the *Evening Standard* they'd plucked from a waste-bin. People hurried past them through the drizzle, scowling, muttering and pushing them as they passed.

'Are we in their way?' Theresa wanted to know. 'Is that the problem?'

'They just don't notice us, that's all. If I were standing here in my feathers –'

'– you'd be locked up as a freak,' Theresa replied. She returned to the business of reading. 'Terrible things,' she sighed. 'Everywhere. Such terrible things.' She passed the paper over to Pidgin. 'Murdered children. Burning hotels. Bombs in toilet bowls. It's one atrocity after another. I think we should find ourselves some little island, where neither man nor angel will find us.'

'And turn our backs on all of *this*?' Pidgin said, spreading his arms and catching a young lady with his fingers.

'Watch your fucking hand,' she snarled, and hurried on.

'They don't notice us, huh?' Theresa said. 'I think they see us very well.'

'The rain has dampened their spirits,' Pidgin said. 'They'll brighten up once it clears.'

'You're an optimist, parrot,' Theresa murmured fretfully. 'And that could well be the death of you.'

'Why don't we find ourselves something to eat?' Pidgin suggested, taking hold of Theresa's arm.

There was a supermarket a hundred yards from where they stood, its bright windows glittering in the puddled pavement.

'We look grotesque,' Theresa objected. 'They'll lynch us if they see us too clearly.'

'You're dressed badly, it's true,' Pidgin replied. 'I, on the other hand, bring a touch of glamour to my dress.'

He had chosen from Raymond's wardrobe the best copy of his feathers he could find, but what upon his back had been a glorious display of natural beauty was now a motley of gaud and fat. As for Theresa, she too had found an approximation of her former state, heaping upon her spine enough thick coats and cardigans (all greys and greens) that she was bent almost double by their weight.

'I suppose if we keep to ourselves we might get away with our lives,' Theresa said.

'So do you want to go in or not?'

Theresa shrugged. 'I *am* hungry,' she murmured.

They furtively slipped inside and sloped up and down the aisles, choosing indulgences: biscuits, chocolates, nuts, carrots and a large bottle of the cherry brandy Raymond had been secretly addicted to since the previous September. Then they wandered up the hill and found themselves a bench outside Christchurch, close to the summit of Crouch End Hill. Though the trees around the building were bare, the mesh of their branches offered the wanderers some protection from the rain, and there they sat to nibble, drink and debate their freedom.

'I feel a great responsibility,' Theresa said.

'You do?' said Pidgin, claiming the brandy bottle from her scaly fingers. 'Why, exactly?'

'Isn't it obvious? We're walking proof of *miracles*. We saw a saint ascend –'

'– and we saw his *deeds*,' Pidgin added. 'All those children, those pretty little girls, healed by his goodness. He was a great man.'

'They didn't *enjoy* the healing much, I think,' Theresa observed, 'they wept a lot.'

'They were cold, most likely. What with their being naked, and his hands being clammy.'

'And perhaps he was a little clumsy with his fingers. But he *was* a great man, just as you say. Are you done with the brandy?'

Pidgin handed the bottle – which was already half empty – back to his companion.

'I saw his fingers slip a good deal,' the parrot-man went on. 'Usually . . .'

'Usually?'

'. . . well, now I think of it, *always* . . .'

'Always?'

'He *was* a great man.'

'*Always?*'

'Between the legs.'

They sat in silence for a few moments, turning this over.

'You know what?' Theresa finally said.

'What?'

'I suspect our Uncle Raymond was a filthy degenerate.'

Another long silence. Pidgin stared up through the branches at the starless sky. 'What if they find him out?'

'That depends if you believe in Divine Forgiveness or not.' Theresa took another mouthful of brandy. 'Personally, I think we may not have seen the last of our Raymond.'

The Saint never knew what his error was; never knew whether it was an unseemly glance at a cherubim, or the way he sometimes stumbled on the word *child* that gave him away. He only knew that one moment he was keeping the company of luminous souls whose every step ignited stars, the next their bright faces were gazing upon him with rancour, and the air which had filled his breast with bliss had turned to birch twigs and was beating him bloody.

He begged for sympathy; begged and begged. His desires had overcome him, he admitted, but he had resisted them as best he could. And if on occasion he'd succumbed to a shameful fever, was that beyond forgiveness? In the grand scheme of things he had surely done more good than bad.

The birches did not slow their tattoo by a beat. He was driven to his knees, sobbing.

Let me go, he finally told the Sublime Throng, *I relinquish my sainthood here and now. Punish me no more. Just send me home.*

The rain had stopped by eight forty-five, and by nine, when Sophus Demdarita brought Raymond back to his humble abode, the clouds were clearing. Moonlight washed the room where he'd healed half a hundred little girls, and where half a hundred times he'd sobbed in shame. It lit the puddles on the carpet, where the rain had poured through the gaping roof. It lit too the empty wooden box where his tortoise had lived, and the pile of feathers beneath Pidgin's perch.

'You *bitch*!' he said to the angel. 'What did you do to them?'

'Nothing,' Sophus replied. She already suspected the worst. 'Stay quite still or you'll confuse me.'

Fearing another beating, Raymond froze, and as the angel frowned and murmured the empty air gave up ghosts of the past. Raymond saw himself, rising from his sonnets, as a syrup of hallowed light announced some heavenly presence. He saw the parrot fly up from its perch in alarm; saw the door thrown open as the neighbours came to complain, and saw them retreat from the threshold in awe and terror.

The recollection grew frenetic now, as Sophus became more impatient to solve this mystery. The ethereal forms of angel and man rose through the roof, and Raymond turned his gaze upon the conjured images of Pidgin and Theresa.

'My God,' he said. 'What's happening to them?'

The parrot was thrashing as if possessed, its plumage dropping out as its flesh swelled and seethed. The tortoise's shell cracked as she too grew larger, giving up her reptilian state for an anatomy that looked more human by the moment.

'What have I done?' Sophus murmured, 'God in Heaven, what *have* I done?' She turned on the sometime Saint. 'I blame you for this,' she said. 'You distracted me with your tears of gratitude. And now I'm obliged to do what I promised my father I would never do.'

'What's that?'

'Take a life,' Sophus replied, watching the speeding images closely. The parrot and the tortoise were stealing clothes, and making for the door. The angel followed. 'Not one life,' it said mournfully. '*Two*. It must be as though this error was never made.'

The streets of north London are not known for miracles. Murder they had seen, and rape, and riot. But revelation? That was for High Holborn and Lambeth. True, there has been an entity with the body of a chow-chow and the head of Winston Churchill reported in Finsbury Park, but this unreliable account was the closest the region had come to having a visitation since the fifties.

Until tonight. Tonight, for the second time within the space of five hours, miraculous lights appeared, and on this occasion (the rain having passed, and the balmier air having coaxed revellers abroad) they did not go unnoticed.

Sophus was in too much of a hurry to be stealthy. She passed along the Broadway in the form of a hovering bonfire, startling atheists from their ease and frightening believers into catechisms. A stupefied solicitor, witnessing this fiery passage from his office window, called both the police and the fire department. By the time Sophus Demdarita was at the bottom of Crouch End Hill there were sirens in the air.

'I hear music,' said Theresa.

'You mean alarms.'

'I mean music.'

She rose from the bench, bottle in hand, and turned towards the modest church behind them. From inside came the sound of a choir in full throat.

'What is it they're singing?'

'A Requiem,' Theresa replied, and started up the steps towards the church.

'Where the fuck are you going?'

'To *listen*,' Theresa said.

'At least leave me the . . .' He didn't get to the word *brandy*. The sirens had drawn his gaze back towards the bottom of the hill, and there, flooding the asphalt, he saw Sophus Demdarita's light. 'Theresa?' he murmured.

Getting no reply, he glanced back towards his companion. Unaware of their jeopardy, she was at the side porch, reaching open the door.

Pidgin yelled a warning – or at least tried to – but when he raised his voice something of the bird that he'd been surfaced, and the cry became a strangled squawk. Even if she had comprehended his words Theresa was deaf to them, transported by the Requiem's din. In a moment, she was gone from sight.

Pidgin's first instinct was to run; to put as much distance as he could between his new-fangled flesh and the Angel that wanted to unmake him. But if he fled now, and the divine messenger did Theresa some fatal harm, what was left for him? A life lived in hiding, fearful of every light that passed his window; a life in which he dared not confess the miracle that had transformed him for fear some witless Christian divulged his whereabouts to God? That was a pitiful way to exist. Better to face the vile undoer now, with Theresa at his side.

He started up the steps with a bound, and the Angel, catching sight of him in the shadows, picked up its speed, ascending the hill at a run, its flaming body seeming to grow with every stride. Gasping with panic, Pidgin raced to the porch, flung open the door and stumbled inside.

A wave of melancholy came to greet him from the far end of the church, where perhaps sixty choristers were assembled in front of the altar, singing some song of death. Theresa glanced round at him, her dark eyes brimming with tears.

'Isn't it beautiful?' she said.

'The Angel.'

'Yes, I know. It's come for us,' she said, glancing back at the stained-glass window behind them. A fiery light was burning outside, and shafts of purple, blue and red fell around the fugitives. 'It's no use running. We're better off enjoying the music, until the end.'

The choir had not given up its *Libera Me*, despite the brightening blaze. Transported by the music, most of the singers continued to give of their best, believing perhaps that this glory was a glimpse of transcendence, induced by the Requiem. Instead of losing power, the music swelled as the doors at the back of the church swung open and Sophus Demdarita made her entrance.

The conductor, who until now had been blissfully unaware of what was afoot, glanced round. The baton fell from his fingers. The choir, suddenly unled, lost its way in the space of a bar, and the Requiem became a tattered cacophony from which the Angel's voice rose like the whine of a finger on the rim of a glass.

'*You*,' it said, pointing its finger at Pidgin and Theresa. '*Come here.*'

'Tell it to fuck off,' Pidgin said to Theresa.

'*Come to me!*'

Theresa turned on her heels, and yelled down the aisle. 'You there! All of you! This is *God's* work you're about to see!'

'*Shut up*,' said the Angel.

'She's going to kill us, because she doesn't want us *human*.'

The choir had forsaken the Requiem entirely now. Two of the tenors were sobbing, and one of the altos had lost control of her bladder, and was splashing loudly on the marble steps.

'Don't look away!' Theresa told them. 'You have to remember this *for ever*.'

'*That won't save you*,' Sophus said. Her wrists were beginning to glow. Some withering blast was undoubtedly simmering there.

'Will you . . . hold my hand?' Pidgin asked, tentatively reaching out for Theresa.

She smiled sweetly, and slipped her hand into his. Then – though they knew they could not escape the coming fire – they began to back away from its source, like a married couple running their ceremony in reverse. Behind them, the witnesses were sloping off. The conductor had taken refuge behind the pulpit; the basses had fled, every one; one of the sobbing tenors was digging for a handkerchief, while the sopranos pushed past him to make their getaway.

The Angel raised her murderous hands.

'It was fun while it lasted,' Pidgin murmured to Theresa, turning his eyes upon her so as not to see the blast when it came.

It didn't come. They retreated another step, and another, and still it didn't come. They both dared glance back towards the Angel, and found to their astonishment that Uncle Raymond had appeared from somewhere, and had thrown himself between them and the Angel's ire. He had clearly suffered in paradise. His cloth-of-gold raiment hung in tatters. His flesh was bloodied and bruised where he'd been repeatedly struck. But he had the strength of an unforgiven man.

'They're innocent!' he hollered. 'Like little children!'

Furious at this interference, Sophus Demdarita unleashed an incoherent yell, and with it the fire she'd intended for Pidgin and Theresa. It struck poor Pocock in his lawless groin – whether by chance or felicity nobody would ever know – and there began its devouring work. Raymond threw back his head and let out a sob that was in part agony and in part thankfulness, then, before the Angel could detach herself, reached up and drove his fingers deep into her eyes.

Angels are beyond physical suffering; it is one of their tragedies. But Raymond's fingers, turning to excrement in that very moment, found their way into Sophus Demdarita's cranium. Blinded by shit, the divine blaze staggered away from her victim, and met a wave of firemen and police officers as they entered the church behind her, axes and hoses at the ready. She threw her arms above her head, and ascended on a beam of flickering power, removing herself from the earthly plane before her presence grazed undeserving human flesh, and began a new game of consequences.

The seed of rot she had sown in Raymond's flesh did not cease to spread on her passing. He was withering into shit, and nothing could stop the process. By the time Pidgin and Theresa reached him he was little more than a head in a spreading pool of excrement. But he seemed happy enough.

'Well, well . . .' he said to the pair, '. . . what a day it's been.' He coughed up a wormy turd. 'I wonder . . . did I maybe dream it all?'

'No,' Theresa said, brushing a stray hair from his eye. 'No, you didn't dream it.'

'Will she come again?' Pidgin wanted to know.

'Very possibly,' Raymond replied. 'But the world's wide, and she'll have my shit in her eyes to keep her from seeing you clearly. No need to live in fear. I did enough of that for all three of us.'

'Did they not want you in Heaven?' Theresa asked him.

'I'm afraid not,' he said. 'But having seen it, I'm not much bothered. One thing though . . .' His face was dissolving now, his eyes sinking away into his sockets.

'Yes?' said Pidgin.

'A kiss?'

Theresa leaned down, and laid her lips on his. The firemen and officers looked away in disgust.

'And you, my pet?' Pocock said to Pidgin. He was just a mouth now, puckered up on a pool of shit.

Pidgin hesitated. 'I'm not your pet,' he said.

The mouth had no time to apologize. Before it could form another syllable, it was unmade.

'I don't regret not having kissed him,' Pidgin remarked to Theresa as they wandered down the hill an hour or so later.

'You can be cold, parrot,' Theresa replied. Then, after a moment, she said: 'I wonder what the choristers will say, when they speak of this?'

'Oh, they'll invent explanations,' Pidgin replied. 'The truth won't come out.'

'Unless *we* tell it.' Theresa said.

'No,' Pidgin replied. 'We must keep it to ourselves.'

'Why?'

'Theresa, my love, isn't it obvious? We're human now. That means there's things we should avoid.'

'Angels?'

'Yes.'

'Excrement.'

'Yes.'

'And –?'

'The truth.'

'Ah,' said Theresa. 'The Truth.' She laughed lightly. 'From now, let's ban it from all conversation. Agreed?'

'Agreed,' he said, laying a little peck upon her scaly cheek.

'Shall I begin?' Theresa said.

'By all means.'

'I loathe you, love. And the thought of making children with you disgusts me.'

Pidgin brushed the swelling mound at the front of his trousers. 'And this,' he said, 'is a liquorice stick. And I can think of no fouler time to use it than now.'

So saying, they embraced with no little passion, and like countless couples wandering the city tonight, started in search of a place to entwine their limbs, telling fond lies to one another as they went.

THE DOG THAT ROARED
Nicola Barker

NELSON MANDELA GOES FREE was the headline on the front page of the *Mail on Sunday*. The young girl whom this story concerns was sitting opposite the paper and the man who had recently bought it from a makeshift stall outside Tower Hill tube station. The headline had grabbed his eye. Although he had already finished reading the leading article, his mind was still full of Mandela's new-found freedom. 'That young girl opposite,' he thought, 'looks like she thinks she's so ancient and worldly-wise, but when Mandela was first imprisoned her mother was probably still at school and she wasn't even thought of.' Time can be such a slow thing, a strange thing.

The young girl felt his gaze and caught his eye with a small yet aggressive snarl. He looked away quickly and began a new article, chastened.

She was resplendent in purple. Everything was purple but her trainers which were by Fila and were a luminous new-white. Obviously her body wasn't purple – she had blonde hair and pale skin – but her eyes were blue with flecks of pinky-mauve at their centre. This colour may have been reflected or it may have been her own.

Although her clothes were purple and sporty in design she was by no means sporty by inclination. She just liked the fashion – or her boyfriend did at any rate – Russell, who was at least a foot-and-a-half taller than her at five-foot nine.

She looked up at him with pinky-violet flecked eyes and said (having dealt with the newspaper reader opposite with consummate skill), 'Give us a gum, Russell, I'm bored.'

Russell reached into his track suit bottoms and removed a packet of gum. Stella watched this process and considered with some disappointment the fact that the removal of the chewing-gum packet had depleted what she had taken to be his shapely genitalia, by a good couple of inches. He proffered her the gum and she took a stick. It felt warm to the touch. She unwrapped it and popped it into her mouth. Russell shifted in his seat and studied the multi-coloured tube map which ran above the top of the window. They were on the District line. 'Three stops to go, Stella,' he said, 'it's only taken twenty-seven minutes so far. No bother!'

Stella chewed meditatively and listened to the conversation of the two people sitting directly behind her. They were two men. One of them was saying: 'I wonder why tube trains should need windows when you only see darkness most of the time anyway. Windows seem gratuitous somehow, like a kind of architectural joke, don't you think?' His companion paused and then answered, 'No. Look at me, I'm not laughing. You really talk shit sometimes.'

Stella looked sideways at Russell, 'You know I hate spearmint but you always buy it. I really hate it.'

He shrugged, 'Well, you don't have to eat it do you? Spit it out if you don't want it. I'm not forcing you to eat the bloody stuff.'

Stella formed the gum into a round pellet with her tongue, inhaled deeply and then spat it from her mouth as though it were a sticky bullet, on to the paper opposite. It clung for a second to the headline and then dropped silently to the floor. No one did anything. Russell looked away. Stella felt a slight pang of disappointment that her behaviour hadn't caused a row. She really felt like a good row. Russell had promised to take her out somewhere special today; on Sunday they always went out. During the week he worked part-time at the Earl's Court arena on the entrance gates, checking tickets, directing visitors. This Sunday it was the final day of Crufts dog show at the arena and he, Russell, had got complimentary staff tickets.

'Go on, it'll be a laugh,' he'd said. Stella didn't think so. She ran a hand through her perm and sighed loudly. Russell touched her arm and whispered, 'How many people on this tube do you think are going to the dog show?'

He paused momentarily and then added, 'Apart from us, that is.'

Stella looked around with dismissive eyes and said loudly, 'The whole tube stinks of bloody dog. Everyone smells of old carpets, old, damp, stinking carpets.'

Everyone pretended not to hear. A couple of women out of Stella's ferocious sight-range sniffed their cardigans casually, trying to look as if this was something they did all the time. One man picked a dog hair from his sleeve. Russell scratched abstractedly under his arm and said, 'I wonder where the dogs all go to the toilet. We'll have to look into that when we get there.'

Stella sighed again, 'I really can't wait.'

The show was packed. People milled and queued and perched and squatted. Some had brought quiche and wine as afternoon refreshments. Others queued for hot dogs, completely oblivious to the irony. Dogs were everywhere, Danes and corgis, poodles and Pomeranians. Stella stood in the middle of it all and radiated ill will. Russell had been deserted at the barrier where he was chatting to a work acquaintance. He had waste disposal on his mind.

All the dogs had been separated into breeds, and each breed was housed (every dog separate with brush-wielding, powder-toting owner at hand) in steel compartments; large metal half-boxes, doggy half-sofas, half-kennels. Stella roamed around awhile on the ground floor, sneered at the judging of St Bernards for a few seconds and then ventured upstairs. She went upstairs so that Russell wouldn't be able to find her, so that he would worry over her whereabouts. 'Serves him right,' she thought. Upstairs she watched some poodles being cut and combed in a special exhibition salon. One of the white, bleary-eyed clients reminded her of her mother. She thought, 'I must recommend that style to her next time she goes for a cut. It looks good.'

As soon as she thought that she might be about to enjoy herself, she moved on and inspected a stall of dog portraits made out of real fur. When the assistant offered her services, Stella laughed in her face. It was that sort of day.

She roamed around some more. Russell was nowhere to be seen. She debated buying a hot dog, and then decided not to. Eventually she wandered into the Toy Dog section. The toy dogs were weird, very tiny and bony. Some were shivery and drippy-eyed. Stella hated them. She marched up and down the rows of boxes like a greedy executioner, a toy-dog sadist. Eventually, as though by instinct, she found the chihuahua. He sat in his box, temporarily ownerless, tiny and bulgy-eyed. Each leg was as thin as one of her fingers. She stopped and looked at him, then muttered, 'You're not a dog, you're a rat.'

The dog's name was Rosetta Vine Bloom Moritz. He had a Swiss breeder. His ears pricked at her mutterings, he stared at her intently and then he said, 'Don't act like I'm deaf or something. Call me a rat again and I'll rip your fucking throat out.'

She wasn't so much shocked by the dog talking as by the bad language that he'd used. She said, 'You ugly rat-dog. Try it. You've got eyes like a frog.'

The dog stood up. His tiny nose quivered as though a bowl of sweet turkey soup had been placed directly beneath it. He said, 'I'm impressed by your grasp of simile. Shame about your dress sense though. Now I know exactly what not to wear this season. You are a cheap tart and you look an absolute nightmare. Sod off.'

Stella moved closer to the dog. She squatted so as to be at his eye level. She stared into his eyes with ill-concealed violence. Rosetta Vine Bloom Moritz stared back, unblinking. He was never out-stared. He sat down again and casually ran his tongue around his lips while purposely revealing his rows of a thousand needle-tiny, needle-sharp white teeth. Stella said 'God knows how you could be entered for a dog show. You'd be better put to use in a laboratory for testing eye-shadow and shampoo.'

He cocked his head slightly, 'You speak from experience, surely. I bet the closest you've ever come to good breeding is a successful bonk in the back of a Sierra. Have you got purple knickers on under that revolting track suit? It would come as no surprise.'

It took a few seconds for this stream of vituperation to enter Stella's consciousness. She digested what he had said and then wondered whether she could get away with punching him. Unfortunately he had turned into a moving target. He had begun to strut up and down his cubicle, occasionally pausing to stand and pose with his legs widely spaced and his tail stuck out straight like a horizontal aerial. After a minute or so of this he looked at her smugly over his shoulder and said, 'I'm a real show dog. I'm perfectly formed. I'd like to see you enter any sort of competition, mental or physical, let alone one of this calibre. There again, if you took off that horrible track suit you might manage to rate quite highly amongst the pugs. You've got a pug's arse from what I can see.'

Stella lost all sense of control. She flattened her hand and drew it back as if she were about to slap Rosetta Vine Bloom Moritz's head off. But he was too wise for that. On uttering the word 'arse' he had spotted the huge frame of his owner–handler over Stella's shoulder. Before Stella could gain the momentum to swing her arm back towards the dog it had been roughly caught by an enormous human paw and given a severe Chinese burn. Stella squealed like a stuck pig as she was hauled up by her still smarting arm and dragged towards the stairs and exit. As they moved the owner shouted to all and sundry, 'This girl tried to abuse my dog. She's sick. She's an animal-hater. She's the lowest form of human scum. I should call the police. Everybody, look at this girl, don't let her near your dogs, she's sick.'

The owner was twice Stella's size. He made her feel very small. In the struggle her track suit had been slightly ripped and crumpled. Everyone glared and tutted. As she was dragged through the exit she thought she caught sight of Russell, but he did not move to help her.

The owner took her to the top of the escalators which led down into the tube station and threatened to throw her down them. Then he let go of her arm and told her to go and never to come back.

She sat silently on the tube, dishevelled, unnerved. On the floor by her foot was a piece of chewed and discarded gum. She bent over, picked it up and put it into her mouth. The grit and dirt stuck in her teeth as she chewed, but she kept chewing.

Rosetta Vine Bloom Moritz won Best of Breed, but didn't get Dog of the Year. He lost by a tail. 'Never mind,' he thought, 'I've been on TV and there's always next year.'

THE CRIME AND SUICIDE OF HARRY D'SOUZA
Ronan Bennett

To change the chapel into a cinema for the film show, the screws
drew long, heavy curtains across the high windows. The curtains
were dusty and badly worn. They made me think, momentarily, of
the musty picture-houses of Mile End and Bethnal Green that I used
to visit in my youth, sometimes with a group of boisterous and
hopeful lads, sometimes with a girl.

But this was no cinema. The semi-darkness, the projector's
whirr, the pale wedge of light – none of these things made it a
cinema. Nor was it, in spite of the garish folk art posters of Christ
and scenes from the Gospels, a chapel. It was the inside of a prison,
and that is something there is never any disguising.

I took a seat at the back. In the rows before me young men had
already forced themselves into high spirits in an effort to enjoy
themselves.

Someone spoke my name.

'Harry.'

The voice was soft, a little hoarse.

Roy took the seat beside me. He inclined his head.

'Always at the back, Harry.' He looked at me with grave eyes.
'What are you doing in the Scrubs?'

'I just finished a lie-down in Strangeways,' I told Roy, whom I
had not seen for a year. 'They're taking me back in a few days.'

'Poxy place.'

'I got moved for a visit.'

'Who you got coming to see you?'

I hesitated.

'Jan.'

Roy considered this for a moment. 'Well, that's good,' he said.
'What's this film anyway?'

I had known Roy for thirty years. It gives a misleading impression of our lives – makes them more desolate than I, at least, felt
them to be – to say most of that time had been in prison, but a lot
of it was. We had worked together outside, two or three times.

Roy was good: level-headed and competent. I had never been to his house, nor he to mine. We had never sat down to a meal together; and when we met to drink it was by chance, not arrangement.

We were good friends.

Roy was doing fifteen for a security van. From what I heard, it had been a tasty piece of work. They followed the van into the Blackwall tunnel, and they had a lorry in front. When the lorry stopped, Roy and his pals boxed the van in, sawed it open and escaped with two hundred thousand. The beauty of it was the tunnel, which kept to itself every forlorn word of the guards' radio messages.

Roy has another thirty months to go.

Last year, Roy's wife killed their three children. Roy and I were in Full Sutton at the time.

How I heard it, Liz got the kids out of bed, got them dressed. They had a light breakfast before she led them to the garage and put all three in the back of the car. She did not open the garage door. She got in the car, gave the kids chocolate and Coca-Cola. She turned on the engine. The eldest twigged and, so the coroner surmised, had tried to escape. But there were child locks in the back. The kid managed to scramble into the front but Liz pinned her down. Mother and daughter were discovered in their final, stifling embrace.

The last time I saw Roy they were leading him away, handcuffed and tranked up, for the funeral.

On the screen an American cop had just saved a hostage from a crazed bank robber. The boys in front booed.

'This is bollocks,' Roy said.

I nodded.

Roy shifted slowly in his seat. I had the feeling he was getting ready to talk about Liz. It was a conversation we had still to have.

'We were married nine years when it happened,' he said after a sideways glance to see if I was willing to listen. 'My second time round, hers as well. She had a breakdown before. When she was nineteen. Something to do with a miscarriage, I don't know. Or it might have been an abortion. I thought she could handle it.'

I kept my eyes on the screen. I have learned over the years you must never say anything – I mean this as a fixed rule – when faced with another's sadness and loss. Whatever words come, they will be inadequate. I have learned to listen. It costs less, and, as long as you do not express anything at odds with the speaker's take on the situation, brings credit – undeserved and, by me, unsought – for being sympathetic. But this was about someone cutting themselves out of time and life, and it was one occasion I would have preferred not to have to listen.

'She was high strung,' Roy continued. 'Just after the marriage, she found out I was seeing this other woman. Said it was cracking her up, that it was all she could think about. I told her I loved her, Harry. What more could I say? But you could see how upset she was. I felt terrible. I just kept wanting to turn the clock back, start again. I told her I'd change. There were other women before, see. Then I got nicked. That was tough on her, but I thought we had it sorted.'

After a pause he added: 'The funny thing is, she never did say anything to me about my work. If I'd done things different . . .' Roy trailed off; it was a line he had attempted before.

There was silence. When he spoke again Roy's voice was harder: 'It wasn't her suicide, Harry. It wasn't her crime.'

I turned to him. I tried to pretend; but the truth was I agreed. It was Roy's crime – that was obvious; and it was his suicide. There is no getting your life back together after something like that. It's over. Admit it, it is over.

Roy said, 'So Jan's coming to see you tomorrow. She's a good girl. Maybe when you get out – when do you get out?'

'In the summer.'

The film ended. I do not like films, I do not like crime films. They never show the criminal in a good light.

I said so to Roy as we were taken back to our cells.

My name is Harry d'Souza and I am in love with a woman named Jan, who, for reasons I do not know, waits for me. She says she loves me, though I am a thief and always have been.

I am forty-two. I'll be forty-three by the time I get out. I am conscious of time. Time for me has always been here and now: the things I wanted and needed were the things I wanted and needed at that moment; and they were what I could discard at will. The future was never something I dwelt on. I am not pitching for effect when I say the most I expected from it was a reasonable run of luck;

and I never kidded myself – luck is like holiday weather: you hope it lasts, but when it breaks there is no point in crying; all you can do is wait for it to pick up again.

I am conscious of distance: distance I put between me and my work and the people I work with; the distance I keep between different parts of my own life. I have always needed a clear view of what was going on around me; I have always had more than most riding on day-to-day decisions.

I learned about time and distance in prison. My last release was in seventy-nine after a ten for armed robbery, out of which I did the six and eight, with another fourteen months tacked on following a fight. I got out, went back to work; but the future let me down and I was back inside within a year.

Jan got her sense of time and distance from the perspectives laid down by an early marriage. Jan got married when she was seventeen. This was twenty years ago. Back then the years in front, she used to say, looked like familiar friends lined up and waiting to greet her. And distance to her meant closeness, always being involved with others: a husband, a family – she was part of some other union. It is not in her nature to be on the outside looking in; she lives to be in.

We have never been lovers, though I have always wanted to be her lover. The postponement of our relationship has made a strange kind of love: sometimes Jan seems close, sometimes very far away.

Jan's visit had been arranged, by letter, months ago, but it got delayed because they took me to Strangeways for a lie-down after some allegations to do with dope. In an empty cell I had time to think about how I got where I was. It was the stage I was at, looking back at things, always ending up with Jan. I do not blame her, or me, particularly. Somehow things just fell out this way. But this distance had to be narrowed down. My options were closing, and I could not trust the weather to clear.

By the time I finished the lie-down I was into the last six months of my sentence, and Jan's visit was on the cards again. I looked at my situation and decided it was time to make a few compromises with the authorities, walk away from trouble, avoid losing remission. Get out on time, for once.

This cost me because I used to imagine Jan could see me in the prison, at my best times, that she could see me when men came to me and asked for advice, or when I faced down a screw. She would know then I counted for something. I knew this was a fantasy, an adolescent fantasy, but I was an empty-handed suitor and had nothing else to impress Jan with, not even in the vain world of my own head.

I had another problem about compromising. In the block at Strangeways there was a screw called Ivan Blair that I had a history with. Although he was not an intelligent man, Blair was attuned to every nuance of prisoners' behaviour. He picked up the rearrangement of my priorities as the snake detects a feint made by its prey, by tasting the air with his tongue. From that moment, Blair provoked me in a hundred different ways every day.

My visits had accumulated while I was in Manchester, and I asked the governor to let me take them somewhere where the conditions were better. Blair opposed this, but I ended up getting moved to London and the Scrubs. Blair said he looked forward to seeing me when I got back.

The night of my arrival there was a picture show. That was when I talked to Roy.

The next morning – the morning of Jan's visit – I woke before five. By ten I was weary, and during the long wait I smoked too much. I was nervous and my throat was sore. Then they called me.

I sat at a laminated table and waited. To my left there was a window, but it was so heavily barred I could see nothing outside. The glass cast back a reflection. It took me a moment to realize it was mine. I sat up straight, as though rebuked.

Jan was coming towards me.

Before I could stand up she leaned over and kissed me lightly on the cheek. We rarely kissed, even this kind of kiss. I felt a sudden release of tension. I felt happy. I was back in London, away from Blair and the Strangeways block; and here was Jan, with kisses.

I had never been able to hold Jan's gaze – it was always too direct, too obviously expectant, and I turned away from her now, searching the tabletop for something of interest.

Our conversation was disconnected. We exchanged bits and pieces of news, nothing that would mean anything to outsiders, and she kept things going when silence threatened to swamp us. Two prisoners passed on the way to their visitors. I caught my reflection again in the window.

She was looking at me, with a smile.

She said, 'Come on, Harry. Time to stop fencing.'

'What?' I said. I was not ready for this, not yet.

Her face suddenly set. She seemed to be assessing something — me, the situation.

'Can I have a cigarette?' she asked.

I opened the packet and gave her a light.

'Do you remember,' she began, 'do you remember what you said in your letter? You sent me a letter.'

'That's right.'

She waited.

'How are things?' I said.

'Things?'

'In general. Are you OK?'

She laughed sourly. With her eyes fixed on me, she slowly shook her head. She sucked on the cigarette, then said, 'I thought, after your letter . . . I didn't expect this.'

'What?' I said.

She crossed her legs. The movement was aggressive and mocking.

I turned and studied my reflection in the glass of the window. I could not see Jan's. I felt something desperately, unpleasantly familiar, something inside me giving way, failure looming.

I heard a tapping noise, Jan drumming her fingers on the table. The impatient tattoo was like a challenge. Without thinking, I put my hand over hers. I had never done anything like that before, not with Jan. The patterns of our behaviour with another person are set down within minutes of the first meeting; I do not believe they can ever be rearranged. With other women I have played many parts: the romantic, the flirt, the rogue, the loyal defender. But with Jan it had been caginess and suspicion from the first.

Jan looked at me sideways. After a moment, she mashed her cigarette into the ashtray and put her hands on top of mine.

'Harry,' she said earnestly, 'I never expected life would turn out a bed of roses. When I was a kid, when I got married, I thought, this is what you do. You have kids, your kids grow up, you get old. That was my mother's life. Christ, Harry, she was happy for two years of her life — the year before she got married and the year after. The rest — what was the rest?'

She paused, then, her eyes downcast, she put her forehead lightly against mine.

'Harry, I love you. I always have. I would have left Derek, you know that, all you had to do was say something. I was sure eventually you would. Because I was always so happy with you, when we had time together.'

'Maybe,' I said, 'it would turn out like your mother.'

'No, no. I know we would be happy. Harry, I waited. Even when it all went flat, I waited. Some other men came around. I didn't want to know, at first.'

'Then?'

'Then I did. You know that. Sometimes I was punishing you. Sometimes I did it for pleasure and didn't think about you.'

The harshness of this made me pull away from her. But she held me fast.

'We have to be honest,' she said. 'If we're to sort things out.'

'Maybe it's best not to say anything.'

'That's always been your way, Harry. But where has it got us?'

She took my hands to her lap. Our foreheads were still touching.

She said, 'I feel sorry for Derek. He treated me badly, especially when I was young. But now I've upset him. I told him I was leaving.'

'You told him?'

'Yes.'

'What did you say?'

'That the time had come, that I had to change my life.'

I pulled back and looked at her. She tugged at my hands in her lap.

'There's no such thing as change,' I said.

'What are you saying?'

'People don't change. They think they can, they want to believe they can. Maybe they change some small piece of their life. Like they get a new job, buy a new house. But the person doesn't change. Is there one person you know that has changed?'

She said wearily, 'Not you anyway, Harry.'

I felt her grip on my hands weaken.

I spoke quickly. 'You say let's be honest. OK. You're leaving your husband, I'll be out in a few months. Great. We get together. Are we going to change? I mean, look at our lives. Are they going to get better?'

In anger, she grabbed the hair on the back of my head and yanked it.

'Yes,' she hissed into my face. 'Yes. They will. But you have to want that, Harry.'

Her grip relaxed. I put a hand on each of her thighs and with small movements tried to let her know I was backing off. She rested her head on my shoulder, as though exhausted. I kissed her ear.

Jan's intensity, her anger, had caused my heart to beat fast; her nearness and warmth were disturbingly erotic.

I moved one hand up to her ribs, my thumb on the side of her breast, covered from view by the way her short jacket fell. I moved the thumb once across the nipple. She flinched slightly. I did it again.

I thought, What am I doing? This is pathetic. I was degrading Jan, who did not have to get her kicks like this – here, in front of these other people – who had a husband and anyone else she cared to have, for she was a good-looking woman. Some of the prisoners and their visitors seemed to be staring. I felt humiliation creep into my bones. I flushed with embarrassment: for me, but especially for Jan.

I heard Jan swallow softly. It was not from sexual excitement. I did not kid myself that what I was doing was driving her mad with desire, but still the sound urged me on.

I got a knee between her legs and she was passive, she let me do it.

I stroked the nipple, and we began to rock, almost imperceptibly. I wanted to put my free hand on her buttocks, to pull her into me still more, but the distance between us ruled that out. Instead, my hand found work at the top of her thigh, clumsily competing against my knee for access to her.

She raised her head. I thought she was going to say, Enough. But she kissed me, and pushed into me strongly, jamming herself against my knee. I strained against her, scrabbling at her; my thumb was no longer flicking at her nipple – I held the breast in my hand and squeezed. I was not gentle.

I broke the kiss. I said, 'I get out in June. My release date is the fifteenth.'

'June the fifteenth,' she said. She kissed me. When I tried to speak she sucked my lip fiercely. I pushed harder against her.

'Harry, Harry,' she whispered.

I wanted to plunge inside her. I screwed my eyes tight shut, bright colours burst in my head. I wanted to fight, I wanted to roar and cry, I wanted to push her against the table and drive myself inside her.

I needed air. I pulled back.

'Are you OK?' she asked; then she laughed, a low, dirty chuckle.

It embarrassed me a little, though I have to say I loved it. All sorts of things were going through my mind: this is what it could be like for us. After June the fifteenth, if I did not fuck things up, we could do this, be together, do whatever we wanted with each other. Jan was right. Of course there is change.

I looked around the visiting room, a sense of fantastic well-being spread through me. I felt alert, strong, sexual, filled with energy. And my energy seemed to fill Jan. There was a new, refreshed brightness about her. Her cheeks had a high colour; there were blisters of sweat on her hairline.

'Say something,' she said.

'It would be too dirty.'

I went to kiss her again, but she avoided my mouth.

She said, 'I'm going to stay with my sister in Wales. She has a cottage she lets during the summer season. I can stay until things get busy.'

'When's that?'

'June'll be OK. But she won't let me stay longer. We don't really get on. I'll wait for you there. Until the fifteenth.'

I was peevishly disappointed. I had assumed she would meet me at the gates of whatever prison I would be released from.

She read me. 'If we've got closer, it's because I kept making the moves.'

'Give me the address,' I said.

She took a long look at me.

'Why should I trust you, Harry? What have you ever done that I should trust you?'

'I don't know what to say to that, Jan. Maybe it's the work I do. It's never been safe for me just to do something because I've wanted to. It's always been plotting, trying to see all the angles, keeping a distance. Or maybe it's just me.'

'I don't understand what you're saying,' she said.

'I've always put things off, important things, until I was sure how they were going to turn out.' The connections in this line of

THE CRIME AND SUICIDE OF HARRY D'SOUZA 27

explanation had seemed obvious when I began, but I was losing myself.

'I know I can't do that any more,' I said, hoping this would be definitive enough.

I do not know if she was convinced; but she said, 'I'll give you the address.'

Something of my elation had been dissipated by the failure to explain myself, but Jan's spirits seemed to have survived my unwieldy reasoning. I watched as she did a half-turn to get to her overcoat, draped over the back of the chair. The movement pushed a breast out and it strained against the wool of her sweater. She twisted a little further. Both nipples stood out hard. It was all I could do to stop myself touching her.

Agitated, I turned away and, seeking distraction, looked into the window: I caught sight of Jan's reflection, and was immediately calmed, reassured. The picture was quite beautiful. There were tricks of light and shadow and prospect: there was a woman, unaware of scrutiny; nothing about her belonged to the world of prisons: in fact, looming out of the darkness, light in her face and hair, she seemed disembodied, quite free of context and position.

I searched the reflection for myself, to locate my place beside the woman. I was hard to find, and I felt a swell of anxiety. The window vibrated, the tiniest tremor – some truck passing nearby – and I materialized into view. But it was not what I had been looking for. The woman was still there, in the foreground, light on her face; and in the shadows behind her a man. But whatever the deceit of plane and perspective, he was half as big again as she. Their connection was false. It was as if the two had been cut from different pictures and pasted together.

'This is the address.'

The words came out of nowhere. I hardly heard her. I hardly saw the paper she handed me.

'I'm glad I came.'

I nodded. She kissed me on the mouth.

'It's going to be all right,' she said as she left.

Blair was grinning when I arrived back at the block in Strangeways. His snake's tongue tasted something unexpected in the air, but he said nothing.

Jan sent me a letter that ended: 'We've come so far, Harry. See you in June. In Wales.'

The letter in my hand, I calculated: one hundred and thirty seven days to go.

The next morning Blair unlocked me. I did not give him the chance to say anything, just drove my fist into the side of his face. He did not go down straight away, and I caught him on the nose and kicked him between the legs, hard.

At the adjudication I lost sixteen weeks' remission. A new release date: October the twelfth.

I travelled to Wales the day I got out. Jan's sister was not friendly. She said Jan had moved on. No one knew where she was.

SUNSHINE
Anne Billson

We came up from Croydon. Evelyn and Marietta attracted quite a bit of attention on the train, probably because of their clown costumes. I tried hard not to feel self-conscious in their company, but it was a relief when we reached Victoria and they headed off towards the District line.

I tottered down the escalator to the northbound platform of the Victoria line. There was a train in the station, and it was already half full; by the time the doors closed, it was crammed. Getting Charlie's guitar out of its case was a bit of a struggle, and I couldn't help poking one or two of the other passengers in the ribs. They scowled, but they didn't complain. Londoners never do.

I waited until the train moved off before I began to sing 'We've Only Just Begun' by the Carpenters, which was one of the songs Charlie liked. I couldn't remember all the words, but it didn't matter, because I filled in the gaps with la-la-la. None of the passengers seemed to mind; they stared straight ahead of them, but I knew that, beneath the deadpan exteriors, they were really enjoying their journey, for once. They were smiling inside.

At least, *most* of the passengers were smiling inside. There always has to be one bad apple, hasn't there? A grouchy man in a grey overcoat huffed and puffed and finally said, 'Could you please *stop* that racket? Otherwise I shall complain to the guard.'

Charlie always said that aggression got you nowhere. If people were rude to us, he said, it was because of their own inadequacies and we ought always to respond with a smile. So I stopped singing for a moment and directed my broadest, sunniest smile at the man. 'Don't be such a spoilsport,' I said to him. 'I'm just trying to bring a little sunshine into your life. Besides, these trains don't have guards any more.'

He turned purple and shrank back, and we didn't get another peep out of him all the way to King's Cross, which is where he and a whole lot of other people got off. I stayed on the train, which was transformed into an altogether more pleasant environment now the crush had subsided. I even managed to find myself a seat.

When I'd had enough of the Carpenters, I took a deep breath
and launched straight into 'Memories', by Andrew Lloyd-Webber.
And I put all my heart and soul into it, because I knew this one was
Charlie's absolute favourite. I sang all the way to Walthamstow and
back.

There was a time when I would have sneered at the type of person
who plays the guitar in public. When I first moved to London, I
was like everyone else: hard-boiled and aggressive, pushy and
acquisitive. When I tore along the pavement with my head down
and my shoulders squared, I expected everyone to scramble out of
the way, and if they didn't, I barged straight into them, and it
served them right.

I had a high-powered job in a publishing firm, and I earned lots
of money, and I spent a lot of money too. But something was
missing from my life. I felt I was going places, but I never seemed
to arrive. There was a gaping void within me, waiting to be filled.

And then, one day, Charlie came along and filled it.

I barely noticed him at first; he was the still centre in the eye of
the rush-hour hurricane. He was hanging around the ticket machines
in Leicester Square station like a homeless person, but he didn't look
homeless – he was too clean and well-dressed, and he smelled of
something expensive.

My Travelcard had expired, and I hadn't got round to getting a
new one, so I was having to use one of those wretched machines. I
had what I thought was the right change, and the small coins were
no problem, but the machine kept regurgitating the fifty pence.
There was a restless queue building up, and the seconds were
ticking away, and I was late, and my eyes were prickling with hot
tears of frustration.

I was pushing the fifty into the slot for the umpteenth time,
when he stepped forward and gently but firmly grasped my wrist.
In a soft voice he said, 'Calm down, little sister. This machine
doesn't take fifty-pence coins.'

'Well, it bloody well *should* do,' I snapped, 'and I'm *not* your
little sister!' And then he caught me with his eyes and I never
looked back.

They were the deepest eyes I had ever seen, they were dark pools
of compassion. I felt an extraordinary wave of emotion well up in

my heart. Some of it was desire, and some of it was the knowledge that, at last, I had found *my other half*.

It was us against the world. We sort of drifted away from the machines as the people rushed by. I forgot about where I was going, and I never went there again. Nor did I go back to work. From that moment on, I had a new job. I was a new person. I was saved.

Croydon was good, he explained, because Croydon wasn't just a town, it was a state of mind. It was a part of London, and at the same time it wasn't London at all. London was a dangerous place. Stay too long in London, Charlie always said, and you would find yourself sucked back into the pit. But you could stand in Croydon, on the edge, and peer into it without falling in.

It turned out that I wasn't the only one who had been plucked out of the pit. In all, there were thirteen of us living in the tiny terraced house in Croydon: twelve women, and Charlie the only man. He only saved women, he said, because only women deserved to be saved. It wasn't his house, but he acted as though it was. Some of the others talked occasionally about the woman to whom it had once belonged, they wondered why she had left, but she was long gone now, and no one knew where.

There were three bedrooms, and it was only natural that Charlie should have the biggest, even though it meant the rest of us were a bit cramped. We didn't mind. It wasn't as though he were selfish about having a room to himself – most nights he helped ease the overcrowding by inviting one or two of us in to share it with him.

After dark we were safely tucked up beneath his wing. But every morning we travelled up to London as though we were regular commuters, and we tried to make a difference.

'Each of us,' Charlie said, 'has the power for good or evil. It is up to each of us to choose.' We'd heard this speech before, but we didn't mind hearing it again.

'Oh Charlie,' whispered Marietta. She was always gazing at him with that gormless expression, trying to attract his attention. But Charlie showed no favouritism. He dispensed wisdom and love with scrupulous impartiality.

'We live in an evil world,' he said, 'but it is up to us to try and make it a better place. It is our duty to spread a little sunshine through other people's lives.'

'I'll spread anything you want,' giggled Nora, but he took no notice of the interruption.

'Be assured,' he said, 'I am not forcing you to do anything against your will. We are equal partners. Let no one say you are my slaves.'

'I'll be your slave, Charlie,' squealed Tricia. I wanted to slap her, but I knew Charlie wouldn't have approved. He was the only one allowed to dispense physical punishment, and he hardly ever found it necessary.

'Look,' said Naomi, 'I'm not so sure I want to stay in this shithole much longer.'

The rest of us groaned. Naomi was always complaining. We couldn't understand why Charlie didn't ask her to leave. But, as usual, he ignored her whingeing. 'Playthings and objects for the opposite sex,' he went on, 'that's all you ever were. Even I used to think like that – but no longer. Now I humbly admit that you women are my equals, indeed – in many ways – my superiors. We're all in this together, toiling towards a common goal. As individuals, none of us can change the world, but – together – we can try.'

There was a breathless hush, followed by a collective sigh of assent. Our twelve faces were tilted towards him, trying to soak up some of his reflected light. He always stood in the brightest part of the room, so that we had come to associate him with the sun. And he always wore white, so that it was sometimes difficult to look at him directly.

We, on the other hand, were encouraged to dress entirely in black. Charlie said black was the least frivolous of all the colours. Women who dressed in black stood more chance of being taken seriously as people. Nevertheless, it was important that we take pride in our bodies, he said. We should never attempt to suppress our natural form, and so the kind of dresses he liked us to wear were black and clingy and finished quite a long way above the knee.

Charlie was so intent upon bolstering our confidence, I didn't like to upset him by complaining that I didn't feel comfortable in the high heels he handed out – they made me feel wobbly and insecure. I suffered in silence – I didn't want him thinking I had no self-esteem, not after everything he'd done.

'So far,' he said, 'you've all been wonderful. Truly I chose wisely when I plucked each of you from the pit, and you followed me home.'

'It wasn't like that at all,' said Naomi. 'I *didn't* follow you. You asked me out, and we went to the pictures and then I came back here to spend the night.'

Several of us shushed her, but Charlie was smiling. 'But you came, Naomi, you came. You came and you stayed.'

'Yeah,' muttered Naomi, 'but that was before I realized I was supposed to be part of a *harem*.' The rest of us tittered in derision. Poor old Naomi didn't get it *at all*.

I'd had my doubts about her for a long time now. Once, at Victoria station, I saw her climbing into a taxi and shooting off towards the West End, though later she tried to deny it. It was obvious she pursued her own agenda during daylight hours, and covered for herself by telling lies. They were lies so extravagant and incredible, they frequently made Charlie laugh out loud. The rest of us were furious, but we didn't dare object. After lights out one night, Marietta admitted that she too had occasionally made up stories in the hope of attracting Charlie's attention. Some of the others confessed they sometimes exaggerated their achievements. I was shocked. It had never occurred to me to do anything but tell the truth.

'But Naomi,' Charlie said, twisting his elegant fingers into a configuration that reminded me of the wings of a powerful bird. 'Haven't you always been free to go?'

'Free to go where? I don't have anywhere *to* go. My boyfriend chucked me out, remember? That was all *your* fault.'

'Shut up, Naomi,' said Lucinda.

'Yeah, shut up, Naomi,' said Tricia. 'If you don't like it, you can leave. No one's stopping you.'

'Ladies, ladies, please,' said Charlie, smiling indulgently. 'Show a little solidarity. You're going to have to stick together if we're going to make any difference at all to this city of ours. Which reminds me, how did you get on with Operation Walrus?'

'It went really well,' I piped up, feeling my face grow warm beneath his gaze. We all fell over ourselves, trying to tell him how we had beamed a little sunshine into the gloomiest tunnels. Evelyn and Marietta had done their clown act on the District line. Jasmine and Tessa had treated the Metropolitan to re-enactments of scenes from *Casablanca* and *Gone With the Wind*. Dawn and Hilary had performed the duet from *Lakmé* all the way to Heathrow and back. Stacey, like me, had gone solo with a guitar and a repertoire of popular songs. 'Good, good,' said Charlie, listening to our cheerful babble. 'Perfect. You are all such wonderful women.' We basked in his approval, but our basking was tinged with disappointment. We had made him smile, but we hadn't made him laugh, not this time. It was rare that he laughed out loud, but we seemed to spend a large portion of our lives trying to make it happen.

At first, I had been reluctant to go back up to London with the rest of them. I was terrified of what might happen when I found myself drawn back into the addictive ebb and flow of city life. But Charlie had gently coaxed me into the swing of things.

The first project he gave me was a solo one – devised especially to give me confidence, he said. I was to buy a Travelcard and roam around the Underground until I found someone listening to loud pop music through leaky earphones. He said it wouldn't be long before I ran into one of these selfish people, who blighted the lives of thousands of their fellow passengers with their *chinka-chinka-chinka* noise. Then I was to whip out my scissors and snip through the lead connecting the earphones to the personal stereo.

For most of the day, I dithered nervously, but, as soon as I'd snipped my first lead and got away with it, I experienced a rush of adrenalin so intoxicating that I grew bolder. For the most part, I operated under the cover of the crowd and made my get-aways while the victims checked their neutered machines in consternation. Towards late afternoon, however, I grew reckless, and leant forward to sever a man from his music in full view of the entire carriage. He bellowed with rage, and it was only due to prompt action on the part of some of the other passengers that I was able to slip away with my limbs intact.

But it was worth it. Later on, when I told Charlie, he laughed so much I thought he was going to have a cardiac arrest.

I was to find out that each of the other women had been through a similar initiation. Once we had crossed that barrier, there was no looking back – we couldn't *wait* to get on that train up to London and do our bit.

It was always Charlie who had the best ideas. When Lucinda suggested we spend the day picking up litter, the rest of us would nod politely, but we couldn't summon much enthusiasm for a plan like that. Charlie's ideas were so much more ingenious. Instead of picking up litter, he said, wouldn't it be much more fun to catch people in the act of dropping it, and *then* pick it up and hand it back to them with a smile on our faces? And just suppose they didn't accept it, and we were to follow them home and post it through their letter-boxes? Charlie was right – it *was* much more fun, even if it did leave Dawn with a black eye and a cracked rib.

Charlie said we were still weighed down by traces of our old, conventional outlook on life, and this was why some of his ideas struck us as off the wall, though once he had explained things, we could never understand how we'd been so stupid. During one of our togetherness sessions, for example, Hilary suggested we spend the afternoon helping tourists. There had immediately been a collective murmur of approval – from everyone except Charlie.

'No, no *no!*' he groaned, slapping his forehead in exasperation. 'No, no, *no!* How stupid can you get? God, sometimes I wonder why I bother with you lot.' We all looked at him in astonishment. Hilary's idea had seemed fine to us.

'Londoners *hate* tourists,' he explained. 'They *hate* them. Tourists travel around in packs and block pavements and jump queues and ask idiotic questions. If we're going to make London a nicer, better place to live and work, we have to *drive the tourists away.*'

And so Charlie hatched Operation Oswald, which involved the misdirecting of as many tourists as possible. If groups of addled Swedes asked for Piccadilly Circus, we would draw elaborate maps to ensure they ended up in West Ruislip. If a party of Japanese announced they were looking for Trafalgar Square, we would go out of our way to see them comfortably ensconced on an express train to Glasgow.

But those old, conventional traces lingered on. I felt bad about the shoplifting, for instance, even though it wasn't as immoral as it sounded. Charlie said you couldn't really call it shoplifting anyway, it was more like *forced sponsorship*. It was better than being a drain on the welfare state, he said. We were strong, able-bodied people, and we could look after ourselves. Besides, no one could have accused us of being selfish, because we never stole for personal gain. We only ever stole for Charlie – clothes and gadgets and toiletries and compact discs and books, and anything he asked us to get, and anything else we could think of while we were at it.

One day, Charlie announced he had dreamt up an extra special assignment for us. He called it Operation Blackbird.

'What's the biggest problem for people who travel by tube?' he asked. 'What's the worst thing about travelling on the Underground?'

We racked our brains, but we couldn't come up with an answer.

'The biggest problem for the London commuter,' said Charlie, 'the single thing that contributes most to his daily misery is overcrowding. There are *too many people in too small a space.*'

'Only at peak hours,' Evelyn said helpfully, but Charlie ignored her.

'There's not much we can do about that,' said Tricia.

'Oh yes there is,' said Charlie. 'We can help to lighten the Underground's load. Today I want each of you to go to an Underground station and pick a man. Choose carefully. Choose a man who looks as though he has spent his life using and abusing women like you. Choose a man who has a mean-looking face, a heart full of stones, and a grim future, and wait until the train is coming into the station and then push him off the platform.'

There was a puzzled silence.

'What?' asked Lucinda at last. 'You mean . . .?'

Charlie looked a little impatient. 'Is it really so difficult for you to grasp? Yes, today I want each of you to push a man under a train.'

Naomi exploded into life. 'You're *joking!*' she shrieked. 'I've never *heard* anything so sick! I'm *out of here!*' She flounced towards the door, then turned back. 'Who's coming with me?'

There was a pause, and then Stacey and Nora shuffled off after her. 'Yeah, the shoplifting was one thing, but this is going too far,' said Tricia. 'Let's go pack.'

Charlie held up his hands, palms outward in what was supposed to be a placatory gesture, though to me it looked like those bird wings again. 'Ladies, ladies, I'll come clean, I'll admit it. Bad joke. It was all a bad joke.'

'Well, I'm still going,' said Naomi. 'I've had enough.'

'Me too,' said Tricia. I was surprised to see her on Naomi's side. Normally she was one of Charlie's most enthusiastic supporters.

'At least let us say goodbye properly,' he said, turning on his most charming smile. 'You're not dashing off right this instant, are you? You can't possibly leave without your goodbye present.'

'Present? What present?' asked Tricia.

Charlie was gazing straight at Naomi now. She knew exactly what kind of present he was talking about. 'Remember, Naomi? Remember when you first came?'

Naomi remembered. She seemed almost to simper. 'OK, OK,' she said. 'We'll go and pack our stuff, and then we can say goodbye properly, and *then* we're out of here.' I wondered why they kept going on about packing, when we shared everything out and none of us had anything we could call our own.

Naomi looked meaningfully at Tricia and Stacey and Nora, but Nora changed her mind and stayed put. The other three clattered off upstairs, and that was the last we ever saw of them.

Charlie turned to the rest of us. 'Any others among you want to leave?'

No one wanted to, or at least no one was admitting to it. I knew what everyone was thinking. We were all thinking that, with Naomi and Tricia and Stacey out of the way, there were only nine of us left. Not only would the two small bedrooms be less cramped, there would be fewer of us competing for Charlie's attention.

And I was thinking that maybe Charlie hadn't been joking after all. But surely he couldn't have been serious? Pushing someone in front of a train was an outrageous idea. On the other hand, I could just imagine his reaction when I came home and described it to him. He would laugh and laugh. He would split his sides laughing. He would find the whole thing *hilarious*.

I looked at the others. How would they know if I chickened out? I could always say I *had* done it, and no one would be any the wiser. If Naomi and Marietta had told lies, then so could I.

I made up my mind. I would go up to London as usual, and I would hang around on tube platforms, and then I would come home and make up a story about having pushed someone on to the tracks. And if – and I meant *if* – if I happened to catch sight of a man with a particularly mean-looking face, I might just sidle up to him and nudge him forwards as the train was coming in. It was all a matter of *if*. I didn't think for one moment that this was actually going to happen.

I looked at the other women again, and wondered how many of them were thinking the same as me.

'Now about this plan,' said Charlie. 'It was just a bad joke, so let's forget it.' And he smiled the most charming smile I had ever seen, and all of us smiled back.

THE GIFT THAT UNWRAPS ITSELF
Glyn Brown

'He wants me to wear a dress.'

'*Does* he, now? And what sort of a dress would that be?'

'A damned tight one. A tight dress.'

'How do you know?'

'Because he told me.' R smacked two mugs of tea down on the circular melamine tabletop. 'Tight, he said. Something that moulds itself to you, like I do.'

'Excuse me, but you know I like my tea in a cup, sweetheart. Mugs are unladylike and ungainly. I don't want to be a nuisance, but I can't drink that.' Dorothy arched her thinly pencilled, Dietrich eyebrows.

'Good God, Mum –'

'If it's too much trouble, I'll do it myself. You know I'm capable of making just the one with a bag in a nice cup, don't you? I'm not exactly *senile*.' Dorothy's charming voice had an edge.

'Don't bother, you're the guest. Oh Mum, stay there ...' Snappily, R snatched up the mug, hurling its contents down the drain with a volley that sent scalding tea lashing up the sides of the chrome sink unit and over the plates stacked on the draining-board. She flicked on the kettle and leaned against the worktop, folding her arms heavily and staring at the ceiling. 'Of course, my tea'll be stone cold by the time I sit down. How stupid. Why don't you drink it while it's hot – ah,' she struck her forehead with a palm, 'impossible, it's in a mug. A Tottenham Hotspur mug, at that.'

'It takes two minutes to boil a kettle,' reasoned Dorothy sagaciously. 'Let's not fuss and fume. Plenty of time for that when it's really called for.'

'Oh, and when will that be?'

'When you start making this dress.'

'*Making* it?' R fairly shrieked. 'You're psychic! So you've got *his* measure.'

Continuing with dharmic calm, Dorothy inquired, 'And does he?'

The kettle sang furiously. R ignored it. 'Does he what?'

'Mould himself to you.'

Steaming, R turned her slim body away and reached for a tea-bag. Over her shoulder, she slung out, 'Isn't that a bit purient of you?'

'The word is prurient.'

'Is it?' hissed R, with the kettle. 'And how would you know?'

'Because I'm not as stupid as you think.' Dorothy was chuckling. She had a winsome and infectious chuckle, but R wasn't in the mood.

'He says to me, wear a dress. Wear this bloody tight dress.'

'No!'

'He did. One that's so tight it shows your erect nipples.'

'Men!'

'I'm outraged. I can't believe it.'

'I can't!'

'Make it – *make* it, Rachel! – out of something tautly slinky, were his words. The man has quarried deep into the textile market. Tactel, he said. He said he'd seen a piece about it in some women's magazine – *Elle*, possibly.'

'He reads women's magazines? Where did he get one of those?'

'Don't look at me, Rachel. I don't buy them.'

'So he bought it himself!'

'Must've done. Went into a shop and bought *Elle*. Bloody hell, what kind of man *is* this? At least if he bought *Playboy*, we'd known what we were dealing with.'

'Tactel, what is that, exactly? Isn't it that pervy fabric you can hardly breathe in? It's got a kind of sheen? He's a pervert, R!'

'Don't I know it. And that's not all.'

'There's never more!'

'But there is. Get this: he has a design in mind.'

'He wants to design you a dress!'

'That's about the size of it.'

'What size?'

'Tiny. Minuscule. A dress, he actually had the audacity to instruct, that's so short it shows your – I can't.' R put her head in her hands. The smoke from her cigarette, upon which she'd been dragging as if it were a life support machine, as if it were an oxygen mask, as if it were really helping her get air into her lungs, danced like a joyous blue streamer up through her lank black hair.

'Tell me!'

R fetched a weary, humiliated sigh. 'So short, it shows your thighs and the merest teasing hint of your . . .'

'*What*?' Rachel's fist met the table with a volcanic punch, her voice was an ear-piercing falsetto. R swallowed glutinously, whispered *sotto voce*, 'nickers.' A dull, plum-dark blush swelled the delicate membranes of her face.

'Oh!' Rachel's trembling hand lurched across the space between them, reached for R's packet of Dunhill Lights and shook one out. She put it between her parted lips, her teeth clamped doggedly, struck a light and considered the flame through narrowed eyes until it burned her fingers, and she dropped the match with a chirrup. She took another, lit the death stick, inhaled deep, deep, deep, and dully said at length, 'I don't know any men like that!'

'I bet you don't. I can quite believe you. Why is it always *my* rotten luck?'

There was a silence. Beyond the window, a chaffinch sang a sweetly tangled if repetitive aria, and the melody flowed liltingly across the room until one of the other women said she was cold and smacked the window shut with a flourish that brooked no argument. It might have been more sisterly if she'd inquired as to the feelings of her neighbours – the day was warm – but this was the Eunice Peabody Women's Centre, and everyone knew that the window-shutter was possibly a) premenstrual b) postnatal c) otherwise hormonal d) pissed off with the world in general and with having to do as she was told by other people, in particular men. The temperature rose, a couple of women took off their jumpers, the bird continued to pour out its refrain, noiselessly.

'What will you do?' asked Rachel.

'Oh,' said R, draining her coffee and beginning to chuck books into her rucksack, 'I suppose I might make the thing. I haven't decided. I'm canvassing opinions.'

Rachel looked alarmed. 'What would happen if you did?'

'I expect he'd tear it off me. That would be consonant with his freakish new behaviour patterns.' R spoke with enervated resignation, concentrating on stacking her books so that they'd fit comfortably against her back and, when this was done, she turned to bid her friend adieu. She got a shock.

'Rachel? Rachel!'

Women clustered in enjoyable alarm, ministering and remarking and offering what advice they could, round Rachel's form, which lay prostrate upon the stripped pine floor.

'You girls. You poor things. Suffering sweetbreads, what kind of dull and boring grave have you dug for yourselves? It's only a dress, after all.'

'I beg your pardon?'

'You heard me, Rap –'

'Please, Mum. Call me R. Just R, not that name you saddled me with.'

'And why not? Although of course I can see the name we gave you, me and your doting father –'

'That petty despot!'

'Myself, I should say, and your loving Dad, all those years ago –'

'Not that many years.'

'In those dear, departed days when the world was innocent –'

'Innocent, my arse! I've seen those fifties snapshots, you in a conical bra, hypocrite, and you say Madonna's a whore.'

'Quite right, and so she may be, in her way, and did I suggest there was something wrong with that? At least she knows how to enjoy herself. Look at her, having a high old time, having I expect the time of her life on it.' Dorothy patted the wavelets of ash-blonde curls where they lapped her nape.

'What's this got to do with the ridiculous moniker you clamped to me like a ball and chain?'

'Just everything, my love, only everything. Consider. Did I want you to traipse along in a joyless grey rut, condemned by a name like Sybil or Clarice or –'

'Or Dorothy?'

'Yes, that's right, or Dorothy, a name whose tiresomely dull effect I myself have spent a lifetime fighting. I did not. That will predispose the world and not in her favour, I told your father, and he agreed.'

'He always did!' spat R with disgust. Had her father no back-bone?

'He did, at that. We were on the same wavelength.' Dorothy, having finished her Cocktail Sobranie, delicately licked the tip of her pinkie, just behind the long, painted nail, and dipped it in a dab of cigarette ash on the table, lifting the grey silt to her pink tongue. 'Ee-yeuch!' grimaced her daughter. 'We thought, let's give her a wildly romantic name, something to encourage reckless abandon.'

'Rapunzel.'

'We told ourselves, she'll let everything down, all those inhibitions people shore up, and her guard, and she'll let down a ladder and invite all sorts of wonderful experience into her life, which, hopefully, she'll live to the absolute fullest. But have you?'

R adjusted the shoulder strap of her beige dungarees. 'No I bloody haven't, you irresponsible old ratbag. Because if I had, I'd probably be laid up right now with every psychological affliction and every sexually transmittable ailment that's going. This is not the naïve 1940s, Mum. Life's dangerous.'

'And it wasn't then?'

'Just don't give me the doodlebug soliloquy again. If I don't know the sound of a doodlebug now from your, I'm assured, extremely accurate rendition –'

'On the nose, my rendition, Rappy, absolutely on the so to speak button.'

'Quite. The dangers we live with in the 1990s are less obvious but finally more insidious, get me?' With a self-important air R bore the ashtray to the bin, emptied it, then scoured its blue glass innards with Ecologic wash-up liquid, kind to whales. 'As for the subject of our current discussion, I've no more to say about my retarded boyfriend's strange request.'

'Poor Rachel. Convent school?'

'Grrr.' R stood up briskly. 'I must be getting on, Mum.'

'It seems so, my love. But what is there to be getting on with, this gloriously sunny morn?'

'Paying bills, telephone calls, hoovering, dusting, typing up the minutes of the meeting. Necessities.'

'Give your wizened mother another half-hour.'

'Sorry, can't. Cup of tea before you go, set you up for the journey?'

Dorothy picked at the black cavern within a pearly back tooth. You could see halfway down her larynx. She had a dark red, gleaming and very deep throat. When she'd finished her excavation she said, 'I'd rather have a gin and tonic. And don't tell me you haven't got gin, I've seen it. For medicinal purposes?'

'Gin helps you bleed, Mum. Understand? For those times when Feminax is useless.'

'Sex was always good for period pains, Rap, I don't know if it's the same in the modern world, but I expect so. A good orgasm relaxes those contracting muscles.'

R felt her forehead with the back of her wrist. 'Jesus Christ.'

'Typical of men. Palaeolithic meathead.'

'You think so? I'm glad about that. I can't tell you how much your opinion means to me.' Trying to breathe rhythmically, R raised her arms above her head in a leisurely arc, keeping her palms open to the sky. 'See, he's asked me about it again, and I don't know what to do.'

'Control your breathing, pet. Don't let that protozoic life-form inside your mindspace.' Diana drew her arms slowly down in front of her. She looked calm and all-powerful, the weak sunshine that filtered through Mr Al Huang's skylight making a halo of her Number One cut. With palms facing each other, she imagined a central column of natural dynamism, drawn to and from the *hara* – a point just below the navel – from where all energy stems. Then she thought about the spinach rissoles waiting to be grilled and eaten with a fresh green endive salad, followed by a pineapple Mivvi. In forty-five minutes, those rissoles would find themselves in the space just behind her *hara*. How would that affect the energy levels?

R thought about him. She could see him now, lying on the bed. She could see his fawn-coloured hair on the pillow, a candystriped pillow that recalled her own happy if obstreperous childhood. Candystripes meant safety. Was he something safe? She glanced sideways towards Diana. Along with the other five members of Mr Al Huang's t'ai chi class, they slowly moved their arms apart again.

'Should I make the dress, Di? That's all I'm asking.' R bit her lip. 'I must have an answer. My head's going round in circles.'

'Make the dress?' Diana hissed out of the side of her mouth. 'Kick him in the bollocks is what you do, lovey. See how he likes them apples.'

'I hear sound which is not rustle of wind in the leaves, nor movement of a field mouse through the long grass,' said Mr Al Huang with the merest hint of irritation. 'Now, we Open the Heart.'

With infinite grace, Mr Al Huang held his arms out before him, parallel with his slim, brown feet, which pointed neatly towards the class. 'Backs of hands are facing each other. Begin to open.'

With one accord, seven diligent disciples swept their arms outwards in a languorous breast-stroke. They were opening up to the universe, here in Hackney. 'Admit the planet into the self,' advised Mr Al Huang. R half-closed her eyes and felt stripes of warmth drop across her face from the slatted skylight. With one eye squinting, she could watch and follow the movement, turning her palms at their outermost point to face each other, and beginning to draw her arms together again until they were back in front of her chest. It felt good to embrace the world. But did that mean everything that was in it? As she pondered, Diana said tersely into her ear: 'After all, what *are* you? A cut-out Bunty doll?'

'I don't think so.' A spoke of sunlight smote R fiercely in the left pupil, and her eye began to water painfully. 'I mean, it never felt like that before.' Having let her attention slip, she saw she was out of step with the class. Her arms windmilled moronically, then she flung them to the sides again to catch up, callously dropping the world. She watched it, like a huge, liquidly lovely blue and white marble, fall to the cold ground and smash.

'Well, that's how it looks to an outsider,' grated Diana. 'None of us could work out what you saw in him in the first place. He's hardly a new man, is he?'

Mr Al Huang directed a gaze of shamanistic intensity in their direction.

'I don't really like the idea of the New Man, *per se*.' Dismally, R realized she didn't in fact know what she *did* like. At least, she didn't know what kind of thing she liked.

Diana smirked. 'But exactly, kitty-cat. What is a new man, after all, but a half-arsed attempt at a woman?' She emphasized the interrogative. She expected an answer. 'Well?'

R felt interrogated, exhausted. 'In which case,' continued Diana, moving forward and blocking the light entirely, 'you're better off with a woman from the start.' Her tone conveyed the irrefutable logic of it. 'At least,' she reasoned, 'a woman never tries to attack you.'

This was confusing, but Mr Al Huang swept them breathlessly on, trilling in a jubilant descant, 'Embrace Tiger, Return to Mountain exercise now. All stand straight, knees relaxed.'

They stood side by side, relaxing their knees. Diana leaned toward R, her heavy earring – a woman's fist inside a silver circle, the fist clutching what looked like a Tampax applicator but was probably a baton in the sisters' race of life – nicking R with the mute savagery of a bee-sting on the cheek, and continued, 'I expect you'll say now he never attacked you. I can see that look on your face.'

'But it's true, he never did.' R felt like a cheap turncoat.

Diana's thorny green gaze was disgusted. 'A fine point in his favour! "He never attacked me." Big of him! Frankly, that sucks.'

R could see two golden eyes. She saw him turn in the bed as he woke, reaching for her, stretching like a bear or a lazy tiger, grinning with equanimity and expecting her unhurriedly. It was hokey, but she realized she was longing for him, as electrically as an eel, and that's all there was to it. You can't fight nature – she'd tried and it had worn her thin. And, if she wasn't mistaken, hadn't that always been Diana's credo? Feeling the earth move under your feet, as Carole King put it, and letting the emotion tell you what your next step should be? That emotion could be a subtle source of energy, if you let it, as sure and as organic as the *hara* itself. Relief spread through her limbs and down her back, hot and tingling, like Vick's Vaporub. Maybe it was worth reminding Diana about that philosophy.

Mr Al Huang was encouraging everyone to sink gradually down from their bouncy knees.

'Well, he wouldn't have been my choice.' Smugly, Diana began to bend. 'I think he's bit of a dunce. For example, why isn't he here doing t'ai chi with you? You'll find that, like most men, he's out of touch with Gaia, the female force, the life force. He's got no plant element in him, no animal, no mystic. He uses the technical brain instead of intuition, when intuition is the only real guide we have.' Her thighbone creaked. 'Ow!' She stamped a foot to sort out her mussed-up musculature. 'Say I'm wrong.'

But R was thinking, and she was listening to Mr Al Huang. 'This movement symbolizes acknowledgement of personal energy and willingness to harness, then release, that energy. Slowly, breathing calmly, bring in arms to gather imaginary tiger.'

R smiled broadly, drenched unexpectedly with ineffable joy. Gradually but deliberately, she gathered the tiger in her arms.

★

On the way to the restaurant, where she spent her evenings trying
to be civil to an assortment of snotty diners, R decided for once not
to cut the usual neurotically time-saving corners. Instead, she took
the scenic route, via Coram's Fields, the place where the sheep are,
just off Russell Square. You're only allowed into this park if you're
a child or if one's with you, but luckily a small girl going to have it
out with a swing was willing to accompany R for the price of
several bars of Cadbury's Old Jamaica. Inside the park, they shook
on it and went their separate ways, the tot hiding her stash down
her jumper. R, at leisure, wandered over the hummocky lawns.
They seemed startlingly green. In the middle of a ring of daisies, she
stopped, gazing down with wonder. Then she knelt. Then, surprising even herself and alerting several parents, she bent right over and
put her face in the lush viridian blades. From woodlouse level, they
seemed tall, illuminated like cathedral windows by the sun behind
them, low in the afternoon sky. R inhaled deeply, filling her chest
with the sensuous pungency of the grass.

'Well, you certainly didn't learn those tricks from me. Oh, I'm
proud of you, infinitely so. But I can't claim the glory for teaching
you your needlework skills.' Dorothy sipped her tea. 'Got any
more biscuits?'

'In the cupboard. What, finished all those Custard Creams?'

'There were five left, don't be miserly.' Dorothy leapt to her
feet and rifled through the dark kitchen cabinets with girlish
gusto. Clutching a fistful of Bourbons, she resumed: 'A good bit of
stitching.'

'Well, unlike some I wasn't playing truant during my school
years.'

'Missed a lot, then.'

'That's how I learned all about tacking, and zigzagging on
elasticated lamé to hold it but keep that important stretch, and
basting and bias binding.'

'Ho hum.' Dorothy yawned rudely. 'Only joking. Myself, I'd go
and buy the thing. But then of course you had a pattern to follow.'

'Yup, that's right. A pretty rude one.' R's eyes twinkled like
twin Dog Stars, two copies of Sirius, in the constellation of the
Greater Dog, the brightest star in the heavens, which gives its name
to those lazy, hazy, overheated dog days.

'Followed it to the letter?'

'No, I improvised a lot. Used some imagination. He said lamé. He didn't say gold.'

'Never thought you had it in you. And that skimpy item is the result. As rude a piece of clothing as ever was seen in the sweatiest New Orleans cat-house.'

'I suppose so.'

'Sexist as all get out.'

'No, it's not! This is a gorgeous dress.'

'Eye of the beholder.' Dorothy dunked her Bourbon.

'Quite. I'm beholding it now, and he will tomorrow, and we'll both think it's beautiful. This dress is an expression of our . . .'

'*Lurve*.' Swabbing up crumbs from the table, Dorothy licked her finger and then waved it triumphantly. 'You, madam, are finally in love.'

'That's, I suppose, true.'

'And it's made a fool of you.'

'What's that?' R sat up and surveyed her licentious crone of a parent. She'd expected at least her mother's blessing in this.

'I don't understand. I've let down my guard. Are you saying I've done the wrong thing?'

An antic bray of mirth filled the stale air. 'Naw, I'm just testing you. Dearie me, I'm merely seeing if you really are in love, and braced for the heady risks, or if you're still caught on the prongs of passionless, nineties indecision.'

R stood up. Her head was pounding. 'I've had enough,' she declared. 'Come on, out of that chair: this is my house and you've had your hour. Put down that tea. You can take your biscuit. Ah no, no buts. Time to surrender, Dorothy.'

'Is this a sense of humour I see before me?' quoth Dot. With unexpected compassion, she smoothed her wayward daughter's shiny hair. 'At last. Hang on to it, gird yourself with it, ducks; it'll be your best defence. For it's a lubricious old, vicious old funfair ride, once you pays your money, and now and again, remember, the machines are faulty.' So saying, she collected her broom and departed with a wink.

What a night! The breeze was a veritable zephyr, a stroking fingertip of a thing that beckoned its way toward R and, by her

side, insinuated itself along her nape – her hair was, for the first
time ever perhaps, put up, and it suited her – and into the delicate
machinery of her ear, kissing the lobe, whizzing around the convoluted cochlea, sighing with emotion in the Eustachian tube. She
wriggled. Wriggling, her thighs rubbed together, one with the
other, and the unusual sensation of ten-denier stockings and the bare
few inches above the stocking-tops set her heart sprinting. No
wonder mum and her friends sold the GIs so many favours for a
pair of nylons, she reflected, biting her lip. God, these tart's duds are
turning me into a simple-minded floozie. The notion made her
want to giggle. She took a left turn, and then a right turn, and she
was almost at his door. She wanted to run. Then she wanted to
stop, but she didn't. She had to keep walking in her tack-slim heels.
If you interrupted the momentum, she'd discovered, you fell over
like a day-old chick. If this was a scene in a movie I was watching,
thought R, I'd be leading the rabble, I'd be chucking popcorn at
the screen and catcalling like billy-o.

Ringing the bell, she heard him running down the stairs, and
that made her shiver. His look when he saw her was one she didn't
recognize. He was formidable, very strange in a dark suit and white
shirt, open at the neck with a bush of chest hair curling out. He
ushered her in but mysteriously refused to touch her.

His sitting room was stark as ever; but it was lit with candles.
They confronted each other, and she realized then that she didn't
know quite what to do. As she faltered, he offered her a wide and
encouraging smile, like a well-wisher waving on an actress from the
wings, and she was filled with languorous triumph. Shucked off her
big, concealing coat, stood there as if on stage, and some tune –
a thing she couldn't place, probably by Test Department or The
Pixies – filled her head, and she thought, drumbeats, he comes to
me with drumbeats. And flugelhorns. All manner of stirring, martial
sounds announce my lover. That had a ring to it, a definite
sonority. Was it Shakespeare or was she making it up? Too damned
delirious to tell.

So this was the thing, this was the traditional, primordial stuff.
Intoxicating. Even though, as of course she knew, he wasn't a
caveman or a Tarzan or thankfully any kind of new man. He was
himself. She felt goatish and wild, and ridiculously sentimental.
'Rapunzel,' he said, making it sound almost good, and on cue she

ripped out the long pin and let down her hair, washed and conditioned and set for thirty minutes on Carmens. Costume drama, like a play, a game for modern lovers. But we're still the buddies we always were, in sneakers and T-shirts, ain't that so, buster? she thought. This was the secret the two of them shared, the thing she'd almost forgotten, and which her mother would never understand, because it hadn't existed in her day, and it was something she mustn't betray by winking in his direction. Her grin got lost in her locks.

Still at quite a distance, still way across the room in the shadows, he regarded her body in its shiny garb. She smoothed her palms over her hips in a nearly natural way.

'Know why I wanted to see you in this dress?'

She didn't answer: tossed her confident head like a Lippizaner. The candlelight caught and danced in her tresses, he strode over in two giant steps and wound his hand into a hank of it, getting a painfully powerful purchase which startled her from her dream.

'It's because I want to watch you take it off. Strip slowly. Tempt me. I want the gift of you. I want the gift that unwraps itself.' The eyes that had seemed tigerish glittered opaquely, pale as a blind man's. She opened her mouth to discuss it, but he moved towards her with a piece of black velvet twisted in his hands, saying, 'It's sexiest with a gag.' Seeing her face, he seemed displeased. 'Have some self-confidence. You can look good in this.'

Now, he alone could speak and he said: 'I thought it was time you grew up, eased out of that denim chrysalis, said So long to your ivory tower. Sure, we know what we said when we met. But this is the modern world, and I can't wait for ever for you to change. I'm hungry. I'm starving.' He seemed ravenous. 'And you're so succulent.'

Something in his voice seemed coated, thickly furred. He raised an eyebrow, the music that she'd heard before – she recognized it now, a cockeyed fairground tune – hummed in her ears, and the room hoicked high its petticoats and danced around her shoulders until she felt sick. She wished she'd never put up her hair; then she'd never have let the ladder of it down. Beyond the moonless windows, the ground seemed far, far away.

Slowly, thinking, This can't be how it ends, she began to undo everything.

A MAP OF THE HEART
Julie Burchill

'Over the actual map of every great city,' said David's friend Matt as they cruised down Baker Street with the top down, the pound up and Sade shimmering on the car radio somewhere in the late eighties, 'we can impose a map of the heart. That is, a map of the places in that city where we have fucked, chucked and fallen in love.'

David took a hand off the wheel, lit a Marlboro and threw the match through the window and looked at his friend, amused but not amazed. It was the eighties, after all, and everyone spoke as if they were trying out for a stint on *South of Watford*. Everyone *tried*; that was why life was such fun, then.

'Who said that?'

'*Me*.' Matt pointed at his chest smugly, as though to distinguish from the other Me who might be off somewhere doing a little light shopping.

'Yeah, but who else?' Matt never said anything unless someone else had said it first; the ecologically sound theory of wit and wisdom.

Matt shrugged. 'I dunno. But it's all Lombard Street to a china orange he's either bent, dead or French. Probably all three.'

David laughed as he swung the jeep up to the kerb outside the cocktail bar; there was blow to be snorted, songs to be sung and slappers to be saveloyed. It was another wonderful night on which to be young, free and single in London, England, 1988.

Six weeks later David lay face down on his bed, weeping.

'Oh, Marie!' he gasped between bouts. 'Marie, Marie! Marie, Marie, Marie!' He rolled on to his back and tears filled up his ears. Drunk on love, he threw up into the bin beside the bed. As luck would have it, it was wickerwork and, like one of the Alaïa bustiers so popular at the time, let out more than it kept in.

David laughed, bitterly he hoped. He watched the sick spreading into the carpet. Fitting, somehow. 'What a tragic farce,' he said to himself, and was sick again.

After a cool decade of putting it about, David had fallen in love at the age of twenty-five with one Marie Machetti, Matt's sister. Like Matt, she was tall, dark and handsome; unlike him she was one of those silent jobs whose personality expressed itself mostly through fiddling with the radio, finding a song it liked and listening to it until another one it didn't much fancy started, when the whole process would begin again. They were mostly car radios because David was with her mostly in cars; Matt's licence had been swiped and he naturally had to take his baby sister, fresh from Cornwall, around a bit.

Yes, David could well recall many a sparkling conversation he had had with Marie:

'So, Marie, do you prefer London to Cornwall?'

She fiddled with the radio. 'Only Way Is Up' filled the car, expanding like methyl cellulose.

'And how's Matt looking after you? Some people find him a bit much!'

'He Ain't Heavy, He's My Brother' assaulted them, after a fashion; a reissue, and just as bad the second time around.

'What did you do in Cornwall?'

'I Don't Want To Talk About It'.

'And have you met any special guy yet?'

'I Should Be So Lucky'.

'How about you coming out with me one night? Without Matt, like?'

'I Owe You Nothing'.

Pretty soon, David got into the rhythm and could match her with 'I Think We're Alone Now', 'Heaven Is A Place On Earth', and once, memorably, 'Get Out Of My Dreams And Into My Car'.

One night, when she was being particularly silent and surly, he found Vanessa Paradis singing 'Joe Le Taxi', and pulled the car up short. 'Go on. Hop it. Do like the lady said and get yourself another driver.' Matt was killing himself in the back seat, as per.

'I don't like taxis,' she said frowning. 'We don't see them much in Cornwall.' She reached out, turned off the radio and, finally, smiled at him. And that was it; he was dead in the water, and some bastard had let down the Lilo.

Marie was a little less dependent on the radio after that, but she still expressed herself mainly through her silences. There was her happy silence, her sad silence, her angry silence (trouble at t' shop in South Molton Street where she was paid a pittance to scowl at anyone stupid enough to want to buy anything), and her anticipatory silence when they were going to a restaurant or club she had high hopes of.

But most of all there was what he thought of as her sex silence; when they went down certain streets, she would squeeze as far away from him as possible, putting such pressure on her door that he feared for her safety and his sanity. She would stare past him aghast, with eyes like black ice: dark, dangerous, treacherous.

The first time it happened, he asked her what the matter was.

'That house. I had a thing with this guy there.' She shuddered, and continued with her attempt to transmigrate through the car door without opening it.

He never asked again. Stone me; it was Matt's map of the heart, no less.

'Face it,' said Matt amiably one day when David mentioned Marie's nasty little habit to him. 'The kid's been in London less than a year – but she's·spread herself around more than a lorry-load of Marmite.'

He knew he was in love, because suddenly everyone was called Marie. There wasn't just Marie Helvin, Marie of Romania, *Marie Claire* the magazine and Marie the biscuit; there was Marie Whitehouse, Marie Archer, Marie Marie (quite contrarie), Proud Marie (of river-boat renown) and Marie the Mother of God.

Perhaps he was cheating here. But Maries did truly seem to be everywhere; having miracle babies on TV, having Lonely Hells in the Sunday papers, serving him cocktails and telling him, 'Hallo, my name is Marie.' (They could have retired on the tips he left them; his dowry, so to speak.)

Then there was the old hit 'Marie, Marie', by Shakin' Stevens – a cheap act to run if ever there had been one; 'Well, you seem so sad/Marie, Marie.' And one night, amazingly, he thought he heard Morrissey singing, '(Marie's the Name) of His Latest Flame' on some unidentified late-night station. He thought he was cracking up; surely The Smiths wouldn't do an Elvis song? He asked Matt, who knew about these things.

'No, you're right. It's cool – eighty-six bootleg. Good song.' He stared hard at Matt. 'Oh my Christ. You've done it, haven't you? Fallen for the little sister.'

'No.' He did the fastest U-turn in history. 'So?'

'So nothing. Be careful, that's all. She hasn't kicked the Cornish shit off her shoes yet.' He tapped the side of his nose. 'Secretive, they are.'

'You're Cornish.'

'I've been up here since I was sixteen, boy – I'm civilized, I am. Put your ear to Marie's twat, and you'll hear the sea. She's a real primitive.'

David made a fist, which he found only marginally easier than making a scale model of the Sydney Opera House out of two egg-boxes and some double-sided Sellotape. He had never hit anyone since he left school; this preyed on his mind sometimes. Matt intercepted him easily.

'Whoah! We're in love!' He threw an arm around David's shoulders. 'Come on – let's go get laid. To celebrate.'

'On your way to visit a slapper?' said Matt when he saw David mooning around the bank one day. 'Don't forget your whip!'

'Who said that?'

'*Me*.'

Matt was a lot quicker – some would say wittier – than David; of that, there was little doubt.

'He's attracted to men *and* women,' David said to him one day of a singing fringe, moderately famous, who patronized their branch. 'What's it called . . .'

Matt snorted. 'Lucky!'

But being in love gave David the edge, he knew. He could honestly say he didn't envy Matt any more; his height, his hair, his habit. Sure, Matt had what the shinies called style. But *he* knew the meaning of Love.

Which was, as far as he could work out, lying in bed staring at the ceiling when not at work or her bidding. And, of course, calling her flat in Holborn to hear her, it had to be admitted, rather unexceptional answerphone message; 'Hallo, it's Marie. I'm not in now, so after the beep please . . .' Her voice trailed off, giving rise to all sorts of vile possibilities, most of which crossed David's mind in the long, dark wank session of the soul. All in all, he felt he was well on the way to establishing a very easy and relaxed relationship with her answering machine, the very opposite of the shy, stilted conversations he had with her in the flesh.

('Did I hear you say your favourite novel was *Mansfield Park?*' 'No.')

He took great care to call her only when he was sure she'd be out; once, he caught her in and was so appalled that he hung up immediately, even though he had called to ask her what time she wanted to be picked up for Sean's bash. This happened a few times over a period of weeks when she was taking odd days off, and David was mortified when Matt said with a wink, 'Marie's got a masher. A real pervo. Gets her on the line, all on her lonesome — and don't say anything!'

'A pervert who likes Pinter, obviously.'

Matt blinked at him. 'Say wha'?'

You dumb fuck, Matt, he crowed silently, behind the crocodile smile. You may be six-two in your silk socks with American retro dream hair and some besotted married woman paying your rent, not to mention habitually beating the birds off with a dick that could act as a rough model of the new super-truncheon the Chief of the Met wants so much to give his boys and girls — but you don't know shit about the ground-breaking British drama of the nineteen-sixties.

David was starting to take comfort in all sorts of pathetic things about Matt. He had to; he was starting to hate him for being, of all things, Marie's brother. Falling in love, it makes much more sense to envy and loathe the sibling rather than the exes. If they're exes, they were at some point sickened-of and dumped. (Our beloved is so glorious, of course, that they could never be the dumpee.)

But imagine what the brother saw!

Marie naked at three; topless at ten; God knows what after that. David's flesh crept, as though someone had pulled a choke-chain of chitlin tight around his neck, as he imagined all the times Matt must have lurked, loomed and hovered (not to mention Hoovered, as some sort of good-guy alibi) outside that foul Falmouth bathroom waiting for Marie to sneak out in a skimpy bath towel, pink-grey from too many reckless tumbles. Disgusting disrespecter of a woman's right to be free inside her own home, her own bath towel, her own skin!

Lucky bastard.

Driving Miss Lazy, David began to know the streets of London almost as well as he had known the back of his father's hand at home in Manchester. The venal villas of Notting Hill; the rich hippies' tinted-windows-and-tincture tack of Bayswater; the chippy verdancy of Belsize Park; Hampstead, smirking; Soho, leering; Fulham, jostling over the cold shoulder of Chelsea to get a better look at Marie, princess of the streets and queen of the city, the X that marked the spot in the A to Z of his heart.

He knew them all. And lodged in the gullet of each postal district was one certain street where Marie, his Marie, had been fucked – badly, brilliantly, who was counting? The point was that it was *out there*.

'You're better than a black cabbie, mate,' Matt said approvingly one night when he'd got them from Southampton Row to Shepherd's Bush in thirteen minutes flat. 'You got the Knowledge!'

David shot a poison arrow of malice at Marie, huddled in the seat beside him. The only knowledge *he* was interested in was carnal.

They'd had one bad conversation too many at one of Matt's mate's dismal, delirious parties. In the kitchen the coke was flowing like Coke and the Perrier was flowing like wine and he and Marie were sitting on the stairs having one of their awful talks, their words sinking sadly like the layers of a *pousse-café* poured by a bad barman. He was inquiring about her holiday plans when she suddenly turned to him – turned *on* him – as near to angry as he had ever seen her.

'Look. Do you want to fuck me?'

Didn't they say honesty was the best policy? 'Yes.'

'Well, forget it. I've got my own troubles.' She stood up unsteadily and stalked off to look for her friend Suzanne.

Later David saw them slow-dancing together to 'Smooth Operator' and had to go into the toilet for a quick one.

What was happening to him? A year ago he'd been a real New Lad about Town, sassy yet sensitive, always ready with a *bon mot* and a ribbed condom. Now he was reduced to having a meaningful relationship with an answering machine and the occasional one night stand with his own fist while the party raved on around him.

Love! You could keep it. Except it was him who had to keep it, now. Like a puppy someone had lumbered him with for Christmas: MARIE IS FOR LIFE. NOT JUST FOR FUN. And it was too late to give it back. He remembered a great old black and white film with Dana Andrews, coolest guy who ever lived – *Night of the Demon*. It was centred on these ancient runes, on a bit of paper; if you got hold of them, whether or not you knew it, you'd soon have the demon feeling your collar. But if you could pass them to some other poor sucker, the curse was off you and on to him.

Love was like that. You were just minding your own business, sitting there talking to some charming stranger, some friend of a friend – and then, without you knowing it, they passed you something; a bit of paper with YOU WILL FALL IN LOVE WITH ME written on it. In *Night of the Demon*, the preferred mode of transmission had been a cigarette packet. He tried to remember, and did; Marie had given him a half-full packet of Marlboro the first night they met, in an uncharacteristic – i.e. suspicious – act of open-handedness. 'Here, have these for the morning – I've got a carton of duty-free at home.' It was probably the longest sentence she'd ever spoken to him. And certainly the longest sentence he'd ever been condemned to.

She'd passed it to him, the bitch, like less vicious girls might give a guy herpes. Who was it had said that love was the most lethal sexually transmitted disease of all? Julie Burchill, probably – and Matt, natch. But he hadn't even shafted Marie, that was the killer. Hah! *she'd* shafted *him*. It was an immaculate misconception, this affair; all of the pain of consumption with none of the pleasure of consummation.

He was still driving her to parties on Friday and Saturday nights; she had relegated him to the category of Just Good Friend.

'Friendship is the booby prize we get for not being good enough to fuck.'

'Who said that?'

'*Me.*'

'Yeah, it sounds like you, for once. Hasn't it ever occured to you that there can be more between a man and a woman than sex?'

'Yeah. Sometimes they buy you clothes, too.'

★

He had stopped playing his Sade records months ago; previously, they had been adequate to express the ups and downs of his Little League loves. But now only Billie, Ella and Sarah could touch those parts of him that Marie wouldn't. He played 'Night and Day', night and day.

> Night and day
> Why should it be so?
> That this longing for you follows wherever I go
> In the roaring traffic's boom
> In the silence of my lonely room
> I think of you
> Night and day.

In his mind's eye he saw the roaring traffic, driving through the gridlocked map of his heart. He saw himself driving her smoothly through the congested valves, her hero, a man in uniform, and he saw her beautiful, dark, fleshy face turned away, away from the side of the street she had swallowed her pride and God knows what else on, mopping up her spilling black hair, as it would be on a pillow when she came. When she came! That was a fucking joke. Because the only coming Marie was going to do for him in the foreseeable future would be coming round to his place from work to get a ride to Matt and Rosie's engagement party this Friday night.

Yes, Matt Machetti had finally met a girl – Rosanna Revere, which just had to be a handle – as gorgeous, gluttonous and vainglorious as he, and of course, they were getting married, which was the most predictable course of action in the late eighties for two congenitally faithless slags. David wished them well, and would be best man.

'Are you going to have an open marriage, then?'

Matt tapped the side of his nose and smiled. 'Ajar, kid. *Ajar.*'

She had knocked on his door drunk, which was a first, half out of her head and her Ozbek. He fed her black coffee and half carried her down to the car. He put her into the passenger seat, and knew with certainty that Marie would be in the passenger seat all her life. Someone would always drive her.

He wound down the window and tried to speak sternly. It was hard when love stuck in your throat like phlegm from heaven.

'Take big breasts,' he told her solicitously, not able to resist looking down her dress. 'Breaths, I mean.'

She giggled, then scowled, and went into her big slump.

He sighed and walked around to the driver's seat. He was a good driver, unanxious and confident. In his car, he calmed down. Not like Matt, who was a maniac. He began to think of Matt, fondly, as though he was dead. He was thinking of Matt so much that he forgot that the party was at Rosie's place in Fulham, not Matt's in Islington. He was actually into Matt's street when it hit him and he turned to Marie and said 'Oh my Christ, I just –'

Her silence silenced him.

She was squeezed as far away from him as possible, putting such pressure on her door that he feared for her safety and, now more than ever, his sanity. She stared past him, at Matt's house, at Matt's flat, with eyes like black ice; dark, dangerous, treacherous, and totally in love.

'Oh, my God.' He said it wonderingly, as if in church, as if in rapture. He stopped the car.

They sat there alone for a long time. Someone was crying. Finally she spoke.

'Like sister and brother, David. You of all people should know what that can mean.' Her hair hung over her face, and she didn't look at him. But she put her hand on his thigh, which was much better. 'Let's go home. We both know the way.'

MEMORIALS
Gordon Burn

Wake and you're back on the news-go-round. Nothing's new. Not a lot is new. Life keeps coming. It keeps coming and coming. So surprise me.

It seems like seconds since I tunnelled home after a standard session of giving it this with the falling-down lotion, drunk as a monkey. And now a shit and a shave and look at me: suited up, almondly aroma'd, batteried and biro'd; the miseried's, the disastered's, the lifelorn's, the victims' (most of all the victims'), friend.

Would you talk to me? Would you tell me your private thoughts and memories? Would you vouchsafe me your keepsakes and momentoes – the ethereally lit studio portrait that leaves a pale space where it was hanging, a light line in the dust where it was standing; the vignetted picture from your wallet? Would you trust me with the home video of the last time you were all together – X removing something from the oven, X red-faced, giggling, shaking a curtain of hair in front of her face to shield it from the camera – before the bombers struck, before the stranger lurched from the shadows? Of course you would. Am I right? I'm not wrong. Believe me. This is my area of operation; my specialized subject; my purlieu; my arena. Beats writing about chocolate bunnies at Easter, I always say. I always say: wind me up and point me at it.

Strictly speaking, I'm not a leg man. A dawn raider. Bish-bash-bosh. Who, what, when and where: what my editor, a Streeter of the old school, likes to call the 'geography' of a story. I'm a colour man. A panner for the significant detail, a delver after the deeper truth. That is, I colour it up. I go in with the second wave. Which these days means that my days are dogged by flowers. My path is strewn with them. Flowers mark the spot.

The flowers come wrapped in all the surfaces of cheap living – klaxon colours, slippery prophylactic textures. As soon as the tape markers are removed, women begin steering children forward clutching thin, apologetic bunches of pinks and gyp and grade-two tulips in flattened cones that imitate laminated wood grain and fake marble, beaten copper and satin-aluminium fire surrounds, duvet and ironing-board covers, silver-frosted ceiling sconces, the technologized treads of trainers, glancing football-shirt shadow-patterns, blistery thermoplastics, the foam-backed leather-like finish of wedding albums.

The effect aimed for in the impromptu pavement shrines marking the site of the latest nail-bomb or child-snatch or brutal sex death is peaceful, pastoral, consolatory – the evocation of some dappled bluebell wood or country churchyard or Dairylea buttercup meadow, a world away from the 144-point hurts of the raw modern city.

In reality, though, the flower-heaped memorials are just another variety of urban utterance. In the first hours, the railway embankments, playing-field perimeters, tower-block entrances and shopping precinct seating islands are transformed as if by flooded lighting or a freak fall of snow. What was concrete and familiar suddenly seems defamiliarized, *derealized*; the backdrop to a dream.

People crowd at the edge of the oddly regular weave of the blankets of flowers, stunned by the scale of what they have made. (I've noticed – but naturally haven't written: it wouldn't get in if I did write it – that an element of civic competitiveness has started creeping in, as if compassion was quantifiable and could be measured in square footage and drift thickness and overall depth of cover.)

But soon (very soon when there has been some weather – a bitter north-easterly clawing at the filmy wrappings, scattering them in shop doorways and bus shelters, pasting them round bollards and railings, throwing them to the wind; persistent rain pounding them into a sodden pulp), they turn into just one more example of urban blight, of city sadness. By the time the story has moved down the page or been buried inside the paper, the memorials start to look like flocks of tick-infested pigeons, or the waterlogged communal bedding in some cardboard city. The poor colours bleed and fade. The soft toys that have been put there, the Snoopys and velveteen bunnies and bag-eyed Pound Puppies, moult and burst along the seams and spill their no longer lovable or huggable wetted kapok guts.

I know I have squeezed a story until its pips are squeaking when the smell of rotted vegetation starts to lift off the bank or trench of remembrances and the mechanical shovels and power-hoses of the refuse departments start preparing to move in. *Under the wide and starry sky, Love's last gift – remembrance, Bitterness serves no purpose and corrodes the soul, A little angel lost in flight*, is the sort of thing it says on the smashed condolence cards they leave in their wake, and I have built up a small collection of these. A selection of them, bordered with butterflies and blurry mis-keyed flowers and cupids, green-stained, the inks running, was posted round my office computer until a protest got up by one of the squeamier pencil-pushers, and including Mahalia, the regular cleaner, who left notes telling me I was a sorryfuck who could empty his own bins, succeeded in having them removed. ' "Life's a shit sandwich" is what they should say', I told them in retaliation, in my bloodier moments. ' "Life's a bucket of warm spit". '

A question that's been bothering me since I woke up this morning (fully-dressed, including battle-wearied Barbour and shoes), is: what did I have to eat last night? I know I had something and I have a reasonably vivid recollection of where I had it: a small, dark, Frenchified place, with amateurish waiters and the dry migrainous smell of new paint; there were pale pink and yellow flowers on the table, a wall hung with peasantware patterned plates, a brass jug on a hook by the door. It's what went into my mouth to blot up the cataract of Jamesons and chasers that remains a blank.

All morning my stomach has been crying out for sustenance and my head has been asking to be put into some quiet, low-lit space. And so, despite the chronic sinusitis and seborrhoeic keratosis, the degenerative arthritis and benign prostate hypertrophy; in the face of dire warnings about cholesterol levels and blood sugar, here we are once more in the bottly light among the pebble-grain glass and the crusted tile mosaic and the brightwork, getting in the first of the day.

Although I am in a job that demands engagement and ingratiation, the glad hand, the lulling smile, and then peptic (ulcer-puncturing) forward propulsion, I find my instincts are all for retreat and withdrawal – to the dim nook, the worn leather, the brown shadows in the old corner. A backwards movement, a compulsive taking to cover, is one that feels engraved in my muscles. As a reflex it is never stronger than when I should be out there, as I should be now, on the loiter, attempting to intrude myself into the life of another stranger.

The cuts have been got together for me by Helen, and it's Helen's arms and hands I can see holding the gnarled clippings in place against the plate of the photocopier. For reasons of speed, I can only suppose, she has run them off without bothering to bring the lid down. The result is that, while I should be reading up the background on the story I'm supposed to be covering – a catalogue of slashings and shootings and other fleeting fish-wrap catastrophes – I find myself drawn instead to these spectral hands and arms which I am intrigued to find I am able to study in forensic detail, in all their cellular particulars. The high contrast throws into relief every grainy pore and follicle; every grooved cross-hatch and complex tonality; the way the fine dark hairs lap around the watch-strap; the triangle of moles below the wrist; the tapered fleshy cushions of the fingers, shot from below (the flash slicing along the wall) and spread flat against the glass.

Helen is not an attractive woman. No kind of sexual *frisson*, so far as I'm aware, has ever passed between us. And yet when I take her disembodied hand and place it near my lap, or lay her arm along my thigh, say – like this – I experience an unexpected but definite stirring.

Do places have memories? Are the chippings and frottings, the rubbing away of the wood grain, the bloom on the brass handle, the grey dead area in the mirror evidence of a place's will to remember? The Mitre, according to a plaque over the bar, was established in 1683, renovated in 1883 and, apart from the inevitable modifications and modernizations, has been altered so little since then it's easy to feel that Helen's isn't the only phantom presence. The highwayman Charles Duval, legend has it, was caught and arrested within the narrow wedge of these walls while sleeping off the effects of the night before. Warren's Blacking, the shoe-polish factory where Dickens was given a job as a boy, virtually abutted it. The Mitre was a favourite watering-hole of the spies, Burgess and Maclean and their crowd, forty years ago, in the early fifties. I imagine the spectres of old boozers stacked up like coats at a party next to me on this faded, recessed bench, and was given an oblique reminder that one day I will be joining them when I approached the bar to order my first drink.

Waiting while the young mick in charge fastened on his greasy bow-tie in the back mirror, I looked up and saw myself on a video monitor that has been placed where the bar staff obviously keep colliding with it with their heads: the lower edge has been blocked off with foam and black electrical tape. The camera was somewhere behind me (I turned and tried but couldn't locate it), and I was standing in a laddered shaft of light that was also invisible to the naked eye. As I looked at the sepia monochrome figure that I was broadly able to identify as me (not *that* short; not *that* fat), I was suddenly made aware that I was watching myself enter the past; I was becoming conscious of the erasure of my presence, and of the volume only temporarily occupied by my body.

A few years ago I watched a woman leap to her death in front of a train at Gloucester Road Underground station. Before she jumped (this was a sign that should have told me what she was planning, I know now but didn't know then), she took her coat, made of a kind of green bouclé material with a pink undercolour, and folded it tidily at her feet. Then she removed her cardigan and placed it on top of the coat. She was plucking at the buttons of the blouse she was wearing when the train came and she hopped forward from the edge of the platform where she had been standing, knees together, like a non-diver launching herself into an echoing indoor pool.

This was an unusual occurrence for me – being an eye-witness rather than having to put a report together based on second- and third-hand accounts. The morning torpor was suddenly charged with a kind of unbelieving delirium. I watched a man come awake at a window on the incoming train and register that something had happened simply by the magnetic wave of excitement, the turbulence on the other side of the glass. Nobody was moving at that point. Nobody moved for what seemed like a long time. And then there was a surge towards, rather than away from, the place where an after-image of the woman seemed to hang in the air, staggered, the way it would be in time-lapse photography. The expressions on the faces of several of the people who went forward to witness what happens when flesh and bones come in contact with bladed titanium reminded me powerfully of something, although I couldn't say at the time what it was. It was only later, half-watching a football match on television, that I remembered: they reminded me of footballers' faces in the seconds after a goal has been scored, and just after they have established brief physical contact with the scorer. In one or two instances, in their inwardness and rapture, they reminded me of the heroes of the back pages themselves.

For a few days, without quite admitting that this was what I was doing, I found myself avoiding Gloucester Road tube and boarding the train at Earls Court or South Kensington. When I did resume my old pattern, I gravitated towards a part of the platform well away from where the woman's clothes had lain and believed I would never be able to travel from there without reliving some aspect of that experience. But I was wrong. Life keeps coming. Time passes. Life crowds in. I can go – have just gone – for months without any detail of the suicide surfacing.

A recurring element in all the cuts with which I'm currently lumbered (one of the great pleasures of the job, after a story has been filed and a line drawn under it, is aiming them), is maps whose inky arrows and star-flashes and blocks of filler Lettratone indicate that they are places where news has suddenly erupted; where the normally only mildly choppy surface of day-to-day living has been violently disturbed. But that was then.

It's now three years since Larry Brown, a policeman, was shot at point-blank range in a courtyard at the front of Orwell Court, a litter-strewn block of flats on the Suffolk Estate in Hackney. The man who ambushed and then killed him gave as his reason the fact that his girlfriend had dumped him the night before. He told detectives: 'I blew your copper away because my girl blew me away. I just did it. The first thing that came into my head was to kill a policeman.'

It's much longer – almost eighteen years – since another policeman, Stephen Tibble, was gunned down by an escaping IRA terrorist on a quiet street in Baron's Court in west London. He was shot twice in the chest and died two and a half hours later in hospital. (Helen's hand, looming out of the blackness, securing a picture of the dead policeman, captioned *Victim*, against the photocopier, has something of the aspect of a blackened hand gesturing from a shallow woodland grave within earshot of motorway traffic.)

Ronan McCloskey was on his fifth day of unsupervised duty as a policeman when he stopped and breathalysed a twenty-two-year-old man driving a Capri in Willesden High Road one night in May, 1987. On the pretext of locking up the car, the man sped away with PC McCloskey trapped half-in and half-out of it. He drove at high speed for half a mile before crashing through a fence at the corner of Dudden Hill Lane and Denzil Road, NW10. Constable McCloskey was hurled against a concrete post and died of head injuries before he reached hospital.

Half the thirty-strong A-shift at Chelsea police station were killed or wounded by the IRA bomb that went off in Hans Crescent, adjacent to Harrods, just before Christmas, 1983.

PC Keith Blakelock was hacked to death with knives and machetes during the Broadwater Farm riot in Tottenham in October, 1985. (An attempt was made to hack off his head, with the intention of parading it on a pole.)

And at the sites of these and other police murders – Braybrook Street, Shepherd's Bush, W12; Montreal Place, off Aldwych, WC2; Higham Hill Road near the junction with Mayfield Road, Walthamstow, E17 – permanent memorials have been erected in recent years: small funerary monuments of Portland stone and granite and white-veined blue marble; important materials in unimportant, sometimes tawdry, settings; desolate reminders of death in tiled hospital rooms; of sudden death on the pavement. Although there are people who bring them flowers, holly wreaths at Christmas and small potted plants, there were always others who, even before the events of recent months, said the memorials were a source of negative energy which they claimed to have experienced as fields and waves of radiation and soft singing static. They believed there was something fetishistic or cultic about them (one woman told me the memorial close to where she lives had been put there to spy on her), and would cross the street in order not to have to pass too close to the bad ju-ju they were generating.

The first attack happened in April last year, in the vicinity of the stone erected in memory of PC McCloskey in Willesden: a young woman gagged and raped in some nearby bushes while walking home from work. The second rape took place in a mews at the rear of Harrods, and this time a knife was used. The rapist struck for the third and fourth times in Tottenham and Hackney, very close to where the officers Blakelock and Brown were killed. The connection between the attacks and their locations remained speculative until the arrival of a set of pictures from the attacker whose existence has been withheld from the public but which I was given sight of thanks to a long-standing sweetheart deal between my paper and the police.

I turned up at the appointed time at the inquiry headquarters and was shown into a cubicle room lined with battered file envelopes on industrial shelving and lighted by a high rectangle window of wired glass. I was brought turbid brown tea in a mug with a faded Metropolitan Police badge on it — *The Badge of Courage* the inscription read — and handed a buff folder by a detective sergeant whose 'Sick bastard' seemed as if it could apply to me as much as to the person in the smudges. It was a transaction loaded with these kinds of ambiguities, and I was aware of his physical closeness, of the close eye-balling he was giving me — on the lookout for some crotch action? Any attempt to palm one of the slippery eight-by-tens? — as I undid the string tie.

The penis in the pictures was that of (probably) a white male — the uncertainty was due to the fact that it was mottled, brown and pink; piebald like a horse. But the weird pigmentation was far from being the most distinctive feature: the shaft — and, in the later pictures, the glans — was pierced with bullet-head silver studs, making it look notched, only semi-organic, and lending it the appearance of some kind of museumized medieval weaponry. The number of studs varied from picture to picture, but they didn't keep sequence with the attacks. They shone with the same value metal sheen as the gold in the declivities of the carved inscriptions of the stubby, phallus-shaped memorials against which they were carefully, semi-erectly posed.

This square is a favourite route for taxis going into the West End from the south and west. There is a steady black stream, sluggish and black as oil, conduited along the northern side and off into the narrow channel to Regent Street, making the turn at the exact spot where WPC Yvonne Fletcher was mowed down, shot in the back, and killed.

The memorial that stands here, the first of the police memorials to go up in London, is white with a granite plaque bearing the standard inscription: *Here fell . . .*, with the name and date. After seven years, the white of the stone is so very white it looks like a keyhole of light projected on to the railings and the tough green-black plants ranged behind it. It is April, too early in the year for the overhead trees to be slaked with dust and particles of carbon, but late enough for the young, lush leaves to throw a cooling shadow, trapping the air underneath. Even on the brightest day the white stone to Yvonne Fletcher has the fluctuating quality of light flickering at the back of a cave.

It has not been violated. It doesn't feature in the pictures. It is maintained in its pristine condition by a woman, a stranger unknown to Yvonne Fletcher at the time of her death, who makes regular expeditions from the small south-coast town where she lives to wash the stone and polish up the granite and set fresh flowers at the memorial's base. It is an activity she feels no compulsion to explain. Attempts were made to get her to sneeze it out in the first months after the memorial was unveiled, but she had made a commitment to remain silent and wouldn't be budged. And in the intervening years, so far as I know, she has been free to go about her janitorial duties undisturbed. But these are slow newsdays. The coincidence of violent death and violent sex at the memorials is red meat. It is a story that has to be kept at a rolling boil. One of the bright young Joe Colleges dredged up a recollection of the woman at morning conference at the beginning of the week. A couple of calls to the budgie at the bill shop supplied likely days and times. And here I am, parked behind the cool stone pillar of a shuttered building with an unobstructed view of the Yvonne Fletcher memorial, poised to invade its guardian's anonymity, ready to pounce.

I had anticipated that she would be approaching from Regent Street to the west, or Piccadilly to the north, which narrowed it down to three streets (and two pubs – the Mitre and the Spanish Patriot, from where I haven't long returned – a final *Adios* to the melt-down hangover with which I started the day, *Buenas dias* to tomorrow's). The route I hadn't counted on was along the gravel path of the formal garden with its lunching office-workers and lurid tulip beds and central statue of William III.

But that's the way she must have come, because now all of a sudden she's there and already absorbed in her work: a medium-built, young-appearing middle-aged woman in trousers, a sweater and a rubberized anorak that she has taken off, folded and placed as padding under her knees. I know from sniffing around there that

she keeps a container of water and a plastic atomizer wedged
between the memorial and the metal fence; she has unpacked spray
polishes and bleaches with emphatic labels and bright child-proof
nozzles and a variety of other cleaning materials which are standing
by waiting to be used. Even before I break cover and take the first
step towards her, I have a vision of her life and a distinct image of a
place I have never known. (Grids of lamp posts, rows of urns and
statues as points of identity and continuity in the vast space. The
smell of real cakes through the doors and windows of the bakery.)

The whole of the south side of the square is undergoing renova-
tion and all the buildings there have disappeared behind a false front
– a simple-coloured, billboard-size façade cartooning the
eighteenth-century classical facades it conceals. Wide orange mesh
covers the spaces of the windows, and men in safety helmets are
visible there in such numbers that I feel like a show put on for their
amusement as I emerge into this hot and intricately enclosed space.
Through the path of the bullet that killed Yvonne Fletcher, through
the accumulation of energies, past the place where her hat had lain,
photographed but untouched, for many hours, a predator closing
and closing on the unalerted woman on her knees.

It is an attitude that prompts a rush of images – darkly radiant,
churchly lit images from pagan ritual and the Scriptures. *Ecce ancilla
Dei. Behold the handmaid of the Lord. The Madonna of Humility.*
Hundreds of associations in a few seconds from far away. But, at
this point, three images predominantly: a man stepping round a
woman who is on her knees with a brush and a bucket and abjectly
imploring to be allowed to go where he is going. A woman
looking up, blinking against the light that has just flooded the
cupboard where she has been forcibly shut away. A woman bent to
the task of scouring a ring of dirt off a bath with the radio playing
some hit from her youth, in the morning after her husband has set
out for the job both of them know in their blood he will soon be
losing and the children have left for school. (No matter how
strenuous our efforts to put a space between them and us, our own
lives constantly invade us.)

There is a tin vase tethered by a chain to the railing at the side of
the stone. Wistaria and lavender in a glass bottle. Primroses in pots
placed in a tricolour basket. I'm almost there now, almost on the
woman, but she still hasn't turned or given any sign that she knows

that I'm approaching. It is as I am about to bring my hand in
contact with the knotty open weave of her sweater, register the
start of alarm, that I notice it has grown as quiet as cancer. Amid all
the noise of the city there is an echo, an experience of quietness
which is almost African in quality. 'Dorothy,' I want to say.
'Dorothy, stand up. Don't cry. Forgive me.' But it is barely dawn
yet where Dorothy is living, in a quiet subdivision near a lake. The
woman glances back at me sleepily, trustingly, when she feels my
hand on her neck and hears the sound of my wife's name.

WAITING TO WAVE
Jonathan Carroll

The weather was not fair. For days since it happened, since the
terrible phone call when she told him in a dead voice she had
decided to stay where she was and wasn't coming back, the weather
had not been fair. For almost two weeks the days were a mirror
reflection of the frightening state of his mind. The mornings started
out too sunny, or else too stormy, then changed in an hour to the
other, then swung back and forth all day between rain and shine, so
one never knew what would be next. Which meant there was one
less place to hide.

Part of him thought the best thing to do was keep busy. Take
walks, go to the movies, put the dog in the car and drive places
they hadn't gone before. But outside or busy, there was this
damned weather or his damned thoughts in between that showed
there's no safe place. Everything will haunt you, all the storms will
find you, everything will remind you she's gone.

He went to a cowboy movie but ten minutes after it started,
began to weep. Luckily there were few people in the theatre so he
only put a hand over his eyes and let the tears fall. What was she
doing while he cried? Was she falling in love in her red and white
summer dress that was his favourite? Summer had just begun down
there. Was she working in the garden she had so proudly described
in an earlier letter?

This was a ghastly part of the torture he meted out to himself: in
his mind he took bits and pieces of what she had said or written
before and slid them together into vivid, awful collages of pain and
loss: he pictured her in that dress, barefoot, digging in this new
garden at twilight. Then from behind, being greeted by the new
someone she had so carefully and vaguely alluded to in their last
conversation. 'Is it only that, or have you met someone new?' She
hesitated and then said half-coyly, 'There's someone I like to talk to,
but you have to understand, it's completely different.' He imagined
her straightening up slowly because she had hurt her back as a
teenager. She had the most prominent backbone he had ever seen.

Turning and smiling that wonderful broad smile at this new man, she would drop the tool she was using and brush off her hands. She had been waiting for him. He had come for her all dressed up. She didn't know whether she liked his cologne. She was very picky about colognes but if they stayed together, after a while she would tell him she didn't care for it. It was time to change and go out for dinner, perhaps to a party. She said she was constantly going to parties now, doing things she had never done in her life. That was the heart of it – everything was so different there and new and she laughed all the time. He had owned that smile for years but no longer did.

The last time they spoke she had said: 'I love you dearly, but . . .' Dearly. Such an ugly little word, a word that diminished him and their years together down to nothing. Grandmothers, ministers, greetings cards all used 'dearly'. Now she did too when she thought about him.

The dog was always happy to go out, which was good. But dogs are like that. Wake them in the middle of the night and say it's time for an hour walk or a big dinner and they're ready. But even the dog . . . From the moment it saw her for the first time, it loved her more than anything on earth. Much more than him. It would have jumped off a cliff, then somehow sprouted wings and flown back if she had told it to. When she was gone, it dashed up to any woman on the street who looked even vaguely like her and howled its delight. And when it actually was her, the dog went mad. Thank God he didn't have to tell it she wouldn't be around any more. Thank God it still ran up to women on the street with the highest hopes but never seemed fazed for long when it wasn't her because next time, next time it would have to be.

He was not a superstitious man but these days he made deals with the gods. He now carried a polished green stone in his pocket she bought for him years ago in the Burlington Arcade on a trip to London. If three things arrived at once that all reminded him of her, that meant he could hope. A white car like hers passed, driven by a woman with lots of hair like hers. On the car, a bumper sticker said 'I love Canada.' She was Canadian. Three things all at once. Wasn't something trying to tell him something? Could he hope? On that trip to London, she had bought a cheap cable-knit cardigan at Marks & Spencer that she adored and wore around the apartment all year long. After that last deadly conversation, he rushed to the closet to see if she had left it on its hook and was thrilled to see it was still there.

He had bought a new car. It was so sleek and full of high-tech gadgets that he nicknamed it 'Terminator'. When he got in and pressed a button, the steering wheel and driver's seat automatically adjusted to his body. There were buttons for person One and Two. He had chosen person Two but now there was no person One. Months ago when ordering it, he had had real pleasure imagining her chauffeuring the two of them around. More and more she had been doing the driving and he liked that. Now it was only the dog in the passenger's seat, silent and all white.

'Would you like to drive?'

On hearing his voice it turned to him, then turned back to look out the window.

Of course the town was haunted. There was virtually nowhere to go or look or be without being reminded of her and their days together. Driving down the street he tried to love the feel of his magnificent new automobile, but there was the store where she bought her lingerie, the restaurant where they'd had that awful meal, and worst of all the café where they'd actually met the first time. That was too painful and he had to look away. He looked away from it every day driving to work. Every day since her call he had to pass that place where it had all begun with such hope and excitement. Why couldn't buildings disappear when relationships did? Everything go away all at once so there was no trace of anything, no tangible proof that anything ever existed. That would be so much easier and better.

There they had walked, there he'd driven her on the bicycle, there she cajoled him into buying her French fries on a cold winter night. Memories like a paper cut, so deep, quick and unexpected that there was no way to guard against them.

He had lost twenty pounds. That was something. For several years he'd talked about losing some weight, so here he was with droopy pants and his belt taken in two notches. That was something, wasn't it? A little perk in this bad time?

What had she lost? What went through her mind these days? Very little, he feared: that tore him. Years together, but then he had heard absolutely nothing from her since that last dead talk. Was this the same woman he had known so long? Or had distance and new circumstances changed her so quickly and hugely that even if she were to come back, she would be unrecognizable? Was he praying for the return of the same woman? He knew nothing. No, that's not true: he knew he was dying, but she seemed to have effortlessly disconnected herself from him and waved bye-bye with what appeared to be the blithest, quickest gesture in the world.

He drove to the river. They had their spot out there too, and the dog was always in heaven when it could be with them and run around at the same time. But this time when he opened the door and clapped at the animal to hop out, it came slowly. The sky was dark again. The dog seemed to know rain was near. Despite all the enthusiasm, it hated bad weather. She told a funny story about walking one evening in the rain for hours while the dog tried to hide in every doorway they passed.

So there they are, the thinner man with his white dog and the wind blowing and the clouds the purple of children's lollipops. They walk and walk. The wind is gusting, the dog runs full speed towards nothing but happiness, the man wears the blue baseball cap she gave him and stuffs his hands deep in his pockets.

He stops when he sees on the other side of an inlet a lone fisherman who's braved the elements today to come out here and try his luck. No one else is around. On one side the man with the dog, on the other the man with the fishing lines. The man with the dog thinks if the other looks up, I will wave at him. There will be luck if he waves back. Somehow that will mean everything. If I can get him to wave back, then my life will change and she will come back and we will face this thing the way it should be faced.

So he waits while the other tends his fishing pole. The dog is jumping around in grass so vividly green in the lowering skies.

'Look up, will you?' He says it out loud, but the fisherman stays at his work.

'Come on, come on. Just look up once. I'll wave as hard as I can. You'll have to wave back. I'll make you.'

The fisherman turns away and bends down to his tackle box. He stays like that a long time, his back to the other. The dog is calm now, sitting on the grass and looking at the water. The wind's begun to gust hard, the clouds are thicker and have stopped moving. His hands are cold so he puts them up under his armpits,

but ready if he needs them. He's waiting for the fisherman to turn
around, even though he knows this whole thing is ridiculous and
pathetic. To think something as small as a wave could change the
line of his life back to what he has been praying for. But he stands
there nevertheless, waiting to wave.

What else is there to do?

MOTHER OF THE CITY
Christopher Fowler

If my Uncle Stanley hadn't passed out pornographic polaroids of his second wife for the amusement of his football mates in the bar of the Skinner's Arms, I might have moved to London. But he did and I didn't, because his wife heard about it and threw him out on the street, and she offered the other half of her house to me.

My parents were in the throes of an ugly divorce and I was desperate to leave home. Aunt Sheila's house was just a few roads away. She wasn't asking much rent and she was good company, so I accepted her offer and never got around to moving further into town, and that's why I'll be dead by the time morning comes.

Fucking London, I hate it.

Here's a depressing thing to do. Grow up in the suburbs, watch your schoolfriends leave one by one for new lives in the city, then bump into them eleven years later in your local pub, on an evening when you're feeling miserable and you're wearing your oldest, most disgusting jumper. Listen to their tales of financial derring-do in the public sector. Admire their smart clothes and the photos of exotic love-partners they keep in their bulging wallets, photos beside which your Uncle Stan's polaroids pale into prudery. Try to make your own life sound interesting when they ask what you've been doing all this time, even though you know that the real answer is nothing.

Don't tell them the truth. Don't say you've been marking time, you're working in the neighbourhood advice bureau, you drive a rusting Fiat Pipsqueak and there's a woman in Safeway's you sometimes sleep with but you've no plans to marry. Because they'll just look around at the pub's dingy flock wallpaper and the drunk kids in tracksuits and say, How can you stay here, Douglas? Don't you know what you've been missing in London all these years?

I know what I've been missing all right. And while I'm thinking about that, my old school chums, my pals-for-life, my mates, my blood-brothers will check their watches and drink up and shake my hand and leave me for the second time, unable to get away fast enough. And once again I stay behind.

You'll have to take my word for it when I say I didn't envy them. I really didn't. I'd been to London plenty of times, and I loathed the place. The streets were crowded and filthy and ripe with menace, the people self-obsessed and unfriendly. People are unfriendly around here as well, only you never see them except on Sunday mornings, when some kind of car-washing decathlon is staged throughout the estate. The rest of the time they're in their houses between the kettle and the TV set, keeping a side-long watch on the street through spotless net curtains. You could have a massive coronary in the middle of the road and the curtains would twitch all around you, but no one would come out. They'll watch but they won't help. They'll say *We thought we shouldn't interfere*.

Fuck, I'm bleeding again.

Seeing as I'm about to die, it's important that you understand; where you live shapes your life. I'm told that the city makes you focus your ambitions. Suburbia drains them off. Move here and you'll soon pack your dreams away, stick them in a box with the Christmas decorations meaning to return to them some day. You don't, of course. And slowly you become invisible, like the neighbours, numb and relaxed. It's a painless process. Eventually you perform all the functions of life without them meaning anything, and it's quite nice, like floating lightly in warm water. At least, that's what I used to think.

Around here the women have become unnaturally attached to the concept of shopping. They spend every weekend with their families scouring vast warehouses full of tat, looking for useless objects to acquire, shell-suited magpies feathering their nests with bright plastic objects. I shouldn't complain. I've always preferred things to people. Gadgets, landscapes, buildings. Especially buildings. As a child, I found my first visit to the British Museum more memorable than anything I'd seen before, not that I'd seen anything. I loved those infinite halls of waxed tiles, each sepulchral room with its own uniformed attendant. Smooth panes of light and dense silence, the exact opposite of my home life. My parents always spoke to me loudly and simultaneously. They complained about everything and fought all the time. I loved them, of course; you do. But they let us down too often, my sister and I, and after a while we didn't trust them any more.

I trusted the British Museum. Some of the exhibits frightened me; the glass box containing the leathery brown body of a cowering Pompeiian, the gilt-encased figures of vigilant guards protecting an Egyptian princess. Within its walls nothing ever changed, and I was safe and secure. I never had that feeling with my parents.

Once my father drove us up from Meadowfields (that's the name of the estate; suitably meaningless, as there isn't a meadow in sight and never was) to the West End, to see some crummy Christmas lights and to visit my mum's hated relatives in Bayswater. When he told the story later, he managed to make it sound as if we had travelled to the steppes of Russia. He and my mother sat opposite my Uncle Ernie and Auntie Doreen on their red leather settee, teacups balanced on locked knees, reliving the high point of our trip, which was a near-collision with a banana lorry bound for Covent Garden. I'd been given a sticky mug of fluorescent orange squash and sent to a corner to be seen and not heard. I was nine years old, and I understood a lot more than they realized. My Uncle Ernie started talking about a woman who was strangled in the next street because she played the wireless too loudly, but my Auntie Doreen gave him a warning look and he quickly shut up.

On the way home, as if to verify his words, we saw two Arab men having a fight at the entrance to Notting Hill tube station. Being impressionable and imaginative, from this moment on I assumed that London was entirely populated by murderers.

A psychiatrist would say that's why I never left Meadowfields. In fact I longed to leave my parents' little house, where each room was filled with swirling floral wallpaper and the sound of Radio One filtered through the kitchen wall all day. All I had to do was get up and go, but I didn't. Inaction was easier. When I moved to Aunt Sheila's I finally saw how far my lead would reach; three roads away. I suppose I was scared of the city, and I felt protected in the suburbs. I've always settled for the safest option.

Look, I've taken a long time getting to the point and you've been very patient, so let me explain what happened last night. I just want you to understand me a little, so you won't think I'm crazy when I explain the insane fix I'm in. It's hard to think clearly. I must put everything in order.

It began with a woman I met two months ago.

Her name is Michelle Davies and she works for an advertising agency in Soho. She's tall and slim, with deep-set brown eyes and masses of glossy dark hair the colour of a freshly creosoted fence. She always wears crimson lipstick, black jeans and a black furry coat. She looks like a page ripped from *Vanity Fair*. She's not like the women around here.

I met her when I was helping with a community project that's tied to a national children's charity, and the charity planned to mention our project in its local press ads, and Michelle was the account executive appointed to help me with the wording.

The first time we met I was nearly an hour late for our appointment because I got lost on the Underground. Michelle was sitting at the end of a conference table, long legs crossed to one side, writing pages of notes, and never once caught my eye when she spoke. The second time, a week later, she seemed to notice me and was much friendlier. At the end of the meeting she caught my arm at the door and asked me to buy her a drink in the bar next to the agency, and utterly astonished, I agreed.

I'll spare you a description of the media types sandwiched between the blue slate walls of the brasserie. The tables were littered with *Time Out*s and transparencies, and everyone was talking loudly about their next production and how they all hated each other.

Listen, I have no illusions about myself. I'm twenty-eight, I don't dress fashionably and I'm already losing my hair. London doesn't suit me. I don't understand it, and I don't fit in. Michelle was seven years younger, and every inch of her matched the life that surrounded us. As we shared a bottle of wine she told me about her father, a successful artist, her mother, a writer of romances, and her ex-boyfriend, some kind of experimental musician. I had no idea why I had been picked to hear these revelations. Her parents were divorced, but still lived near each other in apartments just off the Marylebone Road. She had grown up in a flat in Wigmore Street, and still lived in Praed Street. Her whole family had been raised in the centre of the city, generation upon generation. She was probably one of the last true Londoners. She was rooted right down into the place, and even though I hated being here, I had to admit it made her very urbane and glamorous, sophisticated far beyond her years. As she drained her glass she wondered if I would like to have dinner with her tonight. Did I have to get up early in the morning?

I know what you're thinking – isn't this all a bit sudden? What could she see in me? Would the evening have some kind of humiliating resolution? Did she simply prefer plain men? Well, drinks turned to dinner and dinner turned to bed, and everything turned out to be great. I went back to her apartment and we spent the whole night gently making love, something I hadn't done since I was nineteen, and later she told me that she was attracted to me because I was clearly an honest man. She said all women are looking for honest men.

In the morning, we braved the rain-doused streets to visit a breakfast bar with steamy windows and tall chrome stools, and she ate honey-filled croissants and told me how much she loved the city, how private and protective it was, how she could never live anywhere else and didn't I feel the same way? – and I had to tell her the truth. I said I fucking hated the place.

Yes, that was dumb. But it was honest. She was cooler after that. Not much, but I noticed a definite change in her attitude. I tried to explain but I think I made everything worse. Finally she smiled and finished her coffee and slipped from her stool. She left with barely another word, her broad black coat swinging back and forth as she ran away through the drizzle. Kicking myself, I paid the bill and took the first of three trains home. At the station, a taxi nearly ran me down and a tramp became abusive when I wouldn't give him money.

On my way out of London I tried to understand what she loved so much about the litter-strewn streets, but the city's charms remained elusive. To me the place looked like a half-demolished fairground.

I couldn't get Michelle out of my mind.

Everything about her was attractive and exciting. It wasn't just that she had chosen me when she could have had any man she wanted. I called her at the agency and we talked about work. After the next meeting we went to dinner, and I stayed over again. We saw each other on three more occasions. She was always easygoing, relaxed. I was in knots. Each time she talked about the city she loved so much, I managed to keep my fat mouth shut. Then, on our last meeting, I did something really stupid.

I have a stubborn streak a mile wide and I know it, but knowing your faults doesn't make it any easier to control them. Each time we'd met, I had come up to town and we'd gone somewhere, for dinner, for drinks – it was fine, but Michelle often brought her friends from the agency along, and I would have preferred to see her alone. They sat on either side of her watching me like body-guards, ready to pounce at the first sign of an improper advance.

On this particular evening we were drinking in a small club in Beak Street with her usual crowd. She began talking about some new bar, and I asked her if she ever got tired of living right here, in the middle of so much noise and violence. In reply, she told me London was the safest place in the world. I pointed out that it was now considered to be the most crime-riddled city in Europe. She just stared at me blankly for a moment and turned to talk to someone else.

Her attitude pissed me off. She was living in a dream-state, ignoring anything bad or even remotely realistic in life. I wouldn't let the subject go and tackled her again. She quoted Samuel Johnson, her friends nodded in agreement, I threw in some crime statistics and moments later we were having a heated, pointless row. What impressed me was the way in which she took everything to heart, as if by insulting London I was causing her personal injury. Finally she called me smug and small-minded and stormed out of the club.

One of her friends, an absurd young man with a pony-tail, pushed me down in my seat as I rose to leave. 'You shouldn't have argued with her,' he said, shaking his head in admonishment. 'She loves this city, and she won't hear anyone criticizing it.'

'You can't go on treating her like a child for ever,' I complained. 'Someone has to tell her the truth.'

'That's what her last boyfriend did.'

'And what happened to him?'

'He got knocked off his bike by a bus.' Pony-Tail shrugged. 'He's never going to walk again.' He stared out of the window at the teeming night streets. 'This city. You're either its friend, or you're an enemy.'

After waiting for hours outside her darkened apartment, I re-turned home to Meadowfields in low spirits. I felt as though I had failed some kind of test. A few days later, Michelle reluctantly agreed to see me for dinner. This time there would be just the two of us. We arranged to meet in Dell'Ugo in Frith Street at nine the next Friday evening.

I didn't get there until ten-thirty.

It wasn't my fault. I allowed plenty of time for my rail connections, but one train wasn't running and the passengers were off-loaded on to buses that took the most circuitous route imaginable. By the time I reached the restaurant she had gone. The *maître d'* told me she had waited for forty minutes.

After that Michelle refused to take my calls, either at the agency or at her flat. I must have spoken to her answering machine a hundred times.

A week passed, the worst week of my life. At work, everything went wrong. The money for the charity ads fell through and the campaign was cancelled, so I had no reason to visit the agency again. Then Aunt Sheila asked me to help her sell the house, because she had decided to move to Spain. I would have to find a new place to live. And all the time, Michelle's face was before me. I felt like following her ex-boyfriend under a bus.

It was Friday night, around seven. I was standing in the front garden, breathing cool evening air scented with burning leaves and looking out at the lights of the estate, fifty-eight miles from the city and the woman. That's when it happened. Personal epiphany, collapse of inner belief system, whatever you want to call it. I suddenly saw how cocooned I'd been here in Legoland. I'd never had a chance to understand a woman like Michelle. She unnerved me, so I was backing away from the one thing I really wanted, which was to be with her. Now I could see that she was a lifeline, one final chance for me to escape. OK, it may have been obvious to you but it came as a complete revelation to me.

I ran back into the house, past my Aunt Sheila who was in the kitchen doing something visceral in a pudding basin, and rang Michelle's apartment. And – there was a God – she answered the call. I told her exactly how I felt, begged absolution for my behaviour and explained how desperate I was to see her. For a few moments the line went silent as she thought things through. Once more, my honesty won the day.

'Tomorrow night,' she said. 'I've already made arrangements with friends, but come along.'

'I'll be there,' I replied, elated. 'When and where?'

She said she would be in a restaurant called the Palais Du Jardin in Long Acre until ten-thirty, then at a new club in Soho. She gave me the addresses. 'I warn you, Douglas,' she added. 'This is absolutely your last chance. If you don't show up, you can throw away my number because I'll never speak to you again.'

I swore to myself that nothing would go wrong. Nothing.

Saturday morning.

It feels like a lifetime has passed, but peering at the cracked glass of my watch I realize that it was just twenty hours ago.

I planned everything down to the last detail. I consulted the weather bureau, then rang all three stations and checked that the trains would be running. 'Only connect,' wrote E.M. Forster, but he obviously hadn't seen a British Rail timetable.

To be safe I left half-hour gaps between each train, so there would be no possibility of missing one of them. I bought a new suit, my first since wide lapels went out. I got a decent hair-cut from a new barber, one without photographs of people who looked like Val Doonican taped to his window. The day dragged past at a snail's pace, each minute lasting an hour. Finally it was time to leave Rosemount Crescent.

I made all my connections. Nothing went wrong until I reached Warren Street, where the Northern Line had been closed because of a bomb scare. It had begun to rain, a fine soaking drizzle. There were no cabs to be seen so I waited for a bus, safe in the knowledge that Michelle would be dining for a while yet. I felt that she had deliberately kept the arrangement casual to help me. She knew I had to make an awkward journey into town.

The first two buses were full, and the driver of the third wouldn't take Scottish pound notes, which for some reason I'd been given at the cashpoint. I was fine on the fourth, until I realized that it veered away from Covent Garden at precisely the moment when I needed it to turn left into the area. I walked back along the Strand with my jacket collar turned up against the rain. I hadn't thought to wear an overcoat. I was late, and it felt as if the city was deliberately keeping me away from her. I imagined Michelle at the restaurant table, lowering her wineglass and laughing with friends as she paused to check her watch. I examined my A to Z and turned up towards Long Acre, just in time for a cab to plough through a trough of kerbside water and soak my legs. Then I discovered that I'd lost the piece of paper bearing the name of the restaurant. It had been in the same pocket as the A to Z, but must have fallen out. I had been so determined to memorize the name of the place, and now it completely eluded me. The harder I searched my mind, the less chance I had of remembering it. I had to explore every single restaurant in the damned street, and there were dozens of them.

I was just another guy on a date (admittedly the most important date I'd ever had) and it was turning into the quest for the Holy Grail. It took me over half an hour to cover the whole of Long Acre, only to find that the Palais Du Jardin was the very last restaurant in the street, and that I had missed Michelle Davies's party by five minutes.

At least I remembered the name of the club, and strode on to it, tense and determined. The bare grey building before me had an industrial steel door, above which hung a banner reading 'blUe-TOPIA'. The bricks themselves were bleeding technobeat. In front of the door stood a large man in a tight black suit, white shirt, narrow black tie and sunglasses, a Cro-Magnon Blues Brother.

'Get back behind the rope.' He sounded bored. He kept his arms folded and stared straight ahead.

'How much is it to get in?' I asked.

'Depends which part you're going into.'

I tried to peer through the door's porthole, but he blocked my view. 'What's the difference?'

'You're not dressed for downstairs. Downstairs is Rubber.'

'Ah. How much upstairs?' I felt for my wallet. The rain had begun to fall more heavily, coloured needles passing through neon.

'Twelve pounds.'

'That's a lot.'

'Makes no difference. You can't come in.'

'Why not?'

'It's full up. Fire regulations.'

'But I have to meet someone.'

Just then two shaven-headed girls in stacked boots walked past me, and the bouncer held the door open for them. A wave of boiling air and scrambled music swept over us. 'Why did you let them in?' I asked as he resealed the door.

'They're members.'

'How much is it to be a member?'

'Membership's closed.'

'You told me the club was full.'

'Only to guests.'

'Could I come in if I was with a member?'

The doorman approximated an attitude of deep thought for a moment. 'Not without a Guest Pass.'

'What must I give you to get one of those?'

'Twenty-four hours' notice.'

'Look.' I spoke through gritted teeth. 'I can see we have to reach some kind of agreement here, because the rest of my life is dependent on me getting inside this club tonight.'

'You could try bribing me.' He spoke as if he was telling a child something very obvious. I shuffled some notes from my wallet and held them out. He glanced down briefly, then resumed his Easter Island pose. I added another ten. He palmed the stack without checking it.

'Now can I come in?'

'No.'

'You took a bribe. I'll call the police.'

'Suit yourself. Who are they going to believe?'

That was a good point. He probably knew all the officers in the area. I was just a hick hustling to gain entry to his club. 'I could make trouble for you,' I said unconvincingly.

'Oh, that's good.' He glanced down at me. 'Bouncers love trouble. Every night we pray for a good punch-up. When there's a fight we call each other from all the other clubs,' he indicated the doorways along the street, 'and have a big bundle.'

It was hopeless. My street etiquette was non-existent. I simply didn't know what to do, so I asked him. 'This is incredibly important to me,' I explained. 'Just tell me how I can get in.'

I'd already guessed the reply. 'You can't.'

'Why not?'

'Because you had to ask.' He removed his glasses and studied me with tiny deep-set eyes. 'You're up from the sticks for your Big Night Out, but it's not in here, not for you. You don't fit.'

At least he was honest. I knew then that it wasn't just the club. I'd never be able to make the jump, even for a woman like her. Despondent, I walked to the side of the building and pressed my back against the wet brickwork, studying the sky. And I waited. I thought there might be a side exit I could slip through, but there wasn't. Everyone came and went through the front door. Soon my shirt was sticking to my skin and my shoes were filled with water, but I no longer cared. See Suburban Man attempt to leave his natural habitat! Watch as he enters the kingdom of Urbia and battles the mocking resident tribe! Well, this was one Suburban Man who wasn't going down without a fight.

But two hours later I was still there, shivering in the shadowed lea of the building, studying the lengthy queue of clubbers waiting to enter. When the steel door opened and she appeared with Pony-Tail and some black guy on her arm, I stepped forward into the light. One look at her face told me everything. I was sure now that she'd known I wouldn't get in, and was having a laugh at my expense.

I'm not a violent man, but I found myself moving toward her with my arm raised and I think my hand connected, just a glancing blow. Then people from the queue were on me, someone's hand across my face, another pushing me backwards. There was some shouting, and I remember hearing Michelle call my name, something about not hurting me.

I remember being thrown into the alley and hitting the ground hard. In movies they always land on a neat pile of cardboard boxes. No such luck here, just piss-drenched concrete and drains. My face was hurting, and I could taste blood in my mouth. I unscrewed my eyes and saw Pony-Tail standing over me. The black guy was holding Michelle by the arm, talking fast. She looked really sorry and I think she wanted to help, but he wasn't about to allow her near me. I could barely hear what he was saying through the noise in my head.

'I told you this would happen. He got no roots, no family. He don't belong here. You know that.' He was talking too fast. I didn't understand. Then Pony-Tail was crouching low beside me.

'Big fucking mistake, man. You can't be near her. Don't you get it?' He was waving his hands at me, frustrated by his efforts to explain. 'She's part of this city. Do you see? I mean, really part of it. You hurt her, you hurt – all of this.' He raised his arm at the buildings surrounding us.

I tried to talk but my tongue seemed to block my speech. Pony-Tail moved closer. 'Listen to me, you're cut but this is nothing. You must get up and run. It watches over her and now it'll fight

you. Run back to your own world and you may be able to save
yourself. That's all the advice I can give.'

Then they were gone, the men on either side protecting her,
swiftly bearing her away from harm, slaves guarding their queen.
She stole a final glance back at me, regret filling her eyes.

For a few minutes I lay there. No one came forward to help.
Eventually I found the strength to pull myself to my feet. It felt as if
someone had stuck a penknife into my ribcage. The first time I tried
to leave the alley, the indignant crowd pushed me back. When I
eventually managed to break through, the buildings ahead dazzled
my eyes and I slipped on the wet kerb, falling heavily on to my
shins. I knew that no one would ever come forward to help me
now. The city had changed its face. As I stumbled on, blurs of
angry people gesticulated and screeched, Hogarthian grotesques
marauding across town and time. I milled through them in a maze
of streets that turned me back toward the centre where I would be
consumed and forgotten, another threat disposed of.

I feel dizzy, but I daren't risk lying down. There's a thick rope of
blood running down my left leg, from an artery I think. I'm so
vulnerable, just a sack of flesh and bone encircled by concrete and
steel and iron railings and brittle panes. A few minutes ago I leaned
against a shop window, trying to clear my stinging head, and the
glass shattered, vitreous blades shafting deep into my back.

I can't last much longer without her protection.

The first car that hit me drove over my wrist and didn't stop. A
fucking Fiat Panda. I think the second one broke a bone in my
knee. Something is grinding and mashing when I bend the joint. He
didn't stop, either. Perhaps I'm no longer visible. I can't tell if I'm
walking in the road, because it keeps shifting beneath my feet. The
buildings, too, trundle noisily back and forth, diverting and directing. I feel light-headed. All I know is, I won't survive until
daybreak. No chance of reaching safety now. London has shut me
out and trapped me in.

It's unfair; I don't think I should have to die. I suppose it's
traditional when you screw around with the queen. As the pavement
beneath my feet is heading slightly downhill, I think I'm being led
toward the Embankment. It will be a short drop to the sluggish
river below, and merciful sleep beyond.

I wonder what her real age is, and if she even has a name. Or what would have happened had I learned to love her city, and stay within the custody of her benevolent gaze. Does she look down with a tremor of compassion for those who fail to survive her kingdom, or does she stare in pitiless fascination at the mortals tumbling through her ancient, coiling streets, while far away, suburbia sleeps on?

COLD COLOURS
Neil Gaiman

I

Woken at nine o'clock by the postman, who turns out not to be the postman but an itinerant seller of pigeons crying, 'Fat pigeons, pure pigeons, dove-white, slate-grey, living breathing pigeons, none of your reanimated muck here, sir.'

I have pigeons and to spare and I tell him so. He tells me he's new in this business, used to be part of a moderately successful financial securities analysis company but was laid off, replaced by a computer RS232'd to a quartz sphere. 'Still, mustn't grumble, one door opens another one slams, got to keep up with the times sir, got to keep up with the times.'

He thrusts me a free pigeon (To attract new custom, sir, once you've tried one · of our pigeons you'll never look at another), and struts down the stairs singing 'Pigeons alive-oh, alive alive-oh.'

Ten o'clock after I've bathed and shaved (unguents of eternal youth and of certain sexual attraction applied from plastic vessels), I take the pigeon into my study; I refresh the chalk circle around my old Dell 310, hang wards at each corner of the monitor, and do what is needful with the pigeon.

Then I turn the computer to ON: it chugs and hums; inside it, fans blow like storm winds on old oceans ready to drown poor merchant men. Autoexec complete, it bleeps:

I'll do, I'll do, I'll do . . .

II

Two o'clock and walking through familiar London – or what was familiar London before the cursor deleted certain certainties – I watch a suit-and-tie man giving suck to the Psion Organizer lodged in his breast pocket, its serial interface like a cool mouth hunting his chest for sustenance, familiar feeling, and I'm watching my breath steam in the air.

Cold as a witch's tit these days is London. You'd never think it was November. And from underground the sounds of trains rumble – mysterious: tube trains are almost legendary in these times, stopping only for virgins and the pure of heart, first stop Avalon, Lyonesse, or the Isles of the Blessed. Maybe you get a postcard and maybe you don't.

Anyway, looking down any chasm demonstrates conclusively there is no room under London for subways; I warm my hands at a pit. Flames lock upward.

Far below a smiling demon spots me, waves, mouths carefully, as one does to the deaf, or distant, or to foreigners: its sales performance is spotless: it mimes a Dwarrow Clone, mimes software beyond my wildest, Alberta Magnus AR Chived on three floppies, Claviculae Solomon for VGA, CGA, four-colour or monochrome, mimes and mimes and mimes.

The tourists lean over the riftways to hell staring at the damned (perhaps the worst part of damnation; eternal torture might be bearable in noble silence, alone, but an audience, eating crisps and chips and chestnuts, an audience who aren't even really that interested . . .)

They must feel like something at the zoo, the damned.

Pigeons flutter around Hell, dancing on the updrafts, race memory perhaps telling them that somewhere around here there should be four lions, unfrozen water, one stone man above: the tourists cluster around.

One does a deal with the demon; a broken CD-ROM drive for his soul.

One has recognized a relative in the flames and is waving:

Coooee! Coooeee! Uncle Joseph! Look, Merissa, it's your Great-Uncle Joe that died before you was born, that's him down there, in the Slouth, up to his eyes in boiling scum with the worms crawling in and out of his face. Such a lovely man.

We all cried at his funeral.

Wave to your uncle, Merissa, wave to your uncle.

The pigeon-man lays limed twigs on the cracked paving stones, then sprinkles breadcrumbs and waits.

He raises his cap to me.

'This morning's pigeon, sir, I trust it was satisfactory?'

I allow that it was, and toss him a golden shilling (which he touches surreptitiously to the iron of his gauntlet, checking for fairy gold, then palms).

Tuesdays, I tell him. Come on Tuesdays.

III

Birdlegged cottages and huts crowd the London streets, stepping spindly over the taxis, shitting embers over cyclists, queueing in the streets behind the buses: *chuckchuckchuckchuckchuurck*, they murmur.

Old women with iron teeth gaze out of the windows then return to their magic mirrors, or to their housework, hoovering through fog and filthy air.

Four o'clock in Old Soho, rapidly becoming a backwater of lost technology. The ratcheting grate of charms being wound up with clockwork silver keys grinds out from every backstreet watchmakers, abortionists, philtre-sellers and Tobacconists.

It's raining.

Bullet in-board kids drive pimpmobiles in floppy hats, modem panders, anoracked kid-kings of signal-to-noise; and all their neon-lit stippled stable flirting and turning under the lights: succubi and incubi with sell-by dates and Smart Card eyes, all yours, if you've got your number, know your expiry date, all that.

One of them winks at me (flashes, on, on-off, off-off-on), noise swallows signal in fumbled fellatio. (I cross two fingers, a binary precaution against hex, effective as a superconductor or simple superstition.)

Two poltergeists share a Chinese take-away. Old Soho always makes me nervous.

Brewer Street. A hiss from an alley: Mephistopheles opens his brown coat, flashes me the lining (databased old invocations, magian lay ghosts – with diagrams), curses and begins:

Blight an enemy?
Wither a harvest?
Barren a consort?
Debase an innocent?

Ruin a party . . .?

For you, sir? No, sir? Reconsider I beg. Just a little of your blood smudged on this printout and you can be the proud possessor of a new voice-synthesizer, listen —

He stands a Zenith portable on a table he makes from a modest suitcase, attracting a small audience in the process, plugs in the voicebox, types at the *C:/>* prompt: *GO* and it recites in voice exact and fine — *orientis princeps Beelzebub, inferni irredentista menarche et demigorgon, propitiamus vows* — I hurry onwards, hurry down the street while paper ghosts, old printouts, dog my heels, and hear him patter like a market man —

Not twenty
Not eighteen
Not fifteen,
Cost me twelve lady so help me Satan but to you?
Because I like your pretty face
Because I want to raise your spirits
Five,
That's right.
Five.
Sold to the lady with the lovely eyes . . .

IV

The Archbishop hunches glaucous blind in the darkness on the edge of St Paul's, small, birdlike, luminous, humming *I/O, I/O, I/O.*

It's almost six and the rush-hour traffic in stolen dreams and expanded memory hustles the pavement below us.

I hand the man my jug.

He takes it, carefully, and shuffles back into the waiting cathedral shadows. When he returns the jug is full once more. I josh, 'Guaranteed holy!'

He traces one word in the frozen dirt: WYSIWYG, and does not smile back.

(Wheezy wig. Whisky whig.)

He coughs grey, milk-phlegm, spits on to the steps.

What I see in the water jug: it looks holy enough, but you can't know for sure, not unless you are yourself a siren or a fetch, coagulating out of a telecom mouthpiece, riding the bleep, an invocation, some really Wrong Number; then you can tell from holy.

I've dumped telephones in buckets of the stuff before now, watched things begin to form, then bubble and hiss as the water gets to them: lustrated and asperged, the Final Sanction.

One afternoon there was a queue of them, trapped on the tape of my Ansaphone: I copied it to floppy and filed it away.

You want it? Listen, everything's for sale.

The priest needs shaving, and he's got the shakes. His wine-stained vestments do little to keep him warm. I give him money. (Not much. After all, it's just water, some creatures are so stupid they'll do you a Savini gunk-dissolve if you sprinkle them with Perrier for chrissakes, whining the whole time *All my evil, my beautiful evil.*)

The old priest pockets the coin, gives me a bag of crumbs as a bonus, sits on his steps hugging himself.

I feel the need to say something before I leave.

Look, I tell him, it's not your fault. It's just a multi-user system. You weren't to know. If prayers could be networked, if saintware were up and running, if you could make your side as reliable as they've made theirs . . .

'What You See,' he mutters desolately, 'What You See Is What You Get.' He crumbles a communion wafer and throws it down for the pigeons, makes no attempt to catch even the slowest bird.

Cold wars produce bad losers. I go home.

V

News at Ten. And here is Abel Drugger reading it:

VI

The corners of my eyes catch hasty, bloodless motion – a mouse? Well, certainly a peripheral of some kind.

VII

It's bedtime. I feed the pigeons, then undress. Contemplate down-loading a succubus from a board, maybe just call up a side-kick (there's public domain stuff, bawds and bauds, shareware, no need to pay a fortune, even copy-protected stuff can be copied, passed about, everything has a price, any of us).

Dryware, wetware, hardware, software, blackware, darkware, nightware, nightmare . . .

The modem sits inviting beside the phone: red eyes. I let it rest — you can't trust anybody these days. You download, Hell, you don't know where *what* came from any more, who had it last.

Well, aren't you? Aren't you scared of viruses? Even the better protected files corrupt, and the best protected corrupt absolutely.

In the kitchen I hear the pigeons billing and queueing, dreaming of left-handed knives, of athanors and mirrors.

Pigeon blood stains the floor of my study.

Alone, I sleep. And all alone I dream.

VIII

Perhaps I wake in the night, suddenly comprehending something, reach out, scribble on the back of an old bill my revelation, my new-found understanding (knowing that morning will render it prosaic, knowing that magic is a night-time thing, then remembering when it still was . . .)

Revelation retreats to cliché, listen:

Things seemed simpler before we kept computers.

IX

Waking or dreaming, from outside I hear wild sabbats, screaming winds, tape hum, metal machine music. Witches astride ghetto-blasters crowd the moon, then land on the heath, their naked flanks aglisten.

No one pays anything to attend the meet, each has it taken care of in advance — baby bones with fat still clinging to them, these things are direct debit, standing order. And I see, or think I see, a face I recognize, and all of them queue up to kiss his arse (let's rim the devil, boys, cold seed), and in the dark he turns and looks at me:

One door opens another one slams,
I trust that everything is satisfactory?
We do what we can, everybody's got the right to turn an honest penny:
We're all bankrupt, sir,
We're all redundant,
But we make the best of it, whistle through the blitz,
That's the business. Fair trade is no robbery.
Tuesday morning, then, sir, with the pigeons?

I say no and draw the curtains. Junk mail is everywhere. They'll get to you; one way or another they'll get to you.

Someday I'll find my tube train underground. I'll pay no fare, just: 'This is hell, and I want out of it', and then things will be simple once again.

It will come for me like a dragon down a dark tunnel.

WRITTEN ON MY HEART
Steve Grant

Beryl Mary Holloway sat on a bench by the river, eating a cottage cheese and pastrami bagel and waiting expectantly for the first rush of diet Pepsi after she had finished. She always liked to sit near the Rodin statue, that one of the burghers of Calais, whose lives were saved by the pleas of the queen of King Edward. She'd never been to Calais.

Beryl would sit on her bench, usually alone, and look across at the river, the great grey dishwater sludge with fluffs of white whipped up by the early afternoon wind. This morning she'd finally cracked it; ten thousand pounds worth of voluntary redundancy from her job as a secretary with one of the country's ten biggest unions. She'd just passed a man selling that new paper, the *Big Issue*, and felt guilty, and had offered him ten pounds but he had insisted on taking just the fifty pence. She felt a bit naughty reading about all these jobless statistics when she had only stuck the place so that she'd qualify for the bumper bundle. Still, why not, and what would she spend the money on, that was the most important thing. Dad and Mum had passed on; only child. No relatives worth a Christmas card. In fact, and this was also very naughty, one of her best friends was a woman called Maggie and Maggie was a bag lady. One evening they'd been asked to leave the pub they were in, by the landlord. Cheek. Maybe she should buy Maggie a new bag.

Beryl had always wanted to change her name. When she was little, Beryl's mum had said she had been named for a stone and Beryl had wondered what she meant, as mum was always talking about Aunt Vi's stones and that Aunt Vi had passed one the size of a Cox's pippin and nearly died simply from the sheer agony and had lost blood. But that was when she was little, not even ten yet, and when you were young you did stupid things all the time, like drink painting-set water with lead in it, or swallow forty cherries with the stones still in, and have to listen for the ping on the side of the toilet bowl as mum and dad stood outside counting to see if they were all coming out. Most of Beryl's childhood had been involved with stones in one way or another: Rolling Stones, played too loudly next door. The stones on the bomb-sites near the tube station where she'd play 'kiss-chase' and 'it' and where she fell badly and cut her leg and Martin Blickstead had said she'd die of it, die from poisoned blood. Stone walls. Stone floors. Stone bed. Stone desk. Stone chair. Stone. Stony-faced. Stony-hearted. Stone alone.

So what should she do? Would she keep the flat on? Yes. The flat. *That* was the night it had started, funnily enough. That was the night, after her and Maggie, who was a *kind* person, had been asked to leave, and she, Beryl, had got quite upset with the barman who was probably another one of these clever dicks from Leicester or somewhere like that and they had decided to go back to her flat nearby, and outside her front door was that pile of boxes. That was the night. She wasn't sure who'd actually stacked them in front of the door but as usual it was Brigitte who led the complaining over the next week. 'Well, Beryl, you've got to move all that stuff. It's junk, it's old clobber, it's going to stink, it's going to attract vermin.' Sod her. Sod them. She couldn't help it if Raymond from the charity shop hadn't stopped by to pick it up. And it was all right for Brigitte to go on about how it wasn't worth anything to anybody anyway, but she didn't know how much money it would take to feed one Bangladeshi for a week. And they had said that anything, even waste paper, was wanted. It wasn't her fault that it rained.

'But it's all that stuff,' Dennis had continued a few days later. 'It's all that stuff. It's not just all the papers, Beryl, it's everything else. It's outside. It attracts the pigeons. It stinks.' It didn't stink. 'Why do you collect shopping trolleys, for Christ's sake,' he asked. 'Why do you collect plastic bags? Those cigarette butts in the flower-bed aren't for charity, are they?' Sarky he was. When Beryl had moved into the new flats they had had parties on the terrace. Daisy, who had long gone, married and in Eastbourne, had been an actress then and had been working on one of those early-evening soaps, not one of the bigger ones, but she'd invited a few TV celebs and they'd sat out and danced and Basil, the chef who'd moved back to Middlesbrough, had done the food and all the doors were left open and it was like the Queen's Coronation day. It had been smashing. And Brigitte and her had posed for photos that Basil

took with his smart camera. Basil was always smart, everything was
impeccable. His flat looked twice as big as everyone else's and it was
so white and so tasteful. Things had got a bit nasty. One of Daisy's
actor friends, a large fat man with a bushy beard, had asked Basil
what his favourite record was and Basil had said 'Spirit in the Sky'
by Norman Greenbaum and the actor had laughed so much that he
dropped his glass and smashed it all over the new patio, and Basil
had stormed off and slammed the door. But he was like that;
touchy, but kind. A kind man. A creative man.

Beryl always came to this spot for her lunch, but in a week's time
there wouldn't be any need to come. She would be able to do what
she wanted. She could look for another job, but not until she felt
like it. Maybe she should travel. Brian Smith, one of the union
lawyers, had been talking about America. Washington. He said they
had this monument, which was just a huge, black wall with name
after name on it, all the dead from the Vietnam war. He hadn't
been able to take photographs, you weren't allowed, but he'd seen
all these men in uniform, some of them with crutches and even
some of them in wheelchairs, and they had all been sobbing.
Except, he said, for this group of people from Africa, Nigeria he
thought, who had found it funny. He didn't understand why, but
there was another monument built which was much more old-
fashioned, sort of like the ones in the War Museum when Dad had
taken her on Saturday afternoons. And you could take photographs
of that, and these Africans had been sticking their heads into the
gaps between all these stone soldiers and grinning and shouting
'Watermelon!' loudly as their friends snapped them, and Brian had
said that he had been quite embarrassed but then Africans had a
different attitude to grief. Yes, she thought, and they have so many
problems. Drought. Famine. War. Disease. They probably thought
the Americans were making too much fuss.
    Beryl didn't know if she'd manage to go as far as Washington.
You needed a visa, and someone had told her that they asked you if
you were a Communist and she had been a Communist, funny
though it seemed now, because Jim had been a Communist and
when he'd been at Head Office in London and before he'd told her
about his wife and kids back home in Yorkshire they had gone to
meetings, and she had joined because she was with him and she

thought at the time that she might stay with him for good. But she hadn't. It hadn't worked out. He'd gone back to his wife. He hadn't told her or even rung up, he'd just left a letter that she'd found on the mat and he'd apologized and said that he did care for her but that it was all a mistake and he couldn't leave his family and he hoped he could see her when he was back in London. Well, that was that. For a while she had thought she'd die of it. Was she ever daft. Hadn't even told her he was married. That was Sylvia's happy duty, but when she'd confronted him he'd had the nerve to tell her he was going to leave her. She never believed that, did she? Did she? Wasn't he just looking for a free place to stay?

Enough of that. Maybe she'd pay a visit to Castleford, visit his wife, but you couldn't let it drive you to that kind of nastiness. You couldn't. And she probably knew anyway. They always do, or so she'd read somewhere.

A group of French students were looking at the statue. There were a pair on the edge of the crowd, obviously madly in love, smiling and whispering. There was a boy making a sketch, a very fast sketch. Bits of laughing and larking. They didn't seem too impressed on the whole. It was a replica of the one made in 1896 in Calais and it represented the self-sacrifice of the burghers who were prepared to die to save their city from being sacked, and the chivalry of Edward III, not included, who at the behest of his wife, Queen Matilda or Eleanor or Philippa or something, not included, had spared the lives of these brave people. So it represented courage. Chivalry and Compassion. Good things. And dignity. She had always wanted to come back, and she had read it up in the library. She was fond of this group of dignified men, ready to die for a seaside town, she was glad they'd been spared. She wondered if there had ever been someone called Queen Beryl. It was just about possible, and she thought how beautiful if must be to die for your city, to plead for someone's life, and to show mercy. Yes, to show mercy. It must be wonderful to be asked.

She was always neat and tidy at work. Her neighbours couldn't understand that, how she would go out every morning, dressed in her Burberry copy and her pleated skirt and blouse, and her Selfridge's shoes, with only the smell of the last cigarette giving anything away, and how she could go to work, and keep her job, and still come home to a patio full of 'rubbish'. Their word. They

hadn't really been that bad or anything, Brigitte was a pain sometimes but then she was the tenants' rep, and even Brigitte hadn't
wanted to bring in the association, or get her into trouble because
she knew that Beryl had been off work for a while after Mum and
then Dad had passed away very quickly with hardly a month
between them. She had been depressed, and so they were making
allowances. What right did they have to make allowances?

Most of them lived off the state. Doris in flat fourteen lived with
a drug addict and was once found unconscious in the street. Dennis
on the top floor was the proud gardener now, complaining about
the work he had to do for free, but a few years ago he had been
peeing in the lift every other night and had been on a bottle of
Scotch a day. Barry sublet anyway and shouldn't even be in his flat
but at least he never said anything. Just sloped by, worried sick in
case someone from the association popped by looking for Donella
who was black and female and not pink and bald and spotty and
white as they came.

Brigitte had told her to get help. She had pushed a note through the
door, a newspaper cutting, but Beryl hadn't seen it anyway, because
by then there'd been so much stuff on the doormat. Letters. Bills.
Offers. Competitions. Circulars. Newsletters. Poll tax. Rent demands. Three letters that were probably letters of condolence for
Mum and Dad, but she just left them there. The flats were just too
small. So much stuff and now she'd got no room to swing a mouse.
She needed the space outside, and Dennis and Doris had once said
that it wasn't fair because it wasn't even her space, but it was
outside *her* door, wasn't it? Any moment, any time now, Raymond
would come and take it away. It was part of what she did. She
collected for charity. She couldn't help if it messed up the patio; it
was her bit of the patio, and on the first floor they were expected to
pay extra rent, and they had to put up with Dennis and his mates
from A A banging and sawing and planting and digging, making all
kinds of racket any day that it wasn't raining or snowing. And
Barry's radio when he had the guts to sit outside his door on a
Sunday, when he knew no one from the association would be
round on business.

Now there were no tenants' meetings. Sometimes you never saw
anyone. Some of the new tenants had language difficulties; there

was a girl from Croatia and an old Chinese man who walked
funny, a retired waiter. Chinese waiters were rude, she remembered
when she had been to a Chinese restaurant with Jim after some
meeting at the Conway Hall and Jim had asked him if there was a
downstairs and the man had said something in Chinese and then
said, 'Don't know, you go down and have look, come back, tell
me', and flounced off. Still, China was a place that was fascinating.
They had terrible suffering. She'd seen *The Last Emperor* with Jim
and remembered the newsreels of the Japanese rape of Nanking.
Then there were floods. Earthquakes. Tidal waves. And lots of
different kinds of cancer there, apparently, nose cancer and stomach
cancer. They spat everywhere. And Chairman Mao shot all the
dogs in the seventies and so now there were rats everywhere. Rats.

Rats! How could they get rats on the first floor! Not round that
part of London, too many bloody restaurants, Egon Ronay rats,
maybe. Too choosy. Rats wouldn't eat paper, anyway. Old umbrellas. Shoeboxes full of recyclable paper. Wire-framed baskets. She
hadn't even had any problems in the flat and now there was so
much stuff that she hardly had room to get into the bed and it had
been a small bed. Jim had said that. Good job it's got you in it, he
used to say.

Ten thousand pounds. Maybe she should give it away. Would
they have a party for her? Probably a small one. Nicholson would
make a brief speech, they'd stop work for half an hour or adjourn
to the pub, which she never frequented because she didn't believe in
it, drinking at lunchtime, and you could never get a seat and they
would tell her she'd be missed. But she wouldn't be and she
wouldn't miss them. None of them. Maggie lived rough and she
was nicer than all of them put together. Maggie had been nice to
her after Mum had died, had taken her under her wing for a bit, as
she liked to put it. Beryl thought that maybe Maggie was sad for
her; but she wasn't sad because she loved or missed Mum and Dad,
she was sad because she knew that they had never loved her, that
she had been a chore, an excuse, an irritation. For most of her life.
Named for a stone.

Beryl Mary Holloway sat by the statue of the burghers of Calais in
Victoria Park Gardens, named for the Victoria Park tower of the
Houses of Parliament and from whose flag-pole the Union Jack

swung when the house was in session. It wasn't in session but often she saw them coming and going, some familiar, some faces she knew well like Clare Short, Jeffrey Archer and Virginia Bottomley. People half a world away but it was nobody's fault. What would she do with the money? Her bagel was long finished by now, and the diet Pepsi can empty. Should she put it in a bin, she wondered. Or take it home.

S/HE
Robert Grossmith

It went by a variety of names, from the technical (Gender Complementarity Treatment) through the colloquial (ambisexing, the Switch) to the vulgar (getting lipped, getting boned). Desmond first heard about it on one of the news 'n' views shows he liked to watch while Frida was at her fashion class. Something about advances in the biotechnology of organ-cloning and how the new technique, originally developed for use in sex-change operations, was soon to be made available to the general public. A white-capped surgeon, interviewed in the operating room of her swish Whitechapel clinic, brushed aside the suggestion that there was anything unnatural about GCT: the human body contained ample room for two sets of sex organs, she said; it was an evolutionary accident that we only possessed one.

Frida's account was more impressionistic.

'It's dead simple apparently, only takes a couple of hours, local anaesthetic, you can even watch what they're doing. It's the latest thing, everyone's having it done. Apparently they just connect a few nerve-endings or blood-vessels or whatever they are, and then sort of graft it on. Or in your case – well, I'm not sure what they do exactly in men's cases, I'll have to ask Herm, him and Mandy have just been done. They say they don't know how they ever managed without them. It's transformed their life, they said, their sex life's – well, you can imagine.'

Desmond tried to imagine, but imagination wasn't easy in this inverted alien landscape, and he abandoned the effort with a shrug.

'It's just a fad, like everything. It'll pass.'

He knew that calling it a fad wouldn't deter Frida; on the contrary it would amount in her eyes to a recommendation. Fads were what her life was about, to be in on a fad before everyone else was how she measured her success. Maybe it was her job: working in the make-up department of a movie studio, maybe she was bound to see the world in superficial terms, in cosmetic terms, to see science and medicine as adjuncts of the fashion and entertainment industries. The role of science, to Frida's way of thinking, was to provide people like her with amusing after-dinner conversation and unusual Christmas presents, a tool for provoking the envy and admiration of her friends, of scoring social points.

Take their honeymoon, which they'd spent at Frida's insistence on one of the early, horrendously expensive moon cruises. A poor traveller at the best of times, Desmond succeeded in contracting some rare kind of space bug and spent most of the time ashore throwing up into his helmet. Frida responded by scolding him. To be honeymooning on the moon was the kind of silly obvious pun she enjoyed, one she'd extract a lot of mileage from later. She didn't want him spoiling it by being miserable.

So he knew there'd be little point in opposing her in this latest enthusiasm of hers. She wouldn't be happy till they'd both been kitted out with their new 'complementary' organs, like Mandy and Herm, like the women at her fashion class, like the trendsetters she fondly imagined Desmond and herself to be. 'Everyone's having it done,' she'd said, which was not only untrue but actually the opposite of what she meant. Everyone, in Frida's peculiar usage, meant a select clique of rich style-obsessed socialites and short-lived international celebrities at whose altar she worshipped and whose lead she followed in everything with puppyish devotion. If she'd really thought everyone was having it done, she'd have wanted to be doing something entirely different.

She wouldn't let it rest, she kept coming back to it. She left him notes and obscene drawings before she went to work. She bought an anatomically correct ambisex doll and left it splay-limbed, tumescent, on the kitchen table. She read him items from her fashion and movie magazines: how the Switch was rumoured to have cured everything from shyness to piles, how ambisexuals claimed to feel truly whole for the first time in their lives. Eventually, exhausted, bored, Desmond gave in.

She came home with a catalogue from the clinic showing the different models they could choose from. The organs came in a bewildering variety of shapes and sizes. Here were penises long and short, fat and thin, circumcised and uncircumcised, smooth and sleek as Tampa cigars or bulbous and knobby as comedy vegetables; vaginas resembling huge pink gashes and others like snugly clasped purses, with clitorises that ranged from the button-like to the tentacular. Desmond read:

4/1C BIGBOY. Designed for the discriminating user, the Bigboy features a specially enlarged scrotum guaranteeing frequent and copious emissions together with a delicately ribbed shaft for the ultimate in erotic pleasure. Durable yet highly sensitive, the Bigboy will satisfy both you and your partner for years to come ... *'I never thought such pleasure possible. Now I know how it feels to really satisfy a man. My husband joins me in thanking you for bringing this new dimension to our lives.'* Mrs W., Lyme Regis

37/4A SATURDAY NIGHT SPECIAL. Delight your partner with this compact and unpretentious model which makes up for in comfort and serviceability what it lacks in size. Like the famous pistol from which it takes its name, the 'Special' packs a deceptively powerful punch! Ideally suited for the occasional user ... *'Saturday nights will never be the same again.'* Ms O., New Bristol

62/6F RING MY BELL. A real ding-dong of a model, your bell will be ringing all night long with this high-performance quality vagina! Designed according to the latest bioengineering principles with today's man in mind, this state-of-the-art model features a specially elongated clitoris guaranteeing orgasm upon delirious orgasm ... *'Ring-a-ding-ding!'* Mr P., Staines

The day of the operation arrived – D-Day, Dick Day as Frida had taken to referring to it. On his way to theatre Desmond pondered his impending mutilation. He recalled a comment of Frida's to the effect that having the Switch was no more serious than having a boil lanced or a tooth out, in the days when people used to have boils lanced and teeth out; in fact it was less serious because you weren't losing but gaining something. It was the same argument she used long ago when announcing their wedding plans to his mother: don't think of it as losing a son, Mum, think of it as gaining a daughter. Well Mum, he said to himself as he lay down on the table, you're about to gain another one.

By the time he was under the knife the drugs had begun to take effect. With his legs splayed in the stirrups above him and the surgeon's hands invisibly busy between them, he felt perfectly relaxed, perfectly calm. He was struck by the curiously waxen, polished-looking face of the surgeon, by his perfect teeth and coiffed hair and even tan. Was it his imagination or were all doctors beginning to resemble one another?

He felt a little sore afterwards, nothing more. Before dressing he examined himself front and back in the changing-room mirror and was relieved to detect no obvious signs of disfigurement. Only on a chair with his legs up could the full extent of the damage be seen. He stepped into the kilt he'd brought with him – he categorically refused to wear a skirt in public – and cast one final pained glance at himself in the mirror. What a sight. He'd entered the clinic that morning an ordinary man in a suit. He was leaving it a carnival freak in fancy dress, a hermaphrodite fucking Scotsman.

Later, reunited with Frida at the after-care facility to collect the various lotions and silicone refills required for the operation of their new organs, he found his gaze involuntarily drawn to the crotch of Frida's jeans, hoping not to be met by too manly a bulge.

It was several days before he would allow Frida to inspect the results of the operation, and then only from a distance. She on the other hand flaunted her new gender with exhibitionist zeal, parading naked about the flat, giggling each time it flapped against her thigh, marvelling at its bulbous veiny realism. It was even longer before he plucked up the courage to test the efficacy of his new anatomy in the bathroom. When he finally did so, he experienced such a gut-wrenching sense of plunging bottomless release, as if his body fluids were being bled out of him, drained, strained like water through a sieve, that he immediately contracted his muscles, stood up, turned round and reverted to the more familiar procedure.

Eventually, he knew, he'd be forced to put it to that other, more demanding test. He couldn't hold out for ever against Frida's persistent wheedling requests, her coaxing, her cajoling, her bullying in bed.

'Let me touch it, go on,' she'd half-demand half-plead, 'I just want to see what it feels like. Let me put the lubricant on.'

'A few days more, love, I'm not ready yet. You know what the doctors said about rushing things.'

'A few days more! You're behaving like a prissy little convent girl. I'm not going to eat you, for Chrissakes!'

She had a way with words, did Frida.

He finally settled on the evening of April Fool's Day as the occasion for his deflowering: such a significant event demanded a symbolic date.

They ordered dinner from a Vietnamese delivery service in Leytonstone. A white dinner, in honour of the occasion: sword-fish with almond sauce, followed by a cream *passionel*. Frida's favourite.

He set a candlelit table for two while she changed. She tied her hair in a bun and put on one of his white linen suits, one of the less voluminous ones from a few years back when he still used to go to the gym. It still managed to look as if it had swallowed her. She peered at herself in the mirror and shook her head.

'I can see some serious shopping is called for.'

She took to her role uncertainly at first but with growing conviction, walking, eating, talking as she imagined a man would, hitching the knees of her trousers when she sat down, lowering the pitch of her voice when she spoke. Over dinner they talked about things that didn't matter. She told him about a football game she'd watched on the airbus on the way home from work, the Bulls against the Rams. He filled her in on the latest gossip from the Census Office, how his departmental boss was rumoured to be having an affair with her new PA.

'Oughta be ashamed of herself, woman her age. How old is he, this new boy? Just a lad, I bet. Fuckin' cradle-snatching.'

For a moment he was perplexed. This was not the Frida he knew, she'd always been fiercely approving of relationships between older women and younger men. She claimed women got better at sex as they got older while men got worse, so it was a perfect match. Then he realized that this too was part of the act. She was reacting as she thought a man would react. This was how she thought men were.

Leaving the table to fetch some more wine, he noticed her appraising him from behind.

'Those stockings really suit you, you know. You haven't got bad legs for a man your size.'

He had agreed somewhat reluctantly to wear a figure-hugging leather miniskirt she'd bought him, together with a pair of heels and ridiculous fishnet stockings. He'd never realized before just how uncomfortable women's clothes were.

Over coffee she started coming on to him. She slipped off her shoe and ran the sole of her foot up and down his calf. She pinched his bottom as he leant to refill her cup. She would have stuck her hand up his skirt if there'd been room for it.

As he stood up to clear away the dishes, she pulled him playfully on to her lap – 'Leave those, hon, you can do them tomorrow,' – and began rather too vigorously to goose and kiss and fondle him. With a faint shudder of revulsion he felt her counterfeit member stirring beneath him, filling the loose folds of her trousers and bracing itself taut against his bare suspendered thigh.

'My ding-a-ling, my ding-a-ling,' she sang, the words from a favourite old song of hers, 'I want you to play with my ding-a-ling-a-ling.'

He masked his mounting panic behind a nervous staccato laugh and a grotesque simper.

He undressed quickly while Frida was in the bathroom, ducking beneath the sheet to lie rigid and motionless on his back, legs welded together. She returned reeking of aftershave and clad in a pair of candystriped boxer shorts, which she removed casually, with a leisurely motion, the lights on.

'What about, you know, precautions?'

She laughed, an unguarded feminine laugh.

'Dessie! Didn't you listen to any of what the doctors said? You haven't got a womb, just a vagina.'

She drew back the single sheet under which he cowered and straddled him clumsily with her knees.

'Well, what d'you think?'

It was the first time he'd seen her new organ close up. Against her slight, shapely form it looked savage and monstrous, even though, she assured him, she'd gone for one of the smaller, less exotic models, conscious of his delicacy. Throbbing to its full arching stature under his gaze, it seemed already a natural extension of her body. As penises went, he supposed it was probably a very nice one.

She looked down at it proudly and cupped her scrotum in her hand.

'I'm gonna screw the pussy off you.'

He reminded her of the doctors' advice – take it easy at first, don't force anything – but she paid no attention. She'd already

lowered her head to his loins to work on his redundant member
with her tongue, licking it up and out of the way, clearing a path
for her entry. Reaching blindly for the pot of LubriFem on the
bedside cabinet, she smeared a generous handful of the oily cream
liberally over his labia.

Foreplay had never been Frida's forte, short and sharp and to the
point was how she liked it, she always said. She liked to be taken by
surprise, literally, when bending over a steaming bath or hunting
under the couch for a lost earring.

Sharp was right: when she forced herself inside him he felt she
would split him in two. He felt like a tree forked by lightning, like
a spear was ripping through his delicate entrails. Carried away by
her excitement, she thrust hard and deep, too hard, too deep,
interpreting his cries of distress perhaps as a sign of pleasure. The
pain or pleasure was somehow increased by the curious sensation of
his own penis pressing flat and hard against her hot belly like a twin
of the one inside him. Each thrust was a burning scimitar of pain.
He grabbed her by the shoulders and wrestled her roughly from
him. She fell back with a groan, discharging semen the consistency
of albumen against his upper thigh. He watched the familiar,
remarkable spectacle with a mixture of fascination and disgust,
subsiding into sobs.

Over the following months his relationship with Frida underwent a
change. He had always thought of himself as a basically decent,
tolerant, forbearing sort of person, but faced with Frida's increasingly outlandish behaviour he was at a loss as to how to react. He
could cope with her habit of wearing men's clothes and standing
next to him in the men's toilets when they were out together, of
leering at women walking in Hackney Gardens with an invitation
to him to 'check out the legs/ass/tits on that'. He even acquiesced in
the matter of her new-found sexual proclivities, squeezing what
little hard-earned pleasure he could from their swift and frequent
couplings, aiding her in the pursuit of that much vaunted pinnacle
of ambisexual love, the so-called 'duogasm'. But he drew the line at
being asked to dress in frilly lace underwear the whole time, to
shave his legs and armpits and don a wig in bed, to address his wife
as Freddy and answer to the name of Desirée. He was a man with a
man's needs, he told her, and among those was a need for dignity

and his own self-respect. He reminded her of their marriage vows: do you take this man, this *man*, not this androgyne, this epicene, this ambisexual.

'Oh *yawn*,' she said. 'Times have changed. There's a name for men like you. Unreconstructed males, that's what they used to call men like you.'

It almost made him smile. If there was one thing he wasn't, he thought, it was unreconstructed.

The ambisex look caught on in a big way. Soon every new London High Street boasted a Sextensions or a Clever Dicks where operations were available without appointment. The catch-phrase, at one time so outrageous, that, 'We're all naturally hermaphroditic' had already become a cliché and ever more bizarre variations seemed the order of the day. One man, a Milanese couturier, hit upon the idea of having a vagina, looking rather like an over-sized buttonhole, inserted in his abdomen, and was shown on TV, naked with a hard-on, doing sit-ups ('He looks full of himself,' Frida said, apparently without irony). Another individual had a vagina implanted in each armpit and a penis grafted on to each wrist. A poster of this person, leaning against a telegraph pole with folded arms, was used to promote a new line of stainless cotton singlets marketed by a leading jeans manufacturer. There were records, 'Self-Satisfied' and 'Third Sex', which became instant Number One hits.

No one seemed to have even considered the legal implications. Whether, for example, in the unlikely event of an autosexual union engendering offspring (actually less unlikely now that some militant female ambisexuals had taken to filling their testicular reservoirs with bottled sperm rather than silicone fluid), a person could bring a paternity or maternity suit against themselves. Could a wo/man accuse themselves of rape? No one seemed to know.

There were other developments too, on the medical side. A new model of the miniature organ of choice that grew *in situ* was produced, allowing fashion-conscious parents to ambisex their children at birth. This was itself soon made obsolete by a new drug, Gametene, that could be injected into the foetus during the early stages of pregnancy and so ambisex it naturally in the womb.

Then came the momentous day when Adam Newman (surely a *nom de guerre*) was announced to the world as the First Man to Bear a Child, the foetus of baby Felix having been transplanted to his stomach wall from the body of his wife, killed in a skiing accident when three months pregnant. For a couple of weeks the man was to be seen everywhere, guesting on every TV chat show with little baby Felix cradled in his arms, proudly showing off the scars from his Caesarian section. He was said already to have become one of the ten wealthiest men alive because of lucrative movie and merchandising deals. Toy manufacturers rushed out millions of baby 'Felix' dolls in time for Christmas; they were just like any other doll except they cried *Dadda* instead of *Mamma*.

One day he decided he'd had enough.

They didn't like doing reversals, they said at the clinic. He should have thought of the consequences before he'd had it done. These things weren't to be undertaken lightly, you know. He told them he was through with it, he'd had enough, sew him up, he was going back to being a regular guy, they could fuck themselves.

Frida wasn't back from work when he arrived home from the clinic. Her job took her to out-of-the-way places; she kept irregular hours. He sat down on the balcony and steeled himself for her return with a tumbler of Scotch. She could prepare the dinner tonight.

He was beginning to nod off when he heard her keycard enter the slot.

'What are you doing, sitting in the dark?'

'I've been waiting for my dinner,' he said, 'imagining how it used to be done. Where've you been?'

She dropped her briefcase on the hall carpet and kicked off her shoes, a pair of sensible brown brogues.

'Boy, I'm bushed. What a day I've had!'

Over recent weeks she'd taken to stripping off when she got in from work, preferring to spend her evenings, she said, 'as nature intended'. But this time, when she emerged from the bedroom, she wasn't naked. She was dressed in a complicated leather corset made up of multiple straps and buckles and zippered pouches.

'Are you ready for this?' she said. 'Are you man enough for this?'

She lifted a hand to the nape of her neck and fumbled with a clasp. Desmond felt a wave of sickening apprehension.

'Ta da!'

The corset fell away to reveal the body of an alien from another planet. Attached to her armpits, her breasts, her navel, her wrists, was a crop of phalluses of different sizes, shapes and colours – short stubby pink ones, fat wrinkled brown ones, long tapering black ones – like fruit at different stages of ripeness. Like a tree, a penis-tree. She did a catwalk twirl.

'Well, how do I look?'

He drained the remains of his Scotch.

'Would it be stating the obvious to say – a total prick?'

Those were not good days for Desmond. He hadn't expected to care as much as he did. He hadn't thought it would bother him, having a wife who was more of a man than he was, who was a man eight times over, who had manhood sprouting from every limb, who resembled, naked, some kind of grotesque giant insect. He hadn't thought it would bother him but it did.

He didn't inquire into her new sexual practices, he didn't want to know. The geometry and mathematics of it scared him. Acts of love between polysexuals were, he assumed, complicated affairs.

Sometimes, though, her exploits were difficult to ignore. One night when a despairing excess of Scotch sent him stumbling to the bathroom to throw up, he found her in the shower stall with their upstairs neighbour, fucking him in the neck. Another time she announced she was throwing a 'reunion-party-cum-orgy' for the members of her old fashion class and their partners, and did he want to join them? He declined the invitation, preferring to conduct his own liquid orgy with a bottle of Oblivion at a riverside bar.

The tide turned of course. Tides always turn if you wait long enough.

At first the reports were sporadic and unconfirmed. Then suddenly every TV news show was headlining the 'infant ambisex scandal': across the country babies were being born with penises where their noses should have been, vaginas for mouths. There was uproar. Questions were asked, accusations were made, the President was quizzed. Government ministers held press conferences in which they announced details of a full independent inquiry and 'compensation for the tragic victims of this appalling catastrophe'. There was talk of criminal charges being brought against the drugs conglomerates responsible.

The public reaction was instantaneous. Almost overnight ambisexuality and polysexuality became dirty words. Instead of flaunting their gender, ambisexuals began lying about it or concealing it. A number of sick jokes did the rounds: 'What do ambisexuals call their daughters? Dickhead. What do they call their sons? Cunt-Face.' There was a sense everywhere that some kind of limit of unnatural behaviour had been reached, and that the time was overdue for a return to more responsible standards of conduct.

Desmond didn't buy the official theory. It was too simple, too pat. It looked like a put-up job.

One day at work, on a hunch, he accessed the birth-rate files and ran a socio-economic check over them. It was as he'd suspected: over the past two years the birth-rate among the upper levels of the scale had undergone a staggering decline. Ambisexuals had stopped having children.

It was clear what had happened. Presented with a whole new range of erotic possibilities, ambisexuals had abandoned parenthood for more selfish pleasures. Recreation had replaced procreation. As a result the wealthiest and most influential section of society was rapidly on its way to copulating itself out of existence. Ambisexuality had become the ultimate contraceptive.

This theory was confirmed for Desmond by a report he heard on the radio one night while driving home, where it was announced that trials on the latest model of exo-womb were complete and they were soon to be made available as planned. The doctor interviewed on the report said he hoped many people, 'not just women', would take advantage of this 'safer, more convenient and more civilized method of birthing'. Ambisexual sex might have been out of favour, ambisexual parenting clearly wasn't.

Among the flood of cloying lifestyle-promo films that swamped the nation's screens over the next few months, the following struck Desmond as the most schlocky of them all.

An ageing post-lapsarian couple is shown naked on a deserted beach. The Adamic character is swathed in a thick shaggy pelt of penises, which when erect comes rather to resemble some prickly reptilian armour. Eve's body barely holds together among the multiple lacerations of labia disfiguring her torso. Locked together in a casual embrace, Adam penetrates her back in half a dozen places. Suddenly, as if by accident, his hand strays between her thighs. Eve blushes, removes his hand disapprovingly, draws up a modest knee. 'Adam, don't!' But Adam, the rogue, is grinning lewdly and already unzipping what turns out to have been his costume, stepping naked and uni-membered from the heavy penis suit with its folds of flaccid virilia, which he deposits in a heap on the sand. Eve appraises his nudity with unconcealed curiosity. He is younger and more robust than he first appeared, with a tanned muscular chest and sturdy legs. Against his well-proportioned body his solitary member, cleverly masked during longer shots by a chastely interposed fern, stands out in shocking relief. He reaches up to Eve's neck and locates in one of the orifices at her throat the clasp of the garment she wears. She helps him peel off the flesh-coloured body stocking with its vulval design. This too is discarded – to copulate out-of-shot perhaps with the penis suit. Adam and Eve regard one another and smile. Eve reclines on the bed of warm sand and draws Adam gently towards her. The camera slowly pans to the surf, foaming white at their feet. A voice-over says something about a reversal clinic being open now, near you.

Frida, as he'd known she would be, was one of the first to register for the reversal programme. He was waiting when she returned, candlelit table elegantly set. He wasn't used to seeing her in women's clothes and when she first appeared in the dimly lit doorway, dressed in the simple white frock that she knew he especially liked, he thought he must be hallucinating some wistful spectre of the wife he thought he'd lost. But she was no phantom, she was real. The bandages on her emasculated wrists shone as dully pale in the candlelight as her dress.

She walked across the room in silence, casting him a hesitant glance before lowering herself delicately on to the couch.

'Thought we might have dinner together,' he said. 'It's all prepared. Swordfish, almond sauce, cream *passionel*. Our love-feast, remember?'

He got down from his chair and knelt in front of her, pressing his palms lightly, experimentally, against her pliant breasts.

'Ow, steady on, I'm still sore.'

She smiled.

'You're a good husband, Des, I don't deserve you. I've given you a hard time, haven't I? How have you put up with me?'

He shrugged.

'It's not been easy.'

She rested a hand on his head, curling a lock of hair round her finger.

'Oh darling, do you forgive me?'

'Welcome home,' he said.

Later, in bed, lying beneath him, cushioning his head on her breasts: 'I've been thinking,' she said.

'Yes, my sweet?'

'Well, now this silliness is all over, now things are back to normal, well, I was thinking it might be nice to, you know, start a family.'

He felt his throat constrict, his eyes mist with grateful tears.

'You know it's what I've always wanted. But I can't believe it. I mean you've always been so set against motherhood. Losing your figure and all that. I thought . . .'

'Well, that's the thing, you see. Now there's these new operations available, these, you know, exo-wombs or whatever they're called for men . . . well I was thinking, I was wondering if you might . . .?'

THE RED LINE
Charles Higson

Oval

He had no body hair. Every Friday evening, standing naked before his full-length mirror, he made sure of it. His fingers stroked and probed his skin, and with tweezers, razor and depilatory cream he removed any offending growth. Clean armpits, no ugly squiggles on his chest, no pubic hair polluting his penis and testicles. His golden locks remained, of course, falling around his ears and across his forehead in tight and shining curls. Twice a day he washed his hair, so that it gleamed like precious metal. Once he was clean and smooth all over, he studied himself in the mirror, standing naked and translucent, glistening with baby oil. His skin, pure white and unblemished. His body, plump and rounded, fingernails clean, no mark or blemish anywhere. With his little pink bow of a mouth and his eyes the palest blue, the effect was quite beautiful.

Then he would dress to go out, delighting in the feel of his clothes against his sensitive skin. The creamy luxury of his black silk shirt, the smooth slipperiness of nylon underpants. Then he would put on his white trousers, the evening jacket he'd found in a charity shop, and finally his little red shiny shoes. He was proud of his small feet and hands, they were so dainty and delicate.

Friday night was the highlight of his week. Friday night was karaoke night at The Brunswick. And he was the best. Nobody could touch him, because he was a professional, dedicated, in a different league to the others. He had a routine. He'd worked at it, studied videos to get the moves just right. He was always one of the first up: when the others were still shy and self-conscious he would strut over to the mike knowing that nobody else that evening would be able to come near him. He set the standard against which everyone else was judged. He wasn't just some half-arsed drunk showing off, having a lark. When he went up he was the man himself: he was Bob Seger, the greatest rock singer who had ever lived. When he sang 'We've Got Tonite' and moved just like Bob, every nuance, every gesture perfect, he was aware of the whole pub looking at him in silent awe. And when he finished there would be a thunder of applause, cheers, whistles, shouts of 'Encore!', happy laughter. They loved him. They knew that they had seen perfection.

Bob Seger and the Silver Bullet Band: the very name conjured up such glamorous images. He dreamt that one day he might go on television, do his routine and win a big prize, enough money to be able to afford to go to America, maybe even visit where Bob lived. At least, that was what he had once thought. Now everything was changed. Everything. Why couldn't people just leave things alone, instead of wanting to change, change, change all the time? He thought about it now, as he sat on the noisy, rattling tube train. Remembered the night he'd gone to the pub and the karaoke machine was gone.

Embankment

Berto looked up at the Underground map for what seemed like the hundredth time, and still it made no sense to him. Where was Hackney? The map was a jumble of confusing names. The English language seemed to have no rules. Names didn't sound like they were written. That had been made clear to him after Cathy had left the train and he'd tried to ask a man for help. He hadn't been able to make himself understood and in the end the man had simply laughed and shook his head. It had been humiliating. He hadn't found the courage to ask again. Now he was lost, but he wasn't going to let himself get scared. As long as he was moving it was OK ... If he just sat here on this train, in this warm carriage, he would eventually work out what to do. As long as he acted sensibly and didn't panic, things would work out.

But London was vast and confusing. Not like Venice. In Venice, when he'd met Cathy, everything had seemed clear and easy. Even though they hadn't been able to talk they had understood each other, and as they'd spent most of their time in bed, talking hadn't

been important. So he'd come to England, like she'd said he should
... Only it wasn't what he'd expected. For one thing, she had a
boyfriend. She hadn't told him that before. She'd tried to talk to
him about the boyfriend yesterday in the taxi, on the way to her
place from the station, but he wasn't sure he understood. She'd told
him about something called a 'trial separation' and an 'open relationship', and even though he looked the words up, he still didn't
understand what they meant. So he nodded and went along with it.
To him it all seemed crazy.

She still saw the boyfriend. Last night, his first night in England,
they had all had dinner together. Afterwards the boyfriend had
kissed Cathy goodnight and gone home. Berto had gone to bed
with Cathy and they had started to make love but he could tell that
she was tense, that she didn't really want to do it, so he had stopped.
All those miles, thinking about her, and now this. If only he'd been
able to talk to her about it.

Today had been even stranger. Cathy had been at work, so the
boyfriend had shown him around London. Trying very hard to be
friendly, telling him about everything they saw, too fast for Berto
to understand. That was when Berto realized just how big the city
was, how spread out. You couldn't walk, always it had to be buses
and what the English called the tubes. So he had no sense of the
layout, no internal map.

Berto had only spoken once all day and the boyfriend had
laughed at him. They were by the river where there were some
imposing concrete buildings; a theatre and a cinema and an art
gallery. On a grand scale, as if built from giant slabs. It was very
simple, grey and unfussy, and Berto had said how much he liked it,
how he wished there could be something in Venice like this instead
of all those old buildings which all looked the same and were falling
down. The boyfriend thought this was funny, and Berto supposed
he hadn't said it right. He didn't bother trying to say anything after
that, he left the boyfriend to it, jabbering on and on.

They had stayed out all day, then met Cathy in a Chinese
restaurant. Afterwards they had gone to a party somewhere called
Clapham. He hadn't enjoyed the party. Cathy had ignored him,
spent the whole time with the boyfriend. Everyone had got drunk,
shouting and laughing. He could talk to nobody. He sat on the
stairs by himself and people pushed past him all the time as if he

didn't exist. He had begun to wonder what he was doing in this country.

Luckily, Cathy wanted to leave early, and luckily the boyfriend didn't come with them. But Cathy hadn't been happy. She said she had had an argument with the boyfriend. Berto tried to talk about this but she only became more upset. They had got on the tube, and Berto had said something which made Cathy angry, he had no idea what. She'd shouted at him – too fast, too many words he didn't understand – and at the next stop she got off the train, swore at him (the few words he did understand) and told him not to follow. And like a fool he didn't.

Leicester Square

No more karaoke the barman had said. Karaoke was last year's thing, there wasn't any interest in it any more. Friday night was Dance Night at The Brunswick now. A DJ sat at the back, where the karaoke machine had been, and played endless bang-bang-bang music. *Bang, bang, bang, tss, tss, tss.* All bleeps and funny voices. It was disgusting, and nobody danced, anyway. The pub just filled up with drunks, drug addicts, girls with dirty hair. He hated these people. Desperate, he'd searched for another pub. He found one with a machine not far away, in Stockwell, but they had no Bob Seger. No 'We've Got Tonite' not even 'Hollywood Nights'. It was all Elvis and black disco music. He searched all of South London, but everywhere it was the same. People didn't care about Bob Seger any more.

He took to staying in, standing in front of the mirror for hours on end, shaving and looking at his reflection. He would light candles and with the rest of the room in darkness, he was the most wonderful thing you could imagine. But when he looked out of the window he would see people. Ugly people. Dirty, hairy people. People who didn't know about Bob Seger, or his own perfect karaoke routine. And he knew he had to do something about it. He had to do something about the stubble which was spreading all over London.

Goodge Street

Berto knew he would be OK if he kept moving and didn't panic.
But the map above his head, which before had seemed so clear and
neat and pretty, now made no sense at all. He looked at it and
looked at it but he couldn't find Hackney, where Cathy lived. He
still had her address written down on his little crumpled piece of
paper. He studied it again, as if it might hold some clue, but it was
useless, because he couldn't even find Hackney on the map. He'd
tried following each line, from one end to the other, the blue, the
silver, the green, the yellow, the black he was travelling along. But
they went on forever, and they got tangled in the middle and they
branched and twisted, and he got lost and confused.

They stopped at another station, Goodge Street, in the middle
of the map. Berto wondered if he should just get off and ask someone. But he felt safe in the carriage, it was like a capsule, an air
bubble, bouncing around London. He didn't want the bubble to
burst. The doors closed and they were off again, jostling through the
darkness.

He knew he had once more to try to talk to someone. That would
be the best way. But how? People never understood what he said,
maybe he would be laughed at again. He felt very small and foolish.
He searched the other passengers for a friendly face. There was an
old woman, sniffing and staring vacantly into space. Old people
were no use, they were all deaf. The middle-aged man then? He
was a bit scruffy, asleep, his head lolling on his shoulder. He was
drunk. Drunks were the worst. Berto looked at his watch: it was
nearly half-past twelve. He had to do something. What about the
young woman, then? Women were usually more sympathetic than
men, weren't they? She looked a bit like Cathy. A typical English
girl, with a fresh, pretty, open face. Yes, he could ask her ... Or
the man next to her, perhaps? Dressed funny – all English men
dressed funny. He had a plastic bag in his lap, like so many people
seemed to carry with them, here. He looked the friendly sort. With
curly hair, a face like a cherub from a painting. So many cherubs in
Venice. So many old paintings. Why was he here?

He steeled himself. Go on, Berto, ask the woman ... But then
his eyes caught hers and he looked away embarrassed. A man

shouldn't be like this, helpless. He cursed as the train once more shuddered to a halt. OK, he told himself, before the next stop, then. He would ask her before the next stop.

Euston

Denise looked at the floor; she looked at the torn seat next to her; she looked up at the adverts on the other side. Where did you look on a tube? Anywhere but where was natural, where was comfortable. Anything to avoid looking at someone else. But how did you stop other people looking at you? There – he'd done it again. He'd eyed her up. Jesus! Why had she got on the tube alone? Why hadn't she got a taxi like usual? So she'd saved herself a few pounds, but it wasn't worth it. London wasn't safe for a single woman. Don't look at anyone. Don't talk to anyone.

He was dark-skinned, the man, with thick black hair. Dark eyes. A bit like some of the male models in the Next catalogue. In other circumstances she might have found him attractive. But she knew well enough that rapists weren't all ugly or fat. Every man was a potential rapist. Every time you left your flat you were a potential victim. Every day in the papers there were more reports. Every day on the crime programmes another innocent woman was assaulted. Magazine articles, posters, films, *Woman's Hour*, they all told you the same thing. The city was out to get you.

She laughed sourly to herself when she thought of the taxi option. Just the other day she'd read about a taxi driver who'd attacked a string of girls. She'd tried talking to Neil about her fears, but as usual, he'd been completely unsympathetic. He'd even tried to claim that it was men who were most at risk of assault in London, not women. That was typical of a man. He'd trotted out some statistic, but she wasn't going to be drawn into a stupid male argument about maths. She'd told them about it at the women's group tonight and they'd all laughed, told her once again she should ditch Neil. She frowned. That would be the last women's group she went to in south London. It wasn't worth the risk of travelling back alone late at night.

Oh, God, he was looking at her again, with that look all men

had. The look of a hunter. Cold, superior, in charge. He was
looking at her naked. If only she had something to read, a book to
hide in.

   Camden Town. Half the carriage emptied. There were only four
of them left now, including Denise. The dark-faced man, the man
with the blond curly hair, and down the other end a young bloke
with glasses, too far away to be any help. Shit, it was four more
stops to East Finchley. She looked at the curly-haired man, willing
him to look round. At last he did and she gave him a friendly smile.
But he looked soft, like a child. What use would he be if anything
happened?

   That was it. Never use public transport again. She had to get her
own car. But then there were car thieves, crashes, men in vans
swearing at you, those horrible hyenas in the TV ads . . . Maybe she
should just move back to Nottingham and have done with it.

Tufnell Park

They were both sneering at him now. So bloody superior. So
fucking smug. The girl had actually turned round and jeered at
him. He'd seen them eyeing each other up across the aisle. They
thought they were so clever, didn't they? Thought they owned the
place. The snotty girl and the other one, the dirty-looking man.
Who the fuck did he think he was, the greasy ape? Look at him. He
was just the type who was ruining London. Just the type who went
to discos and clubs – a drug taker, a hooligan. He was covered in
hair, he had black stubble on his cheeks, thick curls crawled out of
the top of his T-shirt, even his hands were hairy. It was disgusting.
It made him feel sick. He shivered and goose-pimples spread down
his arms and back.

   Now look at him, putting on some of those little headphone
things. He could imagine the music – black music. Bang, bang,
bang. The sort of music they played next door and kept him awake
all night. *Tss, tss, tss, bang, bang, bang.* Somebody had to do
something about these people. These spoilers who were ruining
London. Well, that was why he was here, wasn't it? That was why
he'd been riding the Underground all day with his Travelcard. Just
like he used to when he visited Auntie Gwen in Chiswick.

He was ready. He hoped his tape was strong enough. It should be, he'd practised with it in the kitchen till he was sure he had it right. He was impatient to try it out, but he had to wait. There were too many people, still. He would wait, though. This was all that mattered now.

Tss, tss, bang, bang.

Archway

It was comforting to hear an Italian voice, even if it was trying to teach him English. He didn't know why he'd bought the cassette, he'd had it two months and had learnt nothing. There was nothing on the tape to tell him how to find Hackney on the tube. Nothing to tell him how to deal with a crazy English girl with a boyfriend in an 'open relationship'. Nothing to give him the courage to ask someone for help. He knew he would have to soon. The black line on the map just went up and up, finishing somewhere called High Barnet. There he would have to turn and come back again. He couldn't spend the rest of the night travelling up and down the line, like some wandering lost soul. He'd told himself he'd ask the girl by the next stop. But the station had come and gone, and the one after. Stupid, stupid. He had to do something. He had to act like a grown man. He took off the headphones just as the voice was telling him how to buy a loaf of bread.

Highgate

Oh, God. He was leaning forwards. Leaning towards her. He'd deliberately taken off his Walkman and he was going to talk to her. You don't talk to anyone on the tube. Unless ... Oh, God. She jumped up and went to stand by the doors.

Come on, station. It wasn't East Finchley, she'd have to wait for the next train, but she had to do something to get away from this man. Now he was standing, too. She could see his reflection distorted in the doors. He was coming over to her. She shouldn't have moved. She was too far from the curly-haired man in the red shoes. Past the glass wall. Out in the open.

Then lights. The wall rushing past gave way to a platform, posters, lights, the Underground logo, Highgate. The train slowed and stopped, the doors slid open and she was off and running. Don't look back. There was the yellow exit sign. Don't look back. The platform was deserted. She couldn't hear anything behind her, but he was wearing trainers, wasn't he? He could move silently. She passed a poster of a woman, *Hennes*, with a moustache drawn on her face and an obscene message. The whole station seemed deserted, just like that scene in *An American Werewolf in London*. The escalator was endless. She ran up it, two steps at a time. Don't look back. Try not to think about what was behind her. At last she was up. Ahead she could see the ticket collector in his glass box, and she could stand it no more. She had to know. She turned. She was alone. He hadn't followed her.

She smiled and let out her breath. Her quick thinking had saved her life. All she had to do now was get the next train to Highgate.

She turned towards the down-escalator and then a thought struck her. What if there was a man on the platform? What if she had to wait there with him? At this time of night it might be ages till the next train. She pictured her dead body, lying there abandoned, with a moustache drawn on it. But she couldn't leave the Underground here. It was too far to walk to East Finchley. It was dark outside. Taxis weren't safe. Nowhere was safe. A plane could fall out of the sky. She could be blown apart by the IRA. The escalator could burst into flames. The ticket collector could be a rapist . . .

She stood there at the top of the stairs, unable to move. Whatever she did was sure to be a mistake. She began to shake, then tears ran down her face. She couldn't do anything. She was stuck here. Everything had broken down. *Jesus Christ, Denise*, she said to herself. *It's finally happened. You've lost it.*

East Finchley

The dirty bricks of the tunnel wall sped past in a dark smear. He should have followed her. Should have got off this damned train to nowhere and sorted himself out. He looked down the carriage at the man in glasses at the other end. He was reading a book. He had built a wall about himself. So it had to be the other one, the cherub.

Why was he ashamed to ask a man for help? He was a stranger here. Why should he be expected to know his way around?

He turned and walked towards the cherub. And he took it as a good sign when the curly-haired man stood up as well; rose from his seat and came to meet him. Berto noticed he was carrying his plastic bag in a funny way, with his hand down inside it, gripping the sides rather than the handles. But he thought nothing of it.

Berto smiled. '*Scusi.*' And in one quick movement, before Berto knew what was happening, the man took his hand out of the bag and punched him three times in the chest. Berto fell back against the seats, winded. In the half-second before the cherub put his hand back in the bag, Berto saw that he had a kitchen knife taped to his wrist, with four inches of blade sticking out. In panic Berto gasped and sucked in air. His lungs were full of liquid.

With no expression, and without a word, the cherub walked past him to the doors. Berto felt his shirt, it was soaked. He saw that he was covered in blood. He looked down at the young man at the other end, still reading his book. Berto cried out for help, but he didn't know the right words, the English words, and his voice was feeble.

They came to a station and the cherub casually got off the train. Berto tried to get up, but couldn't move. Something ripped inside him. He coughed and sticky, red gloop spattered on the floor. He cried out again, but saw the other man rise and leave the train, too. He was alone. With a last effort he wrenched himself from the seat, but the doors slid closed before he could reach them, and the train was moving once again.

He fell to the floor and lay there watching a trickle of his blood edge across the floor. It reminded him of something. And then he remembered. Of course: the red line – from left to right – the red line on the map. At last it was clear. He'd been shown the way. Follow the red line to the east, there was the station, Bethnal Green. The boyfriend had told him and he hadn't understood at the time. Now he did. Bethnal Green for Hackney. No station where Cathy lived. Follow the red line.

He heard the sound of the train through the floor. *Tss, tss, bang, bang.* He had a map, now. All he had to do was follow the red line as it slowly made its way across the carriage floor.

FAITH

Nick Hornby

'Maybe it's me,' says Paul. 'Maybe it's the smoking. Maybe I've only got, you know, seven thingumajigs per whatsit. Sperms per ejaculation.'

They both stare at the frozen, wobbling image on the TV screen. They are watching an old Preston Sturges film that Paul taped over Christmas – or at least they were, until Sarah went to the toilet and discovered that her period had started.

'Well give up then.'

'I'm going to. And I'm going to put frozen peas down my boxers just before bedtime. That's supposed to help. There must be stuff that you can do too.'

'Like?'

'I don't know.' Things always turn out to be his fault, and the guilt irritates him. 'Pack in drinking. Stop this stupid vegetarian kick. And I reckon you get up too quickly afterwards. You're always going to the loo, or getting a glass of water, or going to turn the answerphone on. It's no wonder nothing ever stays up there.'

Sarah looks at him and shakes her head pityingly. 'Pathetic.'

The video turns itself off, and as if by an awful kind of modern magic, Barbara Stanwyck becomes Jeremy Beadle. He is wearing a huge fake beard and dark glasses, and is thrusting a microphone at somebody contemplating a crumpled BMW. Paul turns the TV off with the remote.

What Sarah can do, he thinks, is feel more positive. For two years they have talked about having a baby – interminable conversations peppered with convoluted subordinate clauses, all introduced by phrases such as 'maybe after', and 'not while'; then there was a period where they played what they referred to as Russian roulette, and used contraception only if there happened to be a plastic case or a cardboard packet within arm's reach.

The dialogue, though, is as nothing compared to the noisy babble of self-interrogation that goes on in her head almost every

minute of the day. Would she like a baby? (Probably, although . . .)
Would she like one now? (Maybe, but . . .) Does she want one with
Paul? (Sometimes, when . . .) What about work? What about
money? What about sleep and friends and smoking and drinking
and travelling and what about eating curry, for God's sake, which
babies don't like and she does, and what about hallo Nellie the
Elephant and goodbye Ella Fitzgerald and what about having to see
Paul's mum and dad all the time because this would be their first
grandchild and what about the pact she made with Julia ages ago
about never ever having a baby no matter who they met or what
their hormones told them?

Sometimes, after she and Paul have made love, she imagines the
lower half of her body as a human Nintendo game. She sees each of
these doubts as a sperm-seeking missile, shattering the tiny heads
into even smaller pieces. It feels as though she and Paul have got
stuck: stuck in their north London flat, stuck in their will-we-
won't-we childless state, stuck with the same friends and the same
restaurants and jobs and things to do, and she cannot see what is
going to free them, propel them into the next stage of their lives
together. There was something she read once, something that she
thinks was supposed to be about politics, but seems to describe their
predicament exactly: 'When the old is dying, and the new cannot
be born, a variety of morbid symptoms appears.' Rows and sulks
followed by childishly intense reconciliations, half-hearted flirta-
tions, unprotected sex followed by these fearful, hopeful waits for
her period . . . they have all the morbid symptoms they can handle.

Even though it is Saturday night, they go to bed early. It's February,
and Michael Fish said that there would be sleet and high winds
tonight; while they're lying in bed they listen to the bumps and
bangs and whistles outside.

'It sounds like there's someone on the roof,' says Sarah.

Paul was thinking the same thing. Their flat is right at the top of
a three-storey house, under the eaves, and they have got used to the
creaks from the tiles a few feet above their heads, but these are
unfamiliar sounds.

'Listen,' says Sarah. 'Listen to that. That's not the wind.'

'How would someone get up there?' Paul asks her.

'Easy. All you've got to do is get from Steve's roof terrace up to ours, and then from the wall on to the roof. The TV repairman did it no problem.'

'But what would anyone want to get up there for? If they wanted to break in, they wouldn't need to go up any further than the terrace.'

They stop talking and listen harder, but the creaking has stopped, and Sarah goes back to her Margaret Atwood while Paul nuzzles her shoulder.

'Not much point in doing it, though, is there?' he says. 'What with your period and everything. If I haven't got many sperm, I don't want to waste them.'

'It doesn't work like that, you berk. Anyway, it would be nice if you wanted to screw for other reasons occasionally. It used to be about lust, not ovulation.'

'Yeah, well. You were younger then.'

She clonks him on the head with the paperback and he kisses her, but she freezes and looks hard at the ceiling.

'Listen to that, now.'

'What? I can't hear anything.'

'It sounds like someone humming.'

'That's the wind.'

'Humming a tune?'

'Humming a tune!' snorts Paul. 'OK, what tune is it?' He can hear it now. It sounds like 'We Are The World'.

'It's that charity song,' says Sarah. 'Not, you know, Bob Geldof. The other one. The American one.'

Paul gets out of bed and gets dressed.

The tiles on the roof terrace are iced over, and Paul nearly slips as he closes the door to the flat behind him. The flat overlooks the football ground, and from the roof terrace you can see the letters SENAL FOOT. Neither Paul nor Sarah are football fans, but they don't mind living this close to the stadium, especially as they're so high up. The excitement seems to rub off on the area, somehow, and at one time the lettering seemed to them to be a hip urban feature, like the pink neon sign that lights up the bedroom, from outside, of one of the characters in *Fame*. Looking down, Paul can see that the street between the flat and the stadium is empty, and the wind is blowing sheets of newspaper and torn-up programmes from the afternoon's game high up into the air. He cannot remember ever feeling this cold in London.

The humming has stopped now. Paul has turned the terrace light on before coming outside, but it doesn't help him to see the roof any more clearly; in fact, as the light is positioned on the wall just under the guttering, it obscures more than it reveals. But even so, it is quite clear that there is a man sitting up there. He is wrapped in blankets and sipping a steaming drink from a plastic beaker. Paul cannot tell whether the man is looking at him or not, but presumes that he must be: the roof terrace is lit up like a stage, and the roof is as dark as an auditorium during a performance.

'Come down at once,' bellows Paul. There is no answer, but Paul can just about see that the man is shaking his head.

'Not until he strengthens the squad,' the man shouts down at him.

'Who?' Paul shouts back. But immediately he knows that this is the wrong question, and that now the conversation will be conducted on the other man's terms.

The figure in blankets points over the road towards the stadium.

'Him,' he yells. 'Old skinflint. He wants to put his hand in his pocket. I'm fed up with it. This is the third year on the trot we've had no midfield.'

While Paul is trying to think of a response (his mouth is open, and he can feel the freezing wind against his fillings), the curtain at the bedroom window is drawn back, and Sarah's face appears. Paul gives her an embarrassed shrug.

'Football,' he mouths at her. She screws up her face to indicate that she hasn't understood.

'Football fan,' he elaborates, but Sarah remains visibly perplexed nevertheless.

'We're never going to win the League with that pair of donkeys chugging up and down,' the man is explaining at a volume sufficient to combat the weather. 'No creativity. No flair. And neither of them have got the pace to get into the box.'

Paul wishes that he followed sport more closely. He has always prided himself on his ability to talk to anyone, but now, talking to this man, ten years of personnel skills seem to have deserted him. All he can remember is a newspaper headline he saw on the tube recently, BUY NOW, GEORGE, but he doesn't really know what these words mean, nor how they can be used as a basis for meaningful discourse. And in any case, he feels that the next thing he says should address the immediate dilemma on his roof, rather than the long-term fortunes of the football club over the road.

'It's not really my problem, though, is it?' The nuances that he is attempting in his voice, the combination of geniality and polite assertiveness, are almost impossible to achieve in these difficult circumstances.

'I never said it was.'

'No. But you're on my roof, you see.'

'Fair enough. But I couldn't get up on the East Stand, and this is the next best thing. I'm not bothering you, am I?'

For the first time Paul is beginning to feel angry, but he is at a loss as to how to convey this when he is already shouting.

'Of course you're bothering us! How do you think I knew you were out here, if you weren't bothering us? You think I come out here every night to check whether there's an idiot camped on my roof?'

The man does not respond immediately, and for a moment they stare at each other, listening to the gale.

'How did you know, actually?' the man asks.

'You were creaking. And humming. Creaking and humming.'

'I'm sorry about the humming. That was just to cheer myself up. And you'll get used to the creaking.'

'I don't want to get used to the creaking,' Paul screams. 'Why should I get used to the creaking?'

'Because I'm not coming down. Not until he's bought a new midfield player. Roy Keane, say. He's still young.'

Paul stands on the terrace until he is sure he has nothing else to offer, and then goes back to bed.

The man is right. They get used to the creaking. They get used to other things, too: cooking for three at dinner-time, and watching Brian slide down the tiles on his bottom until he can reach his steaming food; seeing their pictures in the *Sun* and the *Mirror* and even in the *Guardian*. The photographers discover that they can fit all three of them into the one shot, with Paul and Sarah leaning against the wall and Brian in between them, some fifteen feet above their heads, a huge banner bearing an incomprehensible message unfurled beside him. The couple have perfected a kind of bemused yet patient smile for these photos, and in the *Mirror* Sarah is making a *what-can-you-do* shrug that she finds rather fetching.

They have also got used to dealing with the police, who made one half-hearted attempt to talk Brian down (he retreated right up the slope to the chimney-stack) and then advised them to leave it for a few days. They don't mind; they have not confessed this to each other, but secretly they both enjoy the disruption Brian has brought with him, the buzz, the sense of purpose.

And Sarah in particular is intrigued by Brian, although his certitude wears her out. She cannot imagine what it must be like to be him, to have this one simple thought, this faith, that renders everything else in his life – his work, his family (a wife and two boys, both with eleven first names), his friends and his favourite TV programmes – temporarily insignificant. These people, she thinks. These people with religions and careers that mean everything, love affairs that consume them, hobbies that dominate their every spare moment, children that suck them dry, football teams that drive them on to wind-blasted rooftops ... She, meanwhile, has been landed with a life where everything, lovers and plans and work and friends, just jumble around in her spin-dryer of a head, everything the same size, all tangled up together.

'You must have been thinking about this forever,' she says to him on the Tuesday morning, when she goes outside to show him the first newspaper photos.

'No, not really.'

'When did you get the idea?'

'Just last Saturday. We were so bad I knew I had to do something.'

'And you hadn't thought of climbing up here before then?'

'No. Just saw it as I was leaving the ground. Worked out how I could get up here, went home, got the blankets and the banner and my Thermos, and got on with it. Don't you ever get like that? Get the urge to do something, just because you're so frustrated that you could burst?'

I don't want to burst, she thinks later. Bursting is hopeless, useless, a waste of time and energy. Bursting achieves nothing; it just makes you sit on roofs like a mad person. Is there less lust because that man walks up and down Oxford Street waving a placard about lentils? No, she would say not. Bursting is undignified, and never helps you get what you want.

It takes Brian just over a week to get exactly what he wants. There are tabloid headlines and managerial denials, tooting horns and knots of fans who gather in the street below chanting their support. There are phone-ins and votes of confidence, quotes from former players and plans for a boycott of a forthcoming game. The manager complains bitterly of 'being railroaded by lunatics'; his chairman expresses his 'absolute confidence' in the manager's 'ability to lead this club out of its current crisis', a crisis apparently provoked single-handedly by Brian. On the Friday, Brian decides that he has done enough, and clambers down to a hero's welcome; on Saturday, the team loses at Luton. The manager agrees a fee of five million pounds for Roy Keane on the Monday. Keane scores on his debut and the team start a seventeen-game unbeaten run; in May, Paul and a small group of friends watch from the roof terrace as the crowds fill the streets below, ready to applaud the new League Champions on an open-top bus parade around Islington.

Paul has decided to be an adult about it and invite Sarah to his Championship party, but he does not ask her if she would like to bring anyone else. He understands from mutual friends that there is a someone else, but he has no real desire to meet him, and the roof terrace is much too small to allow for that sort of discomfort.

'You OK?' he asks her as they watch the bus move off.

She nods. 'You?'

He makes a face. 'Been better. I'm glad it's summer, though.'

She cocks her head towards the bus. 'We did our bit, didn't we?'

'We?'

'That's what I said.'

'No, I just mean . . . It's funny to hear you say 'we'. Sorry. I wasn't going to be sentimental.'

'That's OK. I'm sorry . . . you know . . . I'm sorry I messed you about.'

'Well.' He shrugs. 'It wasn't that you messed me about, exactly. It's just that it was all a bit quick. I couldn't really . . . get a handle on anything. You were there, and then you weren't there, and . . .'

*

She has never managed to explain properly to anybody, not even herself, what happened in the days following the purchase of Roy Keane. All she knows is that she found herself explaining to Paul that she was not happy, that there was a hole in her that he would never be able to fill, and that unless she did something to change her circumstances now, this week, this minute, she was afraid that the jumble in her head would continue for ever. So she moved into a friend's place, fell in love with the friend's brother, moved out of the friend's place and into the friend's brother's place, and two months later she was retching stoically into the friend's brother's toilet. It is not possible to tell Paul any of this, however, not in a way that would seem cogent or kind.

'Hey, look!' Paul is pointing down at the street. 'Look! Look who's on the bus!'

Sarah follows his finger, and bursts out laughing. 'I don't believe it! How did he wangle his way up there?'

Brian is standing with the players, catching the scarves and hats that are being thrown towards him. To Sarah and Paul it appears as though it is Brian, rather than Roy Keane or any of the other players or the manager, that the crowd have come to see; Brian, wearing a tie and a blue anorak, simply grins and waves, as though he spends most Sunday mornings listening to a quarter of a million people chanting his name. Paul shakes his head and goes off to get another bottle of wine; Sarah watches until the bus turns the corner and disappears.

FUCK OFF

John McVicar

I always enjoyed sex. I still do. But since I tested HIV positive, not as much.

I was infected roughly a year ago. I suffer no physical effects, nor is there any outward sign of the fatal microscopic infection that lies dormant in my DNA and which will eventually break out, laying siege to my immune system until it crashes and my body becomes a sitting duck to the pneumonias and cancers that will waste and finally kill me. AIDS is cruel to the end. When you die of AIDS, your quality of death is trash.

It will probably be six to seven years before my condition begins to show. In the meantime, I remain what men call 'a looker'. I'm thirty-two years old, dark, lithe, vivacious, some might say intense-looking. There has never been a shortage of men trying to take me out, and there still isn't. But what they see then is not what they get.

I was infected by sex, and the experience, or even the thought, of sex is associated with AIDS. In my mind they are connected, linked. This doesn't put me off sex; it just spoils it a bit. I still get horny, I still want sex and sometimes I have it, but, unless you brainwash yourself, what you know you cannot unknow. Even when I come, I am in the shadow of AIDS.

If you are responsible – and I am – you must take precautions during sex to ensure you don't put anyone else at risk. And it is not as simple as insisting on a condom. I like oral sex but my vaginal secretions are infectious so if the man has a mouth ulcer or a cold sore or bleeding gums or just bit his tongue that morning he is at risk. I can hardly inspect his mouth first, so cunnilingus and *soixante-neuf* are out. Then, there are the ones who do it on their own initiative and, worse, the one who will not take no for an answer. There is always the man who is determined to be the one who will get you to like it. Frontiersmen of the bedroom. They think that opening up new territory gives them the best chance of staking out a claim.

Of course, you can always just say: 'Look, I am HIV positive, so you can't do *that*. But it's perfectly safe to have intercourse as long as you put on a condom and the condom isn't faulty and it doesn't split while we are doing it.' If you say that, the one thing you can be sure of is that you are not going to get a fuck that night. The best you can expect is a long heart-to-heart. And you might end with one of those wheelchair-pushers who want nothing more than to dedicate themselves to an attractive victim. They're really yucky. But some run a mile and the next day tell everyone they know. Others, even if they want to, can't do it because what you've just told them is about as conducive to an erection as a good kick in the balls. When you are HIV positive sex is a minefield, and as for one-night stands, forget it.

HIV puts you on death row and booby-traps your sex life, but it doesn't stop there. Take children. I hadn't really thought about it but vaguely I wanted a child or at least wanted to be able to have one if I decided to. Now, because of the high risk of transmitting HIV to the baby, that option is foreclosed. Unless you are an airhead or just don't care, being HIV positive changes your life in all sorts of unexpected ways that are as different as people are different.

One of my main differences is that I am a computer analyst, and a successful one at that. My forte is debugging programmes that cannot meet the demands placed upon them, or are crashing for the multitude of reasons – including computer viruses – that can cause software to go down. To do what I do, you have to learn to think clearly and rigorously. Now, it is not uncommon for those infected by HIV to think very carefully about their life and, given my work, it was almost certain that I would. I did it, not with a concern to identify the 'if only' clauses, nor did I have any wish to find a scapegoat, and it certainly wasn't a morbid preoccupation, or for that matter an evangelical quest for some AIDS-intensified meaning of life. It was just a search for lessons.

I grew up in Dulwich. My mother is a primary-school teacher and my father a solicitor. They had two other children – I have two brothers, both younger than me. Probably as a result of growing up in the sixties, I knew about sex long before my mother ever mentioned it. I also masturbated from an early age and I could always climax even as a child. I wasn't told by anyone or shown; I just discovered it. Orgasm, then, was never a problem for me, although there were the usual hiccups with men whom I thought I fancied, but found out in bed that I didn't. I had a couple of steamy scenes with other girls when I first went to secondary school but there was nothing particularly crushy about them. Both times we were close friends who occasionally helped each other to come. As for boys, I hardly did anything with one until I was thirteen, and then it was all quite sensible and normal. There was, however, one sexual experience when I was twelve that, while it never went beyond the petting stage, was seminal to say the least.

It involved a much older boy at the school. He was in the sixth form and quite unapproachable to a lowly squid in the second year. Somehow I kept catching his eye and while I had no idea what it was, I knew there was some secret between us. I think he must have engineered it, but one day just after hockey he called me round behind the changing rooms. I was milling around with some other girls, and he caught my eye and jerked his head at me to follow him. I did with my heart pounding, knowing something was going to happen. He had his back to me as he went between the sheds to where they once used to dump coal. When he turned he had his penis out; it was sticking up out of his open trousers.

He said, 'Have you ever done this before?'

I was just looking wide-eyed at his penis and I shook my head in wonderment. I had never seen anything like it. I had seen my brothers', glimpsed some men and dogs and things but nothing like this. It was glistening and shiny and wanting to be touched. I don't know if I put my hand on it first or he did it for me but I know that he held his hand over mine and showed me how to wank him. I remember wanting to do it on my own. I knew I could do it right. As I did it, I thought of it gliding inside me but he didn't try to do anything at all to me. He just stood there groaning slightly, his jaw clenched and his eyes half closed. I kept looking at his face and, of course, he suddenly started grunting and quivering and out shot what the girls at school used to call 'baby juice'. The first time this happened I pulled my hand away in shock and he roughly grabbed it and put it back.

All he said to me as he zipped himself up was, 'Now don't tell anyone, will you.' I said 'No,' but, of course, I couldn't wait to tell my best friends. This sort of encounter was repeated sporadically

with the same boy over a period of about nine months, then he left
and I never saw him again.

Soon afterwards I began going out with boys and I took to sex
like a bird to the air. The experience with the sixth former, though,
gave me a bead on sexual relationships that made sex the purpose of
the relationship rather than the relationship being the purpose of the
sex. That isn't to say the relationship was unimportant, it is just that
my first sexual encounter made the raw physical aspect of male
sexuality extremely erotic for me and I have always been more
inclined to sleep with a man I fancy, but don't particularly like,
than go out with a man whom I like but don't fancy.

I have never been sex-mad in the way that some women and
some men are, although I suspect that men who are like that are
doing it to feed their ego, not satisfy their sex drive. In fact, I think
the way my sexuality was programmed, more towards orgasm than
'love', was rather healthy. It certainly protected me from the
problems of romanticizing sex: even when it was especially intense
and enjoyable, that didn't seem to me a reason to make the
relationship in which it occurred the baseline of your life. People –
women more than men – overload sex; however good the sex, it
can't carry a happy-ever-after relationship or even necessarily provide a solid framework for bringing up children. I have always
looked askance at the idea that sexual enjoyment is a man's entrance
ticket to centre stage of a woman's life.

Obviously, as I look back, I am picking out that part of the
picture that I now feel most reflects me. At the time there were lots
more brush-marks on the canvas. As a teenager, for example, I was
full of the usual dim-witted contradictions. I took on a lot of the
conventions and, in my late teens and early twenties, I tried out
most of what a woman is supposed to do. I fell in love, I was
jealous, possessive, attached great importance to fidelity – but my
heart was not in romance, and even at my most committed there
were encounters with other men that were sex for its own sake and
very little else. Around my twenty-first birthday, I began facing up
to the double standards that were informing my behaviour with
men and I started bearing down on my own hypocrisy.

By the time I left university, ideally sex for me was a means to
have an orgasm with a man whom I temporarily liked and fancied;
it certainly wasn't for having babies, binding you together for life,

or even committing you to being faithful to whoever you were doing it with. I never formalized these ideas, but I remember bulldozing a girlfriend who was banging on about sex being sacred because it created life. I hooted at her that the average person has sex twice in a lifetime to procreate and while the other times may not all be for pleasure, they were nothing to do with babies.

My career took off in the mid-eighties and I began earning huge bonuses on top of a good basic salary. My confidence in running my sex life pretty much as it suited me was boosted by having the means to be completely independent of men. I wasn't constantly hopping from bed to bed but if the fancy took me I did and, if at the time I was involved with someone else, I didn't have any guilts about it. I wasn't married and I wasn't about to get married. I ran my sex life as I did the other parts of my life – on my terms. Those terms included not hurting or exploiting anyone and not trying to impose my standards on others. And what was sauce for the goose was sauce for the gander – any lover who thought that sexual intimacy gave him the right to impose his standards on me was shown the door.

Of course, it wasn't always easy. Most men loathe the idea of their woman having sex or merely reserving the right to have sex with another man. In my opinion their attitude is nothing to do with their needing faithfulness to feel secure about the baby being theirs, and it's fatuous to say they regard women as their property, Well, I know that some men do but I don't mix with them. It is much more about their competitive attitude towards each other. Women are one of the prizes men compete for and I think most of them would much rather be beaten up by another man than cuckolded. You see the same competitiveness in their penis fixation. They desperately want them bigger but more to impress other men than to please women.

I was a free-thinker on sex, who didn't have to do too much thinking about it, since as far as I was concerned I'd got what suited me. In the back of my mind was the vague notion that around my early thirties I'd look around for some man to have a baby with and settle down and stop having affairs or at least be a bit more discreet about them. In the meantime, my love life, while active, was still secondary to the main focus of my life – my work. As a consequence, men were nothing like the problem that, almost without exception, they were to my female friends.

About this time the first tranche of anti-sex AIDS propaganda was issued. Icebergs and tombstones and Just Say No messages and lots of stuff about staying faithful to one partner being the best protection. The big lie was to say that, as far as the risk of contracting AIDS was concerned, every time we had sex with someone we were having sex with everyone they had previously had sex with. In fact, once a person had an AIDS test, as far as that disease was concerned his or her previous sexual history was erased. The thrust of these campaigns was as sick and horrible as the disease. One suspected that the dreadful people responsible for them were rather pleased with AIDS; it was another chance for them to do what they so enjoyed doing – which was to restrict, and meddle in, the sexual lives of others.

In contrast, the message from the pro-sex camp was that, if we all used condoms, the disease would be contained. Apart from the fact that the policy could not and has not worked, my problem with it was that I could not abide condoms. That first sexual encounter had imprinted itself on to my sexuality, and a lot of what I love doing in sex is spoilt by a condom. Apart from my own aversion to them – I am not alone in this – there was also the problem of accidents and faulty ones. As I didn't like the solution being recommended, I gave quite a lot of thought to the alternatives.

Testing is the best method but it has two disadvantages. The HIV antibodies that the test screens for do not appear in the bloodstream in detectable quantities until three months after infection, although the person is still infectious to others. This means that if someone has had unprotected sex in the last three months the test can give a false and, possibly, dangerous reading. So the safest strategy would be to use condoms for the first three months. However, as many of my affairs didn't last that long, this was a counsel of perfection that unless the man insisted otherwise I chose not to follow. I merely insisted on a lover taking a test as soon as we began our affair and left the three-month risk in the lap of the gods.

Incidentally, I began by using the NHS special clinics, but they make such a palaver of it that I got driven into going private. They are reliable enough but not many of the London ones do a same-day service, and none of them will give you the result over the phone. The last straw for me was having to submit to obligatory counselling, which is done by these dreary social-worker types who just got me into a bate. After one particularly infuriating session, I found a Harley Street doctor who was quite happy to give the result of the test over the phone two hours after he'd taken a blood sample.

The other disadvantage of testing as a means to protect oneself from HIV infection is that it cannot work if people are dishonest about their sexual contacts. And most sexually active people are dishonest about sex. Unfortunately for me, my sexual path had bypassed this dishonesty, so I had no appreciation of the difficulty most people have in being honest about sex. Apart from when I was a teenager, I had not made those impossible pacts that lovers usually make with each other to remain faithful and to be honest about any infidelity. Naturally, as I saw my friends doing it, I was aware of the tortuous hypocrisies that people go through to be unfaithful without ever letting on to their partner or, in some cases, even admitting it to themselves. But this was other people, not me. I was like a non-smoker who knows that smokers find it difficult to give up the habit, but has no understanding of how difficult it is. This ignorance was also compounded by a naïve belief that people's awareness of the threat of AIDS no longer makes it tolerable to practise the kind of deceit that is as much a part of sex as the act itself.

In August of 1989, my friend Angela took me to a rehearsal of the Ballet Rambert. She was doing some PR work for Sadler's Wells and said I might find it 'interesting' – meaning I might meet some dishy men. It was all that one would expect from countless TV documentaries that I've seen over the years. A spartan barn of a gymnasium with an upright, hollow-sounding piano and lots of dancers stretching and leaping around all over the place. But the men were delicious and, transparently, as Angela said, they weren't all gay. Whether they were gay or not I did rather look at their bulges. They have codpieces under their tights, but what they leave to the imagination is a pleasure to imagine. Angela kept elbowing me in the ribs and giggling. Unfortunately, I didn't just look, I also fell head over heels in lust.

Gabriel could have leapt out of one of those Häagen-Dazs ads. His brown eyes smouldered, his thick, black hair glistened and he

moved like a dream, all ripply and flowing and expressive. That
evening a gang of us went to Joe Allen's in Covent Garden. I was
bubbling over with excitement and, as I was probably earning more
than all of them put together, I treated everyone to massive exotic
salads and as much wine as we could drink. We were laughing and
talking loudly, with lots of touching and leaning close to make
asides. Friends of the dancers kept coming over to say hallo, and the
table was like a ballet of conviviality. In the middle of all this
exuberance I leant over to Gabriel and asked, 'You are coming back
with me afterwards?' And he did. And he definitely wasn't gay. In
fact, that was the one thing I asked him and he replied that despite
what people believed most male dancers were not gay and he
wasn't one of those who were.

He was big but it wasn't that so much as the way he dominated
and teased me. On the bed, he kept touching me with it and saying,
'You want me to knob you, don't you?' He made me say it, too.
He made me say it over and over again. He would push inside me
just a little, then hold me so that I couldn't move and whip me into
a sexual fervour with his comments and descriptions of what he was
going to do to me. He would talk me into coming and just hold
and watch me as I did. After he'd finished with me, I felt like I was
wafting in and out of an erotic coma.

In the morning, I told him that he could not catch anything
from me because I had regular AIDS tests; I also said that my going
with men was conditional upon them having the test. He listened
with his naughty-boy eyes flicking over my body and a wry
confident grin on his face, but he was perfectly amenable to being
tested. He also had the wit to point out that I'd had unprotected sex
with him without a test. I said he was an exception and that we'd
soon find out if there had been a risk. It transpired that he had been
having an on-off affair with one of the dancers – female – for about
a year or so and had not been with anyone else during that time. It
was all perfectly straightforward: he had a test that afternoon –
negative – and we began to see a lot of each other.

I knew it wouldn't last and didn't particularly want it to, but I
knew I'd enjoy it while it did. In getting the AIDS stuff out of the
way, I also established the ground rules by which I have affairs with
men. I told Gabriel that what I did when I wasn't with him was my
business. I said that I don't do confessions but if I jumped in bed

with someone who hadn't had the test and had unprotected sex – like I had with him – I would tell him and we'd have to use condoms for three months. I said I expected him to extend the same respect to me. I remember kissing him and saying, 'You gorgeous man, I can live with jealousy but not AIDS.'

Real fidelity is honouring your commitments. I was true to him and I thought he was to me.

Gabriel was two years younger than me and, while he was intelligent, he had never disciplined his mind the way he had his body. Sometimes I would become snappy, even ratty, with his half-baked and often received opinions; in turn he would often lapse into the sulks. But we kept it together. About seven months after we met, he came round to my flat without phoning first, which was unusual; he was agitated, looked haggard and was smoking intensely. One of the things I admired about him was the way he could smoke and drink, take whatever drugs were around, even binge on things, then when it suited him stop instantly. The way he was smoking this evening nagged at me but, since I had nothing to hang it on to, it had no significance.

What he had to say came out in a rush. He had been having sex with another male dancer who had told him that afternoon that he was HIV positive. I felt no shock, no anger, no panic. My whole being seemed to dedicate itself reflectively to working out the import of what he'd said. I felt icy and still. In a microsecond, long before he'd finished speaking, my mind had run through the disparate implications of what he was saying. I knew that, if he had it, the odds were that I did too, as our sex was often quite rough. If I did have it, then according to when I contracted it two other men could be at risk. I knew we would have to wait until the morning to find out. I also knew what it was in him that I had misjudged and why, but most of all I knew it was my fault. I had refused to read the writing on the screen.

Despite Gabriel's artistry and bohemian lifestyle, he did not trust himself and was cautious about what he revealed; then there was his over-sensitivity to criticism, even when he rejected the criteria on which it was based. His dancer's affectations were just that – affectations; under pressure he defaulted to the narrow-minded bigotry of his lower-class, albeit respectable, background. Lust, like love, lends enchantment to the view; I hadn't seen his limitations because I hadn't wanted to.

At that moment, however, my clarity of vision and speed of thought put far more than Gabriel's limitations in relief. As I scanned back over our time together, I could see that because he lived a lie much of what he'd been with me had been a lie. A white lie, often a charming white lie, but still a lie. Even now, he was blundering around in guilt and regret like a panicky rat in a closed-off maze, not looking for understanding but merely searching for a gap in the hedge.

There was no point in asking him why he had kept his homo-sexual fling a secret or even why he'd been unable to adhere to the one thing I'd asked of him, which was to tell me if he had unprotected sex. That was the agreement. Such a simple rule, which he'd understood at the time and agreed to follow. But it was in an area – sex – where the real rule was that you lived by double standards. Gabriel's kind upheld fidelity and faithfulness but accepted that as long as you didn't get found out it was OK to connive, cheat and lie to get whatever you could on the side. Of course, when he'd become a ballet dancer, Gabriel had embraced sexual openness but that was merely another convention that he paid no more than lip service to in order to be accepted by his new pack.

He sobbed and begged me to forgive him, which stirred an obligation in me to show some pity. I put my arms around him, not in affection and certainly not lust – that had been cauterized forever by his confession – but in compassion. His sexual morals were deformed. His upbringing had shackled him to an ugly and deceitful approach to sexual relations that opened the door to AIDS. As I dutifully held him, I felt disgusted with myself for letting this moral deformity into my life. The fantasy flitted into my mind of putting my hands round his neck and slowly ridding the world of his malignant character.

Of course, he misinterpreted my embrace and thought I was literally taking him back into my arms. I pulled away from him and shuddered at this obscenity of nature. I sent him home and I haven't seen him since, nor will I by choice. We have spoken twice on the phone. The first was the next morning to arrange our tests – I paid for his, of course. The second time was about a month later. He was drunk or on something and said, 'Look Sarah, we've both got it, so we are not a risk to each other. Why can't we make the best of it and enjoy each other the way we used to?'

I just said, 'Fuck off, you germ.'

That is how I think of him and that's what he is – a germ. He not only infected my body but also my mind. I now lie about sex; I now practise the exact same deceit about sex that caused me to catch AIDS. Of course, unlike the *Germ*, I take precautions to ensure I don't infect anyone else. Nevertheless, in principle, the deceit is just the same. He lied to keep his bisexuality a secret, I lie because I don't want men to know I am HIV positive. I tried being honest and it didn't work. So I am not only HIV positive, my sex life is contaminated with the sort of deceit that I despise and, if that isn't enough, I also have to use fucking condoms.

HARLEY STREET
Hilary Mantel

I open the door. It's my job. I have a hundred administrative tasks, and a job title of course, but in effect I'm the meeter and greeter. I take the appointment cards the patients thrust at me – so many of them never say a word – and usher them to the waiting-room. Later I send them along the corridor or up the stairs to meet whatever is in store for them: which is usually nothing pleasant.

Mostly they look right through me. Their eyes and ears are closed to everything except their own predicament, and they might just as well be steered in by a robot. I said that one day to Mrs Bathurst. She turned her eyes on me, in that half-awake manner she has. A robot, she repeated. Or a zombie, I said brightly. That's what our doctors should do, make a zombie. That would cut down on their practice expenses, give them less to complain about.

Bettina, who takes blood in the basement, said What do you mean, make a zombie? Child's play, I said. You need datura, ground puffer fish, then shake up a herbal cocktail to your family recipe. Then you bury them for a bit, dig them up, slap them round the head to stun them: and they're a zombie. They walk and talk, but their will's been taken out.

I was talking on airily, but at the same time, I admit, I was frightening myself. Bettina watched me for signs of madness; her pretty mouth parted, like a split strawberry. And Mrs Bathurst examined me; her lower jaw sagged, so that the light glinted on one of the gold fillings done cheap for her by Canine, our dentist.

'What's the matter with you two?' I said. 'Don't you read the *New Scientist* these days?'

'My eyes are poor,' Mrs Bathurst said. 'I find the TV is company.'

Of course, the only thing Bettina buys is *Hello*! She is from Melbourne, and has no sense of humour: no sense of anything really. 'Zombies?' she said, articulating carefully: 'I thought zombies were for cutting cane. I never associated them with Harley Street.'

Mrs Bathurst shook her head. 'Beyond the grave,' she said heavily.

Dr Shinbone (first floor, second left) was passing. 'Come, come, Nurse,' he said, startled. 'Is that the sort of talk?'

'She was alluding to the mystery of life and death,' I said to Shinbone.

Mrs Bathurst sighed. 'Not such a mystery really.'

Bettina works in the basement, as I've said, taking samples for a lab. Patients come from practitioners up and down Harley Street, bringing forms with crosses scrawled on them, indicating what tests their blood must have. Bettina extracts some into a tube and puts a label on it. The customers I send her look ill, very ill. They don't like what's coming, but what is it? Just a pinprick. True, we've had some vivisectionists down there, in my time. Bettina is scatty, but skilled in her way, and she doesn't send them out bleeding. Only once, earlier this summer, I remember a young girl stopping by the cubby-hole where I'm housed, and saying Oh: staring at a thin trickle of blood, creeping its way from the crook of her elbow towards the swollen blue veins of her wrist. She was seventeen, anorexic, anaemic. Her blood should have been as pale as herself, thin and green – but of course it was shockingly fresh and red.

I popped out of my door, and put my hands on her shoulders. I had warm and steady hands, back in May. Down you go, I said to her firmly, run down there to Bettina, and ask her for another plaster. She went. Mrs Bathurst was crossing the corridor with a kidney bowl in her hand. I saw her gape, and then she put a hand out to the wall, steadying herself. She looked winded, and as pale as the patient. 'Dear me!' she said. 'Whatever was the matter with that young lass?'

I had to make Mrs Bathurst a cup of tea. I said, 'If blood turns your stomach, why did you go into nursing?'

'Oh no,' she said, 'no, it doesn't usually take me that way at all.' She put her hands around her mug and compressed it. 'It was just coming upon her there in the hall,' she said. 'It was so unexpected.'

Bettina is red-haired, freckled, creamy. When she sits down her white coat parts, and her short skirts ride up and show her baby knees. She's adequately pneumatic and brain-dead, and yet she complains of lack of success with men. They often ask her out, but then she has a hard time to understand what's going on. They meet up with other blokes in some smoky, noisy pub, and – well, I thought Europe would be different, she says — they talk about motorways. Various junctions, their speed between them, and interesting roadworks they may have met. Towards the end of the evening, a few drinks on board, the men say, we hate Arsenal and we hate Arsenal. The landlord wants people to leave; Bettina leaves too, sliding out by the wall from the Ladies to the nearest exit. 'Because not,' she says, 'I do NOT, want their dribble and their paws on me.'

Early in summer she began to say: Men aren't worth it. The television's better; not so repetitive.

'All the same, you need a hobby,' Mrs Bathurst said. 'Something to get you out.'

Bettina wears a little silver cross round her neck, on a chain as thin as a thread. 'That chain'll snap,' Mrs Bathurst said.

'It's delicate,' Bettina said, touching it. In Melbourne, she was drilled to be delicate and sweet. Sometimes she wails, Oh jeepers creepers, I think I've mislaid one of my samples, oh, Geronimo H. Jones! Look, calm down, I say, I'm sure you haven't lost any blood at all. Then she counts up her glass tubes, and checks her forms again and everything's OK. One of these days, something will go wrong, she'll mis-label her samples and some great hairy bloke will be told he's oestrogen deficient and be invited to attend Gland's Menopause Clinic. Still, if there were complaints, they'd just get lost in the system.

Our lot are good at losing complaints. The patients shouldn't think that just because they pay for treatment they're due any respect. Sure, it sounds respectful, the way we put it when we send out the bills:

Dr Shinbone presents his compliments, and begs to state that his fee will be: 100 guineas.

But behind the patients' backs it's more like 'Bloody neurotics! Know-alls! Have the nerve to come in here, wanting attention! Asking me questions! Me, a Barts man!'

You probably think I'm cynical, jaundiced. But I've always found Harley Street a hopeless street, very long, very monotonous, the endless railings and the brass plates and the panelled dark doors all the same. I wonder if the patients dream about it. I do: in these sticky summer dawns, I dream it stretches not just through space but through time. It ends in Marylebone Road and Cavendish Square: in death, and the place you lived before you were born. Naturally, I wouldn't mention anything like this to Bettina or Mrs Bathurst. For the patients' sakes, you have to try to keep cheerful during the day.

Our premises, though, are not designed to lift the spirits. Even if you've never been to Harley Street you've probably got a picture in your mind: leather chesterfields, brass lamps with deep green shades, repro yew coffee-tables stacked with *Country Life* – on the whole, an ambience that suggests that if you're terminal you're at least departing in style. Our waiting-room is not like that. Our armchairs are assorted types, and greasy where heads and hands have rested. We've even one kitchen chair, with a red plastic seat. As for reading matter – old Shinbone brings in his fishing magazines when he's done with them – *What Maggot?*, that sort of thing. I forget now why we call him Shinbone. Usually we name them by their specialities, and he's not in orthopaedics. It must be because of the way his patients look – thinner and thinner, sharpening and sharpening. We see them come in the first time, bluff and flushed, walking bolsters in tweed and cashmere: then we see them get too weak to make it upstairs.

By contrast there's Gland, the top floor endocrinologist. Gland's obese, astonishingly obese; she wheezes as she walks. She treats women for the premenstrual syndrome and for change-of-life upsets: gives them hormones that fatten them up. They come in normal – just a bit thin, hands trembling, very slightly violent and insane – and a couple of months later they're back again, drunkenly cheerful, rolling and puffing, double-chinned, ankles bloated, mad eyes sunk into new flesh. I expect it's Gland's revenge on the world.

I dwell, as I've said, in a small cave, which has an opening into the hall, a kind of serving hatch. Bettina says it's like Piccadilly Circus here; she thinks the expression is original. All our timeshare doctors come tramping in and out. They put their heads into the hatch and say things like: 'Miss Todd, the cleaning is unsatisfactory.'

I say 'Is that so, now?' I reach into my cupboard, and bring out a cloth. 'Doctor,' I say, 'meet the duster. Duster: this is the doctor. You'll be working closely together, from now on.'

Cleaning, you'll appreciate, is not my job. It's done in the night by Mrs Ranatunga and her son Dennis, when I'm not here to supervise them. Mr Smear the gynaecologist, who is Mrs Bathurst's employer, is especially obnoxious if his desk doesn't shine. They don't want to pay out, you see, our doctors – but they still want the red carpet treatment, they expect deference from me like they get from their medical students. Mr Smear is an ambitious man, Mrs Bathurst says, works all hours. He lives in Staines – quite near me, but in rather more style – and in the evenings he does abortions at a nursing home in Slough. Sometimes when he comes to pick up his post from me I say, 'Oh, look, Doctor! Your hands are dirty.' He'll look huffy, hold them up; but yes, there, there, I say. It's amusing then, to see him wildly stare, and scrutinize his cuffs for blood-spots. I take a moral line, you see. I'm not well-paid, but I have that luxury.

Our other full-timer is Canine, who I mentioned before. He has his own little waiting-room, where he puts his pa-tients while their gum-jabs take effect. His trick is to wait until he has one in the chair – a numb-lipped captive, mouth full of fingers – and then start voicing his opinions. Pakis out, hang the Irish, that sort of thing: all the sophistication you expect from a man with letters after his name. I send his patients back into the world, their faces lopsided and their brains fizzing like bombs. Even if they had free speech, would they contradict him? He might hurt them next time.

One thing to be said for Canine – he's not as greedy as the others. As I said, he gave Mrs Bathurst a cut-rate course of treatment.

'Do you have trouble with your teeth, Mrs Bathurst?' Bettina asked: her usual tone, all gush and dote.

Mrs Bathurst said, 'When I was a girl they made me wear a brace. My gums have been tender since.' She put her hand up, as if she were blotting a bead of blood from her lip. She had yellow fingers, and horrible stumpy gnawed-off nails. I thought, it's obvi-ous; she's one of those people who don't like to talk about their childhood. I remember the day that Mrs Bathurst appeared at the door, her P45 in her bag: a woman of uncertain age, sallow, black hair greying, scooped back into wings and pinned with kirby-grips. She wore a dark cape – which she carried well, because of her height. She's worn it all summer though: in August, people stare.

Perhaps it was part of her uniform once, when she was a hospital nurse. It's the sort of thing that's too good to throw away.

It was late June before she gave me a smile and said, 'You can call me Liz.' I tried, but I didn't feel easy; for me, I'm afraid, she'll be Mrs Bathurst for ever. Still, I was pleased at the time that she seemed to want to get on good terms. You see, I've had some problems in my personal life – it's too complicated to go into here – and I suppose I was looking out for an older woman, somebody I could confide in.

One night I said, will you come out? Let's go somewhere! I towed her along to a little French place, a place I used to go to with my boyfriend; if you don't mind, I won't part with the address. It's tatty and dark, infused with a time-warp mixture of Paris garlic and London smog: set in its ways, very cheap, very good.

Mrs Bathurst would hardly eat. She hardly spoke, but spent the evening perched on the edge of her seat, staring at what the waiters were carrying through, and sniffing. The bill came, and I said, 'My treat – really, Liz, honestly.' Right, thanks, she said: yanked her cape from the hook by the door and fluttered off into the night. Bus to catch, I suppose – though I'd always understood she got home by the Underground.

I wanted to like her, you see; but she's one of those people who can't recognize friendship when it's offered. She was more taken with Bettina – though as far as I could see then, they had nothing in common. Bettina came whining to me: 'That woman's always hanging about in my basement.'

'Doing what?'

She pouted. 'Offering to help me.'

'Not a crime.'

'Don't you think she's a lesbian?'

'How would I know?'

'I've seen you drinking tea with her.'

'Yes, but God blast it. Anyway, Mrs. Isn't she?'

'Oh, Mrs.' Bettina said scornfully. 'Probably she's not. She just thinks it sounds more respectful.'

'Respectable, you mean.'

'Anyway. Lesbians often get married.'

'Do they?'

'Definitely.'

I said 'I bow to your worldly wisdom.'

'Look at her!' Bettina said. 'There's something wrong there.'

'Thyroid?' I said. 'Could be, you know. She's thin. And her hands shake.'

Bettina nodded. 'Eyes bulge. Mm. Could be.'

I feel sorry for both of them. Bettina is on some sort of Grand Tour, earning her way around the Old World – she'll stop off and take blood in various European cities, then go home and settle, she says. Mrs Bathurst's own relatives live abroad, and she never sees them.

After our meal out – a disaster, probably my fault – I'd have suggested something else – film, whatever – except that, as I've said, I rent a flat in Staines, thirty-five minutes from Waterloo, and she lives in north London, Kensal Green. What's it like? I asked her. A hole, she said. Mid-summer, she took a fortnight off. She didn't want it, she said, was dreading it in fact – but Smear was going on a sponsored conference, and she wasn't wanted.

The day she was to finish work, she sat with me in my cave, her eyes hidden in her palms. 'Mrs Bathurst,' I said, 'maybe London's not for you. It's not – I don't find it a kind place myself, it's not a place for women alone.' Especially, I didn't say, when they get to your age. After a bit – perhaps she'd been thinking about what I was saying – she took her hands away from her face.

'Move on,' she said, 'that's the way. Move on, every year or two. That way, you'll always meet somebody, won't you?'

My heart went out to her. I scribbled my address. 'Come over, some night. I've got a sofa, I can put you up.'

She didn't want to take it, and I pressed it into her hand. What a cold hand she had: cold like an old buried brick. I revised my opinion on the state of her thyroid gland.

She didn't come, of course. I didn't mind – and I mind less, in view of what I know about her now – but I very pointedly didn't ask her what she'd done with her time. Her first day back, she looked drained. I said, 'What have you been doing, moonlighting?'

She dropped her head, gnawed her lip, turned her big pale face away. She irritated me, at times; it was as if she didn't understand the English language, the disclaimers and the catch-phrases we all have to take on, all of us, wherever we come from. 'Anyway,' I said, 'you've missed all the excitement, Mrs Bathurst. A week ago we had a break-in.' I'd turned up one morning, and there was Mrs

Ranatunga and Dennis. Mrs Ranatunga was in tears, wringing her
J–Cloth between her hands. There was a police car outside.

'Could you credit it?' Mrs Bathurst said. She looked more
animated. 'Drugs?'

'Yes, that's what Shinbone said. They must have thought we
kept drugs on the premises. They ransacked the basement, there was
glass all over the place. They practically ripped the fridge door off.
Bettina's samples 'had been picked up already', Mrs Bathurst said.

'Just as well.'

Mrs Bathurst shook her head, as if the human condition was
beyond her. 'I'll go down and commiserate with Bettina,' she
whispered. 'Poor little girl. What a shock.' One Saturday, after a
long morning at Harley Street, I thought I'd stay in town and go to
the sales. By two o'clock I was worn out from the heat and the
crush. I got on a London tour bus, pretended to be a Finnish
monoglot, and rested my legs on the empty seat next to me. There
was thunder in the air, a clammy heat. Tourists sat dazed on the
traffic islands and in the parks. The trees seemed wetly green,
foliage hanging in great clumped masses, slow-rustling and heavy.
Near Buckingham Palace there was a bed of geraniums – so scarlet,
as if the earth had bled through the pavements: I saw the guardsmen
wilting in sympathy, fainting at their posts.

On Sunday night I dreamed I was in Harley Street. In my dream
it was Monday; this is what people usually dream, who work all
week. I was coming, or going: the pavement was stained – sunrise or
sunset – and I saw that all the Harley Street railings had been filed to
points. I had a companion in the street, matching me step for step. I
said, Look what they've done to the railings. Yes, very nasty points,
she said. Then a big hand came out, and pushed me against them.

On Monday morning I was groggy. I missed my usual train and
arrived at Waterloo twelve minutes late. Twelve minutes – what is
it, against the length of a life? It's the start of a foul day, that's what
it is – because then comes the scrimmage on the Bakerloo line, and
Regent's Park with the lifts broken down. When I made it to the
top I'd got to sprint – otherwise Smear and Shinbone would have
their heads through my hatch, tapping their watch-faces: oh, where
is Todd? I turned into Harley Street. And what did I see? Only Liz
Bathurst heel-toeing it along. I caught up, put my hand on her arm:
Late, Mrs Bathurst! This isn't like you! No sleep, she said, no rest.

You too? I said. My dream was washed away; easily, I melted into sympathy. She nodded. Up all night, she said.

But in the next three, four, five seconds, I began to feel vastly irritated. I can't put it better than that. God knows, Bettina wears me down, so amiable and dumb, and so do the doctors, but suddenly I realized that Mrs Bathurst was wearing me down even more. 'Liz,' (and I snapped at her, I admit it) 'why do you go around the way you do? That cape – dump it, can't you? Burn it, bury it, send it to a car-boot sale. You bloody depress me, woman. Get your hair done. Buy some emery boards, file your nails.'

My nails, she said, my hair? She turned to me, face sallow and innocent as the moon. And then without warning – and I realize I must have offended her – turned on me, drew her arm back, and thumped her fist between my breasts. I careered right back, right into the railings. I felt them dent into my flesh, one bar against my spine and one behind each shoulder-blade. Mrs Bathurst flew off down the street, her cape flapping.

I put my hands behind me, wrapping my fingers for a moment around those disdainful flaking spikes; levered myself away from the railings, and staggered after her. If I'd had any faith in our doctors, I might have asked one of them to look at my bruises. But as it was, I just felt shaken up. And sorry, because I'd been brutal – my fatigue was to blame.

All that day I felt raw. The noises of our house seemed amplified. When the time-share doctors scuffed in and out, I could hear their Lobbs scraping the carpets. I could hear Gland's wheezing and puffing; the snarls of her patients, and the sobs of the patients of Smear, as he pushed in with his cold speculum, and Mrs Bathurst stood by. I heard the whine and grind of Canine's drill, and the chink of steel instruments against steel dishes.

I said to Bettina, is this Monday? Yes, she said; she was so stupid she thought it was a normal question. Ah, I said, then Dr Lobotomy will be in, two-thirty to eight-thirty, first floor, second door on the left. I think I'll get a brain operation, or a major tranquilliser. I was really nasty to Mrs Bathurst today. I laughed at her for wearing that cape.

Bettina turned her strawberry mouth down, just at the corners. Her big pale eyes – unripe fruits – were bulgy with incomprehension. 'I know it's grotesque,' she said, 'but I don't see that it's funny.'

Should I have noticed at this point, that they'd got together, left me in the cold? I lacked insight this summer – that's how Lobotomy would put it. I was concerned – I am concerned – with what's going on in my own head. Yet I've never been so thin-skinned. When the patients come in I seem to see straight though them to the bone. I can hear their hearts flutter, hear their respiration, their digestion, estimate their tick-over speed and say whether they'll be with us for Christmas. It's September now, and I still feel wrecked by London – I am hot, filthy, desperate, when I get back to Staines, for a bath or shower. For comfort I retain this picture in my mind: I'll move, get further out of town, somewhere small and quiet.

Tuesday I bought a bunch of lilies as I came through Waterloo. I pressed them into Mrs Bathurst's hands. 'Sorry,' I said. 'About the cruel remarks I made.'

She flopped them down and left them on the table in the hall: didn't put them in water. I could hardly do it myself, could I? That evening she and Bettina left together. On her way out she just casually scooped them up, without looking at them. I'll never know if they went home with her or went into a bin.

Wednesday, Bettina came up from the basement. She stood inside my door, leaning on the frame. She looked faintly bruised and blurred, as if her outline had become fuzzy. 'I'd like to talk to you,' she said.

'Of course,' I said, rather coldly. 'Are you in some sort of trouble?'

'Not here,' she said, looking around.

'Meet me at one-fifteen,' I said. I told her how to find the French place. They're even cheaper at lunchtime.

I was there first. I drank some water. I didn't think she'd come, thought she'd lose the address, lose interest; her problems were easily soluble, after all. One-thirty, she came flouncing in – cheeks pink with embarrassment, colouring when the waiter took her cheap little rainproof jacket. They brought the menu; she took it without seeing it; she pushed her curly fringe from her forehead and – as I could have forecast – burst into tears. It's been a long, difficult summer. It came to me what Mrs Bathurst said, about the need to move on: I said, 'I suppose you'll not be with us much longer, Bets?'

She locked her eyes into mine; this surprised me, to see those great blue-violet orbs assume a purpose. 'You don't realize, do you?' she said. 'My God, when were you born? Don't you realize I'm seeing Bathurst, most nights now?'

Seeing, indeed. I kept a very judicious silence: that's what you should do, if you don't quite know what people mean. Then she did something odd: her elbows on the table, she put her fingers to the back of her neck, and seemed to massage the scalpline there, and raise her roseate hair. It was as if she were trying to show me something. A moment, and she left it; her hair fell back against her short white neck. She shivered; she drew one hand across her shoulder, slowly, and allowed it to graze her breast, brush her nipple. One of the old waiters passed, and half-smiled at me. As if he had seen this performance before.

'Oh, come on Bets, don't cry.' I extended my hand, let it cover hers for a moment. OK, so you're abnormal, I thought; I should have known, shouldn't I, when you came into my cave to giggle about sexual perversity? 'Lots of people are like it, Bettina.'

'Oh, Jesus,' she said. All her sweetness had gone; she was foul-mouthed, sweating, pallid. 'It's like an addiction,' she said.

'There are support groups. Telephone lines. You can ring up and get advice, and they tell you where you can meet other people who are like you are.' She was shaking her head, her eyes on the check tablecloth. 'There are even clubs – you'll find them in *Time Out*. Anyway, think of it like this – maybe it's just a phase you're going through.'

'Phase?' She lifted her head. 'That's all you know, Todd. I'm like this for ever, now.'

Setting aside my prejudices – which is not easy, and why should it be – I have to say I have no high opinion of Mrs Bathurst. I notice that now she's got Bettina she's suddenly become interested in me. She's asked me to Kensal Green next week. She said, Come round; she smiled, quite broadly, and said, Come for a meal.

LOVE'S SWEET DAUGHTER

John Milne

He came up the stairs to my office two at a time. He was a tall, grey-white haired man, around sixty, and when he arrived he wasn't even breathless, just impatient. There was no stoop to him. Everything about him screamed health, vitality, vitamin pills. I hated him on sight.

'Mr Jenner? Love,' he said, 'Anthony Love.'

He pronounced Anthony with a 'th' not a 't'. He wore a Brooks's shirt, an expensive blue tailored suit and highly polished black brogue Church's.

'Take a seat, Mr Love.' I said.

'Please. An-thony.'

'OK. Take a seat, An-thony.' But he already had. Anthony Love sat back in his seat and crossed his legs. His expensive polished shoes had tiny steel misers on the heels. His face was brown and flat-tanned. His eyes were ice-cold blue.

'Canadian.' I said.

'That's right. But I started off here.'

'At the bottom, I bet.' Why is it colonial types never tell you their father was an earl and they went out with fifty-grand seed money?

'That's right, Mr Jenner. But . . .'

'Everybody's got to start somewhere, I know. What can I do for you?'

'I'm looking for my brother's daughter.'

'Called?'

'Lola. Lola Love, when she was a child. The surname could have changed of course.'

'How old is Lola?'

'Twenty-eight.'

'And she's missing?'

'No. I've just lost contact with her.'

'Why not ask your brother?'

'He's been dead since 1968. I went to Canada five years before that.'

'OK.' I took out a notebook, opened it and wrote at the top of the page, *cooking oil, tea, skimmed milk*. People like you to make notes in this game.

'Why do you want the daughter, Mr Love?'

He smiled and wrung his hands together. Nice sensitive hands, with manicured nails. You could have been a model, Anthony-Love-with-a-'th', if you'd wanted to sell washing-up liquid to rich old men.

'I left here when my niece was a baby,' he said, 'and went up north in Canada. I started up a little oil company . . .'

'. . . sold a little oil. I get the picture. Why do you want the daughter?'

He sighed. 'You're impatient.'

'I'm busy.'

It's not true, I wasn't. The misers on the expensive shoes niggled me. It's a paradox, like the thousand-quid suit on a body that clearly spent much of its life in the gym or on the beach. Mr Love wasn't telling me the truth, the whole truth and nothing but the. All of him was a Freudian slip.

'Got a photo?'

'Not since she was fourteen. Her mother sent me this photo then. It was years after I'd last seen her. It didn't even include a return address.'

He handed me a photograph of a girl in school uniform, leaning against a brick wall. She was a pretty girl with long dark hair. The hair fell half across her face, so that one eye, her nose and half her mouth smiled shyly at the camera. An-thony cleared his throat and swapped feet so that I got a view of the other miser.

'Lola's my last living relative. I want to find her.'

'To leave her your fortune?'

'Not quite yet. How do you know I have a fortune to leave?'

'The misers on your shoes. If a poor man bought a pair of shoes like that he'd simply enjoy them.'

He looked at the underside of his shoe and smiled. 'I'll need an advance,' I said.

He produced a roll, flipped through it till he reached the thousand-pound mark, then laid the notes on the table.

'Will that buy me a few days' attention, Jenner?'

'It certainly will, Love. Where are you staying?'

'Brown's.'

Of course. 'What's the name of your brother?'

'Mark.'

'OK. I'll come to Brown's and tell you when I get some news of Mark, Anthony.'

'Lola. We all know what happened to Mark.'

'Which was?'

'He was murdered.'

Everybody's got to have some luck, if luck is what it is. I found the woman I wanted first time. I spent the morning in St Catherine's House, then headed west on the Central line, chickety-boo, chickety-boo, all the other passengers stare at you. I rose to the street again at Notting Hill and made my way to Ladbroke Grove. Who comes from Ladbroke Grove? No one, as far as I can see.

The house was a full-size Victorian villa. I turned off Ladbroke Grove, walked up the steps to her portico, pulled a bell-chain and waited. Green mould clung to the uncleaned steps. Cracked and flaking cement stucco hung above my head. A couple of yellowing, dirty milk bottles were abandoned in the front garden. It's a bad state of affairs when a person of my standing notices a house is dirty. A grey net curtain moved on the ground floor of the house. I had a glimpse of a hand behind the net. I turned and looked away, knowing I was being studied. Across the street a man's face was at the first-floor window. He had a bald head and his eyes stared steadily. He was studying me; watching, just watching me. People do that in cities. Net curtains, faces at windows. Men stand, half-hidden behind trees, or sit in cars, not reading the newspapers they're holding. Women talk at street corners, crane their necks to watch you pass; rubber-necking. Anonymity is a farce.

Miranda Yale lived in a house worth half-a-million smackeroos and she hadn't had the front swept nor the sashes painted in more than twenty years. It takes all kinds. Perhaps old fruity-pie across the road was watching, just waiting for a new broom. The lock clicked and slid, the peeling viridian paint of the front door swung away from me with a groan. I was confronted with a small, fat woman.

'Can I help you?'

'I expect you can, Miss Yale.' I said.

'How do you know my name? Who are you?'

Her voice was county, a cut-crystal county accent, completely mismatched with the grimy face, the bloated body and the seedy clothes; it was a *Just put the horses away, Jenner, I'm going round the back to see to the gardener* voice.

'I've come to talk to you about Mark Love.'

She looked at me for a moment, blinking in the light of a low sun which peeked through clouds behind me. Cars roared up the Grove, changing gear, fallen rain squeezed under their wheels. *Shhhh* ... the wheels whispered, *shhhh* ... I took my hat off but Miranda Yale stood her ground.

'You're not a reporter,' she said.

'No, I am not. You are Suzanne Miranda Yale and you were once known as Suzanne or Suzy Love or Miranda Love. I just want to have a friendly talk, lady, and it's wet outside and it's not very comfortable standing here talking. What about it?'

'It's not raining now.' She paused. 'And I've never seen a policeman carrying a walking-stick.'

I handed her my card. 'Could I come in and talk?'

She stared up into my face. The eyes behind her washed-out blonde lashes were grey. They almost matched her pale skin. The eyes hardened for a moment, the swollen features creased in concentration.

'Come in?'

I nodded. That was indeed what I had said. She turned and walked inside, leaving the door open. I took one last look at the flaking cement portico, then followed its flaking owner along her hallway.

It was a tall room and about as wide as many people's living-rooms. As I went in I swung the front door shut behind me. The room was very dark suddenly and Miranda had gone except for her voice: 'Do come on in if you're coming,' sounding as if she were talking impatiently to a butcher's boy, or to a household servant who'd asked for an interview. I followed the voice. At each footfall nameless and numberless crumbs and seeds crunched under the soles of my shoes. The drawing-room carpet was worse.

Miranda Love was fifty-three but looked ninety, owing to her

having poured quite a bit of the output of Gilbey Vintners down
her throat since Mark Love had called 'house' in the great bingo
hall of life. When I went into her drawing-room she was holding a
gin bottle up to the light coming through the net curtains. Dust
filtered the shaft of light before it landed on her white, white, near-
translucent white skin. She pursed grey-blue lips and shook the
bottle.

'I'd offer you one but that looks about the end of it.' Miranda
squinted at the gin, poured herself a dribble from the bottom of it,
then waved the empty green bottle.

'It's a bit early,' I said.

Miranda scowled. 'You don't look wholly holy . . . Mr . . .?'

'Jenner. Jimmy Jenner. It's on the card.'

'So sit and tell me your business, Jimmy Jenner-on-the-card.' I
moved a newspaper and sat down on a dusty sofa. More dust
billowed around me. Gin we have none, dust we've got aplenty.

'I'm a private detective. That's also written on my card.'

Miranda grinned. Miranda Love might've been pretty once. She
might've had her house cleaned once too . . . but neither recently.

'You don't need to read the card for that, Jenner. I guessed it
when you rang the doorbell. What's your business with *me*?'

'Well, I want to ask you some questions about your husband.'

'I don't have a husband.'

'But you *did*, right?'

'Since you know so much about it, why don't you tell me?'

I sat with my hat on my knees. I didn't put it on the sofa in case
it caught something. Miranda squirmed in her seat, cupping the last
greasy glassful of gin in her hands. She looked like an albino sea
cow.

'OK. You are the wife of one Mark Thomas Edward Love.
Known as "Chicken" Love. He was a tearaway of this manor,
known for fearlessness and personal sadism. He is believed responsible for several murders before he had his clock stopped by
some equally nasty toerag, *circa* 1968. Did you ever pick up the
insurance?'

'I was the "girlfriend", never "the wife of", and no.'

'Did you ever pick up the body?'

'How old are you?'

'Enough, lady.'

'Well, Mark's body was never found. Just blood on the pavement outside the Jessie Club . . .'

'And a load of witnesses.'

'And a load of witnesses. None of them knew who'd shot him.'

She lifted the glass and sucked the alcohol through her closed teeth. She put the glass down but kept sucking the alcohol backwards and forwards through her teeth, the way thoughtful Americans chew gum, an outward sign of inward thought.

'Let me explain something to you, Mr Jenner. You are not the first man to come here and ask about Mark Love. I'm used to getting visits. About once a year some nasty little pressman turns up here looking for a story. Nowadays it's quite often a presswoman. *They* usually start off polite. *They* usually get their facts at least half-right.'

'OK. But I'm better company. Can I ask some questions or do we have to work our way through a crash course on politeness first?'

Miranda shrugged.

'Get on with it.'

'I know you and Love have a daughter . . .'

'*Had.*' She began picking at the braiding on her dirty blue smocked dress. A black cat strolled in as if he owned the joint. I stood and paced the cat's room for a moment. His eyes followed me.

'I know you had a daughter. Just one?'

'Just one.'

'Where did the three of you live?'

'The three of us never lived anywhere. Lola and I lived here. In this house. And when Mark died we went to Australia.'

'I know. I read in the newspapers about you doing that, Mrs Love.'

'My name is Yale. The newspapers called me Suzy Love but my name is Yale and never was Love. I've never been *Mrs* anybody.'

'And you went abroad when he disappeared, you say?'

'We went to Australia to get away from the publicity that was around when Mark disappeared. I had an uncle in New South Wales and I went to stay with him. I needed to. *We* did.'

'An uncle. Where exactly in New South Wales?'

She wasn't listening. 'We're entitled to private lives, you know. Newspapers.'

'I'm not a newspaperman, Miss Yale.'

'Newspaper publicity. Nobody gave a damn what happened to us. It was the story they wanted. Just because we'd been with Mark. They even changed my name because it sounded better, would you believe that? All because the name "Love" works on some nasty little newspaperman's imagination . . .'

'What sort of man was Love? Apart from the gangster business?'

'*Alleged* gangster business. There was a lot of dirt thrown at anyone from the East End who became successful in the sixties.'

'OK. Alleged. But what sort of *man* was he?'

'Why does it matter?'

She stood. I noticed her legs were bandaged from her ankles up to her hemline. Grey lips, ulcerated legs; Miranda was in a bad way. If her heart didn't give out first she'd end up with a nylon leg like mine.

'Wait there, Jenner.'

'Going nowhere.'

She went out. I paced the filthy room for a minute or two, lifted the net curtain to stare outside, avoided the gaze of Mr Black Cat, who looked at me accusingly. What are you doing here, upsetting my woman? Over the road the nosey neighbour looked at me too. What are you doing here, Mister-with-the-walking-stick?

Miranda came back with a photograph. It showed a slim and attractive blonde dolly-bird of the sixties, clearly Miranda herself. Miranda's swollen features were all present in the dolly-bird, anticipating the gin, just waiting to swell. The Miranda in the picture stood with her arm around a very small child, no more than three years old. The child wore a heavy coat but no bonnet. She had dark hair and dark eyes. Her eyes stared steadily and confidently at the camera lens. Mark Love stood some feet behind them, wearing a dark suit and dark glasses, hands in pockets, leaning against a wall. A line of tall, Georgian-style railings ran by Mark's side and behind the railings were a lot of tall Georgian-style windows and doors. At the end of the railings was a Mark 2 Jag. Mark Love stared out of the side of the picture, as if someone standing just out of the frame had said something very important to him and now he was thinking about it. Mark Love looked about forty, dark-haired, slim, hard-looking. The photo might have been posed by an Italian film-maker.

'That's us. Mark, Lola and me.'

'Who are the fellows in the car?' I could just make out the shapes of two men sitting in the Jaguar.

'Wilkins. An old business colleague of Tom's. The other one's Freddie Philips, our driver. *Mark's* driver . . .'

'Is that the man he disappeared with?'

She didn't answer. We both stared at the photograph a little longer, then Miranda said, 'How did you find me?'

'Newspaper articles, then the Voter's Register.'

'Is that how they all find me?' she asked.

'I don't know. You haven't moved. It isn't difficult. It's not as if you seem to be making any particular effort to hide.'

'I wasn't living here for nearly ten years. When I was in Australia.'

That must have been when they got behind with the cleaning.

'Who else has been here asking questions, Miss Yale?'

Miranda shrugged, picked up her empty glass and stared at it for a while.

'You can have the photograph if you want. I had absolutely loads of them printed. People kept asking for them.'

'Who?'

She shrugged again. 'Everyone.'

'Recently?'

'All the time. It was quite a famous photograph when he had it done. Mark was well known. Do you think I ought to move house?'

'I don't know. It's not up to me, is it?' If she hadn't moved house by now, she simply wasn't going to.

'I have a photograph too.'

I brought out the picture Anthony had given me and gave it to her. Miranda pointed to a big, dusty dresser across the room. 'There's a magnifier in there. Second drawer.'

I fetched it. She rubbed the glass on her dress. I stood over her while she peered into the photo.

'Where did you get this?'

I stopped. Miranda had gone even paler. Her glaucous eyes stared at the glossy black and white of the old photo. For a second her lip might have trembled.

'What is it, Miss Yale?'

She put the photograph down. Now her lip definitely trembled.
'Nothing.'
'It is her, yes?'
She didn't answer.
'Do you recognize the girl?'
'No.'
'Maybe you do.'
'No.' She was silent for a second, but soon regained her haughtiness. 'Who could recognize anything from that?'
'She couldn't have been anyone you might know?'
'No. I've never seen anyone like that.'
'She'd be about the same age as your daughter, Miss Yale.' I held my breath for a second. 'Could it have been your daughter, Miss Yale?'

Miranda took her time. She looked at the photograph in my hand, then at the photograph in hers, then back at the photograph in my hand. The little girl's face gazed out at me, gazed out across the years. Her eyes stared steadily and constantly, now not at the camera lens but confidently into my eyes, seeing my eyes there and looking as if she was about to say something, as if she knew something. I took the glass from her.

'No,' said Miranda Yale. 'No, I'm not able to say who the person in your photograph is. It's a rotten photograph. I've never seen her, anyway.' Now she was doing the trembling-lip job again, very slightly, hardly noticeable, and her voice sounded as if she had bread stuck in her throat. Dry bread.

'And whoever visits here, it won't be my daughter, Mr Jenner. You can be sure of that. Quite certain.'

She paused, letting the lip tremble, then said, 'The reason I came back from Australia was that things were washed up there.'

'You left her there?'

'She died there.'

Suddenly I could hear the voices of some children out on Ladbroke Grove, 'You put that down you put that down you put that down that's mine.' Miranda Yale's face was blank, unemotional. I struggled for some point of communication.

'Hopping the wag from school,' I said, failing.

Miranda Yale cried a little, and while she did it I stood at her window watching the street children rowing over a skateboard.

Eventually a large boy biffed a small one and made off on the board.

'She died a couple of years after her father disappeared. My uncle had an accident in his pick-up truck on a country road in the outback. He was drunk, and he turned it over on a bend. He killed himself and my daughter both.'

Some minutes later and Miranda had been through an entire loo-roll. It lay in crumpled balls at her feet, damp with tears and trodden on as she moved her bandage-wound legs in discomfiture.

'But you lived?'

'I wasn't there. I was with some friends in Sydney when it happened.'

'Drinking?'

Why did I say that? She didn't answer.

'What year was this?'

She made a retching sound, then again, and again. I thought she was puking at first. She covered her face with her hands and retched her grief into her palms, a dry-sobbed sound, all the tears cried out of her now. The pain she suffered was so awful I thought for a minute I would cry too, though I never knew the kid nor gave a damn for her death which had taken place while I was still a kid myself. Miranda took the photo I'd brought from her dirty tabletop, silently pushing it on top of the photo she'd given me, shoving the paper into my hand. It was a 'Goodbye Jenner', as clearly as if she'd had someone around to show me out. Miranda parked her fat jacksie back on the sofa and gripped her empty, finger-greased glass again and wept again. I left as quietly as I could, seeds and crumbs crunching under my soft footsteps. I scraped the soles of my shoes off as best I could on the doorstep and clicked the latch shut behind me. You don't often wipe your feet when you go from a house into the street.

As I crossed the street I could see the face of the bald-headed man in the house opposite, staring down at me from his first-floor window. He dropped the curtain as soon as he saw me looking. I felt like he knew what I'd just left. I felt like thumbing my nose at him. Maybe he could hold his nose for about five minutes while he searched for another loo-roll for Miranda to blub into. Not me. I stood and stared at the man's window for a moment, wondering if he was watching me from behind the net. The bright sun went behind a cloud and rain began to fall again, swiftly, directly. I turned up my collar against the rain and tightened the belt of my mackintosh. Why hadn't she asked where I'd got the photo from? All Miranda would say was that it wasn't Lola, in whose honour we'd had the waterworks session. Scratch Lola Love, Jenner.

I walked a few yards down the road and sat on a low wall, pretending to wait for a bus. I knew he'd come out sooner or later. When he did he was wearing a blue Crombie on his back and a black hat perched on his head, as if he'd been sent out by an over-protective mother. He hung around the bus-stop too.

'You local?' I asked.

'Born and bred.'

'I thought so. I can't figure these buses out, can you?'

He had a Ph.D. in buses, so it took five minutes before he asked me, 'You Press?'

'No. Solicitor's clerk.'

'I saw you visiting the lady opposite. There's no trouble, is there?'

I smiled reassuringly. 'No trouble.' He was waiting to be asked more, so I did. 'I was looking for someone who might have visited her. A young woman. She'd be mid-twenties, with dark hair. Quite good looking, I'd say.'

He shook his head. 'No.'

'Pity.'

'Not here.'

'What?'

'Mid-twenties, you say?'

'That's right.'

'She has a thin face but full features; you know, full lips. All that. Face comes to a nice point, high cheek-bones. She's tall and dark-haired, dresses smartly. Very smartly. She wears a business suit and carries a briefcase. She looks more than a bit elegant. Smart girl, smart clothes, unless I'm very much mistaken . . .' he tapped his head, 'smart brain too. You'd know her if you met her. They have tea in Holland Park. About once a month. But she never comes here.'

Elation. 'What did you do before you retired?'

'I was a Detective Inspector in Bow Street,' he said. 'What division were you in, Mr . . .?'

'Jenner. West End Central. But years later.'

'You don't look like a solicitor's clerk.'

We both laughed.

'And you are?'

'Mr Cook. Plain old Mr Cook.'

'Listen, Mr Cook. In the park. Did you ever see a third person with them? A man in his sixties, grey hair but very fit?'

'No.'

'How about following them?'

'No.'

'Did you follow them?'

'Of course not. But I would have noticed if someone else did.'

'You would. Wasn't Dean Street on your patch, when you were a copper?'

'Maybe.'

We grinned at each other. Now I knew and he knew I knew.

'An obsession?' I asked.

'Unfinished business when I retired. If Mark Love is dead then so am I.'

'You're not dead, sir. Did you just happen to buy a flat here?'

'Everybody's got to live somewhere. I'm not married and it's convenient. Where are you going?'

'Brown's hotel.'

He smiled, we shook hands and he went back into the flats. I flagged a cab. As I got in Miranda was watching me in her turn from the first-floor window. What an actress. The things people will do for their children.

You don't have to wear a tie to go into Brown's but you get better attention if you do. I wore mine to the desk along with a big cheesy smile: 'Like me'. The minion didn't, but was polite.

'Yes, sir?'

'I'm looking for Mark Thomas Edward Love. He's a Canadian businessman staying here.'

'No. We've a Mr Love but his name's not Mark.'

'Anthony. He travels under the name of Anthony. Would you tell him Jimmy Jenner's in the bar waiting to see Mark Love.'

'Yes sir.'

'Be sure to get it right.'

'Yes sir.' This time through gritted teeth. No tip for you unless you smile. That's the game, I have to wear a tie and you have to wear a smile.

Mark came into the bar wearing a beige golfing outfit and soft-fit loafers. His beige sweater had a tiny tartan logo on the front and Mark/Anthony had a tiny pursed look of disapproval on his face.

'How did you know?'

'St Catherine's House. Mark Love's mother only had one son.'

'Maybe you got the wrong Love.'

'Or maybe I'm your brother. I'll tell you what, Mr Love, I'll tell you what I reckon. I reckon London was a bit hot for Mark Love in 1968. Good-looking gangsters were going down to Parkhurst by the busload, and none of them were coming back. So Mark arranged for a lot of his pals to "witness" his demise in Dean Street. Gunshots, blood on the pavement. Starting pistols and a bit of DIY blood-donoring. You were probably already out of the country.'

He smiled. I went on. 'Mark Love went to Canada. His wife, Miranda, went to Australia with their little girl. How am I doing?'

I took out the photograph of Love and his daughter Miranda had given me. Twenty years had passed but it was the man on the other side of the table in Brown's. He knew it, I knew it.

'Not bad.'

'Maybe the plan was to meet later. Unfortunately, Miranda went off the idea. Once she'd got rid of her tough boyfriend, why should she have him back? Why should her daughter have the drawback of a villain like Mark Love for a father? But what to do?'

A waiter hovered by us. Mark Love waved him away.

'What to do, Jenner?'

'I think Miranda let him know their child died in Australia. A tragic accident. Mark took this as a blow. Miranda had to look as if she was destroyed by it too. I went to her house. She's very convincing. You mention little Lola and she comes on like the mother of the nation that just lost the war. But I expect you've been there and had that from her?'

He held up his hands.

'Years later Mark returns from Canada, reckons it's by now safe to come to London and waggle the trees. Where's my daughter, Miranda?'

'I couldn't shake her story.'

'So you wondered if I could.'

'That's about it. Cheer up. You got paid.'

'So I did. But it was a dangerous thing to do. Why, after all this time?'

'I have no one. She's my daughter.'

He waited, and then, 'Did you find her?'

'I know where to find her.'

'Where?'

I tore a page of my notebook and wrote ex-Detective Inspector Cook's name and address on it. I never mentioned the Detective Inspector part.

'He'll tell you.'

Love read it. 'He lives opposite Miranda?'

'Yes.'

Love folded the paper and put it carefully in his wallet.

'And he knows where to find her?'

'Without a doubt.'

'Thank you, Jenner. Thank you.' He stood. 'Can I, er . . . rely on you?'

'Of course.'

He smiled. We shook hands and he went upstairs, no doubt to put on another thousand-quid's-worth of clothes. I fumbled through my pockets for some phone money. Well, I never liked him.

THE BLITZ SPIRIT

Kim Newman

The Shelter was already crowded when he arrived. A wedge of queue stood topside. Men in hats and wide-shouldered double-breasteds and women with Cellophane raincoats over Austerity creations clustered and craned around the entrance. The ARP man on the door lifted the red velvet rope for Frankham without checking his clipboard. The queue muttered but he gave a familiar wave. Most of the civvies recognized him. They wouldn't be here if it weren't for his write-ups.

A barrage balloon caught the searchlight overhead, a low-lying and heavy cloud in December skies. From the depths, band music poured. Three shrills swung 'Don't Sit Under the Apple Tree'. He stood alone in the bare cage-lift as it descended. He was always given elbow-room. It was a sign of respect.

Peter Frankham saw himself in the burnished metal of the cage, looking Nigel Patrick-ish, with thin 'tache and slouch hat, gabardine draped over his shoulders, double length of watch-chain in his waistcoat and ballooning bags. He'd had the look for three months and it wasn't yet through.

The cage rattled open and a commissionaire let him into the Shelter proper.

'There was another bomb in Oxford Street,' someone said. 'Shut down the tube for hours.'

'Don't go on an' on an' on,' he said back.

The dance-floor thronged. Surplus bods huddled in the dark by the walls, tucking into plates of snoek, drinking bombers. Noise was all around: chatter, swing, clatter, siren whines, shrills.

He had passed a stretch of rubble in Oxford Street. It might have been the His Master's Voice shop. The wardens had it roped off and sludgy piles of debris gave off steam where fires had been put out. The whole street was blacked out, Christmas tat turned to sinister black shapes strung from lampposts.

Many in the crowd, men and women, wore uniform. Dancers had jackets undone, sweat-ringed as they jived and jitterbugged, knowing they could die any second. Chippies and touts worked the Shelter on a professional basis. Frankham could spot them a mile off. *Time Out* called him 'Caesar of the Spivs'.

He had no business here. Once he had written a place up, everyone else would go and his actual attendance would be surplus to schedule. But he liked to make snap inspections. Sometimes, he'd pick apart a hole he had built up. These were ephemeral times; nothing stood long. The music got faster.

The band – a young man in a flying helmet surrounded by his instrument panel, flicking switches – pin-balled through 'Coming In On a Wing and a Prayer' and the three shrills were off, replaced by a geezer with a painted tie that hung to his knees, an hour-glass-shaped purple coat and a cigar twice the size of the Old Man's.

The dancers collapsed exhausted and crowds surged in to fill their space. The band went *oom-pah* and the geezer wheezed through impersonations of Benito and Adolf, topping off his sound-bite of an act with 'Der Führer's Face'. The audience knew the routine, and joined in the chorus.

'When der Führer says "We iss der Master Race",

We HEIL –'

An enormous collective oral wet fart resounded.

'HEIL –'

Again.

'Right in der Führer's face . . .'

The Shelter was on its last legs, Frankham thought. Retro was all very well, but it shaded too easily into camp.

He left without even sampling his complementary drink. Outside, as the doors opened, an all-clear sounded.

About eleven, he stopped by Monty's for a coffee-shock. He wrapped a five-pound note in his ration coupon and got the real stuff. Black market, with five sugars. The brush-moustached orderly gave Frankham a smart salute and stumped off on a shrapnel-stiff leg.

'Bit of a prang last month,' he had explained as he plonked down Frankham's mug, sloshing a bit too much in the saucer.

Monty's was in the warrens of Soho, just across from the Windmill. From his place at the counter, Frankham could see the frontage. An audience disgorged from all exits, having just seen *Tonight and Every Night*. Many were whistling the hit, 'Seeing It Through'. The revue was doing better business than *Hello Playmates!* at the Dominion. There was a quote from Frankham on the marquee: 'It's tickety-boo!'

A child-sized figure in a gas mask, trailing a filthy foot of grown-up coat, crept in behind a punter, and started rooting around in the neglected corners. The orderly gave an 'Oi, you!' and shooed the creature out.

'Kids,' he said, 'bless 'em.'

A professorial foreigner was mouthing off at a corner table, surrounded by nodding acolytes as he dipped biscuits in his tea. He had a Viennese beard and a dubious accent.

'Looking backwards is a comprehensible but perilous reaction to the chaos of the present,' Johnny Foreign declaimed. 'Faced with the direst circumstances, it is sometimes natural to wish to return to a time when similar hardships were endured only to be overcome . . .'

Frankham couldn't help but smile. Johnny Foreign was the spit and image of the sinister, sneaky figures on the framed posters behind the bar. CARELESS TALK COSTS LIVES. LOOSE LIPS SINK SHIPS. A definite morale-breaker and no mistake.

A bald little man sidled up to Frankham at the counter and opened his ratty Bud Flanagan coat. His many inside pockets were distended with compact 78s and wire-tape cassettes.

'Slightly bomb-damaged stock,' he whispered out of a corner of his mouth. 'Coupon or cash.'

He had all the sounds: George Formby, Hutch, Gracie Fields, Madonna's Blitzkrieg, the Yank crooners, Hoagy.

Frankham waved the looter away. His wares still had gummy circles where price-stickers had been. He went to tap Johnny Foreign's table and made an exchange with one of the acolytes for an Artie Shaw bootleg.

A family of refugees was holding up foot traffic on Wardour Street. The police were checking papers with some trouble. None of the adults spoke any English, and a sullen, bone-weary schoolgirl was having to translate to her three apparent parents, converting terse British sentences into lengthy Mittel Europa circumlocutions.

The street was blocked off by a checkpoint. Frankham shivered in his gabardine and slipped on his phones, adjusting the wire cassette until swing plugged directly into his brain. The Glenn Miller remix fed his jumping synapses. *Pennsylvania 6–5,000,000.*

'Pass on, please,' said a constable, waving pedestrians by. Soldiers in berets that seemed black in the night shoved the refugees against a wall and patted their pockets for contraband. The *Herald* had run an exposé, indicting bogus refugees as the worst of the black marketeers.

Somewhere, far away, perhaps across the river, was the crump of a big explosion. Another one.

Frankham strode on. He was behind schedule.

The War Room wasn't as overpopulated as the Shelter. It was more expensive and coupons were short since the bank freeze. But after his write-up, it would be the Next Place.

Frankham sipped a reasonable cocktail and leant backwards on the bar-rail with proprietorial insouciance. The dance floor was a map of the European theatre. Hostesses with pointers shoved toy ships and model troop dispositions about. They wore khaki skirts and had their hair done up under peaked caps. They all had sex appeal in buckets.

The Old Man himself, or rather a working simulacrum thereof, sat on the bandstand, bulging his boiler suit like a giant baby, puffing on a jutting cigar, and sampling famous sayings into non-stop swing.

'We shall fight them . . . fight them . . . fight them . . .'

A black couple in US army uniform combined acrobatically, the man standing on Belgium and lifting his scissor-legged partner over his head, vaulting her from Normandy Beach to Peenemunde. Her skirts divided and closed like a snapping trap.

'. . . on the beaches . . . the beaches . . . the beaches . . .'

The dancers were probably with the management. They were too good to be civvies.

Everyone was given a cigar as they came in. Frankham had dumped his in a bucket of sand, but plenty lit up, adding to the smoke-filled room fug that hung under the ceiling, obscuring the lights.

The speciality dancers reached a frenzied climax, dry-humping and rolling across France like the Eighth Army. The Old Man turned a blubbery cartwheel on the bandstand, padding wriggling. Dresden exploded in a three-foot flame which whooshed around the legs of dancers, blowing up skirts to reveal suspenders and camiknickers. Harmless miniature fire-bursts sparked all around, singeing a few, producing squeals of drunken delight.

'Never before . . . I said before,' the Old Man rumbled like a public school Foghorn Leghorn, 'In the field of human conf . . . I said human conflict, has so much, and I mean sooooo much, been owed . . .'

In a sense, Frankham reflected, it was all owed to him.

Frankham had seen it coming a year or so back, when the first big-band tracks leaked into the clubs just as the PM was denying plans had been laid to reintroduce rationing. He had written about it in cutting-edge 'zines, then the overground press. The Blitz Spirit was returning in style. When the Austerity line of fashions hit shops just as the bombing campaign shifted from public transport to department stores, the battle to stay in fashion racked up its first casualties and more eager recruits enlisted. 'Theme Museums' offering realistic simulacra of the darkest hours opened, bombarding the civvies with special effects. Hair salons became barbers' shops, and stylists became skilled in straight-razoring 'taches to pencil lines. De Havilland sound systems swept from the East End into the city, reproducing stuttering swing and syrup sentiment. The British film industry, with Ministry of Information funding, turned out cheap but successful remakes of: *The Foreman Went to France,* . . . *One of our planes is missing* . . . and *The Goose Steps Out.* When the BBC repeated '*Allo 'Allo* and *Dad's Army* to higher viewing figures than the soaps, bombs fell on Albert Square and Brookside Close in retaliation. Euro-talks in Hamburg ground to an unresolvable deadlock, with ambassadors constantly on the point of recall. The spiv look alternated with the uniform style and there was much confusion over just who was entitled to wear British Army combat fatigues. Every West End theatre had its wartime revue running; Andrew Lloyd Webber turned the *Colditz* story into a musical smash while Cameron Mackintosh produced *Every Night Something Awful.* Frankham had already signed for a coffee-table book on the movement. It was to be called *The Finest Hour.*

*

As he emerged into Cavendish Square, a knot of SS skins were being turned away from the War Room. The skinhead Gruppenführer spat abuse at the Tommy on the door, biting down on harsh German phrases like cyanide-filled teeth. The Tommy stood his ground.

There'd been a brief shooting war on Remembrance Sunday, Nouveau Nazis skirmishing with flight-uniformed young men who called themselves the Few. It had been blown up in the papers, but the factions had chased each other up and down Charing Cross Road and St Martin's Lane, trading wild shots and smashing windows.

It was hard to get a cab. Frankham ambled along Margaret Street towards Regent Street and found a corner he could hail from. Standing on the pavement, he was aware of shapes crouched in the alley behind. Three sexless figures lay, their lower bodies swaddled in dirty sleeping-bags. Blank insectile eyes stood out in black-snouted faces. Gas masks.

There was a rush of noise and a whisk of air and Frankham dropped to the ground. Then came the flash and a scatter of hot ashes.

It had been close, maybe a street away. He turned and stood, and saw thin but giant flames shooting up above All Souls, Langham Place and Broadcasting House. That one must have been an incendiary. It had fallen somewhere up on Great Portland Street, near the Post Office.

Fire-engines clanked and people were running towards and away from the explosion. Just standing, he was jostled. He patted the dust from his gabardine and stung his palm on a hot spark.

'. . . *mumble, mumble,*' said a gas mask.

'Pardon?' he said, involuntarily.

'Mustn't grumble,' the gas mask repeated.

'Worse things happen at sea,' another mask confirmed.

In the Troy Club, a Boffin, hand fused with a tumbler of Glenfiddich, tried to explain the nature of ghosts and time.

'. . . a collective wish can summon aspects of the past, invoke them if you will, actually bring into being objects or persons long gone . . .'

Frankham ignored the bespectacled loon and ordered a stiffish

Gin and It. from the barman, who had patent-leather hair, hooded eyes and a white dinner-jacket.

'Close scrape, I've just had,' he said.

'If it's got your name on it, not much you can do, sir.'

Frankham threw the drink at the back of his throat. The stinging behind his eyes calmed him.

'Shook me up, I must say.'

The Troy always had the wireless on. A clubman spun the dial on the waist-high laminated cabinet, trying to find ITMA. He could only get purred news announcements about the latest raids and spun on at random. The wireless coughed out a sample of ranting Adolf, passed John Peel introducing Ambrose, then scratched into 'The Lambeth Walk'.

'Bloody bad show, this,' snorted a Blimp who was having his ear bent by the Boffin. 'Young turks have done for us well and proper. Too many green hands on the tiller, you know. All the good men pensioned off and put out to pasture.'

An airman, barely old enough to raise a 'tache, drank quietly and seriously at the bar, ignoring the Blimp and the Boffin. His hands were shaking almost unnoticeably.

'I should be up there,' he said, thumbing toward the ceiling. 'I was due aloft tonight, but they cancelled the scramble. Bomb or something. Fifth columnists, they say.'

'Very nasty business, sir,' said the barman. 'The enemy within.'

'It's deuced frustrating,' the airman declared, looking at his hands. 'Just sitting here. Not being able to fight back. I'd just like to get one of the bogeys in my sights.'

'Not a man from the Last War on the General Staff,' blustered the Blimp. 'All babies and boyos, with their computer planes and ballistic what-have-you. Don't know the words to "God Save the King" and jitterbug to Yank bands on their leave . . .'

'As a society turns in on its insides,' said the Boffin, 'loses forward momentum in nostalgia, the patterns of time and space itself may bend and bow, and even break. Nobody seems to notice . . .'

'Bloody Yanks. Bet they come in when it's all over, grinning and dispensing chocolate and nylons like bloody manna from Heaven. Heaven, Arizona.'

'We continually try to rethink, to reimagine, the past. It's possible that we actually unpick our destinies, change the situation. Look at all the books: *Fatherland, When Adolf Came, SS/GB, The Man in the High Castle, The Sound of His Horn.* We can wish it otherwise, and otherwise it could very well become . . .'

Frankham looked at his empty glass.

'Another drinkie, sir?' asked the barman.

Frankham ordered one and sprung for another for the airman. He was out of coupons but they knew him at the Troy. The barman could get anything, rationed or not, if slipped a little folded green.

'Think it'll ever end?' the airman asked. 'The War?'

'What War?' Frankham asked, missing something.

The airman didn't answer, just drank. The Troy shuddered, framed pictures of Churchill and the Princesses rattling on the walls. A distant thunder shook the windows. A blind rolled up with a snap, and a voice from below shouted: 'Put that light out.'

To judge from the streaks of angry red in the three o'clock skies, fires had spread. Narrow winding Hanway Street was unaffected by the actual bombardment, but the air was tangy with traces of smoke, the gutters heavy with the run-off from nearby fire-hoses.

Frankham and the airman, whose name was Somerton, had left the Boffin and the Blimp to their fractured conversation in the Club and ventured out in search of a livelier place. Somerton suggested a dancehall Frankham had already written up and written off. Since he was in a ginnily generous mood, he acceded. Who knows, the hole might be looking up. Everything comes around again eventually.

In the sky, dark shapes wheeled and swooped. Somerton looked up, almost with longing. There was a distorted burst of fire and a patter of spent shell-cases sounded a dozen yards away. After a fire-burst, something with a comet-tail of flame plunged downwards.

'Score one for some lucky blighter,' Somerton said.

Oxford Street was still barred to vehicle traffic, but gangs of soot-faced rubble-shifters were swarming over an extensive spill of debris. The fires were dying down and workmen were rooting through for hapless bods who might be trapped. A few disgraceful souls were getting in a spot of Christmas looting, pulling prizes – video recorders, television sets, gramophones – out of the wreckage.

Most wore gas masks and were fast on their feet, no matter how weighted-down they were.

The plane, with swastika markings, had come down in the fountain at the base of Centrepoint. Its bent black fuselage was propped in the steaming shallow waters, hot chunks of wing-metal spread down into Charing Cross Road.

'A bogey,' spat Somerton. 'Messerschmitt.'

Frankham's head was hurting. Behind his skull, things were shifting. He needed more gins. Or fewer.

A souvenir stall opposite Centrepoint was squashed flat by a sheared-off aeroplane wheel. Union Jack bunting was turned to muddied scraps, and Cellophane-wrapped ARP helmets and beef-eater models congealed into crinkling pools of melted plastic. A pair of Japanese tourists – enemy axis aliens – snapped photographs of the stall from every angle, and were apprehended by a couple of constables. Frankham supposed they would be shot as spies.

Somerton wanted a look at the smashed plane. It was some new design, incorporating aerodynamic advances the Air Ministry was not yet aware of. In the empty cockpit, a bank of computer consoles shorted and sparked. The pilot must have hit the silk and come down somewhere nearby.

From the direction of Holborn came the sharp crack of gunfire. Rifle-shots. Then, a burst of machine-gun. Men in uniform trousers and braces broke away from the rescue gangs and seized weapons from a jeep stalled by Claude Gill's.

Somerton crouched down, hauling Frankham out of the line of fire. At a run, Storm troopers charged down New Oxford Street and were greeted by accurate fire. Pinned down between the Tommies entrenched in the Virgin Megastore and an armed police-man who had been hiding in the entrance to Forbidden Planet, the Nazis were cut up properly. They hooted and heiled as bullets hit home.

The air was thick with flying lead. Frankham felt a stab in his upper arm and a hot damp seeping inside his jacket-sleeve.

'Rats,' he said, 'I've been shot.'

'So you have,' Somerton commented.

It was over swiftly. When the last goose-stepping goon was halted, knocked to his knees by a head-shot, some of the civvies gave out a cheer. In the open air, it sounded like the farting response in 'Der Führer's Face'. Only the enemy seemed to have sustained casualties.

Frankham tried to get up and became awkwardly aware of the numbness in his upper chest.

'After you, Claude,' he said to Somerton, waving at the airman to stand.

'No,' said Somerton, helping Frankham up, 'after you, Cecil.'

A Red Cross nurse came over and had a look at him. Her hair was pinned up under her cap. Frankham took a deep breath and it didn't hurt too much. The nurse poked a finger into the blackened dot-like hole in his gabardine, and felt through his jacket and shirt.

'Just a graze, sweetheart,' he said.

'Keep smiling through,' she told him, and left. He glimpsed, in a shop window, a row of civilian casualties by Top Man, all with neatly-bloodied bandages around their heads.

'Proper little angel,' Somerton commented.

'Sometimes, I think it's harder on the women,' Frankham said. 'Yet they complain so little.'

Enough rubble had been shifted to let tanks into Oxford Street. Three of them had been held in reserve near Marble Arch and now they rumbled placidly towards the downed Messerschmitt. Frankham and Somerton gave the Victory-V sign as they passed, and a tank officer, bundled up in thick jumpers, returned the gesture.

'Makes a feller proud,' Somerton said. 'To see everyone doing their bit.'

He woke up with a fearful gin head in some chippie's single bed. He remembered a name – Dottie – and the dancehall, and vaguely supposed he was as far out as Camden or Islington. His arm was stiff and cold, and there was a shifting and uncomfortable girl next to him, face smeared with last night's make-up.

He didn't know what had happened to Somerton or to the girl – Hettie? – he had been dancing with.

Frankham rolled off the bed and hauled himself upright. Dottie – or was this Hettie? – was instantly relieved and filled out the space under the sheet, settling in for more sleep.

He dressed one-handed and managed everything but his cuff-links. The hole in his arm was a scabby red mark. He guessed there was still a lump of bullet inside him.

Outside, he didn't recognize the street. Half the buildings in the immediate area had been bombed out, either last night or within the last month. One completely demolished site was flooded, a small reservoir in the city. The neat piles of fallen masonry were mainly bleached white as bones.

As he walked, his head hurt more and more. Around him, early-morning people busied themselves, whistling cheerfully as they worked, restoring recent damage. There weren't many cars about, but a lot of people were nipping between the craters on bicycles.

There was a tube station nearby, the Angel. It was a part-time shelter, but the trains were running again. A policeman at the entrance was checking papers. Many of the bombed-out were being reassigned to vacant housing.

As he went down the escalator into the depths, Frankham passed framed advertisements for Ovaltine, a Googie Withers film, Lipton's Tea, powdered eggs, Bovril. Every third advertisement showed the Old Man giving the V-sign, with a balloon inviting tourists to share the 'Blitz Experience'.

Suddenly, halfway down the escalator, Frankham had to sit, a shudder of cold pain wrenching his wounded arm. Passers-by stepped delicately around him, and the moving steps nudged him out at the bottom. He found a place to sit, and tried to will the throbbing in his forehead away.

A little girl with curls stepped into his field of vision. Her mother, with a calf-length swirl of skirts and precious nylons, tugged disapprovingly.

'Don't play with the poor man, dear.'

The little girl dumped something in his lap and was pulled away. Frankham looked down at the canvas-covered lump and, with his good hand, undid the bundle. A gas mask tumbled out. He lifted it up to his face and, fumbling with the straps, fitted it on, inhaling the smell of rubber and cotton. Somehow the pain was eased. He drew up his knees and hugged them.

It wouldn't be over by Christmas, Frankham knew. But that didn't matter. London could take it.

DRUG SQUAD SMEECHED MY HOOVER
Lawrence Norfolk

Returning home south of the River from one of his shady northern forays, choking blue Hoover-smeech greets Jerry, my friend and ex-pool partner: the drug squad has paid him a visit.

'Eric!'

Eric: Jerry's flatmate, my ex-schoolmate, and the least likely person to deal with this bad situation. At 8.33 p.m. three men, one woman, one dog, pile in the door, march up and pin Eric to the wall, telling him, 'All right, son, you know what we're here for . . .' and Eric shakes his head. He's in tonight to do some home cooking – rock-cakes.

'Home cooking?' Detective Sergeant Eriksson shakes his head.

'Rock-cakes?' Detective Constable Green tuts. WPC Schneider eyeballs Eric and draws on a pair of black leather gloves.

'Let me talk to him alone, sir . . .' The dog is hopping about and whining.

'Rock-cakes!' shouts uniformed Constable Milligan from the kitchen. 'Gou urth'g jk too, mmnth!'

DS Eriksson prods Eric in the chest. 'Don't kid yourself you're kidding us, kid,' he warns his suspect. 'No rock-cakes cuts the mustard with the drug squad.' The dog takes a shit. Why is any of this happening?

Some months before, not London, somewhere else . . .

A dark blue Morris Marina is flogging down the M4 when eagle-eyed traffic police notice a defective tail-light. They flag the vehicle down, but the driver accelerates away, one hand on the wheel, the other reaching for the polythene bags lying on the back seat which fly out the window, bursting and sending clouds of white powder over the Queen's highway. Mobile unit cops view this activity with suspicion and give chase.

Now the identity of the driver must remain a secret and I'm not completely sure about this, but I think he was someone I used to go camping with when I was twelve. He wore very thick spectacles

and was quite shy. We cooked sausages and argued about the
camping stove he brought. I felt we should build a proper fire.

Meanwhile . . .
    'Mmmth, pretty good rock-cakes, Eldritch.'
    'Eric.'
    'Eric, right. Boys?' DS Eriksson offers the plate.
    'Two minutes alone with him sir . . .' WPC Schneider is buck-
ling on, well, they look like spurs.

And waving off the choking smoke, Jerry makes phone calls to
Jester's Snooker Centre, the Prince Albert, Wig's answerphone, the
Warwick Castle and Janet.
    'What the hell's going on?' Janet wants to know. 'How should I
know where he is? If this is about that six-hundred . . .'
    Their respective benefit scams are in obscure competition due to
a joint tenancy taken out a year back. This isn't why Jerry's calling.
    'Look, Janet . . .,' he says. Janet hangs up.

Orange Land Rovers catch my possible one-time camping partner
somewhere after junction ten. Video-shot from the helicopter captures their perfect boxing manœuvre. The Marina stops. Hesitant
unarmed police approach from left and right. Opaque clouds of
white powder well up inside and press against the windows. Cops
peer in. Helicopter chops the air above, heavy rotors piling on the
down draught. Coke clouds settle down and down until the officers
are small boys with their noses pressed against the glass of the
draining fish tank. Rover the goldfish gasps his last. The car is
empty. The driver's disappeared and the cops have only each other.
I imagine their conversation went something like this:
    'Weirdness afflicts this scene too hugely,' says Motorway Cop
One.
    'Relevant Spaniards will be informed,' mutters his partner. 'No
one gets away with this and gets away with it.'

So now the drug squad is unscrewing Jerry's light sockets and
searching through his complete set of the Arden Shakespeare. Eric is
a hapless bystander. All his rock-cakes have been eaten. DC Green's
stomach growls.

'Hey Eldritch!' shouts DS Eriksson. 'How about some more of those rock-cakes?'

'Eric,' says Eric. 'They've all gone.' WPC Schneider jabs him playfully in the groin. DC Green moves fatefully to the airing cupboard watched by the dog which sneezes, then staggers out to the balcony for a piss.

It's winter and Bermondsey is beautiful tonight . . . and Bermondsey is beautiful tonight. A hundred identical balconies overlook the urban verdure below. Spaceship Brane is grounded on its launch pad; sodium lights mark junctions all about this darkly storied tower. The stars are too far away; possibly we need a bridge of light-years to cross the void.

On the subject of our pool-playing, I remember this: a fine cut off the top cushion to double the black the length of the table. A touch of running side to dodge the kiss, the black running down the angle, the white running clear, myself pulling back. The black drops and my work is done. Why is Jerry looking up the table?

The carpets are up, wires are hanging out the wall, the smoke is acrid stuff. Jerry coughs. 'Eric?' Rock-cake crumbs are strewn about the place and the smoke is pouring from the airing cupboard. Jerry opens the door. I recall the white being dragged across the nap in a flat curve. Choking smoke billows out. The white hangs, then drops. I've lost. Jerry sees a burning dwarf draped in folds of molten plastic, some minor domestic deity that used to be his Hoover.

'Disappeared?'

'Vanished.' The duty sergeant eyes them over the roster.

'Marina, you say?'

'Dark blue. Registration X . . .' The sergeant is already dialling. He knows just the man for the job.

'Yes. Eriksson. E-R-I-K- . . .'

Eric and DC Green stand with PC Milligan watching other X-registered cars troll around the estate below.

'So many criminals out there,' he tells them. 'You wouldn't believe it.' Eric nods.

WPC Schneider strokes him gently with her truncheon.

Detective Sergeant Eriksson's profile appears behind them.

'I have high hopes,' he declares. 'Sorry Eldritch, I'm afraid we're going to have to take you in for questioning.' Eric nods again and the dog pukes horribly over the balcony.

'What about the dog?' Eric asks WPC Schneider as she slips on the handcuffs.

'I feel sort of weird,' says PC Milligan. 'Can you smell burning?'

'It's not our dog,' says Schneider.

After a while I stopped playing pool with Jerry. You have to win once in a while, it's pointless otherwise. I was wrong about the camping, the dog just disappeared and of course the dope was in the Hoover all the time. Sometimes I imagine myself being old and looking back on all this. My bewildered grandchildren are gathered at my feet as I tell them: 'This was back in the eighties, mind you, when London and the drug squad were forces to be reckoned with. Back then your grandad could sink a straight black from anywhere on the table. And when it rained the gutters ran with poison. Great days. Great days.'

NEWMAN PASSAGE or J. MACLAREN-ROSS AND THE CASE OF THE VANISHING WRITERS

Christopher Petit

When I first came to London twenty years ago and didn't know anyone, I haunted cheap movie-houses that were soon to vanish — the cartoon cinema in Victoria Station, the Tolmers, the Metropole, the predominantly homosexual Biograph in Wilton Road, Classics, Jaceys; these were not selective days — and, almost unconsciously, as something to do on Sundays, I started to track down London film locations: a sinister park near Charlton Athletic football ground from *Blow-Up*; a crescent house and a riverside apartment in *The Passenger*; the house on the corner of Powis Square in *Performance*; the Covent Garden pub and Coburg Hotel in *Frenzy*. I would visit these places and feel a little less anonymous, a little more specific, and by patiently stitching them together I made my own map of the city, a limited (and superstitious) one, albeit with more meaning than the official ones I consulted in my negotiations by tube and bus, later by car. Other sites were added to this patchwork. Hilldrop Crescent. Evering Road. The sites of the Whitechapel murders. Rillington Place. Goslett Yard. The Magdala Tavern. The Greenwich Observatory from Conrad's *The Secret Agent*. Other scenes of crimes were added until fact and fiction blurred into myth. The most significant borderline between the two became Newman Passage, known but not discovered properly until seeing the opening of Michael Powell's film *Peeping Tom*, with its sex murder in that alley.

Newman Passage is not a portal, like the archway into Soho in Manette Street, but a partly roofed, narrow alley-way with a hidden dog-leg, out of sight of either end. The lack of clear sight-lines, and the alley's crooked cul-de-sac, are responsible for its sinister reputation and history of sexual assignations. It is the perfect movie location for a murder: Michael Powell noted that it gives you gooseflesh just to look at it and claimed an association with Jack the Ripper (unlikely). According to the wartime writer, Julian Maclaren-Ross, it was known as Jekyll and Hyde Alley and the hidden part of the alley contained a warehouse yard, 'piled high with cardboard boxes into which one sometimes guided girls in order to become better acquainted'.

Newman Passage is the secret heart of a district which, until the end of the Second World War or thereabouts, belonged to Soho: a Bohemian annex, known variously as Fitzrovia and North Soho. Charlotte Street, running north, was its spine, and most of the area's best-known pubs and restaurants were grouped around its bottom end. It was in one of these pubs – the Fitzroy, to be precise – that I first heard of Maclaren-Ross. An old sot buttonholed me (he'd seen me coming) and scrounged gin and orange in exchange for all the famous dead drunks and Soho names he'd kicked about with. Someone else I met ran across him in the early sixties, near the end of his life, in a Turkish bath up around Russell Square. He also told me some of Anthony Powell's novels were based on Maclaren-Ross, but I wasn't interested then in England's dreary past, the war and all that: my life was all future. But somewhere in the back of my mind the ghost of his failure – the shadow lines of my own impending failures – implanted itself and the template of his London imposed itself on my own. I found myself seeking out pubs named by him, without really realizing it (as if guided): the Black Horse in Rathbone Place where a former proprietor had done himself in with three days of purposeful drinking; the Duke of York, former haunt of bums and beatniks; and the Marquess of Granby, where one summer evening a man had been killed in a fight outside while a crowd stood and watched.

Dylan Thomas, drinking bitter, to Maclaren-Ross, drinking Scotch, in the Café Royal: 'Fucking dandy. Flourishing that stick. Why don't you try to look more sordid? Sordidness, boy, that's the thing.' In an age of uniforms and wartime austerity, Maclaren-Ross wore a white corduroy jacket, a large teddy-bear coat in winter, and dark glasses whatever the weather. The gold-topped cane was often in pawn. He belonged to what the Irish writer Anthony Cronin called a 'ruined generation' of artists, ruined because: 'The conditions, the very nature of success and non-success had been altered by public calamity', victims of the saloon-bar life that did for more of them than the war itself. He was usually to be found in the Wheatsheaf with its leaded windows and tartan decoration, at his self-appointed place at the corner of the bar, from which he had usurped a Central European sports writer. As his writing career dwindled in the fifties, his daily routine was increasingly fixed by opening and closing times, and by freelance reviewing's short-term deadlines. A washed-up Maclaren-Ross boasting that he had once been as famous as 'All these Wains and Amises', and complaining that with wartime paper shortages they didn't get as much publicity or do as well financially.

According to one witness, he was in the Wheatsheaf from noon until afternoon closing, followed by roast beef (extra horseradish) at the Scala restaurant, then to the Charing Cross Road for second-hand books and his American cigarettes (Royalty, 'jumbo-size'), then back to the Wheatsheaf for evening opening until ten-thirty closing, and down to the Highlander in Dean Street, which shut half an hour later. Supper and coffee were taken at the Scala, followed by the last tube from Goodge Street. At night he wrote – less writing, in fact, than writing up material that had been rehearsed *ad nauseam* by day in the pub, while holding court, stories that were later transcribed into that strange hand of his that looked like typing, each letter carefully separate. It is a stickler's hand, neat and obsessive, yet curiously unformed, distinctive but without flow, as though the writer were trying to avoid giving too much away (the writing a poison pen might adopt).

Maclaren-Ross in full flight, brooking no interruption, most polished of bar bores, prodigious memory, unimpaired by drink, long after the rest of the assembled company had collapsed.

The narrow topographical boundaries of his life make the slide into obscurity easy to follow, up to a point. He acquired little of the usual baggage that defines people. His addresses were numerous – cheap hotels and rented accommodation. His first marriage lasted only a handful of months. Much later, there was a second wife and even a child (seen pushed around Soho in a pram by the proud father), though that didn't last either. I tried once to trace the son in the London phone book. His mother, I heard, was later linked to Charles Wrey Gardiner, poet and publisher of Grey Walls press, author of anonymous memoirs: *The Answer to Life is No*. Neither lead came to anything. Too much is still left unrecorded. There are too many half-clues, odd names, dead ends, strange disappearances, loose connections and obscurities, like the name C. K. Jaeger, first found easily enough in Alan Ross's introduction to Maclaren-Ross's posthumously published *Memoirs of the Forties*. It was Jaeger's teddy-bear overcoat that Maclaren-Ross wore in winter. Jaeger was a writer too, who'd had, and lost, money when the two of them first knew each other in Bognor Regis in the thirties. At that stage, Jaeger was ahead in the writing game, with reviews printed in the *Evening Standard* and some work on film scripts. They knocked about together selling vacuum cleaners, then looked after other people's gardens until a mowing accident put them in court. We know from Maclaren-Ross that Jaeger had a novel, *Angels on Horseback*, published by Routledge in 1940. There were a number of other novels, now completely forgotten. During the war the two men seem to have drifted apart.

Maclaren-Ross's war was spent partly in the film business with Dylan Thomas, working for a documentary unit until it folded. He believed movies, besides paying well, were the coming medium and that the novel was in retreat. His last publisher, Alan Ross, thought he had what ought to have been a commercial and original talent for films. Yet all that can be traced is some work for Norman Collins at the BBC, a shared writing credit on a daft Canadian co-production called *The Naked Heart*, an adaptation of a romantic novel with a weird list of fellow screenwriters that included C. K. Jaeger (resurfaced); Hugh Mills who was to write *Prudence and the Pill*; and, God knows why, Roger Vadim. The only person I've found with any memory of the film told me the producer was a notorious non-payer and later did a bunk, so it was likely that Maclaren-Ross never collected his fee. There is no mention of *The Naked Heart* in his memoirs (understandably; it is dire). His only other credit was an equally forgotten 1958 B thriller, *The Strange Awakening*.

His enthusiasm for cinema was gargantuan: whole scenes were committed to memory for future recitation. He favoured lugubrious heavies like Sydney Greenstreet, Edward Cianelli and Boris Karloff. According to Anthony Carson, author of a fictional character based on him, Maclaren-Ross saw himself as a sort of frightful celluloid gangster, and geared his appearance to look as sinister as possible. I've seen only one photograph: a BBC still from a television interview done shortly before he died, which shows him as he would have wished, looking gangsterish in dark aviator glasses. There is a resemblance to the actor George Sanders of whom

Maclaren-Ross wrote in praise, admiring the way he imposed blackmail terms, genially, over a gnawed carcass of chicken. Sanders played the sort of villains Maclaren-Ross mimicked, though in private both were insecure. I can see Sanders dying Maclaren-Ross's death by heart attack while worrying about the next piece of work, and vice versa: suicide in a hotel room, with a simple note of dismissal saying that he was bored with the world.

For Anthony Cronin, Maclaren-Ross was first and foremost an actor and possessed an actor's ability to sidestep reality by inventing alternatives. This much is illustrated by an account of a trip to a cinema by the writer Dan Davin, with Maclaren-Ross and the artist, lush and scrounger Nina Hamnett ('Any mun, dearie?'). They trekked off to Chelsea to see Ray Milland in *The Lost Weekend*, not the best choice of film under the circumstances, given their dependence on drink. Davin was thoroughly shaken afterwards and Hamnett had to be given rum before feeling strong enough for the journey back to Rathbone Place and the Wheatsheaf. But Maclaren-Ross, instead of identifying with the alcoholic writer, simply spent the rest of the night impersonating the film's male nurse in the alcoholic ward of the hospital, and: 'Recalling with ever-increasing vividness and pleasure the imaginary mouse which had terrified the alcoholic's delirium'.

Because the career is such a performance, one is invited to see in it the ghosts of other writers' lives. Maclaren-Ross was drawn to those who transcend disgrace and failure or acquire their reputation thanks to some vanishing trick. He had a soft spot too for mysterious biographies hidden behind aliases, such as his fascination over the real identity of the mysterious Cameron McCabe, author of *The Face on the Cutting Room Floor* (1937), a 'brilliant, off-beat detective story' set in the film world, that Maclaren-Ross ascribed to Cyril Connolly and told him so. It was in fact written by a refugee from the Nazis called Ernest Bornemann, later a jazz critic for *Melody Maker*. The review in *Punch* of *The Face on the Cutting Room Floor* – 'No "straight" novel published this month has the literary qualities of this crime story' – is signed Ross Maclaren.

It was Anthony Carson (himself the subject of a Maclaren-Ross essay) who pointed out the physical resemblance to Oscar Wilde, and another source, albeit unreliable and known as the Mad Whore

of Goodge Street, thought he was homosexual. There is no circum-
stantial evidence to make the theory stand up (quite the contrary:
his reputation was for womanizing), but it would make sense: the
secret life, the staying on in Soho, that sexual free-zone at a time
when homosexuality was still outlawed. The point about Maclaren-
Ross is that he encouraged speculation, slipping in and out of a
gallery of roles that included, according to Cronin, 'The Edwardian
masher, the public school man turned door-to-door carpet-seller,
the Riviera playboy, the sex maniac on Brighton pier, the genius
spurned by Wardour Street, even the disdainful literary man, keeping editors at bay'.

If Wilde was the public model, Graham Greene was the private
one – enigmatic, given to vanishing (autobiography: *Ways of
Escape*), perhaps an impostor (fascination for Kim Philby, regarded
success as delayed failure). The two men met once, in 1938, for
lunch at Greene's Clapham home. Maclaren-Ross's account permits
a rare glimpse of the domestic, family man avoided by Greene in
his own memoirs, a role soon to be jettisoned. He was to dump the
family, get away (and, in terms of literary posterity, get away with
it), as Maclaren-Ross's opening image suggests: 'One day in 1956 I
was walking home with a friend who lived off Clapham Common,
when, pointing to a gutted ruin with a façade of blackened brick,
he said: "That used to be a Queen Anne house before the blitz.
Beautiful place I believe. It belonged to Graham Greene." "I
know," I said. "I lunched there once. In 1938", and my friend was
suitably impressed.'

Greene at the time was still only in his mid-thirties, though, seen
here established in the comfortable routines of early middle-age, he
seems older: the silent, elegant Queen Anne home, the domestic
help, the smoothly run household. Greene's own account of struggle,
debt, depression in the period just prior to this differs from
Maclaren-Ross's unruffled picture of a man enviably placed, with
his talk of travel, his discreet, silent wife and racy libel cases. The
unstated and rather moving point of Maclaren-Ross's portrait of the
successful writer is that it was one that he – eight years Greene's
junior – wanted, and anticipated, for himself, but was never to
acquire.

The afternoon ends with Greene dispensing writerly advice to
the aspiring author (and laying down a very false trail) by airily

announcing that he intends in future to stick to writing about home ground, London preferably. 'Oh, I know I've broken the rules several times. But all the same I think an English novelist should write about England, don't you?' It was advice that Maclaren-Ross was to follow, to his detriment, and Greene to disregard, to advantage. Greene's bags were already packed. He left for Mexico, which led to *The Power and the Glory*, and never read Maclaren-Ross's stories as he'd promised. They were returned by Vivien Greene with a note saying her husband was too exhausted. Later in life, Greene would claim that his novels were his children. As for his actual daughter and son, Maclaren-Ross's glimpse of them must be one of the few references in print.

Greene's ability to put distance between himself and the matter in hand was a trait that Maclaren-Ross envied but failed to emulate. Too much of his career was spent getting bogged down. Unlike Greene, he never got away. The war saw him stuck in England (ingloriously; he failed to gain a commission; was discharged for reasons that were never clear). He wrote a bit about army life and the London low life. As Davin observed, he had knocked about a bit, and his first story, about the seduction of a teenage girl, indicates his share of *louche* experience. After the war, there seemed less to write about: with the lights on again, the camaraderie and furtive enjoyment of London's blacked-out nights were lost. Whether from indolence, or from a misreading of the signs, Maclaren-Ross stayed on, a man increasingly trapped in a time zone. The anachronistic mannerisms – sartorial and verbal – became the uniform of a man still on active duty in the front line of Bohemia, long after the rest had died or gone home and settled down. His essay, 'Fitzrovian Nights', says it all: half a dozen pages, perfect in their way, about the thinness and the lure of life as a pub-crawl.

The simplest explanation for his failure is that he fell victim to what was jocularly called Soho-itis, a kind of doldrums leading to a complete inability to get on with anything. To all intents, he had three good years (three!), between 1944 and 1947, when he published half his work, five books – three volumes of short stories and two novels, *Bitten by the Tarantula* and *Of Love and Hunger*, based on his days as a door-to-door salesman.

Dan Davin draws the line at 1955, a hard year for Maclaren-

Ross and in some ways fatal to his talent, and Anthony Powell, who knew him, suggests in *Books Do Furnish a Room* that he got dragged down by a hopeless affair ('– "It's when you have her. She wants it all the time, yet doesn't want it. She goes rigid like a corpse. Every grind's a nightmare." –') which led to the malicious destruction of the manuscript and only copy of a novel he had spent two years on. Powell also refers to what he calls an American-style crack-up, which raises the spirit of the writer whose decline most closely shadows Maclaren-Ross's. Though never famous in the way that Scott Fitzgerald was, his career, if Powell's theory of crack-up is accepted, shares a similar trajectory: early promise, a sense of style – both to the life and to the work – drink, unsuccessful dabbling in films, nervous collapse, financial desperation and eclipse. The pattern of addiction, bankruptcy and breakdown can in both cases be seen as routes of withdrawal into sterile, self-protective, private states, negative versions of the creative privacy on which all writers need to draw in order to write.

The thesis argued by Fitzgerald in *The Crack-Up* is simple and profound: that life has a varying offensive; perhaps the fault is that people are not very good at reading the signs. In Fitzgerald's case, what he thought of as a period of recuperation – retreating from the world to take stock – was the belly of the breakdown ('not an unhappy time'). This took the form of making an inventory of his life, listing possessions, emotional attachments, insults. These lists recall Maclaren-Ross's lists of novels planned but never written that Rayner Heppenstall found so tragic: 'I gazed at these manifestations of sinful pride and marvelled at the purity of the man's ambition and resolve.' But isn't it just as possible to read the opposite into them: to see in them a grand self-delusion, evidence of a literary Crowhurst, forging the route of his own career?

In Maclaren-Ross's deterioration, paranoia played an increasing part. There were days when, with no change to his appearance and invariably in places where he was a regular, he insisted on being addressed as Mr Hyde. Avoiding his many creditors contributed to these Pimpernel fantasies, which, on a deeper level, hid from others the horror of his failure. What glimpses there are of him later on are hopeless and desperate: nights on benches on the Embankment; a ghastly period holed up in Wembley as the unwelcome guest of the Cronins, suffering by then from mild agoraphobia, and 'rasping

away loudly and endlessly at obscure enemies, discovering everywhere plots against his interests'. Maclaren-Ross's hostage host is
also witness to obsessive and barmy fascination for a woman named
Selena that was being dramatized into a film treatment which owed
a large debt to Cocteau's *Orphée*. Maclaren-Ross was given to
consulting the Bible at random, claiming that this way he could
divine Selena's secret thoughts towards him.

Fitzgerald's image of himself in crack-up was of: 'Standing at
twilight on a deserted range, with an empty rifle in my hand and
the targets down'. Coincidence places Maclaren-Ross's in a similar
location for the single most dramatic moment of his life. A bullet
struck his steel helmet while he was in the butts. It was carried in his
pocket afterwards as a lucky charm (not to any great effect, one
might add). Perhaps all writers are superstitious, wrote Greene once,
vaguely, somewhere.

He managed to salvage something of his literary reputation, too late
to enjoy it, with the publication after his death of *Memoirs of the
Forties*, a last revenge on all the doubters, a final triumph (in the
nick of time) that mocked his own death, in keeping with his
admiration for Houdini-like escape acts of all descriptions: 'Hendrik
de Jong, known as the "Top-Hatted Slayer" . . . married his victims
and then bashed their faces in with his bare fists. De Jong . . .
disappeared without a trace while all the ports were watched and
the police patrolled the streets: he was never seen again.'

Similar characters, men who are not what they seem and often
operating under aliases, flit through Maclaren-Ross's pages and are
held up for approval. Many of them, real and imagined, are
forgotten now. Maclaren-Ross's fiction has not lasted and most of
the characters he encountered, apart from Greene and Dylan
Thomas, are little more than literary footnotes. Strangest of all is
the case of G.S. Marlowe, author of *I Am Your Brother* (1935), a once
cultish thriller about a schizophrenic young composer whose repul-
sive mother reminded Maclaren-Ross of one of his landladies.
'snuffling about the Soho markets in search of offal on which to
nourish her other, perhaps imaginary son: a monster product of,
maybe, artificial insemination'. Maclaren-Ross, who was not averse
to importuning successful writers, wrote to Marlowe suggesting
that the story would make an excellent radio serial. This tactic, tried

on Greene too, was not ultimately very successful because, by his own admission, it took Maclaren-Ross twenty more years to break into radio.

Marlowe, whom Maclaren-Ross had imagined being suave and English, turned out to be a bear of a man with a strong foreign accent, confident at dropping names and impressively set up in a plush Kensington flat, which conformed to the standards to which Maclaren-Ross thought every writer should aspire. There was talk of a career in Hollywood, a meeting with Garbo, and a script that he'd written of *David Copperfield*. (Reference works list a single credit on the film, to Sir Hugh Walpole, though Marlowe's claim may not be entirely bogus: Walpole's name, and talk of organizing 'a little dinner party' for Maclaren-Ross to meet him, are mentioned in conversation.) Maclaren-Ross's generous assessment of Marlowe is strangely at odds with the sinister details otherwise noted: curtains drawn against daylight; the plying of whisky; the soporific central heating; the odd stroking of Maclaren-Ross's coat and Marlowe's announcement that he wished he had a coat like it.

At a subsequent meeting, Marlowe is discovered in even more opulent Edgar Wallace-like surroundings with 'dictaphones, telephones and typewriters, [and] a brand new secretary even better-looking than the last'. Marlowe on this occasion plays the harassed, successful writer, up against deadlines. The role is played with consummate skill until an altercation with a laundry man makes Maclaren-Ross realize that Marlowe is as broke as himself. Marlowe announces that he is off abroad to finish his play in peace. This was not altogether as easy as it sounded because by then Britain was at war. His choice of country as somewhere likely to be left in peace by the Nazis showed little political nous: he plumped for Norway. Whether he simply did a bunk Maclaren-Ross never discovered, though in a postscript to the story he met a man years later who claimed to have had a drink in some village with Marlowe, who was alive, though written off as dead by many including his publisher and executors, and enjoying his last laugh.

Maclaren-Ross would be equally obscure today were it not for the myth that he invented for himself. He is his greatest fiction and his life was raided by others for their novels, most notably Anthony Powell, who turned him into X. Trapnel. Even C. K. Jaeger had a go in *The Man in the Top Hat* (1949): '– "I am a writer. I cannot be bribed." ' The proud and preposterous, even tragic, role he invented for himself paid off in the long run – the one decided by posterity. It turned out to be his best work.

A SHORT HISTORY OF THE ENGLISH NOVEL
Will Self

'The sun shone down on nothing new' – Beckett

'All crap,' said Gerard through a mouthful of hamburger, 'utter shite – and the worst thing is that we're aware of it, we know what's going on. Really, I think, it's the cultural complement to the decline of the economy in the seventies coming lolloping along behind.'

We were sitting in Joe Allen's and Gerard was holding forth on the sad state of the English novel. This was all I had to pay for our monthly lunch together: listening to Gerard sound off.

I came back at him. 'I'm not sure I agree with you on this one, Gerard. Isn't that a perennial gripe, something that comes up time and again? Surely we won't be able to judge the literature of this decade for another thirty or forty years?'

'You're bound to say that, being a woman.'

'I'm sorry?'

'Well, in so much as the novel was very much a feminine form in the first place and now that our literary culture has begun to fragment, the partisan concerns of minorities are again taking precedence. There isn't really an "English novel" now, there are just women's novels, black novels, gay novels.'

I tuned him out. He was too annoying to listen to. Round about us the lunch-time crowd was thinning. A few advertising and city types sipped their wine and Perrier, nodding over each other's shoulders at the autographed photos that studded the restaurant's walls, as if they were saluting dear old friends.

Gerard and I had been doing these monthly lunches at Joe Allen's for about a year. Ours was an odd friendship. For a while he'd been married to a friend of mine but it had been a duff exercise in emotional surgery, both hearts rejecting the other. They hadn't had any children. Some of our mutual acquaintances suspected they were gay, and that the marriage was one of convenience, a coming-together to avoid coming out.

Gerard was also a plump, good-looking man, who despite his stress-filled urban existence, still retained the burnish of a country childhood in the pink glow of his cheeks and the chestnut hanks of his thick fringe.

Gerard did something in publishing. That was what accounted for his willingness to pronounce on the current state of English fiction. It wasn't anything editorial or high-profile. Rather, when he talked to me of his work – which he did only infrequently – it was of books as so many units, trafficked hither and thither with as little sentiment as if they were boxes of washing-powder. And when he spoke of authors, he managed somehow to reduce them to the status of assembly-line workers, trampish little automata who were merely bolting the next lump of text on to an endlessly unrolling narrative product.

'. . . Spry old women's sex novels, Welsh novels, the Glasgow Hard Man School, the ex-colonial guilt novel – both perpetrator and victim version . . .' He was still droning on.

'What are you driving at, Gerard?'

'Oh, come on, you're not going to play devil's advocate on this one, are you? You don't believe in the centrality of the literary tradition in this country any more than I do, now do you?'

'S'pose not.'

'You probably buy two or three of the big prize-winning novels every year and then possibly, just possibly, get round to reading one of them a year or so later. As for anything else, you might skim some thrillers that have been made into TV dramas – or vice versa, or scan something issue-based, or nibble at a plot that hinges on an unusual sexual position, the blurb for which happens to have caught your eye . . .'

'. . . But Gerard,' despite myself I was rising to it, 'just because we don't read that much, aren't absorbed in it, it doesn't mean that important literary production isn't going on . . .'

'Not that old chestnut!' he snorted, 'I suppose you're going to tell me next that there may be thousands of unbelievably good manuscripts rotting away in attic rooms, only missing out on publication because of the diffidence of their authors, or the formulaic, sales-driven narrow-mindedness of publishers, eh?'

'No, Gerard, I wasn't going to argue that . . .'

'. . . It's like the old joke about LA, that there aren't any waiters in the whole town, just movie stars "resting". I suppose all these busboys and girls,' he flicked a hand towards the epicene character who had been ministering to us our meal, 'are great novelists hanging out to get more material.'

'No, that's not what I meant.'

'Excuse me?' It was the waiter, a lanky blond who had been dangling in mid-distance. 'Did you want anything else?'

'No, no,' Gerard started shaking his head – but then broke off, 'actually, now that you're here would you mind if I asked you a question?'

'Oh Gerard,' I groaned, 'leave the poor boy alone.'

'No, not at all, anything to be of service,' he was bending down towards us, service inscribed all over his soft-skinned face.

'Tell me then, are you happy working here or do you harbour any other ambition?' Gerard put the question as straight as he could but his plump mouth was twisted with irony.

The waiter thought for a while. I observed his flat fingers, nails bitten to the quick and his thin nose coped with blue veins at the nostrils' flare. His hair was tied back in a pony-tail and fastened with a thick rubber band.

'Do you mind?' he said at length, pulling half-out one of the free chairs.

'No, no,' I replied, 'of course not.' He sat down and instantly we all became intimates, our three brows forming a tight triangle over the cruets. The waiter put up his hands vertically, holding them like parentheses into which he would insert qualifying words.

'Well,' a self-deprecatory cough, 'it's not that I mind working here – because I don't, but I write a little and I suppose I would like to be published some day.'

I wanted to hoot, to crow, to snort derision, but contented myself with a 'Ha!'

'Now come on, wait a minute,' Gerard was adding his bracketing hands to the manual quorum, 'OK, this guy is a writer but who's to say what he's doing is good, or original?'

'Gerard! You're being rude . . .'

'. . . No, really, it doesn't matter, I don't mind. He's got a point,' his secret out, the waiter was more self-possessed, 'I write – that's true. I think the ideas are good. I think the prose is good. But I can't tell if it hangs together.'

'Well, tell us a bit about it. If you can, quote some from memory.' I lit a cigarette and tilted back in my chair.

'It's complex. We know that Eric Gill was something more than an ordinary sexual experimenter. According to his own journal he even had sex with his dog. I'm writing a narrative from the point of view of Gill's dog. The book is called *Fanny Gill*, or *I was Eric Gill's Canine Lover*.' Gerard and I were giggling before he'd finished; and the waiter smiled with us.

'That's very funny,' I said, 'I especially like the play on . . .'

'. . . *Fanny Hill*, yeah. Well, I've tried to style it like an eighteenth-century picaresque narrative. You know, with the dog growing up in the country, being introduced to the Gill household by a canine pander. Her loss of virginity and so on.'

'Can you give us a little gobbet then?' asked Gerard. He was still smiling but no longer ironically. The waiter sat back and struck a pose. With his scraped-back hair and long face, he reminded me of some Regency actor–manager.

Then one night, as I turned and tossed in my basket, the yeasty smell of biscuit and the matted ordure in my coat blanketing my prone form, I became aware of a draught of turpentine, mixed with the lavender of the night air.

My master, the artist and stone-carver, stood over me.

'Come Fanny,' he called, slapping his square-cut hands against his smock, 'there's a good little doggie.' I trotted after him, out into the darkness. He strode ahead, whilst I meandered in his wake, twisting in the smelly skeins betwixt owl pellet and fox stool. 'Come on now!' He was sharp and imperious. A tunnel of light opened up in the darkness. 'Come in!' he snapped again, and I obeyed – poor beast – unaware that I had just taken my last stroll as an innocent dog.

Later, when Gerard had paid the bill and we were walking up Bow Street towards Long Acre, for no reason that I could think of I took Gerard's arm. I'd never touched him before. His body was surprisingly firm, but tinged with dampness like a thick carpet in an old house. I said, trying to purge the triumph from my tone, 'That was really rather good – now wasn't it?'

'Humph! S'pose so, but it was a "gay" novel, not in the mainstream of any literary tradition.'

'How can you say that?' I was incredulous. 'There was nothing obviously gay about it!'

'Really, Geraldine. The idea of using the dog as a sexual object was an allegory for the love that dare not speak its name, only whuffle. Anyway, he himself – the waiter, that is – was an obvious poof.'

We walked on in silence for a while. It was one of those flat, cold London days. The steely air wavered over the bonnets of cars, as if they were some kind of automotive mirage, ready to dissolve into a tarmac desert.

We normally parted at the mouth of the short road that leads to Covent Garden Piazza. I would stand, watching Gerard's retreating overcoat as he moved past the fire-eaters, the jugglers, the stand-up comedians; and on across the parade-ground of flag-stones with its manœuvering battalions of Benelux au pair girls. But on this occasion I wouldn't let him go.

'Do you have to get back to the office? Is there actually anything pressing for you to do?' He seemed startled and turning to present the oblong sincerity of his face to me, he almost wrenched my arm.

'Erm . . . well, no. S'pose not.'

'How about a coffee then?'

'Oh, all right.'

I was sure he had meant this admission to sound cool, unconcerned, but it had come out as pathetic. Despite all his confident, wordy pronouncements, I was beginning to suspect that Gerard's work might be as meaningless as my own.

As we strolled still coupled down Long Acre, the commercial day was pushing towards its postprandial lack of swing. The opulent stores with their displays of flash goods, belied what was really going on.

'The recession's really starting to bite,' Gerard remarked, handing a ten-pence piece to a dosser who sat scrunched up behind a baffler of milk crates, as if he were a photographer of feelings at life's event.

'Tell me about it, mate.' The words leaked from the gaps in the dosser's teeth, trickled through the stubble of his chin and flowed across the pavement carrying their barge-load of hopelessness.

The two of us paused again in front of the Hippodrome.

'Well,' said Gerard, 'where shall we have our coffee, then? Do you want to go to my club?'

'God no! Come on, let's go somewhere a little youthful.'

'You lead – I'll follow.'

We passed the Crystal Rooms, where tense loss adjusters rocked on the saddles of the stranded motorcycles, which they powered on through virtual curve after virtual curve.

At the mouth of Gerrard Street, we passed under the triumphal arch with its coiled and burnished dragons. Around us the Chinese skipped and altercated, as scrutable as ever. Set beside their scooterish bodies, adolescent and wind-cheating, Gerard appeared more than ever to be some Scobie or Brown, lost for ever in the grimy Greeneland of inner London.

Outside the Bar Italia a circle of pari-cropped heads were deliberating over glasses of *caffè e latte* held at hammy angles.

'Oh,' said Gerard, 'the Bar Italia. I haven't been here in ages, what fun.' He pushed ahead of me into the tiled burrow of the café. Behind the grunting Gaggia a dumpy woman with a hennaed brow puffed and pulled. '*Due espressi!*' Gerard trilled in cod-Italian tones, '*Doppi!*'

'I didn't know you spoke Italian,' I said as we scraped back two stools from underneath the giant video screen swathing the back of the café.

'Oh well, you know . . .' He trailed off and gazed up as the flat tummy filling the hissing screen rotated in a figure-eight of oozing congress. A special-effect lipoma swelled in its navel and then inflated into the face of a warbling androgyne.

A swarthy young woman, with a prominent mole on her upper lip, came over and banged two espressos down on the ledge we were sitting against.

'Oh really!' Gerard exclaimed: coffee now spotted his shirt-front like a dalmatian's belly. 'Can't you take a little more care?' The waitress looked at him hard, jaw and brow shaking with anger, as if some prisoners of consciousness were attempting to jack-hammer their escape from her skull. She hiccupped despair, then ran the length of the café and out into the street, sobbing loudly.

'What did I say?' Gerard appealed to the café at large. The group of flat-capped Italian men by the cake display had left off haggling over their pools coupons to stare. The hennaed woman squeezed out from behind the Gaggia and clumped down to where we sat. She started to paw at Gerard's chest with a filthy wodge of J-Cloths.

'I so sorry sir, so sorry . . .'

'. . . Whoa! Hold on – you're making it worse!'

'Iss not her fault you know, she's a good girl, ve-ery good girl. She have a big sadness this days . . .'

'Man-trouble I'll be bound.' Gerard smirked. It looked like he was enjoying his grubby embrocation.

'No iss not that . . . iss, 'ow you say, a re-jection?'

I sat up straighter. 'A rejection? What sort of rejection?' The woman left off rubbing Gerard and turned to me. 'She give this thing, this book to some peoples, they no like . . .'

'Ha, ha! You don't say. My dear Gerard,' I punched him on the upper arm, 'it looks like we have another scrivenous servitor on our hands.'

'This is absurd.' He wasn't amused.

'My friend here is a publisher, he might be able to help your girl, why don't you ask her to join us?'

'Oh really, Geraldine, can't you let this lie. We don't know anything about this girl's book. Madam . . .'

But she was already gone, stomping back down the mirrored alley and out the door into the street, where I saw her place a soft arm round the heaving shoulders of our former waitress.

Gerard and I sat in silence. I scrutinized him again. In this surrounding he appeared fogeyish. He seemed aware of it too, his eyes flicking nervously from the carnal cubs swimming on the ethereal video screen, to their kittenish domesticated cousins, the jail-bait who picked their nails and split their ends all along the coffee bar's counter.

The waitress came back down towards us. She was a striking young woman. Dark but not Neapolitan, with a low brow, short bobbed hair and deep-set, rather steely eyes that skated away from mine when I tried to meet them.

'Yes? The boss said you wanted to talk to me – look, I'm sorry about the spillage, OK?' She didn't sound sorry. Her anger had evaporated, leaving behind a tidal mark of saline bitterness.

'No, no, it's not that. Here, sit down with us for a minute.' I

proffered my pack of cigarettes; she refused with a coltish head jerk.
'Apparently you're a writer of sorts?'

'Not "of sorts". I'm a writer, full stop.'

'Well then,' Gerard chipped in, 'what's the problem with selling
your book? Is it a novel?'

'Ye-es. Someone accepted it provisionally, but they want to
make all sorts of stupid cuts. I won't stand for it, so now they want
to break the contract.'

'Is it your first novel?' asked Gerard.

'The first I've tried to sell – or should I say', "sell out" – not the
first I've written.'

'And what's the novel about, can you tell us?'

'Look,' she was emphatic, eyes at last meeting mine. 'I've been
working here for over a year, doing long hours of mindless skivvy-
ing so that I have the mental energy left over for my writing. I
don't need some pair of smoothies to come along and patronize
me.'

"OK, OK.' For some reason Gerard had turned emollient, placatory. 'If you don't want to talk about it, don't, but we are
genuinely interested.' This seemed to work: she took a deep breath,
accepted one of my cigarettes and lit it with a *fatale*'s flourish.

'All right, I'll tell you. It's set in the future. An old hospital
administrator is looking back over her life. In her youth she worked
for one of a series of hospitals that were set around the ring road of
an English provincial town. These had grown up over the years
from being small cottage hospitals serving local areas, to become
the huge separate departments – psychiatry, oncology, obstetrics –
of one great regional facility.

'One day a meeting is held of all the region's administrators, at
which it is realized that the town is almost completely encircled by
a giant doughnut of health facilities. At my heroine's instigation
policies are fomented for using this reified cordon sanitaire as a
means of filtering out undesirables who want to enter the town and
controlling those who already live in it. Periods of enforced hospitali-
zation are introduced; trouble-makers are subjected to "mandatory
injury". Gradually the administrators carry out a slow but silent *coup*
against central as well as local government.

'In her description of all these events and the part she has played in them, my heroine surveys the whole panorama of such a herstory. From the shifting meaning of hygiene as an ideology – not just a taboo, to the changing gender-roles in this bizarre oligopoly . . .'

'. . . That's brilliant!' I couldn't help breaking in, 'that's one of the most succinct and clearly realized satirical ideas I've heard in a long time.'

'This is not a satire!' she screamed at me, 'That's what these stupid publishers think. I have written this book in the grand tradition of the nineteenth-century English novel. I aim to unite dramatically the formation of individual character to the process of social change. Just because I've cast the plot in the form of an allegory and set it in the future, it has to be regarded as a satire!'

'Sticky bitch.' This from Gerard, some time later as we stood on the corner of Old Compton Street. Across the road in the window of the catering supplier's, dummy waiters stood, their arms rigidly crooked, their plastic features permanently distorted into an attitude of receptivity, preparedness to receive orders for second helpings of inertia.

'Come off it, Gerard. The plot sounded good – more than good, great even. And what could be more central to the English literary tradition? She said so herself.'

'Oh yeah, I have nothing but sympathy for her sometime publishers, I know just what her type of author is like to deal with. Full of themselves, of their bloody idealism, of their fernickety obsession with detail, in a word: precious. No, two words: precious and pretentious.

'Anyway I must get . . .' but he bit off his get-out clause; someone sitting in the window of Wheeler's – diagonally across the street from us – had caught his eye. '. . . Oh shit! There's Andersen. The MD. Trust him to be having a bloody late lunch. I'll have to say hallo to him, or else he'll think that I feel guilty about not being at the office.'

'Oh I see, negative paranoia.'

'Nothing of the sort. Anyway, I'll give you a ring, old girl . . .'

'Not so fast, Gerard, I'll come and wait for you. I want to say goodbye properly.'

'Please yourself.' He shrugged in the copula of our linked arms.

I stood just inside the entrance while Gerard went and fawned over his boss. I was losing my respect for him by the second. Andersen was a middle-aged stuffed suit with a purple balloon of a head. His companion was similar. Gerard adopted the half-crouch posture of an inferior who hasn't been asked to join a table. I couldn't hear what he was saying. Andersen's companion gestured for the bill, using that universal hand signal of squiggling with an imaginary pen on the sheet of the air.

The waiter, a saturnine type who had been lingering by a half-open serving hatch in the oaken mid-ground of the restaurant, came hustling over to the table, almost running. Before he reached the table he was already shouting:

'What are trying to do? Take the piss!'

'I just want the bill,' said Andersen's companion, 'what on earth's the matter with you?'

'You're taking the piss!' the waiter went on. He was thin and nervy, more like a semiologist than a servant. 'You know that I'm really a writer, not a waiter at all. That's why you did that writing gesture in the air. You heard me talking, talking frankly and honestly to some of the other customers, so you decided to make fun of me, to deride me, to put me down!' He turned to address the whole room. The fuddled faces of a few lingering lunchers swung lazily round, their slack mouths O-ing.

'I know who you are!' the waiter's rapier finger pointed at Andersen's companion, 'Mister bloody Hargreaves. Mister big fat fucking publisher! I know you as well, Andersen! You're just two amongst a whole school of ignorami, of basking dugongs who think they know what makes a jolly fucking good read. Ha!' Gerard was backing away from the epicentre of this breakdown in restraint, backing towards me, trying to make himself small and insignificant. 'Let's get the hell out of here,' he said over his shoulder. The waiter had found some uneaten seafood on a plate and was starting to chuck it around, *flotch!* A bivalve slapped against the flock wallpaper, *gletch!* A squiggle of calamari wrapped around a lamp-bracket.

'I'll give you notes from underwater! I'll give you a bloody lobster quadrille . . .' he was doing something unspeakable with the remains of a sea bream, '. . . this is the *fin* of your fucking *siècle!*' He was still ranting as we backed out into the street.

'Jesus Christ.' Gerard had turned pale; he seemed winded. He leant up against the dirty frontage of a porn vendor. 'That was awful, awful.' He shook his head.

'I don't know, I thought there was real vigour there. Reminded me of Henry Miller or the young Donleavy.' Gerard didn't seem to hear me.

'Well, I can't go back to the office now, not after that.'

'Why not?'

'I should have done something, I should have intervened. That man was insane.'

'Gerard, he was just another frustrated writer. It seems the town is full of them.'

'I don't want to go back, I feel jinxed. Tell you what, let's go to my club and have a snifter, would you mind?' I glanced at my watch: it was almost four-thirty.

'No, that's OK, I don't have to clock on for another hour.'

As we walked down Shaftesbury Avenue and turned into Haymarket the afternoon air began to thicken about us, condensing into an almost palpable miasma that blanked out the upper stories of the buildings. The rush-hour traffic was building up around us, Homo Sierra, Homo Astra, Homo Daihatsu, and all the other doomsday subspecies, locking the city into their devolutionary steel chain. Tenebrous people thronged the pavements, pacing out their stay in this pedestrian purgatory.

By the time we reached the imposing neoclassical edifice of Gerard's club in Pall Mall, I was ready for more than a snifter.

In the club's great glass-roofed atrium, ancient bishops scuttled to and fro like land crabs. Along the wall, free-standing notice-boards covered in green baize were hung with thick curling ribbons of teletext news. Here and there a bishop stood, arthritic claw firmly clamped to the test score.

I had to lead Gerard up the broad red-carpeted stairs and drop him into a leather armchair, he was still so sunk in shock. I went off to find a steward. A voice came from behind a tall door that stood ajar at the end of the gallery. Before I could hear anything I caught sight of a strip of nylon jacket, black trouser-leg and sandy hair. It was the steward and he was saying, '. . . of course *Poor Fellow My Country* is the longest novel in the English language, and a damn good novel it is too, right?' The meaningless interrogative swoop in pitch, an Australian: 'I'm not trying to do what Xavier Herbert did. What I'm trying to do is invigorate this whole tired tradition, yank it up by the ears. On the surface this is just another vast *Bildungsroman* about a Perth boy who comes to find fame and fortune in London, but underneath that . . .'

I didn't wait for more. I footed quietly back along the carpet to where Gerard sat and began to pull him to his feet.

'Whoa! What're you doing?'

'Come on, Gerard, we don't want to stay here . . .'

'Why?'

'I'll explain later – now come on.'

As we paced up St James's Street I told him about the steward.

'You're having me on, it just isn't possible.'

'Believe me, Gerard, you were about to meet yet another attend-ant author. This one was a bit of a dead end, so I thought you could give him a miss.'

'So the gag isn't a gag?' He shook his big head and his thick fringe swished like a heavy drape against his brow.

'No, it isn't a gag, Gerard. Now let's stroll for a while, until it's time for me to go to work.'

We recrossed Piccadilly and plunged into fine-art land. We wandered about for a bit, staring through window after window at gallery girl after gallery girl, each one more of a hot-house flower than the last.

Eventually we turned the corner of Hay Hill and there we were, on Dover Street, almost opposite the jobcentre that specializes in catering staff. What a coincidence. Gerard was oblivious as we moved towards the knot of dispirited men and women who stood in front. These were the dregs of the profession, the casual waiters who pick up a shift here and a shift there on a daily basis. This particular bunch were the failures' failures. The ones who hadn't got an evening shift and were now kicking their heels, having a communal complain before bussing off to the 'burbs.

Stupid Gerard, he knocked against one shoulder, caromed off another.

'Oi! Watch your step, mate, can't you look out where you're going?'

'I'm awfully sorry.'

'"Aim offly sorry",' they cruelly parodied his posh accent.

I freed my arm from his and walked on, letting him fall away from me like the first stage of a rocket. He dropped into an ocean of Babel.

Terrified Gerard, looking from face to face. Old, young, black, white. Their uniform lapels poking out from their overcoat collars; their aprons dangling from beneath the hems of their macs. They sized him up, assessed him. Would he make good copy?

One of them, young and lean, grabbed him by the arm, detaining him. 'Think we're of no account, eh? Just a bunch of waiters – is that what you think?' Gerard tried to speak but couldn't. His lips were tightly compressed, a red line cancelling out his expression. 'Perhaps you think we should be proud of our work. Well, we are, matey, we fucking are. We've been watching your kind, noting it all down, putting it in our order pads while you snort in your trough. It may be fragmentary, it may not be prettified, it may not be in the Grand Tradition, but let me tell you,' and with this the young man hit Gerard, quite lightly but in the face, 'it's ours, and we're about ready to publish!'

Then they all waded in.

I was late for work. Marcel, the *maître d'*, tut-tutted as I swung open the door of the staff entrance. 'That's the third time late this week, Geraldine. Hurry up now and change – we need to lay up.' He minced off down the corridor. I did as he said without rancour. Le Caprice may no longer be the best restaurant in London to eat at, but it's a great place to work. If you're a waiter, that is.

NOTHING BUT BONFIRES
Adam Thorpe

'Was it always Shakespeare, Mr Curran?'

I replied in the affirmative.

She took down a quill from the mantelpiece and handed it to me. She had extremely long fingers and nails that were not blunt. I felt the nail of her index finger scrape the inside plumpish part of my own. I held the quill and, for some reason, grunted in amusement, though I think her gesture was absolutely serious. Quills have an obscure relation, in my mind (I now realize), to roll-top desks and thus to the pornographic contents of my father's; though my father never had a quill, nor anything resembling one – not even a fountain pen. It was always biros with my father, the kind that blot.

I turned the quill over in my hands and began to run its plume between my fingers, ceasing this action when I saw that I was ruffling it out of its serried regularity. The nib, I noted, had been idly cut, yet was darkened with use. I decided to smile knowingly with several small nods of the head. I have always found this action to be useful in this sort of situation, when one has no idea of a suitable response. The reaction was rather surprising.

'Gordon, it goes without saying, would rather you kept it, Mr Curran –'

'Kept it?'

'I was going to say, "to yourself", but your eagerness defeated me. That's what comes of a grammar-school education, I am told. A kind of *gauche* eagerness that betrays.'

I was momentarily torn between annoyance at my origins being so contemptuously flushed out (I choose my words carefully – my face was evidentially on fire), and a desire to know whether 'betrays' referred to something more than the original act. Before I could make my reactions known in more than a facial manner, she took the quill from me and held it in front of her:

'Immortal bard, from this pen you flowed. What rivers of blessings poured!'

She said this somewhat automatically, and replaced the quill on the mantelpiece without further ado. Pouring out more tea, she eyed my perplexed demeanour with something of a headmistress's air. Certainly, she reminded me forcefully at this point of Mrs Parkinson, though without the beard of course. I felt as I did once when attempting to cross a dried stream-bed in my fell-walking days, before the accident: every step encountered the irregular instabilities of water-smoothed pebbles. I sipped my tea far too loudly and wondered if I had made an error, wishing to join. Membership naturally assumed a scrupulous ability to keep things secret, one trait I had not (or so I assumed) been vetted for. I had always been a notorious gossip, most particularly in my bank years. But they were long past, I reassured myself. Even Elinor's complaint had been safe in my hands.

'Is the implication,' I began in my firmer tone, though unable to stop myself blinking repeatedly, like one of those old-fashioned motion picture cameras my uncle would entertain the troops with (this is a tic I have since been able to conquer, let me say) — 'is the implication that the quill belonged, actually belonged, to the Shakespeare family?'

For some reason I could not bring myself to say 'Will'. It was not just the humorous rhyme. It was the absurdity of the very idea — his quill unceremoniously dumped on a mantelpiece! I awaited the answer with some trepidation and slightly twitching hands, the teaspoon thus sliding off my saucer in the interim, and making a frightful clatter on the table. I did not retrieve it, despite the small globule of tea it had spilt on the polished surface which I was certain had not been treated against spillage. My hostess gazed fixedly at the spoon, and answered in the affirmative. Then she rose and went to the window.

Drawing aside the stained net curtains, she gazed down at the London traffic. The odd bark of a horn rose up over the rumble, reminding us of the hurly-burly of the streets at this hour. I was certain she would expand, but she continued to gaze down in silence as the astonishing information settled itself on my thoughts as snow upon a stove — for I refused to believe it. Yes, I refused outright and felt like saying so. I stood up, replaced the teaspoon in the saucer, took out my handkerchief and wiped away the globule (peculiarly stricken by the sight of its pale, unerasable ghost on the mahogany) and took a step towards her.

'From whom does this information derive?' I asked, rather assertively I suppose. My heart beat wildly, for she was more than ever like Mrs Parkinson, standing there at the long window, gazing down upon the traffic. Mrs Parkinson had several times taken it upon herself to beat me, alarmingly. My fingers are still stiffer than they ought to be from her notorious raps, and I cannot (however hard I try) rue the day she stepped into a store's open lift-shaft during a blackout, while wishing to grope her way down. Thus enmity is scored deep into the innocent soul, and will no doubt be paid for in the aftermath.

The image of Mrs Parkinson's sprawled and broken body floated briefly before me. Then I saw that my hostess had turned to face us, her form a shapely silhouette against the bright light of the window. Don had not moved from his stool, but it certainly creaked in the corner. Before she could reply to my carefully modulated question, the door at the far end burst open and half a dozen police constables entered, evidently at a point they considered interesting, and my hostess was thrown backwards through the glass, the net curtains billowing wildly where her form had been, tearing themselves upon the jagged edges. The burst of automatic gunfire was still ringing in my ears when I rose from my crouched position and saw myself in the full-length mirror, a pitiable sight, pale and trembling as in the poem. Don was still upon his stool, but from the state of his stomach I knew that he would not be with us much longer. Smoke billowed through the door as the police constables, having shouldered their enormous weaponry, helped themselves to the brown sugar with licked forefingers – as I once did with a similar bowl during a gathering of my mother's yobbish colleagues, being struck for it on the base of the spine (that alone might explain my headaches, were it not for the other and more serious incident).

Nothing of the sort happened, of course! The thought of Mrs Parkinson's violent end had erupted into strange forms that momentarily clouded my vision, and, shaking off the mirage of the constables with some difficulty, I smiled at our hostess, encouraging her to explain. She placed her hands together as in that painting and glanced at Don.

'Does he snuffle?' she asked.

Caught off-guard, I could only reply in the affirmative. 'Don't they all?' I added, which seemed to amuse her.

'They have no nose to speak of. They were bred in boxes too small for them. Or is that chihuahuas?'

She approached me and laid her hand upon my chest, as if to marvel at the heart and its wild antics. Then she looked into my eyes (which were unfortunately and uncontrollably blinking very rapidly once more), and intoned very softly:

'We are Will. We are nothing but Will. We are the cradle for his legacy. We are the wicker basket for his eggs. We are in a speeding car turning a corner when the door flies open and we fall out with the basket. We save the eggs and we do not protect ourselves. The quill is Will's. I hope you realize the table was not treated. Our first meeting is on Monday. At six-thirty. Please be there. *Measure for Measure*. Angelo. Good day, Mr Curran. Give the stool a blow. They get in my throat.'

Don and myself departed.

How it always blows a cold drizzle in London when one is striving to be courteous to the world! I heard the door to the apartment building close behind me and the large knocker bounce with a sharp report before I had engaged with Don's lead and my umbrella, and situated as I was once more in the public arena (let us say I was standing on the pavement), I was jostled several times during my struggle, and I eventually cursed at a low-browed old dame who scuttled away in tears, hauling her ridiculous provender. The street was a sea of umbrellas, most positioned too low, so that for a tall fellow such as myself there was a very real danger of having my throat sliced by the passing barbs. Omnibuses and those foul green taxis shattered whatever calm I still possessed by throwing the gutter's contents over us in glassy sheets, so that by the time I had my articles sorted out I was soaked and shivering, and I crossed the street with far too much haste, considering I had Don to think of. It was pure chance (God rarely comes into it) that a bus's indicator, suddenly popping out by my left ear as I negotiated a jam, did not enter my temple and finish me forthwith.

My rooms were but a five-minute stride from my late hostess, and I prolonged the return by entering a tobacconist's and making much play with the choice of a pipe. I had always fancied smoking one, just as I had always fancied owning an ironmonger's store, but neither fancy had ever borne fruit. The tobacconist was a greasy-faced fellow in white gloves, and his shop gave off an air of spent luxury with its mahogany cabinets and sweetly suffocating perfumes of wax polish and tobacco. A lady with enormous feathers in her hat was shrieking at him about some political mishap or other (she was, he has told me since, a grand niece of Mr Bonar Law) and Don began to grow jittery, forcing me out once more into the chill surrounds without that imagined stem firm between my dentures. I was suffused with a glowing excitement that I could only put down to my recent encounter, and the prospect of at last joining the most select if secretive club in the metropolis, whose legendary status was without parallel amongst the resisting hordes. Glancing up at the sky before I entered my home, I felt as though borne upon a great river, its grey rollings bearing me I knew not whither, save it was out of disappointment and the dull thump of self-commiseration: being situated above a bank, that last is no idle metaphor.

Imagine how I spent the intervening weekend! I threw myself upon my Shakespeare, I railed and simpered my part, I scanned every line with a light pencil to ensure rhythmic exactitude (I knew already their views on this), I wept at my character's chill perfidy. A breakfast of buttered toast was all my fare on the Saturday, and on the Sunday I dined with great cheer at the corner Lyons, spilling the sauce bottle with a poorly gauged rhetorical gesture, my book propped against the condiments. The whole steamed-up interior rocked and roared with appreciation as I flung myself without a single metrical error through the opening speech, and the waitress, handing me a great mauve mug of freshly brewed tea, said that one was 'on the house'. How those brazen, unconstrained days come back to one in all their goldenness! Only the sinister presence of a bank official I remembered from my clerical years reminded me of my proper existence.

Chipping the mark of former users from the lip of the mug with my nail, I mused on time, and history, and a little on the arts, until the bank official had departed with a low grunt, leaving only the redolence of his uncertain bowels to mar my happiness.

The Monday could not have arrived too early. I dealt with the tea chests brusquely, prompting remarks from my fellow-workers that only fed my eagerness to be finished, to be enclosed by something quite other. Fragments of the immortal lines left my lips and floated in the enormous space beneath the girders, jostling undiscerned with curses and the cacophony of piped accordion bands, the demotic fare of the docks. The sudden tang of wine from a broken vessel deep in the straw of a chest I had split open too severely caused me to rail against the injustice of my lot, until the supervisor silenced me with his baton. Nursing my bruises (he would always strike on the elbows), I limped home through the slush of the sudden chill, flinging from my person the ragamuffins and their scabrous elders as I traversed the bridge, scorching my coat against a chestnut-seller's erubescent brazier, catching my heel in a poorly placed rat trap. Even the tray of the blind muffin-seller could not tempt me that evening: his weeping sockets above the taped lint sought me as they always did, but I darted past like a man possessed (which indeed I was), barely heeding the spittled obscenities he flung after me.

Ushered into the back room as Big Ben struck the half-hour, my skin still glowing from the scrub I had given it in the filthy apartment washroom, I knew at once that I was treading unplumbable depths. I had donned a ruff and garters for the occasion, but the twelve gathered already were clad in cloaks of a most sombre hue, holding them across their faces like spies. I heard the clop of a horse and dray outside (we looked out on to an ignominious back street, its sewage filling the air with its stench) and the bored screech of a street vendor selling oranges, and wished I was anywhere but within. My cream lace ruff stuck out alarmingly, and only the intervention of my hostess saved me from the embarrassment of tears: she ordered us all to sit, and begin.

I have to say that my reading was exemplary: however troubled my proper self, the performer in me triumphed. The copy I was given (we were forbidden to bring our own) was barely legible, so blotted was the ink, but my cues were accurate, and my tone ruthless. At the end, breathless from exertion, I looked up and every eye was upon me.

'A most remarkable showing,' came a voice from within a hood. 'Most remarkable.'

'Quite outstandingly spoke,' said another.

'Welcome,' whispered a third, his ravaged face (no doubt the effect of the bombings) managed a smile. 'I am Gordon.'

They clapped unevenly. I stood and bowed. My hostess opened
her mouth to speak, but at the very moment of my highest award
(that which might have come from her lips) there was a scuffle
beyond the door and the maidservant entered with a jug of brimming ale and thirteen tankards upon a squeaking hospital trolley.

Who cares if I vomited into the river that night, under a gentle
fall of snow?

When the river froze the next day, I was among the first upon
the ice. We slipped and scrambled, Don and I, over the great
gleaming freeze, and not even the hiss of the brazier as it sank, the
terrible cries of the idiot chestnut-seller as he drowned, could stain
my joy.

I was heedless of danger in those days.

Heedless – and thus magnificent in my nefariously double life!
Never mind that that subsequent meeting had me chafing at the
tight bit of Barnardo, or the dull inanities of the Doctor in *King
Lear*, or various servants and retainers whose names are so inconse-
quent they escape me – I delivered each part with the relish that
comes from true adoration, in which (to adapt an otherwise con-
temptible phrase from the 1989 Committee of Regeneration's
Annual Report) the slippage of a single tooth brings the engine to a
halt. I looked upon this period as an apprenticeship of the most
valuable kind, in which personal regard is subsumed beneath a
desire to act in accord with the whole, in which the glances of my
hostess and the twitches of Gordon's mouth were reward enough,
and in which the acres of my personal silence (as the others
bellowed or hissed or ranted through the play) had about them the
beauty and calm of a great plain, broken only by a single tree that
takes upon itself the importance of a landmark. Indeed, on the one
occasion I was given a character who, despite his presence in the
dramatis personae, had no lines whatsoever (I think the vessel was,
alas, *Anthony and Cleopatra*). I said nothing about it beforehand, but
sat, as Gordon's spittle flung itself across the room, with my eyes
firmly shut throughout, proud in my mute perfection, and taking
my hostess's proffered peppermint afterwards with what I can only
describe as a theatrical gesture.

That was, in some ways, my finest hour.

Was it this abject lack of self-regard that spelt our doom? Were we blind to the signs as a muffin-seller is blind to the urchin that steals from his tray? Did I, in some way, become careless in my devotion, once walking to a meeting in the plumed garb of a courtly retainer with only my gabardine as cover? Was that delirious reading in the Lyons corner house the spark that sizzled the long trail through worsening days to the ultimate horror of what happened?

I had not an inkling of it as I stepped between the foul seepages of the shattered sewerage that August evening of, I think, 1992. An omnibus, stranded by the curfew, winked its electric lamp forlornly in the darkness. Smoke from some unrecorded incident stung my throat and, since I was to be the Second Gentleman in *The Winter's Tale*, had me soon sucking on a large pastille bartered for several cuds of tobacco from a syphilitic vendor of medicaments who had dared the guns. Having no lamp, I was wet to my knees in evil-smelling fluids by the time the house of my hostess hove into view, and I spent the first five minutes donning my garb in her hallway. How that stench still brings it all back! My hostess eyed my plain white robe with reckless longing, for I had just related to her its glorious pedigree — how it had indeed been smuggled from the Apollo wardrobe by the stage door as the zealous mobs tore down the plush and ripped up the infamous boards, and how I had acquired it only by careful negotiation in an ill-lit upper room in Eastcheap, flourishing my brass-rubbings.

She massaged the sleeve between her fingers, while her mouth — which only the previous month had been bruising itself upon the part of Desdemona — quivered with unexpressed emotion. Even I, who have not once dared even the stews of Oxford Street, might have laid a kiss upon them, if Gordon had not been re-erecting the hatstand next to us — a particularly low-flying gunship having just shaken it from its screw.

She raised her eyes, that met my own.

'Theatre,' she whispered, kissing the hem. 'The grease of the paint! The dust of the boards! The lights that blind! Oh!'

She let out a moan that had Gordon turning his head as he hammered the antlers back into place with the heel of his stouter shoe (he also being afflicted with a club-foot, as it happened). He cleared his throat demonstratively.

'I'm looking forward very much indeed to your Second Gentleman,' he proffered, with a spasm of his good eyelid.

'Rogero,' I replied, with an immodest haste I can only explicate by reference to my hostess's proximity, and the heady whiff of her perfume.

'Rogero?' Gordon growled, pausing in his work. I noticed that where the hatstand had been hammered back, a crack had appeared in the sallow distemper. This did not strike me at the time as in any way an omen. I waited for the gunship to pass overhead once more, its proximity again threatening to undo Gordon's efforts, sending judders through my bottom teeth, and causing my hostess to glance upwards so anxiously that I had an all but irresistible desire to take her in my arms.

'He has a name,' I said, in the ensuing and rather intense quiet. 'His name is Rogero. He is addressed as such by the First Gentleman, whom I believe Stuart is interpreting tonight.'

Gordon nodded cursorily. There was an ominous pause, the nature of which even my hostess appeared to be aware of, dropping the fold of my garment and bringing her fingers up to my lips, as if to quieten me. But I continued regardless, feeling her sharp nails scrape the base of my nose as I spoke.

Here comes a gentleman that happily knows more. The news, Rogero?

I paused again. Far off, the crackle of automatic weaponry punctuated the otherwise still warmth of a Bloomsbury night. I adopted, all but unconsciously, the posture I had practised for the role of the Second Gentleman, both hands high in the air, right foot forward.

Nothing but bonfires. The oracle is fulfill'd: the King's daughter is found. Such a deal of wonder is broken out within this hour that ballad-makers cannot be able to express it.

I hurried the lines, of course. I was not performing but illustrating. My delivery had little passion to speak of, and took but a few seconds. How strange then, to think of those lines as being the last ever enunciated without the confines of that house – and possibly anywhere in the capital (I cannot speak for the provinces) since the advent of the Great Retainment, its wind-fluttered hills of smouldering paper blocking the omnibuses just weeks after this dreadful episode.

'Thank you,' said Gordon, nevertheless, 'thank you. I fancy that to be a quite remarkable rendition, Rogero.'

We went upstairs to where the others were waiting, nibbling the corners of their manuscripts. Barely had we settled into our wicker chairs and cleared out throats when the door, under our startled gaze, began to splinter. Through a split in the panel we each of us, with a chill of realization, discerned the small steel head of an axe. Yet no one so much as swore. The great white ruffs (I had caused a fashion in my own small way) may have rasped against beards as heads turned, and my robes, suffused with my hostess's floral scent, shuffled their folds as I leant forward to view the phenomenon, but otherwise there was an absolute quiet from us all, even when the instrument of destruction paused – its owner no doubt catching his breath between his florid oaths before the renewed onslaught that was to see us exposed within seconds to the enormous weaponry of the special constables and their mangy but savage dogs.

Alas, that the terrified grip on my thigh was not our hostess's, but the First Gentleman's! And he it was, so it turned out, who had sold us for some insignificant number of guineas and a mere clutch of confiscated long-playing records. (The quill, however, was trampled underfoot and lost in the ransacking, much to his reported disappointment.) Looking back on that episode and its terrible aftermath, I see now that Stuart's performances lacked both conviction and zeal. I had, foolishly, put this down to a certain fear once known as 'fright of the stage'. And so it probably was, but of a different sort from (or is it *to* – I forget these days!) my own.

I had never said anything about his shortcomings, of course. Gordon always gave him parts slightly larger than mine, and any adverse comments would have been regarded as mere rancour, when the truth was very different. The truth, I begin to realize, is always different, as a tree is when viewed even from adjacent angles. And now that I have been rendered permanently mute, like the others (except my hostess, who kept her tongue but lost – Oh, horrible! – her eyes), the calm of my vast plain is undisturbed by so much as a single item of foliage, or the shimmering mirage of such.

NIGHT MOVES

Mark Timlin

I was sitting in a pub in the Elephant and Castle on a cold morning in early January. Early enough so that the Christmas decorations were still up. Not my favourite time of the year. Not my favourite part of the world, and not my favourite pub either. But I was meeting a bloke. An old acquaintance. He had some work for me. He owned an electrical goods warehouse in Lee Green, and he was losing a lot of gear. It was positively flying out of the door, he reckoned. He had a staff of about twenty, and he hadn't got a clue which of them was at it. So he asked if I'd have a nose round. I was meeting him in the boozer because he didn't want anyone to know he was hiring me. The idea was that he'd put me in as a relief driver or something. Working undercover. Not the best job I've ever had, but I needed a new set of tyres for the motor, and needs must. He was late, and I was already starting on my second pint of watery lager. At almost two quid a pint, it wasn't cheap, and I was bored enough to work out how much tread I could get for the money I'd spent.

The place was morning quiet. A couple of geezers in one corner working out the black economy price for a bit of roof work and, sitting at the bar, a big bloke in his early thirties. He was huge across the shoulders, like someone who worked out a lot, wearing a mid-blue suit, white shirt and tie, and knocking back the large Scotches as quickly as the barmaid could fill his glass. He had a familiar look. But a lot of geezers who hung around the Elephant had similar, and I didn't know him.

Anyway, just as the hands of the clock behind the bar reached high noon, the pub door opened, and two more faces came in Both in long navy blue double-breasted overcoats. They were a hard pair, but I'd've been willing to bet the nanny-goats were real cashmere. They looked like they had a couple of stalls down East Street, a resprayed Roller on an N or M plate each, bought on the drip, parked outside the council flats that their brassy missuses kept like little palaces, whilst their hubbies were chasing scrubbers down the Old Kent Road on a Saturday, when the boozers don't shut till two in the morning.

Now one of these two I *did* know. Definitely. His name was Chris Tennyson, and we'd gone to the same grammar school together. Even though it was twenty-five years later, I'd've known him in a minute. Not that I was about to chat about the best years of our lives. I didn't see him as a leading light in the Old Boys' Association, any more than I was.

He didn't see me, sitting where I was, out of the way between a fruit machine and the Rock-Ola. The pair of them just walked over to the ice-cream in the blue suit and Chris put his hand under his coat and dragged out a short-barrelled revolver that looked like a .357 magnum from where I was sitting, and the other geezer let his coat fall open and pulled up a sawn-off pump-action shotgun on a piece of electric cable that was slung over his shoulder. Chris put the barrel of the pistol under the geezer in the blue suit's chin and pulled the trigger, and most of his head splashed across the notice-board where details of the pub's pool, darts and football teams' fixtures, printed on exercise-book paper, were pinned up. Then he stepped back, and the other character pulled the trigger of the pump and blew a great big hole just where the top button of the geezer's mid-blue suit jacket was. Even though the bloke's body was hard, solid and muscular, the shot was so close and so powerful that loops of hot, red blood snaked off his torso and slapped on to the wall behind him, and the front of his suit smoked and burned briefly. This took less time than it takes to tell, and my ears were still ringing from the noise of the gun-shots, and the bar was full of blue smoke and the stink of gunpowder, and worse: the smell of the inside of a human body ripped open and suddenly exposed to the air.

Then it was all over. The bloke in the blue suit had been blown clean off his stool by the shotgun blast, and landed in an untidy heap on the carpet. Chris and his mate started backing towards the main door, keeping the guns they were carrying moving in slow arcs across the empty air in front of them. The barmaid, who I couldn't help noticing had got some of the geezer in the blue suit's brain on the front of her jumper, started screaming. A relentless sound like a car alarm going in the middle of the night, with no one taking a blind bit of notice.

As they reached the door, Chris caught sight of me, and that's when I saw recognition in his eyes. Just for a moment, before he put the gun back under his arm, and his mate let the pump drop back under his coat, which he quickly buttoned up. But I knew he'd recognized me, just as I'd recognized him, and I knew it meant trouble. Big trouble.

They pushed through the door, and I stood up from where I was sitting, picked up the glass I'd been using and walked up to the bar. The geezers who'd been doing a bit of business looked at me before they hit the trail to anonymity, leaving just me and the barmaid, who was still screaming, and the corpse of the guy in the blue suit all alone. There was a drying-up cloth on top of the counter and I used it to wipe my fingerprints off the glass. I looked at the barmaid, and she looked at me, and still screaming she reached out her hand towards me. I ignored it. Maybe not the nicest thing I've ever done in my life, and if I hadn't recognized Chris Tennyson, perhaps I'd have acted differently. Maybe I would have answered that keening plea, and taken her hand and comforted her. Instead I started to walk across the carpet towards the door. When I was less than halfway there, a door behind the bar opened and a smallish, moustachioed man in an open-necked shirt, braces and dark grey suit trousers came through. He stopped on the threshold. Christ knows what he thought had happened.

Above the barmaid's racket I said: 'Call the police. And look after her. She's not hurt.' Then I turned and walked the rest of the way towards the door and out into the street. My car was parked around the corner and I went and got in it and drove off.

I parked it again in a twenty-four-hour NCP in Holborn and started hitting the pubs. When the pubs shut, I went to Gerry's club in Dean Street. When that closed, I went round to see Helen at Troy's off Tottenham Court Road, and when she slung me out of there I walked down to the Piano Bar in Brewer Street, where I got into a conversation with a transvestite who was more attractive than most of the women I'd met lately, and stayed there until they finally shut at three-thirty.

I abandoned the car to the four winds and caught a lobster home. I had the driver drop me at the top of my road, and wandered slowly down, checking out the parked motors as I went.

I didn't see anything that struck me as suss in the freezing night air, and I let myself in at the front door of the house and walked up the stairs to my flat on the top floor.

I put the key in the door, opened it and stepped inside. I touched the switch on the wall, and the dim forty-watt bulb I'd put in the centre fixture struggled into life. I hate too much light.

They were sitting waiting for me. Chris Tennyson on the bed, his mate in the armchair. Chris held the .357. His pal, the sawn-off. I froze, still with one hand on the switch, the other on the edge of the door.

Shit, I thought. Why the hell did I have to go into that lousy pub, today of all days?

'You're late,' said Chris conversationally. 'We thought you were never coming. I was just saying you must have gone case with some bird.' He grinned. 'But never mind. You're here now. Come on in, mate. Long time, no see.'

For one split second I thought about turning and running, slamming the door behind me. But I knew the magnum would chop it to pieces and me with it before I got to the top of the stairs. And if the magnum missed, the spread of the shotgun's load would blow a hole in my back big enough to park a car. I'd seen what it had done to the geezer in the pub. So I just stayed where I was.

'Come in and shut the door,' instructed Chris. 'We need to talk.'

I did as I was told, and stood in the middle of the room facing the pair of them. Chris nodded his head, and his mate put the shotgun down next to the chair, got up, and carefully avoiding getting in the line of fire walked round behind me and frisked me through the heavy coat I was wearing against the weather.

'He's clean,' he grunted, and walked back, sat down and picked up the shotgun again.

I was, as a matter of fact. Clean as a whistle. And all of a sudden I wished that I had a little .25 stuck in my sock or somewhere else similar.

'How long has it been?' asked Chris, casually.

I shrugged. 'Years,' I replied. 'I was in 4C, and you were in the sixth form.'

'You've got a good memory.'

I nodded. 'How did you find me?' I asked.

'Easy. You're famous round here.'

'You too, now,' I replied. 'I bet you're on everyone's most
wanted list.'

He smiled easily. But then he always had. 'One of those things,'
he said. 'Except no one but you knows who did it.'

'What about the barmaid, and the other people in the pub?' I
asked.

'They're no problem,' said Chris. 'No problem at all. You're the
only fly in the ointment as far as we're concerned. A very large fly.
A bluebottle, almost.'

I ignored the comment and the veiled threat that went with it.
'What did the geezer do? The geezer you shot.' I asked.

'He owed us money,' said the other face. He had a deep voice.
'He was taking the piss. We couldn't let him do that. We had to
make an example. Otherwise they'd all think they could do it.'

I didn't ask what he owed them money for. Or who he was.
That wasn't my main concern.

'So what happens now?' I asked.

'We've been discussing that,' said Chris. 'All day.'

'And?'

'And, I'm afraid we've come to only one conclusion.'

'What's that then?'

'Well, sad as it may seem, you know who I am. We didn't
expect anyone to be in that boozer who'd recognize either of us. It's
not where we operate normally, see.'

I didn't say a word or move or anything. But I saw.

'Now me,' he went on. 'I'm all for letting sleeping dogs lie. But
Chesney here,' he nodded towards his mate, 'he's of a different
persuasion. He hates loose ends. And unfortunately, Nick, you
come into the loose end category.'

'So?' I said.

'So we're going to have to make sure that you don't let it slip
who I am.'

'I suppose there's no point in me saying I didn't see a thing.'

'No point at all,' said Chris. 'Because.' He shook his head sadly.
'We'd always be wondering if . . .' He paused. 'Say something else
came up concerning you. You might want to do a deal for what
you saw today.'

There was no point in arguing. It was a logical point of view,
after all. 'So what happens now?' I asked.

'Now the three of us take a little ride together. Over Epping way, maybe. What do you say, Chesney?'

'The forest's nice this time of year,' Chesney grunted in reply.

'If we're quick we'll be there before it's properly light,' said Chris. 'And then . . .' He didn't bother finishing the sentence. 'I'm really sorry, mate,' he continued.

And do you know, I sincerely believe that he was.

The three of us went downstairs and out to the street. It was still dark and even colder than when I had come in, if anything. Or perhaps it was just me. Maybe I was anticipating some far-flung corner of an Epping Forest field that would be for ever south London.

'The car's this way,' said Chris, taking my arm and leading me across the pavement. All was silent in the street and I took one last look back up at the window of my flat, and suddenly realized I badly needed to take a piss.

I was just about to mention it. You know how it is – you should always go before you leave home – when all of a sudden the street was lit up as bright as day as a whole bank of searchlights bathed us in their brilliance like a trio of actors taking centre stage. Behind the searchlight's beam I could see the blue flashing lights of maybe half a dozen police vehicles as they started to rotate, and an amplified voice said: 'Armed police. The three of you stand still and raise your arms.'

I couldn't believe it. Not twenty minutes before the street had been clean, and now there were dozens of blue-clad figures moving around behind the lights, and with a roar of its rotors, a police helicopter rose behind the houses on the opposite side of the street and added its Night Sun, thirty million candlepower searchlight, to the beams that transfixed us like insects on a piece of white cardboard.

'You in the middle,' the amplified voice barked. 'Stand still.' That was me. 'You, on his left, move two paces to *your* left. Now.' Chesney did as he was told. 'You on his right, move two paces to *your* right. Now.' Chris obeyed. 'All three of you, on your knees,' the voice continued, 'keeping your hands in the air.'

We all complied. The pavement was hard, cold and gritty through the material of my trousers.

When the three of us were kneeling, the voice went on. 'All three of you lie face down, keeping your hands away from your bodies. Now.'

We all fell forward, breaking the fall with our hands and ended up lying flat out like three fishes on a slab.

When we had done what the voice commanded, I heard the noise of rubber-soled boots on the road, and we were surrounded by armed police officers. They all carried Hechler and Koch automatic weapons, and as I peered up from my uncomfortable position on the freezing pavement I noticed that the guns were all set on full auto with the safety catches off. I just hoped that no one's finger slipped on the trigger.

The three of us were thoroughly searched, and Chris's revolver, Chesney's shotgun, plus a flick-knife and heavy-duty brass knucks which he was also carrying were taken away. Then we were handcuffed and led to three separate cars. I don't know where the other two went, but I ended up at Streatham police station where the custody officer took my watch, cigarettes, lighter, keys, and what money I still had left, from me. I didn't have a belt, braces or shoelaces, but he took the scarf I was wearing, so that I couldn't hang myself with it, and I was put into a holding cell in the basement and left alone. I wasn't charged, or allowed to make a telephone call, or even given a cup of tea, and no one said much. But at least there was a lidless toilet in the cell so that I could finally relieve my aching bladder.

Without my Rolex I couldn't tell how long I'd been there when a uniformed constable and two plain-clothes coppers came to fetch me and take me to an interview room. But it had to have been a couple of hours, if not more.

Once inside the cheerless room, with only a tin desk, fastened to the floor, three chairs and a twin-deck cassette player for furniture, the senior of the two detectives, who introduced himself as DI Graves, gave me my cigarettes and lighter back and sent the constable to get me a cuppa before we settled down with his partner, DS Conroy, for a little chat.

'You're a very lucky man, Sharman,' said Graves, as I took a drag on my third Silk Cut in fifteen minutes, and sipped at the plastic cup of hot water that might have been shown a tea bag in a previous life. 'Very lucky indeed.'

I nodded. 'I wouldn't have given a lot for my chances if you hadn't turned up. How did you know where to find me?' I asked.

'We'll talk about that later. First of all we'd like to talk about the shooting that occurred yesterday morning at the Elephant and Castle.'

'I had nothing to do with that,' I said.

'No one said you did. In fact Christopher Tennyson has made a full statement in which he confesses to the crime and clears you of any involvement. He's told us everything.'

'That's very magnanimous of him, considering I hadn't seen him for twenty-five years until yesterday morning. It was a pure coincidence that I was there at all. Just my bad luck.'

'Which confirms our feelings on the matter,' said Graves. 'You two were at school together, I understand.'

I nodded. 'But don't get all choked up with sentiment. We weren't exactly bosom buddies. I just knew him in passing. That was all. What I'm more interested in is how you knew who I was? I'm not known in that pub. How come you were waiting for me tonight, or this morning, or whatever time it was? Or had you followed them to my place?'

'No. It was you we were looking for. We've had a car outside your place since early last afternoon, waiting for you to get home. When the officers inside the car saw Tennyson and Chesney Himes arrive about two this morning, and they fitted the descriptions we had of the two men who shot and killed Jack O'Connor yesterday, and it looked like they were staying, reinforcements were called. By the time you got home the place was surrounded.'

'I didn't see any sign when I walked down the street.'

'You weren't supposed to. This isn't Amateur Hour, you know.'

'And you waited for me before you went in. How thoughtful.'

'We weren't *entirely* sure that you weren't webbed up with the killing, and we figured that nothing much would happen until you got home. Anyway it's easier to nick bodies in the street than inside a house full of civilians. We knew you'd have to come out sooner or later.'

'Meanwhile they could have topped me inside my flat while you lot were polishing your guns outside.'

'It was a chance we had to take. A calculated risk.'

'Thanks a lot. If the chance ever comes up again, just remember it's my life you're taking a calculated risk with, not half a quid on the favourite at Sandown Park.'

He grinned, but said nothing.

'But how did you know it was me in the pub in the first place?' I asked for the third time.

He clicked his fingers and his oppo gave him a slim, pink file that he'd been holding. Graves put it flat on the table in front of him and opened it. It contained one sheet of thin white paper.

'You were supposed to be meeting someone called Paul Kennedy yesterday morning? About a job he wants you to do?'

I nodded again. 'That's right,' I said.

But how the hell did he know?

'He was late.' Not a question. A statement.

'That's right,' I said again.

'When our first blokes arrived on the scene, a couple of minutes after you left, in answer to the landlord's 999 call, Paul Kennedy rang the pub to apologize for keeping you waiting. One of the officers took the call. Your name rang lots of bells with him. You have a very interesting past.'

'It's had its moments,' I agreed.

'We got your details out of the computer. That's why we were waiting. To talk to you about what you'd seen. We really didn't think that if you were going to be involved in a hit, you'd have someone ring the boozer five minutes after it went down and ask for you by name. But then you never know.' He shrugged. 'Stranger things have happened.'

Another nod. Good for Paul, I thought. He always was a polite bloke. That was half the reason so much stuff was going missing from his warehouse. He cared too much for his fellow man to get ruthless. I definitely owed him one. More than one in fact.

'I'm glad you were there,' I said. 'I wouldn't have given much for my future health if you hadn't been.'

'We try to oblige occasionally,' he replied. 'Despite what you read in the papers. But you really should have stayed where you were, in the pub. Done the right thing. Acted like a good citizen.'

When I didn't say anything in reply, he went on. 'A favour for old times' sake? For an old school friend? It nearly cost you your health.'

'Who said I was doing Tennyson a favour?' I asked.

'Weren't you?'

'No. Not particularly. I just didn't want to get involved.'

He looked at the ceiling. I wondered how many times he'd heard those words before: 'I just didn't want to get involved.'

'We're all involved,' he said. 'In a manner of speaking.'

'You're right,' I said. 'And who was O'Connor? The bloke who was shot?'

'A local boy. Used to be a handy boxer so I'm told. But he fell on hard times. His eyes went. He supported his mother, or tried to. Got into debt with Tennyson and Himes. That's their game by the way. Lending money at exorbitant rates. A right pair of sharks. Anyway, O'Connor couldn't pay the interest on what he'd borrowed, let alone anything off the principal. They shot him as an example to others. One thing's for sure. They won't be missed by the local council estates. They're a couple of pieces of garbage that are well out of the way.'

Until a couple more pieces of garbage pick up the business, I thought, but didn't bother to mention it. 'That's all right, then,' I said instead. 'So I take it you won't be needing me any more today.'

'We'd like a statement before you go if you don't mind,' said Graves, pushing a statement form and leaky ball-point in front of me. 'Otherwise I don't think we'll be needing you at all. Both our friends are trying to outdo each other in the cough stakes. It looks like the whole incident has been cleared up to everyone's satisfaction with the minimum of grief.'

Except to poor old Jack O'Connor and his mum, I thought, as I lit another cigarette, picked up the pen and pulled the statement form in front of me.

TURNING THIRTY
Lisa Tuttle

I walked into the pub off the Gray's Inn Road and saw him slouching at the bar, and it was as if no time had passed.

The pub was one where we'd often met, and which I'd not visited since. I went in there today because I wanted a drink. It wasn't nostalgia or anything; to tell the truth, I'd hardly taken in where I was. The pub just happened to be the one I was passing at the moment I realized I really could not face the tube just then without a little lubricant.

With the end of our affair, we'd ceased to see each other. It wasn't something that had to be arranged: we had never moved in the same circles, and our one mutual acquaintance had moved to America soon after she'd introduced us. About two years after the last goodbye I had seen Nick in Holborn Underground station: I was on the down escalator and he was ascending; I don't think he saw me. The sight of him sent me into such a spin that I actually forgot where I was going.

Now at the sight, so familiar five years ago but not since, of my one and only adulterous lover, I came unanchored in time. I felt a little jolt, as if I'd seen a ghost, and then I shivered as that old sado-masochistic cocktail of lust and anger and loneliness began to spread throughout my system, and I went up to him with a sort of casual, sort of wicked grin, the way I used to, as if we'd planned this meeting and I was pretending we hadn't.

He was exactly the same. Those might have been the same pair of jeans, the same denim jacket, the same Doc Martens he'd been wearing the evening I'd first put my hand on his thigh under the table in the Café Pacifico. It was maybe not quite the same haircut, but definitely the same wire-framed glasses, the same blue eyes, and the same slightly crooked front teeth that showed when he grinned the same loopy grin.

Which he did, hugely, at the sight of me, and I realized he was honestly pleased to see me. He'd never been one to disguise his feelings, unlike every other man I'd ever been with.

'You look wonderful,' he said.

'You look like a refugee from the seventies. Still. And I'll bet they're not even Levi's – Marks and Sparks' own brand, am I right?'

'I was never a slave to designer labels, and, as you can see, success hasn't changed me.'

'You're successful?'

'Meet my backer.' He introduced me to the man he'd been drinking with; despite my hopeful first impression, he wasn't alone. I was about to make my excuses, but the man in the suit beat me to it: cordial smile and nods all around, and he was off. Nick ordered me a whisky and dry ginger and I didn't stop him, although I didn't like the mixture. It was what I'd always drunk with him, and that he still remembered pleased me.

We gave each other cautious, curious looks.

'Well,' he said.

'Your backer?'

'I'm making a film. Didn't you know? There was a piece about me in the *Face*. In April.'

'I must have missed that issue.'

'I did a film for Channel Four. Part of the four-minute film series. *Ratphobia*. Did you see it?'

'No. Sorry. I didn't know. The *TV Times* is another one of those must-reads that I just don't . . . You should have sent me a card.'

'I would have. But you told me once a long time ago never to darken your door again and that included your office mail.'

I didn't know what to say to that because it was true, and he sounded hurt. I was always saying things to hurt and then feeling abashed by my success. An awkward silence fell, for about twenty-three seconds, and then my drink arrived.

'Cheers.'

'Confusion to your enemies.'

I would have to stay at least until I'd finished my drink, and all at once that seemed too long. We had nothing to say to each other; we never had. Back in the days when we were seeing each other, if we weren't making love we were either flirting or fighting; there was nothing else for us, no comfortable middle ground, none of the common interests on which friendships are built. He hadn't the least

understanding of, or interest in, my work, and as for his, well, at
the time when I knew him his film-making aspirations had pro-
gressed no further than production work on a couple of pop videos.
He spent a lot of time talking himself up to various people who
might help his career, and when he talked to me, too often the same
well-practised, self-aggrandizing phrases came rolling out. I hated it.
Not only because I mistrusted people who tried to impress me, but
because I felt he wasn't talking to me at those times, but performing
for an imaginary audience. So I would not admire; I refused to be
impressed. And I did my best (in a phrase of my grandmother's), to
cut him down to size.

Sometimes I didn't even have to try. How could the names he
dropped impress me if I'd never heard them before? I know he
found my ignorance of famous film directors and musical megastars
difficult to credit. But although he was only four years younger
than me, we belonged to different generations, culturally speaking.
I'd stopped paying attention to pop music in about 1978, whereas
Nick still bought singles and read things like the *Face* and *NME*.

'You still working in the same place?' he asked suddenly.

'And still doing the same thing.' I wondered if he remembered
what it was.

'That's good,' he said. 'I guess you're happy?'

'Well, I need the money. It's easier working than finding a
backer.'

'You're not kidding! But really, it's a great project. I've got a
script by – d'you remember that book that came out a few years
ago, the one everyone was talking about, a big novel about –'

I gulped at my drink and felt an unexpected pleasure at the
warm, bubbly kick of it.

Then Nick was excusing himself, ordering another round before
he left and before I could stop him. It occurred to me that I could
slip away while he was in the loo. On the other hand, I wasn't
ready to go home, and I didn't particularly want to go somewhere
else and drink alone. The first drink had mellowed me, but I
wanted more.

As I put my empty glass on the bar I looked up and saw Nick
walking towards me, a sight from the past I never thought I'd see
again. Maybe because we were both married and always met in the
centre of London, well away from both our homes, my most

common image of Nick is of suddenly picking out his figure against a background of strangers in some public place, coming towards me along the Tottenham Court Road, weaving among the tables in a large restaurant, or between the other drinkers in this very pub.

He had one of those long, awkward bodies you often see on adolescents. Even now, past thirty, he looked as if he hadn't quite grown into it. Totally unathletic, of course, with a stooping, hip-slung stance. Watching this once so familiar body come towards me, I was seized with lust.

Lust is, for me, a particularly intense variety of memory. I can't imagine feeling it for a stranger. For someone I've just met I might feel interest or attraction, but not lust – no more lust than love. Nick was the first man for whom I ever felt lust without loving, and even with him it was hardly lust at first sight. I thought him attractive in a kind of young, funky, non-threatening way. My reasons for contemplating sex with him had more to do with my feelings for my husband than for Nick. I was furiously angry with Peter, desperate to right the balance of our dying marriage by taking a lover. When Nick made it obvious he was attracted to me I felt a resurgence of a female power which Peter had all but destroyed in me.

What started out of curiosity, anger, loneliness and revenge became something else after the first kiss. Sex, when we got to it, was explosive, quite unlike anything I'd expected, or experienced, before. It was wonderful and terrible. I'd never had orgasms so violent. Afterwards I hated him for making me feel so intensely, hated him because I wanted him so fiercely and specifically.

Now I began to remember, in a pornographic, filmic rush. Positions we had used in our fierce and frantic couplings those few times we had the opportunity – on the floor, against the wall, in the bath, as well as in the beds. Even more powerful, because I'd always been left wanting more, were memories of our more public embraces, on the street, under bridges or in doorways, when we had no time, or nowhere to go, yet were desperate with desire.

It was just then, in my unusually vulnerable state, that the music began. It came from the jukebox: a plaintive love song first popular about twelve years ago. The summer I fell in love with Peter that song was to be heard on every radio, at every party, from every jukebox in the land. It was no longer in the charts, of course, hadn't been for a long time, but it had remained popular enough for unlucky coincidence to strike, years later: it was the song Nick had chosen as a background to his seduction of me, in this pub, five years ago. He couldn't have failed to notice the effect it had on me, and as I never told him that I associated it with falling in love with someone else, it became from that night 'our song'.

And there it was again. No wonder I forgot what year it was. I realized Nick hadn't gone to the loo at all – he'd been remembering old times and he wanted to see if 'our song' had lasted the years. I hated him and loved him for it. I could no more fight the effects of that song than I could have resisted a massive shot of muscle relaxant. Already weakened by whisky and lust I hadn't a prayer against the power of a sentimental song.

He saw me slumping and put his arm around me. I burst into tears.

'I've missed you too,' he said.

When I stopped shaking he walked me over to the table in the corner farthest from the bar where, in the old days, we'd often spent hours drinking and driving each other crazy. He had seemed determined either to undress me or to get inside my clothes with me, and I had fought him off like a reluctant virgin, my occasional delicious lapses into surrender always broken by the fear of public indecency.

It was like old times. He was just as I'd remembered – I was just as I'd remembered, roused to a pitch of desire I'd nearly forgotten. It was as if we had spent only weeks apart, not years, just as in those days the weeks apart had felt like years.

'Don't.'

'But you like it.'

'I didn't say I didn't like it, just don't.'

'But why?'

'Someone might see.'

'So?'

I struggled without success to trap his hands. 'I'm no exhibitionist. Anyway, you're the movie buff. Didn't you see The Accused?'

He gave a soundless laugh. 'This isn't that kind of bar.'

'And I'm not that kind of girl. Can we talk?'

'We'll only end up fighting.'

'I need another drink; so do you.'

He looked at our empty glasses and sighed. When he got up to go to the bar I followed.

We drank; we flirted; we fought. And all of a sudden the barman was calling time. That couldn't be right. But the clock on the wall said it was, and I looked around and realized we were the only customers left.

We walked all the way down to Holborn tube station, hand in hand, like innocent lovers. The hour and the darkness gave us that freedom. Just before we reached the station he pulled me into a recessed doorway, one that had been overlooked by the homeless sleeping in others. As he kissed me, he slipped his cold hands into my layers of clothing, seeking flesh. I felt a reckless pleasure and did nothing as he eventually managed to bare one breast. I'd barely had time to feel the cold before his hot mouth left mine and closed around the nipple.

Then the heady sensation stopped. 'You're driving me crazy,' he said, low-voiced. 'This is no good. I want to make love to you. Come back with me.'

'To Kent? Your wife won't mind?'

'I'm on expenses. We can get a hotel room. I said I might have to stay overnight . . . In fact, I do; I've missed the last train.'

All our lovemaking had been in dark corners or in cheap hotels. We'd only spent the whole night together twice. I'd planned and chosen nights Peter was away, but Nick had had to call home, once from a pay phone in a station, once from the hotel room. I remembered how much I had hated those phone calls, which I'd tried not to hear. Did he say 'I love you' before he said goodbye? Afterwards, when he'd said it to me, I'd hit him. That had been the next to last time we'd seen each other.

All those old feelings were still there, as volatile and immediate as the touch of his lips. I wanted sex with him, violent and annihilating, but I couldn't deal with the emotions of before and after.

'I can't,' I said abruptly, pushing him off, fixing my clothes. 'I haven't missed my train and I'm not going to.' I began walking towards the station.

'I'm sorry,' he said humbly. Although we'd both been married, both, therefore, equally guilty, I'd reserved the role of the innocent. Of course, the husband I betrayed had already betrayed me, but I didn't tell Nick that. From his readiness to shoulder all the guilt I guessed that I was not the first woman his wife might have cause to hate. This, of course, added to the anger I felt at him and at faithless men everywhere.

'If you knew how much I've missed you – how much you still mean to me – can I see you again?'

'I don't think so,' I said. 'Nothing's changed. Has it?'

He looked very sad. 'I guess not.'

I had a ticket, he didn't, so I pushed through the turnstile and left him without looking back.

In my mind, though, I never stopped looking back. I had plenty of time to think, for it's a long journey from Holborn to South Harrow, with a long, cold wait on the platform at Acton Town making it even longer at that time of night. Yet with all the time I had to think, I really didn't think at all. I was moving on automatic pilot, going through motions learned a long time ago, while in my head, playing again and again like some cheap, sentimental, incredibly powerful song, was the memory of Nick: the rasp of his whiskers on my face, the taste of whisky on his tongue, the strength of his arms around me, the light in his eyes, his voice whispering in my ear, his face.

Tears came to my eyes and then dried up. Older recollections – highly-charged sexual moments – mingled with the memories of a few hours before. Things he'd said to me, things we'd done. Even more powerfully: all the things we hadn't done.

I was fairly drunk. Feeling no pain, as they say – except in my heart. As I walked up the hill from South Harrow station I cursed myself for not having gone with him, for not having seized a precious few hours of joy. Why did I always worry about what came next, why was I so desperate never to be caught out, always to behave correctly? What was the big deal about faithfulness and propriety, and getting home before dawn? It had never made me happy.

All too soon I was standing on the doorstep, trying to dig out my key from the clutter in the bottom of my handbag. I couldn't find it, but that didn't mean a choice between dumping everything out on the ground or ringing the bell – long ago, and without telling Peter, I had hidden a spare as insurance. The brick was still loose and the key was still there. It was a bit stiff turning in the lock, but it let me in.

The house was dark and silent. He hadn't even left a light on for

me. I felt annoyed and yet relieved that I wouldn't have to hide my
guilt and lie. With luck, I wouldn't wake him. I switched on the
light in the corridor and opened the bedroom door and then I
stared in horror feeling everything, my own sense of identity,
swirling madly.

The bedroom furniture had changed. The bed was in a different
position. And in the bed, sleeping beside Peter, was a woman.
Peter's wife.

Not me – I wasn't Peter's wife any longer. I wasn't anything to
Peter. Not since our divorce had become final, more than two years
ago. And for two years before that we had ceased to live as man
and wife.

I stared and stared as if seeing a ghost, but the only ghost in that
house was me, the ghost of myself as I had been five years ago,
when I was turning thirty. Meeting Nick tonight had brought that
troubled young woman back to life, made her more real than the
woman I thought I was now, thirty-five and single, living in a
shared flat in Kilburn, with a room and a life of her own. What sort
of a life was it that could vanish so completely after a brief meeting
with an old lover?

The ghost I had become stared and stared, unable to move,
unable to think of how I could explain my presence when they
woke, as they would at any moment, and found me here, more
than four years out of my rightful place.

THE GIFT
Nigel Watts

Gordon is a good lad. He's a bit rough, but his heart is in the right place. My arms won't bend as well as they used to, and even though my sleeves are baggy, we still manage to get one hand jammed painfully back on itself. He liberates the hand and then tugs the pyjama trousers while I jiggle myself in the chair. The leatherette seat is cold against my bare skin.

There's a knock at the door. That makes a change. Once they would have just walked in. 'Gordon? Phone call for you.'

'I'm busy.'

'It's Bill.'

Bill is the Centre director, and doesn't like to be kept waiting. Gordon looks at me and then at the door.

'Go on. Off you go,' I say.

He takes my towelling dressing-gown off the back of the door and wraps it round my shoulders.

'I won't be long.'

He turns off the bath-tap and leaves.

I wheel my chair to the window, but it's frosted glass, impossible to see through. We're north facing here, a view I know well.

Things *have* changed. I remember when this used to be a village. Not much of one, admittedly, but a village none the less. Hedges, fields, a single paved street, a church, a patch of grass we called the Green; even a water-pump. I remember a white shire horse roped to a stake. The omnibus to London, open-topped in summer, was a two-hour journey. Now we *are* London.

I have lived here almost as long as I can remember. Though my medical condition was apparent from birth, I lived my first eighteen months within the matrix of a normal, albeit stressful, family unit. I was probably a baby much like other babies; but even in the blessed days of emergent self-consciousness, when my hands and mouth were my primary organs of perception and the world was nothing more than an extension of myself, I had become a package, though cumbersome, that had already been labelled: congenitally imbecilic.

It is reported that, despite the pall my condition cast over others, I was an unusually happy baby. Which sadly was not the case with my parents: my father died from undisclosed causes soon after my birth, and my mother – the person from whose body I evolved – left me, Jack and Josephine (my brother and sister) with Aunt May, took a bus fifty miles to Brighton and threw herself off the pier. She died, not as one might expect, from drowning, but from snapping her neck upon impact with an underwater concrete support. I have often speculated as to why she should have chosen Brighton for the site of her suicide: I know of no family connection with the town. And neither have I been able to establish why a young woman would wish to kill herself. Through my youth I had assumed, and was not persuaded to the contrary, that her suicide was the act of an ashamed woman; myself being the source of that shame. Now, I doubt that it was so, but the accusation was enough to scar my early years.

I go to the mirror. It has misted over with steam from the bath and all I can see is a myopic picture of a white-haired man. Myself, I presume.

Aunt May, with two children of her own, agreed to adopt Jack and Josephine, but I, six months short of my second birthday, and clearly destined for a life of dependency, was placed within the Chelsea Home for the Handicapped. I, of course, remember nothing of this; what scant information I have of my past has been gleaned from the incomplete medical records that exist. Jack, Josephine and Aunt May visited me once or twice, but when they sailed to Australia a few years later, omitting to leave a forwarding address, the golden thread between my hapless family and myself was stretched taut. This was in 1925, when the journey to Australia took fifty days and cost little more than a hundred pounds.

When I compare my life to the mainstream, as occasionally I am still wont to do, I feel as if I have been transplanted from a parallel universe into a world which, though recognizable, for some reason is far more unruly than that for which I was designed. Here, action only approximates to intention, for somehow I have been allocated the body of a person for whom the telegraph lines between will and muscle have been brought down in a storm. Happily, there are others – congenitally maladroit – from my universe, which affords some comfort of understanding. And so we gaze at each other, boggle-eyed fish out of water, mouthing the air hopelessly, waiting to be picked up by the tail and dropped back into our natural medium.

My dressing-gown is slipping, and the more I try to retrieve it, the further off my shoulder it slips. Somebody walks past the door, but I don't call out.

As a young man I used to envy the ease with which the more able-bodied negotiated their world, but the older I grew, the more apparent it became that my portion of eternity (as William Blake, another Londoner, would have it) seemed no more full of frustration than theirs. I was born into humility: I am a stranger to physical autonomy. I miss walking no more than an ambulant person misses flying.

Oh, but I *do* miss flying. For how many years have I wished I could fly? Since I was a child perhaps and I realized my limbs would never be able to describe the movements my mind imagined. Since I realized that the running and jumping of other people were for other people alone. Since I realized that I was bound to this wheelchair; that these spastic jerks were the extent to which my arms would allow themselves to be subjugated.

Apparently there is a modern fashion to pretend disability is a linguistic tyranny, that if the words 'normal' and 'abnormal' were abolished, so the condition, undefined, would likewise be abolished. The truth is, though I have the dexterity to brush my teeth (though now, my teeth are plastic and cleaned in a fizzy solution at the end of the day), I would not be able to screw the cap on the toothpaste. *I* call that disabled. I'm not an idiot, but I *am* a cripple.

I look around the bathroom: it makes a change to be in such an environment. There is so little space left in my bedroom that I have had to give away my cupboard, and the table with a lamp on it. It's just me and my bed now.

The dressing-gown is nestling in a heap round my haunches. I try pulling it back up, but it has caught on the chair and no matter how much I tug, it won't move. I'm getting rather chilled. I hope Gordon comes back soon.

I suppose my love of flight has a lot to do with the view from the dormitory. After my early start, I was moved to my present domicile when the Chelsea Home was closed down. The air was cleaner here, considered to be more prophylactic than the damp river air. In those days, the view was almost all fields. This was farmland then. There always seemed to be so much sky, and it was always changing: clouds, flocks of starlings, stars. I remember the look of the cornfields in the summer, swallows screaming overhead, a bright orange sun at sunset. As I grew older, I became aware that, to the able-bodied who came to the dormitory to dress and wash me, the view was hardly spectacular, but these were people who had holidayed in the Alps, bicycled through the Lake District, walked through forests, forded rivers, climbed trees. For me, who had done none of these things, my vista was a rich and fascinating panorama.

Buildings grew up over the years, and the village become suburbia. Road traffic increased, telegraph wires began criss-crossing the sky, buildings grew upwards and outwards, spreading towards the horizon like a pool of lava consuming the fields. The sky shrank. It had become a town, pavements on either side of a tarmacked street, a hardware shop, a greengrocer's. The church remained, but the view was obscured. I watched the shops change over the years: now it's all computers and video-hire stores. And suddenly we have a London postcode.

But even with the change, there was always something to watch: shoppers, traffic, birds, trees. From my perspective of the third floor I was luckily afforded a bird's-eye view over the rooftops of most of the neighbourhood, a perspective those at street-level lacked, and yet I wasn't so high as to miss the street-level activity. Fortunately I had excellent eyesight.

An architectural stroke of luck had given me a stone ledge just below my window. Telegraph wires had been fixed to it, which became a favourite meeting place, a kind of avian forum. I never tired of watching the birds. Sparrows were my favourites, although for the summer months when the swallows and house martins appeared from north Africa my allegiance shifted.

Once a seagull landed on the ledge, though we must be many miles from the coast. And one year a frequent visitor was a robin, perching on my window-ledge, cocking his head at his reflection in the glass. He was so tame I'm sure that if I'd been able to open the window, he would have flown in.

It was a red-letter day when I was first moved from a dormitory into a private room. I had watched the regime change over the years. We were called idiots at first, a generic term of breathtaking indiscrimination. Some of us were strapped into our beds, the others left to soil themselves in high-sided cots, twenty to a room. All the offcuts swept under a single carpet. Change was slow in coming, but even the competent among the inmates had little sense of injustice. We knew no different.

Some time later we became known as spastics, and we began to have rights. Now my medical form is marked: *cerebral palsied*, and suddenly I have my own room, and staff knock on the door before coming in.

It took me weeks to become accustomed to the luxury of lying awake with no sound other than that of my own breath. I decorated the walls with pictures, had my own knitted rug beside my bed. A television stood in the corner, though for some reason, I couldn't make it work.

Though my new arrangements were undeniably luxurious, the view was dull. I had been moved up a floor, which denied me visual access to the street. And even worse, that side of the building faced a new supermarket. Though I still had the sky, there was no ledge upon which birds could congregate, no telegraph wires either. Just row upon row of identical houses.

I think I would have despaired had it not been for the presence of an elm tree, the top branches of which I could see from my chair.

After a week I asked if I could be returned to the dormitory, but the staff said I had to keep up with the times. I was assured that I would soon get used to it. I didn't protest, but I could feel myself drowning in cement.

At first the piped music was enjoyable, but as with the television I found it was beyond my ability to control. I enjoyed listening to music, but I enjoy reading more, and this constant noise made reading impossible. When I told the staff, I was informed that the music was there for all our benefit, and that I was being selfish in denying it to others. When I persisted, asking them to disengage my speaker, I was given earplugs. Due to the manual dexterity needed to insert these small wax pellets, a staff member had to put them in for me at the beginning of each day. And thus I was presented with a stark choice: constant noise or constant deafness. I chose deafness.

It was less of a disability than I had anticipated. Apart from being unable to hear the intercom when staff spoke to me, I found little disadvantage. Of course, I missed the birdsong, but I found myself capable of imagining it.

And then after the first month I was presented with a bill. Now that I was a private client, they informed me, I was liable for taxation. Apparently it was to cover the cost of the radio and television. I, of course, could not pay. I have no family, and no private income. I asked if they could take the technology away, but they said it was not possible. I would have to be set to work.

And so I was given the task of counting words. At first I tried to make sense out of the lists, but the words were random. Occasionally there would be an apparent connection, but generally, there wasn't. Though I asked, nobody could tell me the purpose of the lists, or my purpose in counting them. Nobody knew: it was a government scheme for which I was to be paid one penny per one hundred words. During the first month I had spent hours by the window, enjoying the birds in the treetops. But now I had to restrict my window-gazing to snatched moments.

I found my mind wandering with the monotony of the task. I began to find myself day-dreaming, staring blankly out of the window, lost in thought. It was always the same fantasy, and with each passing day, it became more detailed and more vivid.

It is always the same time of day in my dream: twilight with the street lights coming on. And it always begins the same way. I am falling through the window, head over heels, the bricks of the wall flashing before my eyes. I fall in slow motion, tumbling freely as though there is no ground beneath me. I am going to die, but I don't mind. If this is my last moment, this is how I want it to be: flying at last. The ground rushes towards me, and without knowing what I am doing, I give the slightest movement of my arms and swoop like a paper aeroplane, missing the road by inches. I climb, the momentum carrying me as high as the rooftops, the darkening sky above me.

I haven't died. I begin a circling descent, sliding through the air on my abdomen, turning and rolling. I am aware of a high whooping sound, and I realize it is coming from my mouth. I have never been so happy. I am a bird, a fish in water, a leaf on the wind.

And then an angel appears. He varies from day to day, but usually he is tall and blond. We fly side by side. The flying is effortless: not flying so much as gliding. I can cut through the air like a knife through water, rising thermals lifting us to a thousand, two thousand, three thousand feet. I look at my body, my arms and legs straight and graceful, my spine bending easily for the first time.

We fly out of the city, over the identical roofs, over the snaking grey roads, out of London and into dark green countryside. And then we come to the sea. I have only imagined sandy beaches before, lighthouses, fishing-boats, and here they are. The moon is like a sickle and we swoop low over the sea, chasing the foam on the waves, a cloud of moving silver beneath the surface of the water: a school of mackerel. We spiral higher and higher until the horizon becomes curved and even the birds have been left behind.

And then we're flying home. I follow him as he leads me over cornfields, through empty villages, past churches, a shire horse roped to a stake. And then the roads, the traffic, orange street lights, the identical roofs packed closer and closer until we are in London again. And though I return with a sinking heart I always know that beyond the darkness are fields and rivers and space.

I loved these journeys. They even began to creep into my dreams at night. During the day, of course, my productivity declined and I soon discovered I was unable to earn sufficient to pay my bills. I knew they couldn't evict me, and I wondered how the situation would be resolved. I soon learnt.

One morning two workmen appeared with sheets of plasterboard and lengths of timber, and by the evening a partition had divided my room in two. If I was incapable of paying, my room would be reduced in size. A simple enough equation.

It was not a great inconvenience. Mine was a large room, and even a reduction by half did little to confine me. It *did* bisect my window, but I could still see the tree.

Walking and running: the heritage of which I have supposedly been cheated. It is flying which is the true motion: gliding, swoop-ing, circling in the air: this is the ultimate human evolution. Sitting by the window, forcing myself to count words, I couldn't believe that one day I wouldn't fly, that one day my aching shoulders wouldn't sprout wings and lift me away from the city. As long as I had my window and my imagination, I had my escape.

Debts mounted every month, and every month the room was reduced in size. First lengthwise, and then across the width. I tried counting words faster, working into the night until my eyes stung with tiredness and I nodded off over the lists. But I couldn't keep up with the payments, and so with each month my room got smaller. It was reduced in head height so that my helpers had to stoop when they came in. Finally I was living in a corridor, just wide enough for my chair and my bed. At one end was a tiny door, at the other, a tiny window.

Yesterday was the first day of the month. I am in arrears of nearly three months now. There is only one thing left for them to take away. My window.

I'm aware of someone standing behind me and I start. I can see someone in the corner of my eye. I move the chair round and there he is at the door. My angel.

I can't say anything. I'm aware of my head bobbing up and down, but I can't control it.

He walks past me to the window and opens it. I have my eyes on him. He is exactly as I imagined him. Tall and handsome, with blond hair and strong wings that brush the floor as he walks. I follow his gaze and together we watch a pair of pigeons circle and fly off: it will soon be too dark for them to fly.

He turns to look at me. 'I see you like birds,' he says.

It takes me almost a minute to get the word out. 'Yes.'

'But you never fly with them.'

I give my most eloquent gesture: a shrug of the shoulders. I'm cold from the draught and he lifts my dressing-gown back on to my shoulders and ties the belt. He turns back to the window and continues to gaze out in silence. The light is fading from the sky. The street lights flicker on. It is twilight.

'Why are you here?' I ask him at last.

'I've brought you a present.' I can't see the expression on his face in the dusk, but from the sound of his voice I imagine he is smiling.

'Where is it?'

He laughs quietly, but says nothing.

'Show me,' I say.

He pushes the window wide open, a gust of air fluttering the hem of his gown. The empty street is expectant, waiting for something to happen. A light is switched on in the opposite house and the curtains pulled shut.

He moves my chair to the window, standing behind me. Then

he indicates the street with a sweep of his arm, and as his arm completes the arc, he lifts me from under my armpits until I am standing. I find myself on my feet for the first time in my life. I panic, my arms flailing.

'Relax,' he whispers in my ear. 'I've got you.' He leans forward so that we are half out of the window. My sight drops to the pavement. It is a long way down.

'Do you trust me?' he whispers in my ear.

'I –'

And then he pushes me.

The ground rushes to meet me. I am tumbling head over heels, bricks flashing before my eyes. Without knowing what I am doing, I give the slightest movement of my arms and swoop like a paper aeroplane.

READ MORE IN PENGUIN

In every corner of the world, on every subject under the sun, Penguin represents quality and variety – the very best in publishing today.

For complete information about books available from Penguin – including Puffins, Penguin Classics and Arkana – and how to order them, write to us at the appropriate address below. Please note that for copyright reasons the selection of books varies from country to country.

In the United Kingdom: Please write to *Dept. EP, Penguin Books Ltd, Bath Road, Harmondsworth, West Drayton, Middlesex UB7 0DA*

In the United States: Please write to *Consumer Sales, Penguin USA, P.O. Box 999, Dept. 17109, Bergenfield, New Jersey 07621-0120.* VISA and MasterCard holders call 1-800-253-6476 to order Penguin titles

In Canada: Please write to *Penguin Books Canada Ltd, 10 Alcorn Avenue, Suite 300, Toronto, Ontario M4V 3B2*

In Australia: Please write to *Penguin Books Australia Ltd, P.O. Box 257, Ringwood, Victoria 3134*

In New Zealand: Please write to *Penguin Books (NZ) Ltd, Private Bag 102902, North Shore Mail Centre, Auckland 10*

In India: Please write to *Penguin Books India Pvt Ltd, 706 Eros Apartments, 56 Nehru Place, New Delhi 110 019*

In the Netherlands: Please write to *Penguin Books Netherlands bv, Postbus 3507, NL-1001 AH Amsterdam*

In Germany: Please write to *Penguin Books Deutschland GmbH, Metzlerstrasse 26, 60594 Frankfurt am Main*

In Spain: Please write to *Penguin Books S. A., Bravo Murillo 19, 1° B, 28015 Madrid*

In Italy: Please write to *Penguin Italia s.r.l., Via Felice Casati 20, I–20124 Milano*

In France: Please write to *Penguin France S. A., 17 rue Lejeune, F–31000 Toulouse*

In Japan: Please write to *Penguin Books Japan, Ishikiribashi Building, 2–5–4, Suido, Bunkyo-ku, Tokyo 112*

In South Africa: Please write to *Longman Penguin Southern Africa (Pty) Ltd, Private Bag X08, Bertsham 2013*

READ MORE IN PENGUIN

A SELECTION OF OMNIBUSES

The Cornish Trilogy Robertson Davies

'He has created a rich oeuvre of densely plotted, highly symbolic novels that not only function as superbly funny entertainments but also give the reader, in his character's words, a deeper kind of pleasure – delight, awe, religious intimations, "a fine sense of the past, and of the boundless depth and variety of life"' – *The New York Times*

A Dalgliesh Trilogy P. D. James

Three classics of detective fiction featuring the assiduous Adam Dalgliesh. In *A Shroud for a Nightingale*, *The Black Tower* and *Death of an Expert Witness*, Dalgliesh, with his depth and intelligence, provides the solutions to seemingly unfathomable intrigues.

The Pop Larkin Chronicles H. E. Bates

'Tastes ambrosially of childhood. Never were skies so cornflower blue or beds so swansbottom ... Life not as it is or was, but as it should be' – *Guardian*. 'Pop is as sexy, genial, generous and boozy as ever, Ma is a worthy match for him in these qualities' – *The Times*

The Penguin Book of New American Voices
Edited by Jay McInerney

'Traditional, well-crafted, poignant tales rub shoulders with ones from the inner city which read like bulletins from a war zone ... At their best [these stories] shake you up, take you some place you've never been, and dump you into some weird life you've never even imagined' – *Mail on Sunday*

Lucia Victrix E. F. Benson

Mapp and Lucia, Lucia's Progress, Trouble for Lucia – now together in one volume, these three chronicles of English country life will delight a new generation of readers with their wry observation and delicious satire.

READ MORE IN PENGUIN

A SELECTION OF OMNIBUSES

The Penguin Book of Classic Fantasy by Women
Edited by A. Susan Williams

This wide-ranging and nerve-tingling collection assembles short stories written by women from 1806 to the Second World War. From George Eliot on clairvoyance to C. L. Moore on aliens or Virginia Woolf on psychological spectres, here is every aspect of fantasy from some of the best-known writers of their day.

The Penguin Collection

This collection of writing by twelve acclaimed authors represents the finest in modern fiction, and celebrates sixty years of Penguin Books. Among the stories assembled here are ones by William Boyd, Donna Tartt, John Updike and Barbara Vine.

V. I. Warshawski   Sara Paretsky

In *Indemnity Only*, *Deadlock* and *Killing Orders*, Sara Paretsky demonstrates the skill that makes tough female private eye Warshawski one of the most witty, slick and imaginative sleuths on the street today.

A David Lodge Trilogy   David Lodge

His three brilliant comic novels revolving around the University of Rummidge and the eventful lives of its role-swapping academics. Collected here are: *Changing Places*, *Small World* and *Nice Work*.

The Rabbit Novels   John Updike

'One of the finest literary achievements to have come out of the US since the war ... It is in their particularity, in the way they capture the minutiae of the world ... that [the Rabbit] books are most lovable' – *Irish Times*

READ MORE IN PENGUIN

A SELECTION OF OMNIBUSES

Zuckerman Bound Philip Roth

The Zuckerman trilogy – *The Ghost Writer, Zuckerman Unbound* and *The Anatomy Lesson* – and the novella-length epilogue, *The Prague Orgy*, are here collected in a single volume. Brilliantly diverse and intricately designed, together they form a wholly original and richly comic investigation into the unforeseen consequences of art.

The Collected Stories of Colette Colette

The hundred short stories collected here include such masterpieces as 'Bella-Vista', 'The Tender Shoot' and 'Le Képi', Colette's subtle and ruthless rendering of a woman's belated sexual awakening. 'A perfectionist in her every word' – *Spectator*

The Collected Stories Muriel Spark

'Muriel Spark has made herself a mistress at writing stories which seem to trip blithely and bitchily along life's way until the reader is suddenly pulled up with a shock recognition of death and judgment, heaven and hell' – *London Review of Books*

The Complete Saki

Macabre, acid and very funny, Saki's work drives a knife into the upper crust of English Edwardian life. Here are the effete and dashing heroes, the tea on the lawn, the smell of gunshot, the half-felt menace of disturbing undercurrents . . . all in this magnificent omnibus.

The Penguin Book of Gay Short Stories
Edited by David Leavitt and Mark Mitchell

The diversity – and unity – of gay love and experience in the twentieth century is celebrated in this collection of thirty-nine stories. 'The book is like a long, enjoyable party, at which the celebrated . . . rub shoulders with the neglected' – *The Times Literary Supplement*

READ MORE IN PENGUIN

A SELECTION OF OMNIBUSES

Italian Folktales   Italo Calvino

Greeted with overwhelming enthusiasm and praise, Calvino's anthology is already a classic. These tales have been gathered from every region of Italy and retold in Calvino's own inspired and sensuous language. 'A magic book' – *Time*

The Penguin Book of Lesbian Short Stories
Edited by Margaret Reynolds

'Its historical sweep is its joy, a century's worth of polymorphous protagonists, from lady companions and *salonières* to pathological inverts and victims of sexology; from butch-femme stereotypes to nineties bad girls' – *Guardian*

On the Edge of the Great Rift   Paul Theroux
Three Novels of Africa

In *Fong and the Indians*, Sam Fong, a Chinese immigrant in a ramshackle East African country, is reduced to making friends with the enemy. Miss Poole runs a school in the Kenyan bush in *Girls at Play*, and in *Jungle Lovers*, the fortunes of a dedicated insurance salesman and a ruthless terrorist become strangely interwoven.

The Levant Trilogy   Olivia Manning
The Danger Tree • The Battle Lost and Won • The Sum of Things

'Her lucid and unsentimental style conveys the full force of ordinary reality with its small betrayals and frustrations but, at the back of it, images of another and more enduring life emerge' – *The Times*

The Complete Enderby   Anthony Burgess

In these four collected novels Enderby – poet and social critic, comrade and Catholic – is endlessly hounded by women. He may be found hiding in the lavatory where much of his best work is composed, or perhaps in Rome, brainwashed into respectability by a glamorous wife, aftershave and the *dolce vita*.

READ MORE IN PENGUIN

A CHOICE OF FICTION

No Night is Too Long Barbara Vine

Tim Cornish, a creative-writing student, sits composing a confession: an admission of a crime committed two years ago that has yet to be discovered. 'A dark, watery masterpiece ... suffused with sexuality, which explores with hypnotic effect the psychological path between passion and murder' – *The Times*

Peerless Flats Esther Freud

Lisa has high hopes for her first year in London. She is sixteen and ambitious to become more like her sister Ruby. For Ruby has cropped hair, a past and a rockabilly boyfriend whose father is in prison. 'Freud sounds out as a clear, attractive voice in the literary hubbub' – *Observer*

One of the Family Monica Dickens

At 72 Chepstow Villas lives the Morley family: Leonard, the Assistant Manager of Whiteley's, his gentle wife Gwen, 'new woman' daughter Madge and son Dicky. Into their comfortable Edwardian world comes a sinister threat of murder and a charismatic stranger who will change their lives for ever. 'It is the contrasts that Dickens depicts so rivetingly ... she captures vividly the gradual blurring of social divisions during the last days of the Empire' – *Daily Mail*

Original Sin P. D. James

The literary world is shaken when a murder takes place at the Peverell Press, an old-established publishing house located in a dramatic mock-Venetian palace on the Thames. 'Superbly plotted ... James is interested in the soul, not just in the mind, of a killer' – *Daily Telegraph*

In Cold Domain Anne Fine

'A streamlined, ruthlessly stripped-down psychological family romance with enough plot twists and character revelations to fuel a book three times as long, as wicked and funny as anything Fay Weldon has written. Anne Fine is brilliant' – *Time Out*

READ MORE IN PENGUIN

A CHOICE OF FICTION

Mothers' Boys Margaret Forster

'Margaret Forster has a remarkable gift for taking huge social issues and welding them into minutely observed human dramas that are perfect portraits of the way we live now . . . The story grips and the heart bleeds for these good mothers who are, like all mothers, never good enough' – *Daily Mail*

Cleopatra's Sister Penelope Lively

'A fluent, funny, ultimately moving romance in which lovers share centre stage with Lively's persuasive meditations on history and fate . . . a book of great charm with a real intellectual resonance at its core' – *The New York Times Book Review*

A Private View Anita Brookner

George Bland had planned to spend his retirement in leisurely travel and modest entertainment with his friend Putnam. When Putnam dies George is left attempting to impose some purpose on the solitary end of his life. 'A beautiful book that one is impelled to read at one sitting and finishes with a deep sense of sadness' – *Evening Standard*

The Constant Mistress Angela Lambert

Laura King is a liberated, intelligent and successful woman. Although she has never married, hers has been an active and emotionally fulfilled life. Suddenly, at the age of forty-four, she learns that she is suffering from a rare liver disease and has only a year or two to live. In typically flamboyant style, Laura invites her ex-lovers to dinner . . .

The Rose Revived Katie Fforde

When May teams up with Sally and Harriet, it is the best day's work she's ever done. Each of them needs money, badly. Which is why they are reduced to working for Quality Cleaners under the watchful eye of 'Slimeball' Slater. When they discover it is *them* being taken to the cleaners, they set up as an independent team – and that is when things really begin to take off.

READ MORE IN PENGUIN

A CHOICE OF FICTION

Felicia's Journey   William Trevor
Winner of the 1994 Whitbread Book of the Year Award

Vividly and with heart-aching insight William Trevor traces the desperate plight of a young Irish girl scouring the post-industrial Midlands for her lover. Unable to find Johnny, she is, instead, found by Mr Hilditch, pudgy canteen manager, collecter and befriender of homeless young girls.

The Eye in the Door   Pat Barker

'Barker weaves fact and fiction to spellbinding effect, conjuring up the vastness of the First World War through its chilling impact on the minds of the men who endured it ... a startlingly original work of fiction ... it extends the boundaries not only of the anti-war novel, but of fiction generally' – *Sunday Telegraph*

The Heart of It   Barry Hines

Cal Rickards, a successful scriptwriter, is forced to return to the Yorkshire mining town of his youth when his father, a leading voice in the 1980s miners' strike, suddenly becomes ill. Gradually, as Cal delves into his family's past and faces unsettling memories, he comes to reassess his own future.

Dr Haggard's Disease   Patrick McGrath

'The reader is compellingly drawn into Dr Haggard's life as it begins to unfold through episodic flashbacks ... It is a beautiful story, impressively told, with a restraint and a grasp of technicality that command belief, and a lyricism that gives the description of the love affair the sort of epic quality rarely found these days' – *The Times*

A Place I've Never Been   David Leavitt

'Wise, witty and cunningly fuelled by narrative ... another high calibre collection by an unnervingly mature young writer' – *Sunday Times*. 'Leavitt can make a world at a stroke and people it with convincing characters ... humane, touching and beautifully written' – *Observer*

READ MORE IN PENGUIN

A CHOICE OF FICTION

The Ghost Road Pat Barker
Winner of the 1995 Booker Prize

'One of the richest and most rewarding works of fiction of recent times. Intricately plotted, beautifully written, skilfully assembled, tender, horrifying and funny, it lives on in the imagination, like the war it so imaginatively and so intelligently explores' – *The Times Literary Supplement*

None to Accompany Me Nadine Gordimer

In an extraordinary period before the first non-racial elections in South Africa, Vera Stark, a lawyer representing blacks' struggle to reclaim the land, weaves an interpretation of her own past into her participation in the present. 'With great dexterity and force Gordimer combines all these stories – career, colleagues, political struggles, sexual love, identity, family – into a compelling narrative' – *Daily Telegraph*

Of Love and Other Demons Gabriel García Márquez

'García Márquez tells a story of forbidden love, but he demonstrates once again the vigor of his own passion: the daring and irresistible coupling of history and imagination' – *Time*. 'A further marvellous manifestation of the enchantment and the disenchantment that his native Colombia always stirs in García Márquez' – *Sunday Times*

Millroy the Magician Paul Theroux

A magician of baffling talents, a vegetarian and a health fanatic with a mission to change the food habits of America, Millroy has the power to heal, and to hypnotize. 'Fresh and unexpected . . . this very accomplished, confident book is among his best' – *Guardian*

English Music Peter Ackroyd

'Each dream-sequence is a virtuoso performance on Ackroyd's part. In his fiction he has made a speciality of leap-frogging time, so that the past occupies the same plane as the present. Never before, however, has he been so chronologically acrobatic, nor so confident' – *The Times*

PENGUIN AUDIOBOOKS

A Quality of Writing That Speaks for Itself

Penguin Books has always led the field in quality publishing. Now you can listen at leisure to your favourite books, read to you by familiar voices from radio, stage and screen. Penguin Audiobooks are produced to an excellent standard, and abridgements are always faithful to the original texts. From thrillers to classic literature, biography to humour, with a wealth of titles in between, Penguin Audiobooks offer you quality, entertainment and the chance to rediscover the pleasure of listening.

You can order Penguin Audiobooks through Penguin Direct by telephoning (0181) 899 4036. The lines are open 24 hours every day. Ask for Penguin Direct, quoting your credit card details.

A selection of Penguin Audiobooks, published or forthcoming:

Sense and Sensibility by Jane Austen, read by Joanna David

Cleared for Take-Off by Dirk Bogarde, read by the author

A Period of Adjustment by Dirk Bogarde, read by the author

A Short Walk from Harrods by Dirk Bogarde, read by the author

A Good Man in Africa by William Boyd, read by Timothy Spall

The Road to Wellville by T. Coraghessan Boyle, read by the author

Jane Eyre by Charlotte Brontë, read by Juliet Stevenson

Wuthering Heights by Emily Brontë, read by Juliet Stevenson

The Secret Garden by Frances Hodgson Burnett, read by Helena Bonham Carter

Oscar and Lucinda by Peter Carey, read by John Turnbull

Heart of Darkness by Joseph Conrad, read by David Threlfall

The Winter King by Bernard Cornwell, read by Tim Pigott-Smith

The Naked Civil Servant by Quentin Crisp, read by the author

Great Expectations by Charles Dickens, read by Hugh Laurie

Middlemarch by George Eliot, read by Harriet Walter

Zlata's Diary by Zlata Filipović, read by Dorota Puzio

To the Hilt by Dick Francis, read by Martin Jarvis

The Vulture Fund by Stephen Frey, read by Colin Stinton

PENGUIN AUDIOBOOKS

The Prophet by Kahlil Gibran, read by Renu Setna

Virtual Light by William Gibson, read by Peter Weller

My Name Escapes Me by Alec Guinness, read by the author

Thunderpoint by Jack Higgins, read by Roger Moore

The Iliad by Homer, read by Derek Jacobi

More Please by Barry Humphries, read by the author

Goodbye to Berlin by Christopher Isherwood, read by Alan Cumming

One Flew over the Cuckoo's Nest by Ken Kesey, read by the author

Nightmares and Dreamscapes by Stephen King, read by Whoopi Goldberg, Rob Lowe, Stephen King et al.

Therapy by David Lodge, read by Warren Clarke

An Experiment in Love by Hilary Mantel, read by Billie Whitelaw

Rebecca by Daphne du Maurier, read by Joanna David

Hotel Pastis by Peter Mayle, read by Tim Pigott-Smith

How Stella Got Her Groove Back by Terry McMillan, read by the author

And when did you last see your father? by Blake Morrison, read by the author

Murderers and Other Friends by John Mortimer, read by the author

Nineteen Eighty-Four by George Orwell, read by Timothy West

Guardian Angel by Sara Paretsky, read by Jane Kaczmarek

History: The Home Movie by Craig Raine, read by the author

A Peaceful Retirement by Miss Read, read by June Whitfield

Frankenstein by Mary Shelley, read by Richard Pasco

The Devil's Juggler by Murray Smith, read by Kenneth Cranham

Kidnapped by Robert Louis Stevenson, read by Robbie Coltrane

Perfume by Patrick Süskind, read by Sean Barratt

The Secret History by Donna Tartt, read by Robert Sean Leonard

The Pillars of Hercules by Paul Theroux, read by William Hootkins

The Brimstone Wedding by Barbara Vine, read by Jan Francis

READ MORE IN PENGUIN

The Time Out Book of New York Short Stories
Edited by Nicholas Royle

This breathtaking collection of original short stories on one of the world's most exciting cities reflects the diversity of New York and the state of the art of the short story in America and Britain today.

It contains original stories by 23 cutting-edge American and British authors:

Mark Amerika	Brooke Auchincloss
Thomas Beller	Christopher Burns
Jonathan Carroll	Jonathan Coe
Rikki Ducornet	Christopher Fowler
Edward Fox	Maureen Freely
Samantha Gillison	Steve Grant
Charles Higson	Liz Jensen
Russell Celyn Jones	Cris Mazza
Michael Moorcock	Kim Newman
Joyce Carol Oates	Lisa Natalie Pearson
Elisa Segrave	Lynne Tillman
Elizabeth Young	